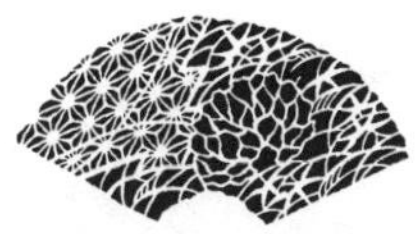

Be a Woman

Be a Woman

HAYASHI FUMIKO AND MODERN JAPANESE WOMEN'S LITERATURE

JOAN E. ERICSON

University of Hawai'i Press
Honolulu

Printed in the United States of America

02 01 00 99 98 97 5 4 3 2 1

Library of Congress Cataloging-in-Publication Data
Ericson, Joan E., 1951–
Be a woman : Hayashi Fumiko and modern Japanese women's literature / Joan E. Ericson.
p. cm.
Includes translation of "Hōrōki" and "Suisen" by Fumiko Hayashi.
Includes bibliographical references and index.
ISBN 0–8248–1884–9 (alk. paper)
1. Hayashi, Fumiko, 1904–1951—Criticism and interpretation.
2. Japanese fiction—20th century—History and criticism.
3. Japanese fiction—women authors—History and criticism.
4. Hayashi, Fumiko, 1904–1951—Translations into English.
I. Hayashi, Fumiko, 1904–1951. Hōrōki. English. II. Hayashi, Fumiko, 1904–1951. Suisen. English. III. Title.
PL829.A8Z63 1997
895.6'344—DC21 97–18939
CIP

University of Hawai'i Press books are printed on acid-free paper and meet the guidelines for permanence and durability of the Council on Library Resources

Book design by Kenneth Miyamoto

Cover illustration: Self-portrait, oil. Painted sometime before 1933, and used as the frontispiece of Hayashi Fumiko's second poetry anthology, *Vestiges.* (Courtesy of Hayashi Fukue)

In memory of

Leona Ericson

and

Meiō Masako

and

for Jim

despite his advice

Contents

Preface

I first became familiar with Hayashi Fumiko's writing during the mid-seventies—when I was teaching French for the continuing education division of Sophia University in Tokyo—through Ivan Morris' translation of her story "Downtown."[1] Morris' translation successfully conveys the gritty backdrop of the postwar urban landscape and the resilience of the female protagonist. As I found in reading the Japanese, however, he also took considerable liberties with the text, particularly in the opening passages, where the setting is completely recast. For example, Morris invents "a parked car, at one of those innumerable bombsites scattered through downtown Tokyo." Gone is the "long, narrow road, crowded with a succession of small buildings, under whose eaves Riyo [not Ryō] scurries." Salmon might seem too extravagant for a laborer's hut, so it becomes cod. A man on a bicycle, asking directions to the Katsushika borough offices, completely disappears, as does a pair of rubber boots and a considerable portion of the protagonist's interior monologues. There are many modifications of objects that are inevitable in any translation: a *hachimaki* (a rolled headband) becomes a red kerchief, and a charcoal-burning *shichirin* (a cylindrical terra cotta grill, used outside or on earthen floors) becomes an iron stove emitting the warm sound of crackling wood. Overall, the translation appears less disjointed and the tone more upbeat than the Japanese.

These observations are not offered to indict Morris. Good translation is exceedingly difficult and necessarily reflects changes in the times and in the expectations of the audience. But I mention the differences to underscore the significance translations have in determining how a Japanese author is understood by the overwhelming majority of those outside Japan. Translations serve as points of entry to literatures that are otherwise inaccessible. And because so little is ever translated (as of the late 1980s, Japanese was twentieth among the languages most frequently translated into any other language), the works selected have a decisive influence on how Japanese writing is perceived and evaluated in the context of world literature. As the number of non-Japanese who can read moderately sophisticated Japanese literature in the original remains minuscule, Japanese writers must rely on others to present their craft and imagination to the world.

Even the most successful translations, however, also confront an additional problem: Few foreign readers have anywhere near the background in literary history or culture that native speakers bring with them to reading their literatures. Moreover, most translations are presented without much attempt to set them in their proper context. To be sure, there is much that can be gained from launching, untutored, into "international" literature, and I have often enjoyed the unanticipated perspectives or representations that challenge my preconceptions and affect me, educate me, in ways that few introductory essays ever have. But I am also sure that a more nuanced, sophisticated, artful interpretation can be rendered if readers begin with a richer grounding. My work attempts to recover a literary history that has been neglected in the standard surveys of the modern canon and present it in a way that will make the reading of specific texts both more rewarding and more challenging, asking the reader to interrogate not only works of a single author but the categories through which women and Japanese culture have been read.

I began this study of Hayashi Fumiko (1903–1951), an especially prominent "woman writer," more than ten years ago. I intended to scrutinize the ways in which she has been categorized by her gender; to shed some light on the history of gendered literary classifications; and to explore how Hayashi sought to engage, subvert, or exploit such practices. When I presented my preliminary findings in Tokyo in 1985, at what was then called the Association of Orientalists in Japan, I was taken aback by the dismissal of my cautious questioning of the stigma associated with the terms "woman writer" (*joryū sakka*) and "women's literature" *(joryū bungaku)*. It was my first paper presentation in Japanese, and the polite conventions that I had worked so hard to absorb did not lend themselves to sharply honed scholastic debate. I was dismayed by some of the hostile responses from the audience. "How can you use French terms like 'genre' and 'gender'? They don't apply in Japan," I recall an apoplectic senior professor retorting. Even more astonishing were the sincerity and great efforts with which several older women—some not even in attendance—sought to reassure me that there was nothing in the least uncomplimentary about these labels. Since that time, however, there has been a striking revision in the terminology. In the wake of a series of feminist critiques, the principal terms that had been used for at least fifty years to characterize most modern women's writing—"woman writer" and "women's literature"—have been stricken from the pages of the preeminent literary journals as demeaning, inappropriate, or simply archaic.

I have translated Hayashi's *Diary of a Vagabond* (1928–1930) and "Narcissus" (1949) not only to bring two of her most successful works to the attention of English-speaking readers, but also to illustrate how the concept of "women's literature" was stretched to cover an enormous range of literary writing in ways that obscured the intentions and achievements of the author. My analysis of these texts, which emphasizes historical context and illustrates the complex contradictions of gendered literary categorization, is designed to achieve two objectives: to caution against the tendency in certain literary circles today to adopt ahistorical—even antihistorical—readings of texts, and to encourage readers, many of whom may be encountering Hayashi's works for the first time, to explore their own interpretations in light of and in response to the world in which the work was written.

Readers knowledgeable about recent western feminist theoretical discourse on difference, "getting personal," reading autobiographically, or decentering the self, may find the critical categories and cited literature wholly unfamiliar. There are no references to the post-structuralist, postmodernist debates that dominate contemporary literary criticism and gender theory in European languages. I seek to avoid the presumption that western theories are the sole measure for any scholarly assessment of gendered literary categorization in Japan. The Japanese debates and dynamics are worth recovering and scrutinizing on their own terms. Sharp-eyed readers may recognize the subhead "Feminine, Feminist, Female" in my concluding chapter as taken from Elaine Showalter's 1979 essay "Toward a Feminist Poetics," but I use the phrase ironically to underscore the contrast in the categorization and reception of writing by women, intending to alert the reader, who may be familiar only with western discourse, that Japanese discourse on gender is different. Those familiar only with western debates would do well to appreciate the nuances of the Japanese perspective and experience.

Until recently, discussion in English about gender in modern Japanese literature, or literary criticism of modern works by women, has been exceedingly rare.[2] My primary goals are to recover that aspect of literary history and to broaden the focus of inquiry, so that gendered institutional practices that influenced writing and reading receive fuller consideration. In Japan as well, however much the environment has changed recently, much work is needed to establish how "feminine," as a cultural stereotype, was imposed—and then appropriated and manipulated—by women. Contemporary Japanese feminist critics are more in sync with both their Anglo-American and French counterparts than the debates on which I focus might indicate. They treat, for example, the textual play of meaning in "male" literature that cannot be bound by authorial intention, and also interrogate the distinction between male and female voice.[3] Nevertheless, the history of how modern women writers have been misrepresented remains crucial to reinterpreting their contributions to literature.

I am no gender theorist. And I prefer my literary theory in small doses. Readers seeking more explicitly theoretical approaches well versed in western literary criticism should consult the sophisticated English works on Japanese literature that have appeared in the last half-dozen years, though none of them addresses the issue of gender.[4] Rather than joining in the rush to theory, I continue in my old, reprobate ways, translating and trying to make accessible major literary works by reconstructing a history of the writer and the era.

I should also express my qualified agnosticism about the question of a distinctive women's voice. Even though I criticize the conception and attribution of the term "women's literature" in modern Japan, I do not assume a complete isomorphism between women's and men's literary works. My assumptions about a "women's voice" are rather like my understanding of the difference in physical strength between the sexes. While men are generally perceived to be stronger than women—the average man being stronger than the average woman—the variations within each sex are at least as great as the difference between the average strengths. And since women who receive roughly comparable nutrition and medical care as men have far lower mortality at every age group, even in utero, they could justifiably be viewed as the stronger sex. Similarly, we should recognize the wide range among women's voices and be willing to consider, in assessing why and how literature is created and received, not only aspects of literary aesthetics, but also the gendered nature of social and institutional factors, such as the forms of education for writers and readers, the size and character of readership, and the outlets for publication, which, with many others, shape the writer and the canon.

Interpreting the work of many women writers would require first a recovery from neglect, if not oblivion. But Hayashi was an especially prolific, prominent, and popular writer who, at certain points in her career, as Donald Keene observes, "was the most popular writer in the country."[5] In beginning an assessment of her life and work, one is confronted with an embarrassment of riches. Many of her publications were ostensibly about herself. Hayashi's published accounts of her life, however, are notoriously full of contradictory assertions and evasions. And we lack much in the way of archival materials, unpublished letters, and even the originals of her famous diaries from the mid-1920s, which she revisited as the source of successive "autobiographies." Moreover, her published works are so extensive, and in many cases so mediocre or prosaic, that a complete reading would risk desensitizing one to what was, at times, extremely effective and innovative. The appeal of Hayashi's best works remains readily apparent today. Accessible, unaffected, she often addressed the dilemmas of impoverished women and explored the female identity in unstable, alienating environments. Yet the way in which she has been categorized has consigned her to the margins of the modern canon.

Hayashi attracted me also because of circumstances surrounding her "home town" of Onomichi, which she depicts with great affection in many of her early works. I grew up as the daughter of Lutheran missionaries in the neighboring town of Mihara and often visited Onomichi to go to the chrysanthemum doll festival and to take the ferry to the island of Mukaigashima in the Inland Sea. The ferry trips were part of my monthly childhood ritual to visit the closest American family within Hiroshima prefecture. Although I was born the year Hayashi died, my childhood memories enable me to appreciate some of the atmosphere she evokes from the earlier era, notably the tiny fishing vessels that continued to serve as both workplace and home to many families in the 1950s. I also recall, as the last family in our Mihara neighborhood to bring a television into the home, that one of the first programs I watched was the year-long NHK serialization of "Uzushio" (Swirling eddies) in the early 1960s, based on Hayashi's *Hōrōki* (Diary of a vagabond). The NHK version remains only a dim memory for me, but it sparked a revival of interest in Hayashi in Japan, including reprints of her work and critical evaluations of her place in Japanese literature.

My research on the reception of women writers in general, and of Hayashi Fumiko in particular, addresses the often elusive body of literary criticism and also includes consideration of their popularity and their place in popular imagination. I found rich resources and knowledgeable, helpful staff in the Kindai bungakkan [Modern literature library], the Diet Library, the Chūō Public Library, and the libraries of Tokyo University, International Christian University, and Meiji University, all in Tokyo. Two visits to the Onomichi public library were rewarding not only because of its unique collection of local materials on Hayashi, but also because I had the opportunity to discuss Hayashi with the Hayashi Fumiko kenkyū kai (Hayashi Fumiko Study Group), which has compiled two books on this local heroine. The considerable discrepancies between Hayashi's ostensibly autobiographical accounts and the information uncovered by this group in extensive interviews of local people who knew Hayashi colored my reading of her work.

Hayashi Fumiko's husband, Hayashi Ryokubin, graciously helped to dispel some myths and to flesh out her personal habits and quirks. After Fumiko's early death, Ryokubin entered her niece, Fukue, one of the members of this extended household, into the Hayashi family registry, and he continued to reside in the house in which he and Fumiko had lived.[6] Since my interview with him in 1985, Ryokubin has died, and Fukue has donated Hayashi's house to the city of Tokyo as a site of historic literary interest. It has been transformed into a handsome museum displaying her memorabilia. Fukue now lives nearby with her widowed sister and has been very accessible and generous in sharing stories about her famous aunt.

I have also made a pilgrimage to Kagoshima and Sakurajima and collected locally published material on Hayashi, whose mother was from that area. Hayashi has been enshrined in a variety of ways; for example, she is commemorated by the local elementary school in its school song.[7] Rather more remarkably, on the back of an ordinary tourist map of Sakurajima, I found an effusive ditty entitled "Hayashi Fumiko sanka" (In praise of Hayashi Fumiko), complete with musical score. The musical notation indicates that it should be sung "with emotion" *(omoi o komete)*. Its first stanza opens with one of Hayashi's best-known poems—"The life of a flower is short, and bitter are its days"—yet edits the line to fit the music.[8] The anonymous lyricist adds: "Across the channel literature shines." This process of enshrining her in the public memory continues. Most recently, in Moji (adjacent to Shimonoseki, and rival claimant for the site of her birth) in March 1995, a renovated "Taisho roman" building opened, housing, on the ground floor, an haute cuisine restaurant, and upstairs, two rooms dedicated to Hayashi Fumiko memorabilia (and one to Albert Einstein, who, as they say, "slept here").

I should declare that, in the critical appreciation that follows, I write with profound personal gratitude to Professor Donald Keene, as supervisor of my dissertation. All the exceptional accolades apply—for prompt, meticulous reading of my manuscript, for sound advice, and for the incredible wealth of information he was always ready to share, an accessibility and depth that is reflected in his exemplary scholarship. And I remain particularly indebted for his gracious acceptance of an intellectual approach that differed from his own. It became increasingly clear in the course of our exchanges that my assessments of the influence of gendered categories of literary classification, and of the social dynamics that underlay the arrival of women writers in the 1920s, he considered to be a sociological undertaking, and separate from the study of the literature that was produced.

I would be remiss if I did not include, in discussing my research, my experiences in teaching a course on Japanese women writers at Mount Holyoke College. Teaching gave me an opportunity to present my ideas and to respond to the interrogation of my bright and uninhibited students. The course forced me to come to terms with very great stretches of history and to reexamine literature written by women from the pre-Heian through the modern period. Such a perspective has led me to qualify much of my earlier thinking and to recognize the persistence, albeit one that constantly took new forms, of what have been perceived to be male and female literary styles. My students' healthy skepticism has persuaded me to reconsider the experience of the 1920s and 1930s as only one of the many lineages shaping the context and content of modern Japanese women's literature. My students helped me understand my own research as a single element in a much larger set of issues relating to women writers in Japan and throughout the world.

Mitaka, Japan

Notes

1. Ivan Morris' translation appeared initially in 1956 under the title "Tokyo" in Keene's anthology *Modern Japanese Literature,* and then as "Downtown" in his own anthology, *Modern Japanese Stories.* Hayashi's original title had the kanji for Shitamachi, but she indicated in kana that it should be read "Dauntaun." My translation of the title would be "The Low City."

2. Essays in Schalow and Walker, eds., *The Woman's Hand,* make a considerable contribution in these areas.

3. Egusa and Urushida, eds., *Onna ga yomu nihon kindai bungaku* (Readings by women of modern Japanese literature); Egusa et al., *Dansei sakka o yomu* (Women reading male Japanese writers); see especially Seki's article, "Dansei = dansei monogatari to shite no *Ningen shikkaku*" (Male = No longer human as masculine voice).

4. Notably, Fowler, *The Rhetoric of Confession;* Wolfe, *Suicidal Narrative in Modern Japan;* Karatani, *Origins of Modern Japanese Literature;* Fujii, *Complicit Fictions;* Treat, *Writing Ground Zero.*

5. Keene, *Dawn to the West,* 1142.

6. The caption of a photograph of Ryokubin and Fukue describes the couple as "Hayashi Ryokubin and his wife (Fumiko's niece)." Onomichi dokusho kai, *Onomichi to Hayashi Fumiko—arubamu* (Onomichi: Onomichi Public Library, 1984), 70.

7. The third stanza of the school song of of Kaishin shōgakkō on Sakurajima has her: "Blooming into the world as a literary flower . . . To render service to the world, daily she studied" which, even by the standards of school songs, struck me as a bit of a reach.

8. The poem is a favorite for commemorative stone cenotaphs that stand, among other places, in front of the school in Onomichi that Hayashi attended, and near the inn in Sakurajima where her mother had worked. The poem reads *Hana no inochi wa mijikakute, kurushiki koto nomi ōkariki.*

Acknowledgments

This study began over a decade ago as a doctoral dissertation at Columbia University. I am grateful to many faculty who advised me on its conception and development. I am especially indebted to Edward Seidensticker, for guiding my initial reading of Hayashi Fumiko; to Carol Gluck, for demonstrating, during my apprenticeship as her research assistant, the merits of sustained labor in bringing a book to fruition; and most of all to Donald Keene and Paul Anderer, for generous support and criticism of the dissertation.

During the mid-1980s, I learned much from the late Miyoshi Yukio about contemporary Japanese literary concerns in his seminar at Tokyo University, and I gained immeasurably from the friendship and discussions with Karatani Kojin and Meiō Masako during our weekly dinners. A decade later, Nakayama Kazuko and Fujita Kazumi would inspire and stimulate me to complete my work; I owe them more than I can express. In the intervening years, I benefited from the counsel of many friends and colleagues. I must single out Brett de Bary and Ted Fowler for reading the early stages of my work; thanks to Paul Schalow, Janet Walker, and Amy Heinrich for encouragement of my approach; and special thanks to Dick Minear, who returned incisive comments to me more quickly than I thought humanly possible. Christopher Drake, Hakuta Chisato, Matsumoto Tomone, and Yamamura Mariko advised me on points of translation.

I had the pleasure of completing this manuscript in Tokyo, and I believe it reflects the concerns of Japan-centered conversations to which I have sought to contribute. Watanabe Sumiko and the rest of the participants in the Shin feminizumu hihyō no kai confirmed for me the value of addressing women authors within the terms of the Japanese literary and intellectual traditions. Ogata Akiko shared her interest in Hayashi Fumiko and *Nyonin geijutsu,* and I thank her for inviting me to the book celebration for Wakabayashi Tsuya. Sata Ineko, Tsushima Yūko, Setouchi Harumi, and Mochizuki Yuriko offered their perspectives as writers, and Urushida Kazuyo and the habituées of *Jo-an* illustrated the benefits of a women's space. Tasaka Sumiko and the Hayashi Fumiko Study Group at the Onomichi Public Library graciously shared their findings with me, and Hayashi Fukue shared her family albums and lore.

A doctoral dissertation grant from the Japan Foundation (1984–1985) enabled me to begin research in Japan, and two summer faculty grants from Mount Holyoke College helped to continue the project. It was completed during 1994–1995, while I was initiating a new study on Japanese women's journals in the early Showa era, on a Senior Fulbright Research Grant and summer grants from the National Endowment from the Humanities and the Northeast Asia Council of the Association for Asian Studies. It is certain that adding two daughters to my family was a singular event, and I have hopes that, without such wonderful diversions, this next project will be completed in a more timely fashion.

I am grateful for permission to reprint sections of this book. Portions of the argument were adapted from "The Origins of the Concept of 'Women's Literature' " in *The Woman's Hand: Gender and Theory in Japanese Women's Writing,* edited by Paul Gordon Schalow and Janet A. Walker, with the permission of the publishers, Stanford University Press, © 1996 by the Board of Trustees of the Leland Stanford Junior University. Chapter 5 appeared as "Hayashi Fumiko and the Transformation of Her Fiction" in *Currents in Japanese Culture: Translations and Transformations,* edited by Amy V. Heinrich, Columbia University Press, 1997. The translation of "Narcissus" appeared in *Asian Cultural Studies* Vol. 21 (April 1995): 71–84.

PART ONE

LITERARY HISTORY

1

Reading a Woman Writer

Japanese women writers occupy a preeminent position in the classical literary canon, a phenomenon that many observers, both Japanese and western, have noted as an anomaly in world literatures.[1] Literary histories have also commonly noted that, after an earlier period of dominance, Japanese women writers were eclipsed and virtually silenced before their reemergence in the modern era.[2] Today, any sizable Japanese bookstore contains a section dedicated to women writers. Bookstores usually promote the latest winners of the Women's Literary Prize and current bestsellers. They also carry an impressive array of works, principally fiction, by women. Since the early 1980s, a wide selection of stories by modern Japanese women writers has been translated into English,[3] attesting to the recognition that these writers are now beginning to receive even beyond their own frontiers. But a western reader might easily miss the connotations borne by the terms "woman writer" *(joryū sakka)* or "women's literature" *(joryū bungaku)* until recently.[4]

The implications of Japanese gender-based literary categorizations are difficult to summarize both because of ambiguities and inconsistencies in the terms' use in literary criticism and because of the conflation of literary aesthetics with the far more pervasive and deep-rooted attitudes toward gender differences in society. While many modern literary critics have treated "women's literature" and "woman writer" as value-neutral terms,[5] there has been a presumption that "women's literature" referred to a specific literary style—principally characterized by sentimental lyricism and impressionistic, non-intellectual, detailed observations of daily life—and that a "woman writer" wrote in this fashion. While this style has been popular with readers, critics have often disparaged it. Even among those critics who denied any explicit disapproval of the style, the effect of categorizing the works of modern Japanese women writers by the gender of their author has been to segregate this body of work from the modern literary canon.

In the past decade, the terms "women's literature" and "woman writer" have come under increasing criticism for their limiting and derogatory connotations. Japanese feminists have substituted the term *josei* (female) for *joryū* to avoid the implication of a specific "style" (a literal translation of *ryū*).[6] While "women's literature" *(joryū bungaku)* previously referred mainly to works written in the modern period,[7] in contemporary feminist usage, *joryū bungaku* is relegated solely to the classical canon when, it is argued, "women's literature" did mean a specific—and highly regarded—style of writing.[8] In the early 1990s, such feminist critics as Ueno, Egusa, Urushida, Saegusa, and Yamashita began a far-reaching reappraisal of modern literary classics as "male literature" *(danryū bungaku)*. Their work provoked a firestorm of debate.[9]

The curious mixture of reactions to these concepts among women writers I have interviewed demonstrates, the contradictory legacies of categorization by gender. Setouchi Harumi (b. 1922) advocated the elimination of all such distinctions, including not only the literary concept but the special prizes and societies honoring women writers that have grown up over the past fifty years and have played an important role in promoting many women's literary careers. Sata Ineko (b. 1904) denied that there was a stigma to the term, yet mentioned parenthetically that she was pleased when critics wrote that she did not seem like a woman writer. Tsushima Yūko (b. 1947) observed that the notion of "women's literature" as a specific style no longer reflected the diversity of approaches employed by women writers. She expressed annoyance that there was still a segregated space in bookstores for women's literature, separate from general literature. Yet she excused the practice on the grounds that readers were used to this division, and admitted to haunting these sections herself to see what had been newly published.

Tsushima expressed the dominant interpretation; which is that the segregation of women's literature cannot be understood as a case of contemporary discrimination, but reflects a tradition harking back to classical antiquity. When women writers point to exceptions to categorization of women writers solely by gender, they are certainly correct. There has always been a permeability to the concept of women's literature. It never applied to all women writers, nor to all the works of those who were thought to write in that style. This partial application of the term poses an initial problem for the contemporary reader. Since those few women who received the highest critical praise were generally not characterized as "woman writers," nor was their work viewed as "women's literature," did most women who wrote earn the label "woman writer"? At the core of such a categorization, then, was a judgment of the writer's merits. Women might publish in prestigious journals, but their work fell into categories that prejudged their contributions as marginal and outside the literary mainstream. Why women have remained marginal within the modern Japanese canon cannot be explained without serious consideration of the institutional practices and social processes that determine who gets published, who constitutes the readership, and how a work is received—in addition to how the literary aesthetic is conveyed.

Presumptions of Difference

The biography of the writer Miyamoto Yuriko (1899–1951) written by her husband Miyamoto Kenji, a Communist Party leader, to accompany the fourteen volumes of his wife's collected works published soon after her death in 1951, was designed to distance her from the category of women's literature. Miyamoto Kenji presented his wife not as a woman writer *(joryū sakka)* but as an important figure in the literary canon, as an intellectual writer of the Proletarian school, carefully locating each of her works within the broader literary and political framework of the time. He used the terms *josei* (female) or *fujin* (lady) rather than *joryū* in reference to both Yuriko and other women whose works he discusses, such as Tsuboi Sakae (1899–1967), Sata Ineko (b. 1904), Nogami Yaeko (1885–1985), and Hayashi Fumiko.[10] Miyamoto Kenji argues that women who did not have strong personalities or a distinctly individual writing style were grouped together with other women by default, despite the fact that there were no literary groups of female writers or established literary journals for their work. His biography of his wife illustrated the gender stereotypes that determined whether and where a woman could publish, and the ways in which women authors could internalize those expectations. For example, Yuriko's first published story, *Mazushiki hitobito no mure* (A flock of the poor, 1916), was initially rejected by Takita Tetsutarō, the editor of *Fujin kōron* (Ladies' forum), because she did not write simply enough for the readership of his magazine. Yuriko was elated by this rejection, for she took it as a vote of confidence in her artistry.[11]

Women writers often shared disparaging preconceptions of their work. For example, Yosano Akiko, another woman writer, had praised Yuriko at the outset of her career for her "rationality, in contrast to the sentimentalism of so many fledgling women writers."[12] Even such female literary critics as Itagaki Naoko, who challenged the conventional critical neglect of and condescension toward women writers, set them apart from the trends and tendencies in the literary mainstream.[13] Yet from the 1920s on, numerous women writers—Hayashi Fumiko, Hirabayashi Taiko, Miyamoto Yuriko, Sata Ineko, Tsuboi Sakae, and Uno Chiyo—from many strata of society caught the popular imagination. Their writing was not limited to a particular literary genre or form; it included autobiographies, histories, and dramas, as well as poetry and fiction. But the diversity of styles, temperaments, and approaches notwithstanding, the public, the critics, and even the writers themselves accepted the convention that most women wrote women's literature *(joryū bungaku)*, and that any female author could be labeled as *joryū sakka rashii* (like a woman writer).

Itagaki's history of women's literature from the vantage point of the mid-1960s demonstrates the immense range and considerable accomplishments of women writers in the 1920s. Despite the close mirroring by women of the dominant styles in the mainstream literary arena, Itagaki argues, women wrote within a separate sphere. "The women writers of the Taishō period . . . dealt with womanlike *(joryū rashii)* material and worlds and brought out characteristic feminine *(onna rashii)* qualities. Therein was born the appeal of women writers and their raison d'être."[14] In her view, the women writers of the 1920s distinguished themselves from earlier women writers by their characterizations of contemporary social problems.[15] Proletarian school literature echoed this focus with a more political edge.

Writing in the early 1970s, the leftist critic Odagiri Hideo echoed some of Itagaki's themes, illustrating society's reluctance to use the same terms for women writers as for men. He praised the "socially conscious" confessional fiction of several well known women writers, but he continued to characterize them as a single group. In his view, they shared commonalities that separated their work from men's.[16]

The distinctions drawn between "masculine" and "feminine" women writers helped to cement the notion of a separate "women's literature." For example, Kitagawa Noriko's comparison of the works of Hayashi Fumiko and Okamoto Kanoko (1889–1939), which analyzes the differences of gender attributes in writing style and content, followed the practice of separating Okamoto Kanoko from other "women writers."[17] Unlike most critics, she relied on quantification to enumerate the differences.[18]

Kitagawa identified and grouped fifteen elements of structure and style, such as the number of kanji and the complexity of the sentences, but also the number of periods. Correlations were evaluated through factor analysis.[19] Many of the more striking points of comparison, however, derive simply from the illustrations she selected: She found, for example, that while both writers used original similes, Hayashi's were more vivid and natural—"barking a question like a stray dog," "eyes like a beast," and "soiled like the slippery guts of a fish"—or that Hayashi stood out in her use of onomatopoeia, such as *kirakira, giragira, torotoro, dorodoro, herahera, berabera,* to convey leaden sounds and to represent action situations as strong, heavy, and wild. Kitagawa analyzed ten works by Okamoto and two by Hayashi and concluded that the decided differences—

including the use of words that could be declined *(yōgenkei)*, the number of modifiers, and the adoption of a written style *(bunshōkei)* as opposed to conversational style—indicated Okamoto's masculinity, as opposed to Hayashi's femininity.[20]

Kitagawa's comparison of Hayashi is notable for its close textual analysis, which is a departure from the often wholly arbitrary and artificial judgments reached by many other literary pundits. Nevertheless, her ahistorical approach has cut Hayashi's works off from the social and intellectual context in which they were composed, and her factors appear to have been selected largely for convenience, not to test a specific intellectual question. But the more general problem of her approach is its reification. The distinctive elements and measurements of Hayashi's work—among them less frequent use of kanji, shorter, simpler sentences, and a realistic, concrete portrayal of what is close to the author—are presented as representative of a "women's style." Striking differences between Hayashi's works are subsumed under supposed commonalities. Her imagery, language, and point of view are taken as emblematic of women's writing, diminishing the author's originality and neglecting both issues of intentionality and traits shared with other authors, male or female.

Bracketing Women Writers

Japanese feminists who thoroughly reject the notion of a specific "women's style" in modern literature nevertheless often continue to bracket women, to examine these writers and their works as a collective whole, to make comparisons principally between these women, and to isolate them from the rest of literary history.[21] The objective of this approach has been to avoid the critical standards of "male" literature and to rescue from obscurity contributions by individual authors or collective enterprises by women that produced such pioneering feminist journals as *Seito* (Bluestockings, 1911–1916) or *Nyonin geijutsu* (Women's arts, 1928–1932). But efforts to reclaim this neglected history run the risk of segregating and distorting it. Grouping women writers in literary histories still remains a convention, although the presumptions underlying "women's literature" have fallen into disrepute. Even within the American academy, authorities as dissimilar as Donald Keene and Masao Miyoshi have bracketed modern Japanese women writers, albeit without relying on any presumption of inherent gender difference in styles. This persistence of addressing women writers as a group despite the absence of a specific "women's style" raises additional problems in reading a woman writer and assessing her work. How Keene and Miyoshi have represented the women's works illustrates some of the difficulties of incorporating gender as a central issue in the study of modern Japanese literature.

Keene's magisterial history of modern Japanese fiction, *Dawn to the West*, surveys the lives and works of seven women writers in "The Revival of Writing by Women" (one of his twenty-seven chapters) with characteristic judiciousness, providing informative summaries that are, on the whole, generous and sympathetic.[22] With considerable elegance and economy, Keene's short portraits convey in salient details and excerpts, not only each author's specific contributions, but also something of her appeal for contemporary readers. He invests his descriptions with his own sense of appreciation and pleasure. Keene notes the general hostility toward women writers, in the dismissive attitudes of male literati and the critical disdain that has kept their works from being taken seriously, but his principal interest is clearly in the appraisal of the specific circumstances surrounding an individual author and her work. His thesis is that, though a sizable number of women writers gained prominence in the 1930s, only in the postwar era, when women had the freedom to express their views fully, did most of these authors produce their best work.

Keene's command of the enormous sweep of literary history is unparalleled. Sometimes, however, he takes certain assumptions about larger social dynamics for granted. His introduction to the "revival" that ended "many centuries of silence"[23] in literature by women, for example, scarcely begins to address the character of sex discrimination and the significance of gender in what was written and read. This briefest of introductions is, however, very much in keeping with his approach in most other chapters and with his overwhelmingly biographical emphasis. Keene seems ambivalent about whether there is much intellectual justification for grouping these women writers together.[24] He acknowledges, for instance, the striking dissimilarities of their work, but suggests that collectively they "shared many frustrations," apparently a reference to discriminatory attitudes and practices. Yet Keene attributes critical disparagement and condescension—"these [popular] women were often known more for their love-life than for their criticisms of society or the beauty of their prose styles"—to the limited subject matter about which women could write with authority, as a result of "social restrictions on woman's activities, which prevented these women from gaining personal knowledge of most nonamatory aspects of life in Japan."[25] Here his emphasis is clearly on the progressive, liberating effects of the postwar reforms and the ways in which they opened new possibilities for women, in literature as in other areas. But surely the negative criticism that women writers faced, in the 1930s and after, was not always earned; nor was the literary imagination of every woman writer stunted, however pernicious or pervasive the restrictions. After all, the lives of Heian court women, who produced such justly heralded prose, were anything but worldly.

Keene does not clearly specify how postwar reforms helped women to address "the position of women in Japanese society." Only in the works of Miyamoto Yuriko can we see how political freedoms were crucial to her indictment of the militarists. Yet even in a novel like Miyamoto's *Fūchisō* (The weathervane plant, 1946), her husband's recriminations for her having joined the Japanese Literature Patriotic Association and her defense of inescapable, grudging collaboration are expressed in terms of situational ethics—not in terms of gendered perspectives on the capacities and limits of resistance. Similarly, the postwar writings of Hayashi Fumiko, Sata Ineko, and Hirabayashi Taiko, cast a cold eye on the harsh, distasteful choices that most women had to make and suggested that the Manichean contrast of collaboration or resistance misrepresented women's experiences. But these evaluations did not follow from an easing of censorship, the granting of the franchise, or formal equality under the law. One is tempted to draw almost the opposite conclusion from Keene: that when the postwar reforms lifted long-standing restrictions on women's rights, women writers aptly perceived the limits of these changes and sought to explore a landscape no longer dominated by sharply contrasting political polarities.

Keene's approach has mirrored the dominant tradition in Japanese literary scholarship, in treating gender as straightforward and the category "woman writer" as unproblematic. My work to date has sought to challenge the inadequacies of gender-based categorizations and also to examine the ways in which women writers—Hayashi Fumiko in particular—could subvert as well as invoke literary conventions.[26] Keene's reading of Hayashi Fumiko is perceptive, and he has a fine eye for detail, but in relying on her major biographers, he takes Hayashi at her word. For example, Keene, citing Fukuda, takes virtually all early biographical details from incidents in her *Hōrōki* (Diary of a vagabond, 1928–1930), including those far more sensational allegations against former lovers, by then deceased, made in a postwar sequel. Or consider how Keene quotes Hayashi's self-mocking admission that "the only ideal I ever had was to get rich quick." Lest the reader conclude that she was merely a grasping social climber prone to confession, this passage, from her *Diary*, is a flight of fantasy in a depiction of an impoverished childhood (her parents were itinerant peddlers). More typical of her self-portrait is the sentence that follows, which reads: "When it rained for days on end and drenched the cart my stepfather rented, we ate only squash and rice gruel for every meal. It was depressing even to pick up my bowl."[27] Keene, to his credit, does not indict her for her lack of social or political consciousness, but notes the "absolute frankness" with which she portrayed her struggles. Like many male authors, however, Hayashi was perfectly capable of dissembling her past to fit the occasion.[28]

Details of Hayashi's life, taken from her ostensibly autobiographical works or from the commentary that she would append, have been accepted unquestioningly by Keene and her biographers. Hayashi recounted, for instance, and her biographers repeated,[29] how her immensely popular *Diary* had been driven from the pages of the monthly *Nyonin geijutsu* after six installments for political reasons. In fact, her work ran for two years, even after a portion of the collected installments had become a runaway best-selling book. Hayashi apparently wanted to dissociate herself from the feminist and increasingly radical venue in which she had made her début, and to associate herself with the more mainstream journals where she would later publish her work. What we miss in Keene's assessment of Hayashi—and of women in general—is the critical scrutiny, so evident in his treatment of, say, Dazai Osamu or Mishima Yukio, that interrogates the way in which literary imagination engages and transforms experience and personality, rather than simply mirroring them.

Masao Miyoshi, in *Off Center,* has an altogether different objective from Keene's both in the thrust of his criticism and in his specific chapter, "Gathering Voices," which seeks to locate the work of Japanese women writers squarely in the context of gender dynamics and the struggle against sexist oppression.[30] Miyoshi contributes to the theoretically sophisticated literary criticism of recent years, which has recast the way academics read modern Japanese literature.[31] He presents a trenchant and insightful characterization of literary form of the *shōsetsu* (usually translated "novel"), sketching its myriad lineages and specifying its distinctive elements, to prevent it from being subsumed under the model of the western novel. His indictment of the decline of critical exposition, of the displacement of written discourse by easily digestible "conversations" (interviews, dialogues, roundtables), and of the effects of this decline on conformity and consensus, are perceptive and persuasive. Miyoshi seeks engagement across a much broader terrain than literature, or even cultural studies, scrutinizing the discourse on contemporary trade frictions and U.S.–Japan relations more generally. But the heart of his recent work focuses on critical assessments of literary forms and writers.

Miyoshi offers a radical assessment of the effects of postwar reforms on women, namely, that very little changed. In his view, legal reforms failed to affect social or political practices, and deep-seated assumptions of women's proper place persisted. He is surely right in observing that sexism remained endemic in the political culture and in the workplace. Though his discussion is brief and his evidence largely anecdotal, there is little doubt that discrimination remains inescapable for all but a very few Japanese women. I believe his emphasis on an appraisal of women's experiences as a group is a necessary precondition to discussing the specific contributions of women writers. His essay, however, is marred by an uneven tone and emphasis, too many sweeping synthetic assertions, and altogether too few assessments of specific literary works.

Miyoshi's "Gathering" is rather thinly populated. Aside from a fine, insightful discussion of Miyamoto Yuriko, only Enchi Fumiko and Tsushima Yuko (neither of whom is discussed by Keene) receive more than the briefest summary.[32] Despite the inclusion of active, contemporary writers, the list of those deemed worthy of extended consideration is extremely short. All are from the upper middle class. Compared to Keene, Miyoshi gives less information about fewer writers—and little analysis of their literature. But the brevity of these discussions is even more striking when compared to his lengthy assessments of Tanizaki, Mishima, or Oe. Even his surveys of postwar *shutaisei* (subjectivity) or of contemporary "Japan-bashers" depict a more densely populated terrain than does his treatment of women. A third of the "Gathering" essay is over before the first Japanese woman appears, though a cast of several dozen familiar European intellectuals races across the page as Miyoshi seeks to situate the struggle of feminists in Japan in a global context. To read what women wrote in light of the shifting character of sexism may require more time and attention, and the limitations of a single essay may have impelled Miyoshi to adopt stylized syntheses and to offer the reader too few examples.

His opening discussion of the "repressive conditions of modernity" for women focuses largely on legal codes and state restrictions. But his treatment of resistance as a heroic stance of an enlightened few—and these from the upper middle class—is very odd. He condemns the great unwashed masses, even the feminists among them, for falling short: "A full awareness of equality in race, class and gender was beyond [their] comprehension."[33] The standards by which he judges these women are so sweeping and uncompromising that few in even the most fashionable academic department could satisfy them. Miyoshi appears to be employing a peculiarly archaic concept of false consciousness that seems completely out of step, not only with current approaches to feminism or agency, but even with his own admonitions against the condescension of First World feminists toward Third World women.[34] One gets very little sense of how an individual woman might have resisted repression, why or how women made particular choices or compromises in specific historical contexts, or how their choices were perceived by their contemporaries. Miyoshi jumps to condemn without revealing much of the experience of these women—compromises, capitulations, and all.

It is apparent that Miyoshi is principally concerned with the adoption of a feminist perspective within an academic program more than with the ever-baffled, ever-resurgent efforts of actually existing women. This is the only explanation I have for the curious inversion in his discussion of global struggles (along the axis class/race/gender) and the way in which intellectual problems are studied and taught in the academy. The inversion is already tipped in his initial perspective on race, where antiracist struggles and analyses are characterized as having failed to amount to much until they were "gathered into a discursive context," and this only recently. In a perplexing selection from the enormous array of first-rate intellectual antiracist work, Miyoshi cites Hobson, Lenin, and Luxemburg, as if casting against type. If he is on somewhat firmer basis in describing how ground was grudgingly ceded to feminist criticism—and the remarkable transformation of literary scholarship in the past two decades—surely he does not mean that the struggle against sexism is determined principally by what happens on the panels of the MLA. Like the global antiracist struggle, feminism, if it is meant to be truly global and emancipatory, must reflect concrete historical conditions and scrutinize the means by which women have sought their goals.

In his discussion of Japanese women writers, Miyoshi has a penchant for hyperbole in place of reasoned exposition. Prior to his survey of the younger generation of postwar writers, Miyoshi posits that, despite the lack of a vibrant feminist movement—"the dominant gender ideology is hardly contested"—women will be, or at least remain the last hope to be, the agents of a radical transformation of society. Their marginality invests them with this unique capacity: "Japan's egress from the cycle [of production and consumption] is incumbent upon its women." Miyoshi characterizes the goal of such a transformation as an escape from "a routinized, dehydrated [?], or even de-eroticized life, with few dreams, little grace, and no criticism." But surely these desiccated specters are most often found, statistically speaking, haunting the hallways of higher learning in departments of literature. Perhaps the most puzzling assertion on these pages is that women's enormous transformative potentiality ("not yet an actuality") derives from, shades of biological destiny, their increasing "free time," envisioned as the time after children (or without children or in-laws, and including the hours freed by "improvements in household efficiency") and before death. Unencumbered housewives, so his reasoning goes, will develop a sensitivity to their shallow, empty lives and to the "predicaments of industrialized wealth" and recast both personal relationships and the world economy, because they will have time on their hands for critical scrutiny of their lives and the world at large. It is nice, I guess, to hear that women may be able to do something constructive after the kids leave the nest, even if the prospect is hedged as a "possibility." And I am attracted by the challenge to "wrench men from their 'utopian' unintelligence." But, if liberties of this sort are all too common in contemporary criticism, they by no means do justice to what women writers wrote, or to the circumstances that they continue to confront.

Engaging Gender

Recently, a Japanese feminist critic called for a reconsideration of the role of gender in shaping the modern literary canon, particularly to "exhume and reconsider the work by women writers who have been unjustly forgotten."[35] Curiously, this call failed to address those women writers most familiar to contemporary readers. Hayashi Fumiko was one of a considerable number of women writers who achieved popularity and fame from the late 1920s on. The experiences of this generation suggest a more complex dynamic than mere invisibility or neglect by critics or the reading public. Hayashi's work and its reception reveal the contested character of gender boundaries, yet confirm the centrality of gender in shaping a woman writer's reputation. A close scrutiny of her writing and its reception demands an historically grounded appraisal to capture the mechanisms through which gender operates and, even more important, the means that an individual woman writer employs to engage or exploit the boundaries of her gendered world.

In his 1953 analysis of Hayashi Fumiko and women writers in general, Nakamura Mitsuo presented the clearest description of the prevailing conventions of women's literature as they existed. Nakamura separated women writers into two groups: those similar to men and those having a "female sensibility," who write "women's literature."[36]

> There are generally two types of women writers [*joryū sakka*]. On the one hand are those who are closer to men or who give the reader the feeling of outdoing men, rather than being women. Presently such writers as Miyamoto Yuriko are of this type. I think that Hirabayashi Taiko [1905–1972] also belongs to this pattern. Even male readers, when we read these writers, do not need to be conscious of the fact that they are pieces written by women.
>
> Furthermore, the writers themselves do not wish to be so considered. And female readers too, while they recognize feminine elements in those works, no doubt sense in the writer a certain degree of masculinity, and admire the writer for completely separating herself from the weaknesses of her sex. There is more of a sense of sexual attraction than sisterly affection in their admiration.
>
> However, the special characteristic of Hayashi Fumiko as a writer is found in the opposite situation, in the fact that she remains feminine throughout, and that feminine quality is at times so strong as to be overpowering. . . . Hayashi Fumiko had an unusually strong female sensibility and female faults, but without discarding those elements, she let them mature to fruition.[37]

Perhaps because he presumed common conventions that the audience would accept as natural and self-evident, Nakamura failed to define what constituted masculine or feminine sensibilities, faults, or styles.

In keeping with the permeable categorization of women's literature since the 1920s, Nakamura did not equate sex with gender. But the objections to Nakamura's characterization of Hayashi Fumiko as quintessentially feminine, a judgment shared by his contemporaries,[38] are not due simply to a lack of specificity in definition. There is no indication of the fluidity of gender distinctions, and differences are treated as unchangeable. Femininity or masculinity is not treated as a conscious choice, an identity that authors can adopt or discard at will.

Surveys of modern Japanese women writers that seek to introduce their work to English-language readers make major contributions in overturning stereotyped Orientalist images of the aesthetic sensibilities of Japanese women, and thoughtfully introduce a cross-section of modern women's fiction.[39] Noriko Mizuta Lippit and Kyoko Iriye Selden aptly identified the contradictory legacies of what they translate the "female-school." While encouraging and lending legitimacy to the literary contributions of modern women, the notion of a separate and distinct female style set expectations that tended to restrict women writers to such subjects as "the mysterious female psyche, motherhood or female eroticism."[40] Like Vernon, Lippit and Selden reject the inadequacies of this categorization, segregating by gender, and illustrate the myriad ways in which individual women writers sought to explore unconventional gender identities and various literary styles. Yet both works suggest that, underlying the diverse array of modern women's styles and themes, there remains a shared realm of experience, a core, that constitutes a distinct female perspective. Vernon is far more unequivocal. For her, enduring gender differences are readily apparent in the thematization of female characters.[41] The perception of an inherent difference in the female literary voice continues to be a sharply debated issue in Japan, as elsewhere.

A literary history that focuses on an individual author differs significantly from both introductory surveys of the field and biographical sourcebooks, however useful these may be for other purposes. When viewed through a close, extended scrutiny of the writing of a single woman, literary conventions appear not as fixed or as determining, but as negotiable. Presumptions about gender differences in literature could, as Lippit and Selden argue, restrict or enable what women wrote. But neither an author's strategies for invoking or contesting the gendered institutional practices of the publishing industry nor the deep-rooted sexism underlying her work's critical reception is easily encapsulated. Shifts in strategy reveal changes in both individual sensibilities and the larger social environment. I follow Venon's delineation of the evolving voice of individual authors and their confrontation with gendered institutional practices—without presuming inherent gender differences. Central to my inquiry is the attempt to interrogate how women writers sought to negotiate the terrain.

Looking at an individual author alone shifts the critic's focus from the broader pattern and commonalities of experience to seeming anomalies—the particular or the unique. There are clear risks to this approach, including loss of perspective and a tendency to misplace emphasis. The critic may find herself highlighting and privileging all things from the vantage point of one person. But focusing on a single author shifts the emphasis to the innovations, the originality, and the distinctive qualities of the writing and the writer.

Recent Japanese feminist interpretations promise a wholesale revision of canonical literature. The central focus has been twofold: to recapture the works of women writers that had been neglected and in essence lost and to reevaluate the merits of the canonical male writers. Perhaps it is understandable that those women who have contributed the most important analyses to this revision have sought to break new ground and have largely left behind the discussion of works by prominent women writers, in which women critics and historians had long played a dominant role. I shall try to show that the new feminist perspective makes a return to this familiar territory all the more informed, surprising, and urgent. "Women's literature" as a concept of critical discourse referring to a specific literary style in the modern era is dead. I do not mean to resurrect it. But I do mean to reexamine its impact, its origins, how it operated, how it influenced the work and the reception of a prominent woman writer, and how such a perspective can help us to understand, appreciate, and enjoy her work more.

Notes

1. Morris, *The World of the Shining Prince,* 211; Kato, *A History of Japanese Literature.,* 1:170–188.

2. See Vernon, *Daughters of the Moon,* 17–32; Keene, *Dawn to the West,* 1113.

3. For a comprehensive list of modern literary works by women in English translation, see the bibliography compiled by Midori McKeon and Joan E. Ericson in Schalow and Walker, eds., *The Woman's Hand.*

4. The term *joryū bungaku* has previously been translated as "female-school literature" (N. Mizuta Lippit and K. Iriye Selden, *Stories by Contemporary Japanese Women Writers,* xiv) or "feminine-style literature" (Vernon, *Daughters of the Moon,* 137), but I have chosen "women's literature" because it conveys some of the ambiguity that in Japanese facilitates conflation of an author's gender with a specific literary style.

5. Yoshida, "Kindai joryū no bungaku," 10; Ikari, "Nihon no kazoku seido to joryū bungaku," 53–54; Kikuta, "Nihon no koten bungaku to kindai joryū no

bungaku," 73–74; Muramatsu, *Kindai joryū sakka no shōzō,* 258; Moriyasu, "Nihon bungaku ni okeru josei no ichi ni tsuite," 1–2.

6. Tomioka, *Fuji no koromo ni asa no fusuma,* 107–108; Yuri, "Josei sakka no genzai," 74; Endō Orie, "Kotoba to josei," 36.

7. Classical literature *(ōchō bungaku)* was not conventionally categorized according to the gender of the author, and the reference for women writers of the court was usually "female" *(josei)* or "court lady" *(nyōbō)* rather than *joryū.* Fujii, "Tsukurimono no jukusei," 87–89.

8. Negoro, *"chō joryū bungaku no kotoba to buntai,* 1; Kanai, *Heian joryū sakka no shinzō,* 1–10; Muramatsu and Watanabe, *Gendai josei bungaku jiten,* 1.

9. A sampling of the recent debate can be found in special issues of journals. Cf. *Masei to bosei: Onna no me de bungaku o yominaosu* (Witches and mothers: Rereading literature through women's eyes), *Shin Nihon bungaku,* special issue (Winter 1992); *Feminizumu no shimpuku* (Feminism's pendulum), *Gunzō,* special issue (October 1992); *Feminizumu no kotoba—josei bungaku.* (The vocabulary of feminism—literature by women), *Kokubungaku,* special issue (November 1992); *'Dansei' to iu seido* (The institution called "male"), *Nihon bungaku,* special issue (November 1992).

10. A rare use of the term *joryū sakka* appears only in reference to the expectations of Yuriko's mother, a graduate of the Peers girls' school, who saw her own literary ambitions in her daughter's future and wanted her to become a *joryū sakka.* Miyamoto Kenji, *Miyamoto Yuriko no sekai,* 17–18.

11. Ibid., 7–8.

12. Ibid., 137.

13. See Itagaki, "Genkon nihon no joryū bundan."

14. Itagaki, *Meiji, Taishō, Shōwa no joryū bungaku,* 106.

15. Ibid., 117.

16. Odagiri, *Gendai no sakka,* 172.

17. Compare Kamei Katsuichirō, "Horobi no shitaku," 242–260 (originally published in *Bungei* in April 1939, shortly after Okamoto Kanoko's death), and Yamamoto Kenkichi, "Okamoto Kanoko no bungaku" (originally published in *Mita bungaku,* April 1940), other critics who considered Okamoto different.

18. Kitagawa, "Okamoto Kanoko no shōsetsu no buntai ni tsuite."

19. The dubious origins of factor analysis should alert readers to the implicit biases of this approach: see Gould, *The Mismeasurement of Man,* 237–272.

20. The works by Okamoto were *Tsuru wa yamiki* (The crane is ill, 1936), *Konton mibun* (Chaotic unfinished self, 1936), *Boshi jojō* (Mother and child lyricism, 1937), *Nikutai no shinkyoku* (The physical divine comedy, 1937), *Kingyo ryoran* (A profusion of goldfish, 1937), *Yagate gogatsu ni* (Soon in May, 1938), *Pari sai* (Bastille day, 1938), *Kawa akari* (River lights, 1939), *Nyōtai Kaiken* (A woman's body, 1939), and *Seisei ryūten* (Lively wandering, 1939); those by Hayashi Fumiko were *Hōrōki* (Diary of a vagabond, 1928–1930) and *Ukigumo* (The drifting clouds, 1949–1951).

21. See Imai, Yabu, and Watanabe, eds., *Tanpen josei bungaku kindai* and *Tanpen josei bungaku gendai.*

22. In *Dawn to the West,* Keene offers profiles of Nogami Yaeko (1885–1985), Okamoto Kanoko (1889–1939), Uno Chiyo (1897–1996), Hayashi

Fumiko (1903–1951), Miyamoto Yuriko (1899–1951), Sata Ineko (b. 1904), and Hirabayshi Taiko (1905–1972). An earlier chapter of the book focuses solely on Higuchi Ichiyo (1872–1896); and other writers, such as Tanabe Kaho (1868–1943), Tamura Toshiko (1884–1945), Tsuboi Sakae (1899–1967), and Yosano Akiko (1876–1942), receive passing references. Yosano is also discussed in Keene's volume on poetry. In keeping with Japanese convention, Keene does not discuss writers who are still active.

23. Keene, *Dawn to the West,* 1113.

24. In spring 1984, I took notes for a colloquium at the East Asian Institute at Columbia that coincided with the publication of this volume. When pressed by a member of the audience for the justification for grouping women writers in this fashion, Keene responded that he had initially dispersed his discussions of female authors through other chapters, but that, at the recommendation of his editor, he had brought them together.

25. Keene, *Dawn to the West,* 1114.

26. See Ericson, "Hayashi Fumiko and the Transformation of Her Fiction," in Heinrich, ed., *Translations and Transitions.*

27. Hayashi, *Hōrōki,* 10.

28. See Ericson, "Hayashi Fumiko" in Gessel, ed., *Modern Japanese Novelists.*

29. Fukuda and Endō, *Hayashi Fumiko: Hito to sakuhin,* 104; Hirabayashi, *Hayashi Fumiko,* 109; Keene, *Dawn to the West,* 1141.

30. Miyoshi, "Gathering Voices," in Miyoshi, *Off Center,* 189–216.

31. For examples, see note 4 to the preface.

32. Miyoshi does present a highly attenuated paragraph-length assessment of Hayashi Fumiko, Hirabayashi Taiko, and Sata Ineko. Other writers from a younger generation merit only a favorable reference as "critically alert and historically intelligent" (Kono Taeko [b. 1925], Ariyoshi Sawako [1931–1984], Tomioka Taeko [b. 1935]) or a dismissive condemnation (Oba Mineko [b. 1930], Yamasaki Michiko [b. 1936]). In the epilogue to Miyoshi's volume, Yoshimoto Banana (b. 1964) is added to the unfavorable list.

33. Miyoshi, "Gathering Voices," 195.

34. Ibid., 193.

35. Ueno, "Atogaki," 400.

36. Nakamura, "Hayashi Fumiko ron," 94–112.

37. Ibid., 95.

38. Nakamura was not alone in such a judgment. Tamiya characterized Hayashi as "the representative woman writer in our country" ("Kaisetsu," 221).

39. Vernon, *Daughters of the Moon;* Lippit and Selden, *Stories by Contemporary Japanese Women Writers.*

40. Lippit and Selden, *Stories by Contemporary Japanese Women Writers,* xiv.

41. Vernon, *Daughters of the Moon,* 138–139.

2

When Was Women's Literature?

Women's contributions to the classical Japanese canon were considerable, far greater than women's contributions to, for example, English or French literature. The earliest extant book in Japan, the *Kojiki* (Record of ancient matters, 712), dating from the Nara period (685–793), is said to have been recited by Hieda no Are, a female royal attendant, and transcribed by the male scholar Ō no Yasumaro.[1] Perhaps the greatest of all Japanese poetic anthologies, the *Manyōshū* (The ten thousand leaves, 759), includes selections by more than 130 women poets. But the accomplishments of women writers during the Heian period (794–1185) stand above all others for their enduring influence on succeeding generations. Why women were central to this era's literary canon may be explained in part by the crystallization of a poetic aesthetic that elevated pure *yamato kotoba* (native Japanese language) accessible to women even as it sought to mirror the ideals of classical Chinese, the domain of men. The *Kokinwakashū* (Anthology of ancient and contemporary poems, 905) illustrates this emerging aesthetic; it was written, probably, in hiragana, the "women's hand" *(onna no te* or *onnade)* that, by the tenth century, was considered the sole script suitable for women.[2] Prose classics by Heian court women, such as Michitsuna no Haha's *Kagerō nikki* (Kagerō diary, or The gossamer years, c. 974), Sei Shōnagon's *Makura no sōshi* (The pillow book, c. 996), Murasaki Shikibu's *Genji monogatari* (The tale of Genji, c. 1010), or Takasue no Musume's *Sarashina nikki* (Sarashina Diary, or As I crossed a bridge of dreams, c. 1050), are held up as standards for Japanese literature.[3]

The interplay of language and gender in classical Japanese literature both confirms and qualifies Wittgenstein's dictum that "the limits of my language mean the limits of my world."[4] In the court literature of the Heian period, language demarcated the gender-specific divisions between two literary arenas. Realms restricted to men consisted of official documents and such literary works as poetry, prose, and diaries written in literary Chinese. A notable exception was *waka* poetry, which was written in hiragana and often signed. Because the conventions of men's formal sinicized styles often permeated unacknowledged works, literary scholars have been able to attribute a Heian author's sex based on linguistic gender markers.[5]

Having been denied formal education—specifically, the extensive training needed to write in classical Chinese—high-born women employed a written form that more closely approximated spoken Japanese. This form let them express their private emotions and perceptions in both fiction and poetic diaries in ways that were intimate, immediate, and lyrical. The conventions that excluded women from government and so-called serious matters helped them create an apt vehicle for portraying the nature of social relations and the subjectivity of experience.

The boundaries between gender-divided literary realms were, however, permeable. A few women, such as Empress Shōtoku (718–770) and Princess Uchiko (807–847), wrote Chinese poems. Most literary women, despite their limited education, learned and used some Chinese characters.[6] Yet for women to flaunt their erudition was a breach of court etiquette. Although Murasaki Shikibu chafed at the sobriquet "Our Lady of the Chronicles," earned because of the sophistication of her literary style and her reading of literary Chinese,[7] she was not above disparaging her contemporary, Sei Shōnagon, for littering her writing with Chinese characters.[8] Women were expected to restrict themselves to informal forms of expression and highly personal observations or emotions. Such expectations must have prompted Ki no Tsurayuki (870?–945?), the principal editor of the *Kokinwakashū*, to adopt a female persona in his *Tosa nikki* (Tosa diary, 934–935), a travel diary that begins: "Diaries are written by men, I am told. I am writing one nevertheless, to see what a woman can do."[9] Despite the artifice of a female identity—"the author declares 'she' cannot understand poetry composed in Chinese, the language of men . . . "[10]—the diary has a formal sinicized structure and lacks the introspection characteristic of Heian women's writings. But pretending to be a woman allowed the author to include a collection of *waka* poems and, perhaps more important, to express grief over the death of a daughter.

It seems appropriate to qualify Wittgenstein's limits in several ways when considering gender roles in literature. Despite the inescapable influence of social and literary conventions, an author's choice of language is also determined by affiliation, which links the work to other literary and intellectual traditions, and intention.[11] However sharply defined and closely guarded, boundaries remain porous, in part because of their artificial character. Women may be expected to act in specific, limited ways, but, like men, they remain capable of expressing their own creativity in ways that may challenge or subvert expectations. Trespassing—or simply "passing"—and impersonation are not unique to the Japanese experience. Henry Louis Gates, Jr., has written of the long tradition in American letters of adopting a language and an identity to present, often with painstaking verisimilitude, supposed first-hand accounts of lives and cultures only imagined, notably in the ersatz slave narratives written by whites or free blacks for the abolitionist press.[12]

Despite women's preeminence in classical Japanese literature, and despite the importance of the heavily feminine tradition of poetry and diaries, the strong female voice seems to have died out in Japanese literature by the early modern period.[13] The apparent absence of women writers from the mid-fourteenth through the mid-seventeenth centuries has often been explained by the growing codification and integration into Japanese society of Neo-Confucian precepts.[14] But the transformation of women's role in literature appears to have begun in the earlier medieval era, when changes in laws affecting individual inheritance and property rights increasingly subordinated women.[15] Although on occasion women's names can be found in linked-verse *(haikai no renga)* poetry and travel diaries of the Edo period, what has survived in the literary canon is almost entirely written by men.[16] For the most part, however, female poets operated outside male circles, composing their works in separate women's poetry matches. The term for their poetry, "women's linked verse" *(nyōbō renga),* denotes something distinct and different from the work of their male counterparts.

The scarcity of female authors in the literary histories of this period does not preclude the existence of women who were writing. Anthologies from the first decades of the twentieth century indicate the variety and diversity of women's literary efforts during the Edo period. In 1901, two anthologies devoted to women writers were published. One of these, *Joryū bungaku shi* (A history of women's literature), included biographies and excerpts of works by women from the early medieval era up to the end of the Edo period. In 1918–1919, the same publishing company produced a four-volume *Joryū bungaku zenshū* (Collected works of women's literature) which included tales *(monogatari),* histories, random jottings *(zuihitsu),* travel diaries, and poetry by thirty women writers from the Edo Period. This collection emphasized the importance of poets of *waka* and *haikai*, especially Kaga no Chiyojo, Chie no Uchiko, and Sessho Kaka, as well as the diverse accomplishments of Arakida Reiko (1732–1806).[17] But neither of these anthologies treated women writers as sharing a common literary style. The terms "women's literature" *(joryū bungaku)* and "woman writer" *(keishū sakka)* referred only to the sex of the authors.[18]

The attempt to recover literary work by women from the Edo period early in this century could not rely on standard histories or interpretations. Most women represented in the anthologies I have mentioned shared their work within their circle of friends and acquaintances, and relied on hand-copied—not printed—texts. In 1916, the woman poet Yosano Akiko (1878–1942) wrote a biography of Arakida, whose own extensive oeuvre had not been published during her lifetime.[19] As one of the handful of women prominent in the literary world around 1910, Yosano Akiko sought to establish a literary lineage of women writers in the recent past, building a bridge between the widely heralded but distant literary achievements of classical antiquity, and the contemporary world, where female authors were rare.

From the end of the nineteenth century, women writers began to publish. In some circles they were received enthusiastically. In 1895, *Bungei kurabu* (the Literary Club) published a special issue entitled *Keishū shōsetsu* (Women's fiction) devoted to contemporary women writers of the Meiji period.[20] This publication was so popular that a second issue appeared two years later under the same name.[21] But critically acclaimed women writers were generally treated as exceptions—in ways that revealed many critics' scarcely veiled disdain for women's abilities. For example, a critic praised Tanabe Kaho's *Yabu no uguisu* (Nightingale in the grove, 1888) as "surprisingly complex (considering the author was a woman)."[22] And Hoshino Tenchi, who reviewed Higuchi Ichiyō's story *Umoregi* (A buried life, 1892), commented, "Not only is the conception unusual, but the style is so incisive it makes one doubt the work was written by a woman."[23] Furthermore, Tsubouchi Shōyō praised Miyamoto Yuriko's *Mazushiki hitobito no mure* (A flock of the poor, 1916) as "unwomanish," with few short sentences.[24]

Some have viewed such assumptions about women's abilities and styles in the modern era as emblematic of the emerging segregation of women's literature. Akiyama Shun, for instance, in his 1980 essay "Ima joryū bungaku to wa nani ka" (What is women's literature today?), argued that "the concept of 'women's literature' was first made in modern Japanese literature, as seen in references to Higuchi Ichiyō, because it was thought to be far different in character from the so-called male writer's intellect *(chisei)*, a Western scholastic intellect."[25] Akiyama suggested that the disparagement of women writers by such Meiji intellectuals as the author Kunikida Doppo did not derive from a feudalistic patriarchy, but from a Meiji (male) elitist attempt to monopolize western intellectual work. The constellation of attitudes women writers confronted directly affected the nature of their published work. Recent research has uncovered how Higuchi's male mentor, Nakarai Tōsui, edited early drafts of her stories to conform to expectations of how a woman should write.[26]

The specific characteristics attributed to the work of women writers, however, as well as assessments of whether any given writer conformed to those expectations, were rapidly changing from the last decade of the nineteenth century. Although his observation about how the founders of modern Japanese literature reshaped the prejudices that confronted women writers is acute, Akiyama fails to cite specific examples of use of the concept "women's literature" that would allow us to assess how the term was meant. Aside from Akiyama, most other literary critics and historians, including Higuchi's American biographer, Robert Danly, have not categorized Higuchi Ichiyō as a writer of "women's literature."[27] References to "women writers" or "women's literature" may not have suggested a common style but, as in the anthologies of Edo Period women writers, served solely as gender identification. By asserting a separate and distinct literary category from the 1890s on, Akiyama presumes a continuity in the perception of women's writing that stands apart from the enormous transformation of social attitudes, including those toward gender, aesthetic tastes, and institutional dynamics in commerical publishing.

Discontinuities and the Modern Female

Why did the concept of women's literature as denoting a specific style emerge when it did? Examining what women wrote and how their writing changed, for example, during the 1920s, will not answer this question. Such an examination would assume that the label was earned rather than ascribed and would tend to separate the production and reception of literature from its broader historical and social context. The segregation of women writers was not simply attributable to an endemic sexism, however deep-rooted that may be in Japanese society. Why women's literature took on its modern meaning when it did is best explained by the growth of women's literacy and the emergence of journals targeted at a female audience, as well as to a reaction to the shifting gender roles of the Taishō Period.

Literacy—the ability to read kana and simple kanji—was widespread by the early twentieth century even among women. The percentage of girls completing the four years of primary education rose dramatically, from 18 percent in 1875 to 72 percent in 1900 and 97 percent in 1910.[28] Discussions of the social changes of the Meiji era too often neglect the consequences of this rapid increase in elementary literacy among young women, but evidence from other areas of the world demonstrates the enormous significance of women's literacy in empowering women and improving the quality of their lives.[29] Most newspapers and journals printed kana alongside kanji, so that reading material was accessible even to those with very modest education.

But women's access to most forms of higher education remained limited until the 1920s, and even then, professional or university training remained extremely rare. Women were not allowed to enter standard high schools, but were tracked into either special women's high schools (whose enrollment soared nationwide from 12,000 in 1900 to more than 300,000 in 1925) or vocational and normal schools (the total enrollment in both of these types of schools reached almost 23,000 by 1925). Universities first admitted women in 1915 (by 1930 there were only eighty-one women enrolled) and restricted their entrance to a very small, if often extremely talented, few.[30] Nevertheless, by the 1920s the educational and social reforms of the Meiji era had created a mass female readership.

Female readers, whose numbers were swelled by the matriculates and graduates of high schools for girls, were increasingly capable of reading moderately sophisticated literary works. Moreover, while the higher educational institutions remained largely sex-segregated, the quality of young women's education improved following the educational reform of the 1910s. By the mid-1920s, graduates from girls' high schools constituted 10 percent of their age cohort in the general population. Maeda Ai has argued that these graduates were the core readership of women's journals.[31]

The growth of women's magazines coincided with the growth of women's advancement into urban, white-collar occupations. Such fields as nursing and elementary school teaching were open to women in the Meiji era, but the numbers of women in them increased rapidly during the second and third decades of the twentieth century; the number of women nurses jumped from 14,000 in 1914 to more than 42,000 a decade later, and women elementary school teachers, who accounted for 37.5 percent of all elementary school teachers in 1912, were 47.5 percent in 1922. The journals often featured profiles of exceptional women—actresses, physicians, or reporters—who broke barriers to gain entrée into more glamorous or well paid fields, but most white-collar female workers worked at more conventional sex-segregated jobs. A survey of working women in Tokyo published in 1923 found 18,274 clerks, typists, and office workers, 8,500 telephone operators, 5,000 waitresses, 2,445 school teachers, and 1,500 actresses and entertainers.[32] Margit Nagy reminds us that whie-collar women were a distinct minority. Of twenty-seven million women in the nation in the year of the survey, 3.5 million were in the paid labor force, 2.6 million of them in manual labor jobs.[33] The majority of wage-earning women in the modern tertiary sector (as opposed to those working in the family shop) were single, between education and marriage, and contributed to their parental household income.[34] Their wages gave them disposable income and the ability to make discretionary purchases of such items as women's magazines.

In the following year, 1924, the Tokyo Social Affairs Department surveyed nine hundred women workers, principally office workers, clerks, nurses, and telephone operators, to determine what they read. Of these eight hundred subscribed to a newspaper, and 740 subscribed to a women's journal.[35] These figures underline the striking degree to which urban wage-earning women in the tertiary sector constituted a core of devoted readers and a significant market for journals that promoted writing by women. The survey's finding is at odds with the stereotype Aono Suekichi presents in "Women's Demands on Literature," namely, that women's magazines largely fulfilled the fantasies of housewives and house-bound middle-class daughters—"to imbibe the intoxicating freedom of women's liberation in the world of fiction . . . [specifically] in popular literature in women's magazines."[36]

The modern era did not invent distinctions between appropriate spheres for men and women, but as the pace of social change accelerated from the Meiji period on, and as the norms of family organization, occupations, schooling, and government were increasingly challenged, the boundaries between the sexes were policed with increased vigor. The state recruited intellectuals for a campaign promoting a separate sphere for women as "good wives and wise mothers" *(ryōsai kenbo)*.[37] But efforts to elaborate distinctions between men's and women's roles in politics, education, work, and the family tended to founder in the sea change of social transformation. The concepts of masculinity and femininity, particularly the ways in which power was linked with gender and the declining norms of domesticity and submissiveness, changed in ways that were beyond the power of the state or its minions to control.

While the blurring of gender norms, as well as campaigns to reinvent them, was evident beginning in the 1880s, both escalated during the first decades of the twentieth century. Donald Roden writes that growing ambivalence to gender-dictated roles during the 1920s "captured the imagination of a cross section of the literate urban population in a manner that was simply unthinkable in the heyday of 'civilization and enlightenment' [in the Meiji era]."[38] He argues that this process was rooted in late Meiji shifts in attitude that subverted the conventional notions of male "household head and stalwart provider" and fueled the image of a "new woman [who] exuded . . . a firm self-confidence and an emotional independence from the patriarchal family."[39] The popular media projected the shifting ground of gender identities. Mainstream and, especially, women's magazines—not only the feminist flagships *Seitō* and *Nyonin gejitsu*, but also less activist more long-lived publications—dissected changes monthly.[40]

Women's growing presence in new occupations during the boom years of the First World War fueled the image of working women. The independence, self-confidence, and self-sufficiency of many young working women shattered conventional gender roles. In the decade following the great earthquake of 1923, the media fixated on the symbol of the *moga*, or modern girl, to represent not only a decadent libertine but, in a broader sense, a threat to the social order. "The trumpeted promiscuity of the Modern Girl, who moved from man to man, was thus but one aspect of her self-sufficiency. She appeared to be a free agent without ties of filiation, affect, or obligation to lover, father, mother, husband or children—in striking counterpoint to the state ideology of family documented in the Civil Code and in the ethics texts taught in schools."[41] In the context of such shifting gender norms, conservative critics' call for a return to the "natural" distinctions between men and women became much more influential. Nogami Toshio warned of the degeneration that would follow from a blurring of "spiritual differences" between the sexes and from the "deviant conditions that have arisen . . . [where] women who perform men's work have significantly increased in number."[42] In 1922, General Ugaki Kazushige decried "the feminization of men and the masculinization of women and the neutered gender that results [as] a modernistic tendency that makes it impossible for the individual, the society, or the nation to achieve great progress. . . . Since the manliness of man and the femininity of woman must forever be preserved, it is imperative that we not allow the rise of neutered people who defy nature's grace."[43] Such sentiments were hardly original, but only in the 1920s did the reaction gain a critical mass. Educators and representatives of government ministries

> waged a vociferous campaign—in the name of bourgeois gentility, natural order, and civilized morality—against the perceived distortions and excesses of Taishō culture. These included feminism, homosexuality, recreational sex, and the blurring, whether intended or not, of the sacred and inviolate lines between the masculine and feminine. The defenders of respectability spared no effort in championing the immiscibility of the sexes with long-winded explanations of male aggression and female passivity, of male rationality and female hysteria, of man's destiny to work outside and woman's to stay at home, and of the necessity to prevent the "masculinization" of feminine language.[44]

In the wake of the rising tide of reaction, the concept of a separate "women's literature" took form.

The Crystallization of a Category

The dominant trend in Japanese literature in the first decades of the twentieth century was to emphasize the interiority of the author in what came to be known as the I-novel (*watakushi* or *shishōsetsu*). While it has not been uncommon to attribute this fixation on the self to emulation of western tradition, Edward Fowler has traced its roots to classical Japanese literary traditions and to the structure of the language itself.[45] Women's classical confessional diaries offered a wellspring for this preeminent genre of modern Japanese letters. Given women's greater opportunities for education and the growth of a sizable female readership, especially among the urban middle classes, it is not surprising that women of the modern era adopted similar confessional forms to express their world. In fact, the most successful modern authors, both male and female, were influenced by this "feminine" tradition. Women writers were quite candid about themselves, revealing secrets about their lives, loves, and search for survival in a manner as sensational and indiscreet as their male counterparts'.[46]

Interiority and modern psychological narration were tied to a transformation of literary language through the movement toward *genbun itchi* (unification of spoken and written language). Karatani Kōjin has characterized this profound rupture in literary traditions as a prerequisite for modern realism and confessional forms, because it did away with the immense diversity of styles and genres of Chinese-influenced literature *(kanbungaku)*.[47] But the triumph of *genbun itchi* also made literature far more accessible to women readers and writers, who could increasingly appreciate it and even participate in it through a language that did not have to be taught separately. Modern women's writing has often been linked to this transformation of literary style: Tanabe Kaho's *Yabu no uguisu* (Nightingale in the grove, 1888) is said to have been inspired by Tsubouchi Shōyō's *Tōsei shosei katagi* (The characters of modern students, 1885–1886), which advanced the cause of *genbun itchi;* Higuchi Ichiyō's first stories were inspired by the financial success of Tanabe's novel.[48] Women's literature as a distinct style, however, emerged only in relation to the principal conceptual antinomies of literary criticism in the 1920s.

The term "I-novel" (a literal translation of *watakushi shōsetsu*, which may be better rendered as "confessional or personal fiction") was coined in the early 1920s as a slightly derogatory description of a literary tendency that had begun in the late Meiji era. In a 1921 issue of the literary journal *Kaizō* (Reconstruction), *watakushi shōsetsu* was described as "no more than an extension of a chronicle, lacking in reflection."[49] Yet in a few years, in the hands of such influential writer-critics as Kume Masao, *watakushi shōsetsu* (including *shinkyō shōsetsu* "mental attitude fiction") became the standard for judging literary merit.[50] Critics found the works of the new Proletarian school lacking according to this new standard and dismissed them as mere didactic moralizing. Confessional literature was considered "pure literature."[51] By the early

1930s, a preoccupation with the "national character" or "peculiarly Japanese features" as the essence of artistic expression began to restrict permissible literary forms and, in the wake of state repression, Proletarian literature died out.[52] Despite their presumption of familiarity with literary people and personalities, which might be expected to limit their readership, by the mid-1930s works in the I-novel form had achieved preeminence in the contemporary canon.[53]

Women writers of the 1920s also often favored a confessional style. Their work, however, was not generally categorized as *watakushi shōsetsu,* but as *jiden shōsetsu* (autobiographical fiction).[54] The notion that "women's literature" constituted a distinct style must have derived from the presumption that women's autobiographical fiction was somehow different from the I-novels men wrote. The implications of such a distinction were not widely perceived at the time. Only a few observers, for example, Shintō Junko, who argued that literature labeled to indicate that it was written by women implied that the work was a poor piece of writing *(dasaku)* or inferior *(akusaku)*,[55] have noted the negative connotations attributed, through this division, to women's writing.

"Women's literature" does not constitute a literary school in the same sense as the Kenyūsha (1885–1903) with their journal *Garakuta bunko* (Rubbish heap library), the Romantic writers (1889–1904) with their journal *Bungakkai* (The world of literature), or the White Birch Society (1910–1920), who published in *Shirakaba* (White birch).[56] Neither did the "women" of "women's literature" form an informal group like Natsume Sōseki's coterie, where aspiring male writers gathered around an established master. Women writers grouped by critics shared no unifying tradition, no school, and no journal. Consequently the term did not do justice to the diversity of perspectives and approaches of those labeled. To call someone a "woman writer" said nothing about the author's relation with other literary, intellectual, social, and political trends. And the seeming simplicity of the term facilitated conflating the author's sex with her style. The label "woman writer" connoted an inevitable destiny when, as a critical assessment, it should have been only a contingent association. The stereotyping encouraged neglect of any transformation or change in an author's style and obscured artistic maturation and development.

The concept of women's literature as a distinct style of writing developed as a residual category, defined not so much by intrinsic criteria as by its relation to other conceptual distinctions in the criticism of the 1920s. Some women writers wrote short, simple sentences and gave realistic, concrete portrayals of what was close to the author; so did many men. A writer's—any writer's—variation in language and style was at least as great as the presumed variations between the sexes. The boundaries of women's literature were demarcated by two sets of conceptual antinomies—the pure and the popular, the confessional and the autobiographical. These oppositions were always imperfect, and allowances were made for exceptions, but in most cases they implicitly devalued the work of women writers as merely popular and aesthetically second rate.

The distinctly separate identity of "women's literature" in the critical discourse ensured its treatment as unequal. Even as the work of women writers exhibited enormous change between the 1930s and the 1970s, its classification as "women's literature" defined (though without defining) what women wrote and how it was perceived. Despite this, a separate women's style was neither universally acknowledged nor encouraged by male critics and writers. A 1949 questionnaire in the resurrected *Nyonin geijutsu* solicited a range of responses to the question "What are your expectations for women's arts?" The critic Ara Masato wrote, "Separating men from women must be stopped as quickly as possible." The poet Kimata Osamu, a student of the poet Kitahara Hakushu, replied, "I look forward to the birth of a woman artist who does not need the special designation 'woman' *(joryū)*." And the poet Horiguchi Daigaku answered, "To become an artist who overcomes being female *(josei)*." While a few respondents celebrated women's difference, most either challenged the concept of gender-based art or disparaged what was perceived as female. The artist Suda Kunitarō wrote, "I look forward to art that is not imitative. That is because I believe that women especially have this imitative nature." Takii Kōsaku, a writer and follower of the confessional writer Shiga Naoya, anticipated that, once women had higher education (like men), they would produce sensitive, detailed, and beautiful works. Hinatsu Kōnosuke, a poet, thought that, up to that time, women writers had been spoiled, and inferior work had been accepted "because they were women." In the same questionnaire, the query, "What literary work could have been written only by a woman?" prompted the answer "none," or identified several western works. Kimata Masato alone cited specific examples by a Japanese woman, Sata Ineko's recent works *Michi* (Road) and *Kyogi* (Falsehood). Most respondents dismissed the question's premise. Odagiri Hideo replied, for example, "I do not think there are any exceptional works in that category"; Fukuda Tsuneari said, "There are none among high-quality works, only among pulp fiction."[57]

Champions of women's artistic sensibilities often have been equally unequivocal. In the early 1970s, Okuno Takeo asserted that men needed to take on a woman's voice to write. He viewed Japanese fiction since the Meiji era as feminine *(joseiteki)*, and even went so far as to suggest creating a "men's style" *(danryū)* literary prize as men's talent decreased.[58] Such a prize would parallel the separate prizes for women writers already in existence, and presumed that such special recognition should be granted only to second-rate authors. Okuno asserted that women could write fiction best, because they possess capabilities analogous to those of the medium in shamanism and can change into the characters they portray.[59]

Female writers and critics have also argued that women writers possess unique characteristics. Itagaki Naoko assumed that women naturally wrote simpler, less intellectual fiction.[60] Kumasaka Atsuko began her article on Hayashi Fumiko and Okamoto Kanoko with the premise that there are "inherently feminine" sensations, notably *onnen* (hatred), which comes from "the consciousness of being a victim."[61] Many have reiterated assumptions about separate men's and women's styles of language that have been conventions since classical antiquity. But a study in the May 1967 issue of *Kokubungaku* that compared vocabulary in literary works by men and women concluded, contrary to expectations, that the women's works contained fewer expressions of emotion *(kanjōteki hyōgen)* and more examples of independence and objectivity *(jiritsusei kyakkansei)* than did the works of male authors.[62]

The assumptions that underlay the prevailing gender classifications were playfully ridiculed in Setouchi Harumi's 1962 top ten stipulations for success as a woman writer

- Be a woman.
- Be masculine.
- Don't be too beautiful.
- Have natural talent.
- Have a high opinion of yourself.
- Jealously defend your self-interests.
- Don't try to be a good wife.
- Have the courage to "strip" and bare all in your writing.
- Be endowed with property.
- Be content in your loneliness.[63]

Setouchi's elaboration of each of these points, qualifying them in ways to make them seem "reasonable," if not natural, underscores the list's bitter humor. Her message, however much couched tongue in cheek, is brutally clear: To write, women must be prepared to fight with no holds barred, because it's a cruel, a merciless, and, most of all, a man's world.

A Categorical Revision

Through the first four postwar decades, the terms *joryū bungaku* (women's literature) and *joryū sakka* (women writers) seemed to be thoroughly ensconced in the literary lexicon. The concepts periodically served as the organizing themes in special issues of the two most influential academic literary journals, both named *Kokubungaku* (National literature).[64] Articles in these issues—the September issues of *Kokubungaku* (I) in 1962, 1976, and 1985, and the July 1976 issue of *Kokubungaku* (II)—usually presented assessments of a modern writer and the themes of her work, treating their categorization as natural, self-evident or, at least, given. But dissatisfaction with the inadequacies of the categories was already being clearly expressed by the early 1980s, particularly in "conversations" that referred to the contemporary scene. For instance, in a roundtable discussion published in the December 1980 special issue of *Kokubungaku* (II), which focused on the trajectory of women's writing since Higuchi Ichiyō, the literary critic Kawamura Jirō emphasized recent changes in the utility of the term *joryū bungaku*: where it had once meant a style of literature, now it referred only to the gender of the author: "Formerly, if you just said *joryū bungaku*, somehow, you had an understanding of what kind of person the authors were and what they were doing . . . [but] the term *joryū bungaku* doesn't mean anything anymore in our current situation."[65] In Kawamura's view, the category that once denoted a literary style no longer captured the diversity of approaches employed by women writers. However, "from a woman's perspective, the term *joryū bungaku* may [still] evoke a sense of discrimination or express a prejudice."[66]

The women writers in the discussion, Tsushima Yūko and Takahashi Takako, echoed the declining significance of the distinction that "women's literature" conveyed. Takahashi suggested that the former tendency of women writers to take an antagonistic stance toward male writers had been eclipsed by the growth of personal freedoms and experimentation in contemporary literature. Tsushima expressed the consensus that this process would continue: "The image conjured up by *joryū sakka* will probably be different even from that of one generation ago." Just as the term *keishū sakka* was outmoded, so too the term *joryū sakka* would probably fall into disuse.[67]

Yet the projected passing of the term *joryū sakka* was met with reservation. Kawamura, responding to Tsushima's observation about the negative connotations of *keishū sakka*, suggested that though male critics and publishers imposed such terms on women writers, and these terms restricted the forms of acceptable expression, the net impact was positive for women writers. Kawamura suggested that restrictions on women writers that kept them out of the literary mainstream had focused their energies and provided a driving force to their work that was now missing. And all the participants persisted in drawing distinctions between male and female types of literature, either of which, they concluded, may be written by men or women.

In Kawamura's view, objectivity characterizes masculine works, and subjectivity feminine works. Takahashi suggested that such qualities were determined not by the sex of the author, but by the style of writing. Kawamura concurred, proposing that women writers increasingly exhibit what he called the masculine traits of rationality, objectivity, and self-awareness. He also pointed to the feminization of male writers, such as Nakagami Kenji, who, he argued, sought to incorporate the femininity of chaos.[68] Takahashi admitted that she was a bit masculine *(danseiteki)*, or perhaps androgynous, while Tsushima, she felt, remained feminine *(joseiteki)*. All agreed that a woman writer was not necessarily feminine.

Despite the presumed permeability and shifting specificity of gender roles among contemporary writers, both authors in the roundtable continued to maintain that women convey distinct qualities in their works. While they themselves did not consciously write as women, the female writer, so they argued, can look within herself for an accurate portrayal of female characters. Tsushima noted that fictional characterizations dealing only with the male world were unconvincing, and that the incorporation of women's perspectives was increasingly necessary for significant works of literature. Takahashi suggested that the marginality of women in Japanese society allowed them a distinct advantage in capturing the complex nature of human beings.[69]

This discussion previewed many of the central elements of the next decade's debate. The terms *joryū sakka* and *joryū bungaku* had lost their validity, certainly in reference to a specific style of modern literature. Yet distinctions between masculine and feminine styles and notions about the unique literary voice of women remained. It would be naive to expect such pervasive and long-standing social distinctions to disappear from literary expression, but neither are such distinctions static and unchanging.

The rejection of the terminology *joryū* in the mid-1980s did not stem from a particular theoretical breakthrough or universally acknowledged influential essay. It appeared—at first inconsistently—in a variety of venues and works. Tomioka Taeko's " 'Onna no kotoba' to 'Kuni no kotoba' " ("Women's language" and "the nation's language") served as a precursor to the shift, criticizing the nature of the boundaries and contradictions inherent in the notion of linguistic differences appropriate for separate spheres.[70] In May 1986 a special issue of *Kokubungaku* (II) entitled *Josei—sono henkaku no ekurichūru* (*Ecriture* of the changing female) showed how the ground was shifting: Several of the main articles used *joryū bungaku,* but an equal number, and the issue's title, used *josei*, not only in reference to "women's history" or "debates on women," where the term had long been standard, but also in reference to literature.[71] Mizuta, in relation to the representation of women's sexuality and to the writer Okamoto Kaneko—a woman often treated as a "masculine" exception—twice wrote *josei bungaku*.[72] Yet neither Mizuta nor any other contributor to this volume directly addressed the prevailing practice of categorization. Nor, despite the editor's choice of *écriture* for the title, did anyone discuss French feminism's approach to "woman" as a "writing-effect." Yonaha Keiko's *Gendai joryū sakka ron* (The debate on contemporary women writers), also published in 1986, was adamant in rejecting the implications of the term *joryū bungaku,* but continued to use *joryū* to elaborate on the fundamental difference in literary voice of "those who can give birth."

Far more indicative of the changing terminology was the 1987 anthology of modern women writers, *Tanpen josei bungaku kindai* (Modern women's short stories) edited by Imai Yasuko, Yabu Teiko, and Watanabe Sumiko. Even in this volume, the editors' stated objectives—"to present works by women writers, selected by women, that represented women from a contemporary perspective"—did not explicitly condemn the *joryū* categorization, and many of the accompanying biographical essays and criticism were inconsistent in their application of the terms, or avoided gender references altogether.[73] For example, Iwabuchi Hiroko uses both *josei* and *joryū* in reference to Miyamoto Yuriko and other women writers, while Ogata Akiko avoids any use of either in discussing Hayashi Fumiko.[74] Despite the volume's inconsistencies, it was riding a wave of revision. Since then, almost every major publication about modern women writers has followed its lead.[75] Yet, as Imai Yasuko points out in her 1993 commentary on Kurahashi Yumiko, a male critic could write *josei* and still ooze condescension toward women. She quotes a particularly egregious example: "When I read the works of Kurahashi, I am filled with admiration for her intellect. The ranks of women writers (*josei sakka*) who, for the most part, rely on emotion, are not devoid of intellect. However, I cannot help but think there is something different about Kurahashi's intelligence or, more colloquially, her smarts, which sets her apart from other women. . . . Kurahashi's brain is more masculine, or androgynous. You could even say that it has uniquely evolved, even more than the average man's."[76]

The new terminology coincided with increasing recognition of the diversity of women's experience. The Equal Employment Opportunity Law (EEOL), stripped the "protective" regulations that had limited women's corporate overtime or night shift work and adopted "male" standards for the workplace, was a benchmark in this process. It passed over the objections and protests of many feminists and activist organizations. This legislation enabled a small minority of women to join the "comprehensive" (*sōgō shoku*) career track for management and supervisory personnel. The majority remained in the general clerical category, which offered no prospects for advancement. Perhaps more significantly, a growing percentage of working women—and the majority of the growth in jobs—was relegated to part-time positions, with no benefits, no job security, and low wages.[77] The increasing disparities in women's work experiences resulting from the law helped to undercut assumptions of commonalities among women. Although these trends in the workplace coincided with the perception of differences among women authors, the use of *josei* probably has little to do with the broader social dynamics. Literature in Japan has rarely reflected the pulse of popular debate. The dramatic campaigns against sex tours or the prominence of pornography by the Women's Action Group from the late 1970s and early 1980s, to say nothing of the live-ins (*gasshuku*) of the Lib movement in the early 1970s, had next to no visible impact on how literature by or about women, was read.[78]

The shift in terminology is probably best attributed to two principal factors internal to higher education. One indirect contributor was the late arrival of women's studies *(joseigaku)*—late compared to the United States, Britain, or even, say, India—as an institutionally recognized and influential part of the academy. The Ministry of Education retreated only grudgingly from its long-standing skepticism about the field, but by 1986, nine research centers or institutes of women's studies (sometimes labeled as women's culture or education) had been established, and a small but rapidly growing number of four-year colleges and universities had begun to offer courses in it.[79] Once it had established a toehold, women's studies began to provide a kind of protection against victimization, although it had as yet little institutional support. But by the mid-1980s, female academics had begun to adopt far more explicitly feminist perspectives. These academics increasingly aligned with, and even superseded, the movement-oriented activists as the most dynamic and visible contributors to feminist debates. Their efforts brought at least terminological changes to the Japanese literature departments, which have arguably been universities' most intellectually conservative domains. Hostility from male peers and administrators has severely limited the progress of gender as a focus of intellectual inquiry. Where terminology is concerned, however, the institutional validation of the "g-word" has disrupted literary discourse. The diversity and innovations of modern women writers could no longer be lumped together and dismissed under a single derogatory label. The influence of female sociologists, notably Ueno Chizuko[80] and Ehara Yumiko,[81] also affected the terms used. The publications in which they set out their perspectives on gender difference and, in the case of Ueno, willingness directly to address the place of women in literature were widely read. In almost the reverse of the American experience, Japanese sociologists since the mid-1970s have been freer to embrace gender as their defining focus and their core intellectual problem. Literature, as a discipline, has come to adopt at least some of these perspectives as the writings of sociologists expanded beyond their disciplinary domain.

Notes

1. Konishi, *A History of Japanese Literature*, 1:161. The sex of Hieda no Are remains contested. The original Japanese edition of this book does not unequivocally state that Hieda no Are was a woman.

2. Ibid., 2:140–142; Bowring, "The Female Hand," 49–56.

3. Readers should note that none of the given names of these authors is known: Two of the authors are known only by their relations to historically identified men, and even the most renowned classical author, Murasaki Shikibu, is known only by her father's court title (Shikibu) and the appellation of a principal character in *The Tale of Genji* (Murasaki, or "lavender").

4. Wittgenstein, *Tractatus Logico-Philosophicus*, 115.

5. For insight into this matter, see Miyake, "The *Tosa Diary,* in Schalow and Walker, eds., *The Woman's Hand*. See also Miyake's "Women's Voice in Japanese Literature" and Bundy's "Japan's First Woman Diarist."

6. Keene, *Anthology of Japanese Literature*, 162–164.

7. She was tagged with this particular label because of the presumption that she had read the *Nihon shoki* (The records of Japan) (720), written in literary Chinese. Bowring, *Murasaki Shikibu,* 137–139.

8. Ibid., 131.

9. Quoted in Keene, *Travelers of a Hundred Ages*, 20.

10. Ibid., 21.

11. Gilbert and Gubar, in *No Man's Land,* 1:171, discuss the notion of affiliation as a means of asserting choice and continuity.

12. Gates, " 'Authenticity' or the Lesson of Little Tree," 27.

13. Keene observes that there was a hiatus of about three hundred years (c. 1358–1681) when works by women writers were absent (*Travelers of a Hundred Ages,* 175, 264). Mulhern's 1994 sourcebook, *Japanese Women Writers,* gives profiles of fifteen women in the classical era and forty-three in the modern, but not one from the Muromachi era (beginning 1336) to the 1870s.

14. Vernon, *Daughters of the Moon*, 27–28; Chabot, "A View of Tokugawa Women and Literature," 55–56.

15. Mass, *Lordship and Inheritance in Early Medieval Japan,* 9, 49, 101–106.

16. Notable exceptions include Inoue Tsūjo (1660–1738), Iseki Takako (1785–1845), and Takejo, whose *Kōshi michi no ki* (A record of the road to Kōshi, 1720) was published in 1807 (Keene, *Travelers of a Hundred Ages*, 328–340, 376–382). Yanagawa Kōron (wife of Yanagawa Seigan, 1789–1858) stood out for her compositions of *kanshi*, or Chinese poetry (Keene, *World within Walls*, 555).

17. Arakida Reiko's work—*renga* poetry, histories written in kana, classical fiction (*gabun*), travel diaries, and love stories—takes up all of the second and part of the third volume in the four-volume set. Arakida's love stories, such as *Goyō* (Five leaves) and *Hamachidori* (Plover), have a Heian setting. Other authors also evoked Heian themes and models: Takabatake Tomi (d. 1881) chose the pen name Takabatake Shikibu, reminiscent of Heian women who are known to us today only by the court title Shikibu and a given name not their own. Uden

no Yonoko's travel diary (1806) was described as having the literary form and aptitude of Sei Shōnagon's *Pillow Book*. Furuya Tomoyoshi, *Joryū bungaku zenshū*, 3:5.

18. *Keishū sakka* (a woman gifted in the arts; literally [one from the] bedroom [who] excels), a predecessor to *joryū sakka*, was more widely used in the Meiji and Taishō eras than it was later. Women writers and critics came to view the term as outmoded and pejorative, but it did not suggest a specific style of writing.

19. Yosano Akiko, *Tokugawa jidai joryū bungaku.*

20. Mawatari, "Joryū bungei kenkyū," 35.

21. The issues included works by Tanabe (Miyake) Kaho (1868–1944), Higuchi Ichiyō (1872–96), Koganei Kimiko (1870–1944), Wakamatsu Shizuko (1864–1896), and Tazawa Inafune (1874–1896), among others. For a discussion of these two special issues and a complete list of authors, see Shioda, *Meiji joryū sakka ron*, 261–262, and Danly, *In the Shade of Spring Leaves,* 149.

22. Keene, *Dawn to the West,* 167.

23. *Jogakusei* (December 1892), quoted in Keene, *Dawn to the West*, 173–174.

24. Miyamoto Kenji, *Miyamoto Yuriko no sekai,* 7.

25. Akiyama, "Ima joryū bungaku to wa nani ka," 125.

26. Seki, *Higuchi Ichiyō o yomu,* 48–51.

27. Okazaki, *Japanese Literature in the Meiji Era.*, 174–178; Keene, *Dawn to the West*, 165–185; Karatani, *Origins of Modern Japanese Literature*, 135.

28. Kaigo, *Nihon kindai kyōiku shi jiten,* 93.

29. Women's increased literacy is associated with a decline in maternal mortality and physical vulnerability, an improvement in nutrition and health, and greater real income. For a disturbing account of the costs of low literacy (among other factors), see Sen, "More than 100 Million Women Are Missing."

30. These figures represent women attending the institutions that were designated "university" *(daigaku)* under the old educational system, and do not include women enrolled in normal schools for teacher training, women's colleges, or other specialty schools. Kaigo, ed., *Nihon kindai kyōiku shi jiten,* 108.

31. Maeda, "Taishō kōki tsūzoku shōsetsu no tenkai (ge)," 651.

32. Tōkyō shi shakaikyoku (Tokyo city social affairs department), *Shokugyō fujin ni kan suru chōsa* (A survey concerning working women [1923]), 16. Note that some white-collar jobs, notably nursing, are absent from the survey.

33. The 900,000 working women who did not do manual labor were classified as holding *chitekirōdōsha* or mental labor jobs. Nagy, "Middle-Class Working Women during the Interwar Years," 202.

34. On the marital status and motivations of these women, see ibid., 205–209.

35. Maeda, "Taishō kōki tsūzoku shōsetsu no tenkai (ge)."

36. Quoted in ibid., 814. Aono Suekichi (1890–1961) was a prominent Marxist critic and advocate of Proletarian literature.

37. Nolte and Hastings, "The Meiji State Policy toward Women," 158–159; Garon, "Women's Groups and the Japanese State," 10–15.

38. Roden, "Taishō Culture and the Problem of Gender Ambivalence," 43.

39. Ibid.

40. See also Rodd, "Yosano Akiko and the Taishō Debate of the 'New Woman.' "

41. Silverberg, "The Modern Girl as Militant," 246.

42. Nogami, quoted in Roden, "Taishō Culture and the Problem of Gender Ambivalence," 46.

43. Kazushige, quoted in ibid., 52.

44. Ibid.

45. Fowler, *Rhetoric of Confession,* 28–29.

46. For confessional fiction in English translation, see Tayama Katai, *Quilt,* translated by Kenneth G. Henshall, and Shiga Naoya's *Dark Night's Passing;* for works by women in this vein see Hirabayashi Taeko's "Self-Mockery," as well as Uno Chiyo's *Confessions of Love* and "This Powder Box."

47. Karatani, *Origins of Modern Japanese Literature*, 69–75.

48. Danly, *In the Shade of Spring Leaves*, 28; Keene, *Dawn to the West*, 167.

49. Chiba, "Bungaku no ichinen," 185.

50. Kume, " 'Watakushi' shōsetsu to 'shinkyō' shōsetsu," originally published in 1925 in *Bungei kōza.*

51. In the 1920s, Proletarian literature attracted a large number of proponents, both writers (Kobayashi Takiji, Hayama Yoshiki, Hayashi Fusao, Kuroshima Denji) and critics (Aono Suekichi, Nakano Shigeharu). Recent observers have agreed with earlier critics' low opinion of it—for example, Keene comments on its "stylistic immaturity and awkwardness of techniques" (*Dawn to the West,* 599)—although their reasons are unrelated to its contrast with *watakushi shōsetsu.* For a critical appraisal of Proletarian literature, see Arima, *The Failure of Freedom*, 173–213.

52. But consider also the tenacity and sophistication of those who opposed the rise of jingoism, as represented in Silverberg, *Changing Song.*

53. Kobayashi Hideo, "Watakushi shōsetsu ron," originally published in 1935 in *Keizai ōrai.*

54. See, for example, Itagaki, "Shōwa no joryū sakka," 32; Yoshida, "Kindai joryū no bungaku," 16; Kōra, "Jiko to Tō no shinwaka," 110.

55. Shintō, "Hirabayashi Taiko," 48–49.

56. With only a few exceptions, such as Higuchi Ichiyō's association with the Romantic writers and their journal *Bungakkai,* or Sō Fusa's (b. 1907; nom de plume of Katayama Fusako) tie with Hori Tatsuo and the modernist school, literary schools rarely allowed women to participate. For example, the White Birch Society, particularly active and influential in the 1910s, excluded women from the pages of its journal primarily because it relied on its own members, fellow students from the all-male Tokyo Imperial University, for contributions. Endō Yu, " 'Shirakaba ha' to joryū bungaku."

57. Joryū bungakusha kai, ed., *Nyonin geijutsu* (January 1, 1949), 67, 127.

58. Okuno, *Joryū sakka ron*, 15.

59. Ibid., 259–260.

60. Itagaki, *Meiji, Taishō, Shōwa no joryū bungaku*, 2.

61. Kumasaka, " 'Onnen to shite no joryū bungaku' ", 79.

62. The data for this comparison were highly selective and cannot constitute a conclusive refutation of conventional wisdom. For example, Hayashi Fumiko's

Bangiku (Late chrysanthemum) and Hirabayashi Taiko's *Watashi wa ikiru* (I will live) were the two works chosen as representative of women's literature. The *Kokubungaku* study is quoted in Tsukada, "Joryū bungaku no josetsu," 31.

63. Setouchi, "Joryū sakka ni naru jōken."

64. I refer to *Kokubungaku kaishaku to kanshō* (National literature: Commentary and appreciation) as *Kokubungaku* (I), as it was founded first, in 1945, and *Kokubungaku: kaishaku to kyōzai no kenkyū* (National literature: Commentary and teaching materials), founded twenty years later, as *Kokubungaku* (II). They are independent of one another and are produced by different publishers.

65. "Joryū o tsukihatarakasu mono," 6.

66. Ibid., 8.

67. Ibid., 10.

68. Ibid., 21. Describing chaos as a feminine trait echoes the distinctions of yin and yang in Chinese divination.

69. Ibid., 14.

70. Tomioka's " 'Onna no kotoba' to 'Kuni no kotoba' " was published in 1983 as part of a year-long serial in the journal *Fujin kōron*; the collected essays were published the following year in *Fuji no koromo ni asa no fusuma.*

71. *Kokubungaku* (II) 31/5, *Josei—sono henkaku no ekurichūru,* (May 1986) included Mizuta, "Josei ron no yukue" (The direction of debates on women) and Sone, "Gendai bungaku ni okeru josei no hakken" (The discovery of women in modern literature).

72. Mizuta, "Josei ron no yukue," 70.

73. Imai, Yabu, and Watanabe eds., *Tanpen josei bungaku kindai,* 1–2.

74. Iwabuchi, "Kaisetsu," Ogata, "Kaisetsu," both in Imai, Yabu, and Watanabe, eds., *Tanpen josei bungaku kindai.*

75. For instance, in the 1990 biographical dictionary of 380 modern Japanese women writers, from the 1880s to the 1980s, edited by Muramatsu Sadataka and Watanabe Sumiko, and rather misleadingly titled *Gendai josei bungaku jiten* [A dictionary of contemporary women's fiction], but also in successive special issues of *Kokubungaku* (I), *Kotoba to josei* [Women and language] (July 1991), and *Kokubungaku* (II), *Feminizumu no kotoba: josei bungaku* [The language of feminism—women's literature] (November 1992) and in other anthologies (Imai et al., 1993; Josei bungaku kai 1994) geared for university students.

76. Kurahashi, quoted in Imai Yasuko, "Kaisetsu," 23.

77. The Ministry of Labor's *Labor Force Survey* showed a sharp rise in the number of working women, from 15.5 to 20.1 million between 1985 and 1993. Part-time women workers increased dramatically from 3.33 to 6.23 million. Japanese women have the lowest wages, as a percentage of men's, in the industrialized world, and Japan was the only nation in which women's wages, so measured, fell during the 1980s (United Nations Development Programme, *Human Development Report*, 21–22, 191; Japan Statistical Association, *Historical Statistics of Japan*, 250; Statistical Bureau, Management and Coordination Agency, *Japan Statistical Yearbook, 1993/94*, 110. Among women working full time, average monthly cash earnings fell (in enterprises with more than thirty workers) from 53.81 percent of men's wages in 1980 to 49.55 percent in 1990. Wages for women in smaller enterprises were lower both in absolute and in relative terms. Women

working part time made approximately half as much per hour as women in full-time work made. (*Japan Statistical Yearbook, 1993/94*, 119, 126.

78. Four women's studies organizations had been established by the late 1970s, but the activists and were largely separate from academic discourse, without dialogue or interaction. Some well known activists expressed outright hostility and scorn for academics. Cf. Miki Soko, "What Is Women's Studies—without the Spirit of Women's Liberation—For?"

79. Tachi, "Kōtō kyōiku ni okeru joseigaku no." Nevertheless, by many standards, the pace of these gains was glacial. Only in 1994 was the first degree-granting program in women's studies" established, at Ochanomizu Women's University, and this was for a Ph.D. only.

80. Ueno, *Onna wa sekai o sukueru ka* and *Onna to iu kairaku.*

81. Ehara, *Feminizu to kenryoku sayū* and *Feminizu ronsō.*

3 Women's Journals

The category "women's literature" came to mean the kind of style that would appeal to women readers partly because of changes in the publishing business in the early twentieth century. Contemporary observers noted how editors and publishers tailored their publications to specific audiences, either all or some portion of the women's market.[1] This practice was aided and abetted by the continuing notion that women had a distinct—and separate—place in society. Two kinds of women's journals developed. The first type consisted of commercially oriented, mass-market magazines that often, but not always, advocated the "good wife/ wise mother" concept of the "traditional" Japanese family.[2] The second offered forums for social and political reform or took as a mandate the education of women. Sometimes these magazines served as serious literary venues for women.

Several of the early women's journals, such as *Jogaku zasshi* (Women's education magazine, 1885), a Christian journal oriented toward improving women's status, or *Sekai fujin* (Women's world, 1907), dedicated to women's education and rights, were launched with a reforming mission. But their zeal was often short-lived, particularly in the face of official hostility (*Sekai fujin* was banned within two years of its first issue), and they generally did not provide an effective artistic forum. The editors of *Jogaku zasshi,* however, were able to establish a mainstream literary journal entitled *Bungakkai*, which later helped Higuchi Ichiyō to popularity.[3] Journals like *Bungakkai* were rare. Usually male publishers and editors of general-interest journals would establish women's magazines to supplement their flagship publication.

Hiratsuka Raichō (1886–1971), a graduate of Japan's first women's college, founded the explicitly feminist journal, *Seitō* (Bluestockings), in September 1911, gathering together a small staff of like-minded women college graduates. Hiratsuka had gained considerable notoriety from the newspaper coverage of her "failed love suicide" with the married naturalist novelist Morita Sōhei in March 1908. Morita's fictionalized account of the event, *Baien* (Smoke), serialized in *Asahi Shimbun* in 1909 and 1910 had only added to it. The whiff of scandal continued to haunt Hiratsuka and her associates throughout *Seitō*'s short life. She and her staff were pilloried in the press as a threat to public morality, as much for their personal affairs and public acts as for the intellectual content of the issues, although these remain astonishing for contemporary readers.[4] In the inaugural issue of *Seitō*, Hiratsuka began her lead article by referring to the myth of the sun goddesss, Amaterasu, in the founding of Japan: "In the beginning, woman truly was the sun . . . now she has become the moon—shining by the light of others, dependent on others for a living, with a face as pale and ashen as an invalid's."[5] Her condemnation of women's status in Japan was unmistakable but, by evoking the idea of a golden age, she suggested that women could rise again. *Seitō* declared that its mandate was "to gauge the progress of women's literature, to exhibit natural talent, and hereafter to give birth to women's genius."[6] The journal lasted only four and a half years before it was finally closed for "disrupting good morals and manners," but during its short life, it challenged pervasive conventions about marriage and the role of women in Japanese society.[7]

Seitō initiated a series of highly contentious public debates on chastity, abortion, and prostitution. It ran provocative articles that resulted in the ban of a succession of issues. These celebrated the sexuality and infidelity of a married woman (April 1912), called for women's liberation through Marxist revolution (Februrary 1913), and condemned the illegality of abortion and the hypocritical imprisonment and abuse of women punished for it (June 1915).[8] Although some present-day critics dismiss its literary contributions, this journal, particularly in its first two years, provided a much-needed venue for women's writing, publishing works by Yosano Akiko, Nogami Yaeko, Okamoto Kanoko, Hasegawa Shigure (1879–1941), Mori Shigejo (1880–1936; wife of Mori Ogai), Koganei Kimiko (1870–1956; sister of Mori Ogai), and Kunikida Haruko (1879–1962; sister of Kunikida Doppo) among many others.[9]

Seitō, the best known and most influential of the pioneering feminist journals, is still a touchstone for contemporary feminists. The monthly Shin-feminizu Hihyō Kai (New feminism study group), which I attended in 1994 and 1995, shows the continued interest in the contributions of this journal. The focus of this group of a dozen female intellectuals and academics was to scrutinize *Seitō* issue by issue, dissecting one issue each month. Shin-femi meetings sometimes also included a presentation on some other writer or issue, but the first half of every five-hour meeting was given over to interrogating the contents of a specific issue, reexamining the concerns and artistry of this early feminist publication. On some points, our group departed from widely repeated assertions of the origins and intentions of the journal. For example, Mikiso Hane, among others, cites the journal's own statement of purpose to characterize it, at least initially, as a literary journal that increasingly got involved in social issues.[10] Most members of Shin-femi agreed that Hiratsuka had initially opposed the inclusion of literature, but that others who supported the journal, especially Ikuta Chōkō, convinced her that it was necessary to assure the journal's visibility, popularity, and even its acceptability to the authorities. The draft statement of purpose was changed from "women's self-awakening" (*joishi kakusei*) to "women's literature" *(joryū bungaku)* for this reason.[11]

In 1915, editorship turned over to Itō Noe (1895–1923) who, at age twenty, pushed broader social perspectives, questioned even more sharply the prevailing social practices, translated articles by such foreign feminists as Emma Goldman, and scathingly condemned sanctimonious charity and narrow-minded morality. From the outset, the journal emphasized the freedom to love and the acceptability of an unmarried women's loss of virginity, arguing that strictures on women's expression of sexuality were introduced, or at least heavily stressed, by Christian missionaries. With Itō at the helm, this issue would be emphasized and incur the censors' ire, eventually forcing an end to publication in February 1916. Itō herself would be publicly involved with an older, married man, Ōsugi Sakae (1885–1923), who was simultaneously involved with another socialist activist, Kamichika Ichiko (1888–1981). In 1916, Kamichika stabbed Ōsugi in the neck, and her arrest and detention created a scandal. On September 16, 1923, long after the journal had ceased publication, Ōsugi and Itō, who were continuing to work as activist organizers in a working-class district, were murdered by police.

Other feminist journals were also published in the Taishō era and, like many political or avant-garde publications, tended to die young. But feminist journals were perceived as less influential and less well known than the anarchist journals *Aka to kuro* (Red and black, 1923–1924) and *Bungei kaihō* (Literary liberation, 1927), the Proletarian journals *Tane maku hito* (The sower, 1921) and *Bungei sensen* (Literary front, 1924) or the dadaist *GE GIMGAM PRRR GIMGEM* (1924). The feminist journal *Saffron* (1914, March–August), edited by Ōtake Itsue, was published by the same press, and had many of the same contributors, as *Seitō*, but it was exclusively literary, with lush illustrations, translations (including several works of Oscar Wilde), and many contributions by Kamichika Ichiko. *Beatrice* (July 1916–April 1917), edited by Yamada Tazu, Imai Kuniko (1890–1948), and Ikuta Hanayo (1888–1970), took its title from the character in Dante's *Inferno* and had an all-female staff. It published works by many of the women associated with *Seitō*. *Uuman karento* (The current woman, June 1923–December 1926), edited by Miyake Yasuko (1890–1932), and *Shojochi* (Virgin soil, April 1922–January 1923), edited by the influential male author Shimazaki Tōson (its title was taken from Turgenev's story), had both a literary and an educational focus. *Shojochi* received considerable criticism from other feminists. *Nyonin geijutsu* (Women's arts, 1923), edited by Hasegawa Shigure and Okada Yachiyo (1883–1962), put out only two issues before ceasing publication in the wake of the Great Kanto Earthquake.[12]

The majority of "women's magazines" were unconnected to any feminist movement or activist editor. Women's journals that targeted the broadest cross-section of women readers grew rapidly, particularly after World War I. By the mid-1920s, *Fujin kōron* (Ladies' review, founded 1916) and *Fujin kurabu* (Ladies' club, founded 1920) had monthly circulations of at least 100,000, while those of *Fujo kai* (Women's world, founded 1910) and *Shufu no tomo* (Housewives' friend, founded 1917) had reached 250,000.[13] Maeda Ai estimated that in January 1925, women's magazines sold 1.2 million copies.[14] The twentieth-anniversary issue of *Fujin sekai* (founded 1906) alone had a print run of 600,000. Fourteen women's magazines were being published monthly by the mid-1920s. Readers of these publications, by their sheer numbers, formed a critical mass that influenced what was being written, and by whom.

By publishing in women's journals, women writers became more visible and strengthened their reputations. The literary pages of at least two newspapers with national circulation, *Asahi Shimbun* and *Yomiuri Shimbun,* reflected the growing status and legitimacy of women's journals among the reading public. By the summer of 1930, *Asahi Shimbun* was running regular features on contemporary women writers, while *Yomiuri Shimbun* presented monthly reviews of the forthcoming articles in major women's journals. This coverage of women writers and the journals in which they published no doubt helped earn them popular recognition. But the newspapers did not invent the interest or the audience. They mirrored—even while they stimulated—the public's new found enthusiasm for women's literature.

Women's journals opened new possibilities for publishing and income that changed literary careers, and not just women's. Ōya Sōichi was one of the first to assert the influence of women's journals on the *bundan* (literary guild).[15] In 1926, Ōya compared the growth of women's magazines to new colonies:

> What one must call the remarkable phenomenon of the increase in women readers in recent years has influenced popular writing in much the same way that the discovery of a vast new colony might

> influence the country. Thus the sudden development of women's magazines influenced Japan's *bundan*, much as the growth of the spinning industry's China market reconstituted the Japanese financial system. Popular writers' incomes rose proportionately in relation to the development of women's magazines.[16]

Yet in his view, increased incomes and circulation served only to debase the value of the literary works, as new avenues for writing catering to popular tastes unleashed a flood of "slipshod works." Writers could now publish popular literature without the self-discipline needed to write in the confessional style that dominated the literary high ground. The new outlets for publication undermined the tight control over access and acceptable style that had characterized the *bundan*.

Ōya was not alone in criticizing the so-called slipshod literature that focused on modern and faddish facets of life. (Particular culprits were atmospheric stories about "places of assignation, geisha, cafes, waitresses, cards, *shōgi*, mah-jongg, billiards, and baseball . . . [that] flooded the market.")[17] The writer and critic Satō Haruo had voiced a similar opinion about the debasement of the *bundan* several months earlier in "On the Life of the Literary Man" (*Shinchō*, September 1926). Yet Ōya stood alone, however, in emphasizing the central role of women's journals in the surge of popular literature. He also blamed the supposed decline in standards on the *bundan* itself because of its system of distinguishing between serious and popular (i.e., written for money) literature. "Short pieces of confessional fiction in general magazines *(sōgō zasshi)* or literary magazines, and popular novels *(tsūzoku chōhen)* in newspapers or women's magazines—this was the general rule of thumb for the inhabitants of the *bundan*."[18] In Ōya's view, its acceptance of hack writing in women's magazines by established authors undermined the *bundan*'s foundations when such magazines began to offer a lucrative alternative to "serious" literary efforts.[19]

Muramatsu Sadataka's disparagement of mass-market literature, written in the 1950s, reflected the same widespread bias against women readers.

> Many of the readers of newspaper fiction are women *(josei)*. It is not an exaggeration to say that they are represented in particular by housewives who, after having seen their husbands off to work, are satisfied with reading the next newspaper installment at the kitchen table. They have this in common with readers of women's magazines. For these women, the most appealing subject matter is family based, particularly when it is fraught with the complications of love affairs of a married woman or a married man.[20]

Women's Arts

In 1928, the playwright Hasegawa Shigure resurrected the title *Nyonin geijutsu* (Women's arts) to launch the most influential feminist journal since *Seitō*. *Nyonin geijutsu* was explicitly run by women and written for women readers. It ran from July 1928 to June 1932, with a total of forty-eight issues.[21]

Nyonin geijutsu sought to showcase literature by women. Hasegawa, its editor, acted as a mentor to a succession of fledgling writers. When organizing the inaugural issue, Hasegawa, along with Ikuta Hanayo, paid a visit to each potential contributor, even taking a taxi to Kamakura to encourage Yamakawa Kikue (1890–1980) to join. Actively involved in the journal from the outset were Kamichika Ichiko, Imai Kuniko (1890–1948), Sasaki Fusa (1897–1949), and Hirabayashi Taiko. Those whose work appeared in the first issue did not share a common literary style, ideology, or educational background, unlike their male counterparts. In an interview with Setouchi Harumi, Enchi Fumiko (1905–1986) later described how Hasegawa had attempted to include a diverse collection of forms, styles, and themes, encouraging writers to try new approaches: Enchi attributed both her own drama *Banshun sō ya* (Late spring evening of merriment) and Hayashi's shift from poetry to the prose *Diary of a Vagabond* to Hasegawa's influence.[22] Enchi characterized Shigure as "unstinting in her support . . . never speaking negatively about women writers *(joryū sakka)*," and explained how she had gone to great lengths to help Enchi produce her play at the Tsukiji theater, even giving out specially made presents to the audience.[23]

At first the journal cast itself as a female version of *Bungei shunju* (Literary age). It considered itself a force to be reckoned with, employing elaborate public relations campaigns, holding parties with the press in attendance, and adopting *zadankai* (roundtable) formats that presented the participants as serious intellectuals or literary luminaries. Its peak circulation was about 10,000 copies, which was a considerable achievement, although it fell far short of the more commercially oriented "women's journals."

Mikami Otokichi (1891–1946), Hasegawa's husband, provided at least some of the journal's financial backing. Seeking to make amends after an extramarital affair, it is said, he offered his wife a ring worth 20,000 yen. She instead asked for the ring's cash equivalent in order to start a journal for new writers.[24] Whatever the merits of the tale, it is clear that a journal of *Nyonin geijutsu's* size and quality, without significant advertising revenues, had to tap considerable financial resources beyond its sales. Mikami's commercial success made the journal's existence possible.[25]

Nyonin geijutsu's distinctive elements are readily apparent when it is compared with two other women's journals, *Fujin kōron* (Ladies' review) and *Shufu no tomo* (Housewives' friend). Both of these journals antedated *Nyonin geijutsu* by more than a decade. By the mid-1920s, they were both commercial successes, with circulations of 100,000 and 250,000, respectively. *Fujin kōron* was launched in 1916. A sell-out special issue of the mainstream intellectual journal *Chūō kōron* (Central review), *Fujin mondai* (Women's issues) in July 1913 had indicated the commercial viability of a women's journal.[26] From the outset, *Fujin kōron* projected itself as a "serious" journal for educated middle class-women—although kana were included next to the kanji—running numerous debates on various aspects of women's rights, but also more practical advice, such as "How to Treat Your Maid."

The July 1928 issue of *Fujin kōron* was typical, containing some four dozen short articles on a diverse array of subjects—current events, movie reviews, an ongoing series of one hundred movie stars' biographies, reminiscences of hometowns, and one poem. Advertisements for *Chūō kōron* books, nursing bras, diaper covers, Lion toothpaste, tinned crab meat, and Quaker Oats, among other products, also appeared. There were four selections of literature: three serialized novels by men and a prize-winning short story, "Futatsu no kekkon" (Two marriages), by Kageyama Yuriko. This story depicts two high school girls pledging to each other, upon graduation, never to marry; when one does shortly thereafter, her friend is crestfallen, equally disturbed by the loss of "our little nest" and her partner's loss of virginity. The denouement has the two women reconciling, vowing their friendship, and espousing a reliance on their bonds and commitment to each other that will last long after their men have left them or died.

Shufu no tomo (Housewives' friend) was founded in 1917. Its expressed goal was to help the average housewife. It was a purely popular magazine, with none of the intellectual pretenses of *Fujin kōron*. In *Shufu no tomo,* too, kana ran alongside all kanji, and there was an impressive amount of advertisement. The July 1928 issue included a range of practical advice about medical treatment, children's education, beauty, fashion, handicrafts, sewing, cooking, and overcoming bad habits. In addition, there were tips on purchasing and running summer houses, and investing in the bond market. Many of the advertisements were for food items, but there were also some for venereal disease, and for abortifacients (for "starting your period again"). One of the journal's distinguishing characteristics was the scores of photographs of young women at the beginning of each issue. Typically these photos were informal, though obviously posed. They often featured young women in kimono standing beside a tree, or in western clothes, tennis racket in hand. At first glance they look like *omiai* (formal introductions to explore the possibility of marriage), but many of the women in them were already married. Perhaps we should view them as representations of women in the equivalent of some social register.

The July 1928 issue of *Shufu no tomo* contained seven serialized novels. Three were anonymous, and four were by men. The novel "Hiaburi" (Burning at the stake) by Mikami Otokichi, begun in January 1928, illustrates common themes of the period. It followed the twists and turns of a working girl, Rinko, who embraces the ideals of living virtuously and aspires to become a "good wife," while facing difficulties related principally to the scoundrels where she works. One distinguishing characteristic of *Shufu no tomo* was its inclusion of a regular column of letters from readers commenting, advising, or simply rooting for characters in the serialized fiction: "Please let Rinko stay with her boyfriend Shinsaburō and not be forced into a relationship with her boss Ishihara," or "We working women understand this very well and have suffered because of such harassment," and "Rinko, don't give in!" Mikami's "Hiaburi" had originally been scheduled to last for a year, but its run was extended, by popular demand.

From its premiere in July 1928 *Nyonin geijutsu* stood out both for the serious intellectual quality of its contents and for its explicitly feminist orientation. All of the articles were written or translated by women. The journal's look was extraordinary for a "movement" publication: handsome cover, several high-gloss photographs, and perfect binding like the mass-market women's journals. But it had very few advertisements—in the first issue, three publishers and a shoe store. Kana were included only next to some of the kanji in Hasegawa Shigure's play *Umashi hime* (Sweet princess). Inside the front cover is a striking photograph, taken in Moscow, of a small group of intellectuals—three women and two men—that included Chūjō Yuriko (who later married Miyamoto Kenji) and her lesbian lover Yuasa Yoshiko (1896–1982), who is dressed in a man's suit and has extremely short hair. The contents of the issue had *jihyō* (current debates, for example, evening newspaper coverage of the Japanese military presence in China, in comparison with that in the American publication *The Nation;* the closure of the journal *Josei;* and Ikami Sugiko's election as representative to the Pan-Pacific Women's Organization), *hyōron* (criticism, including "A Definition of So-Called Female Culture," "Feminists and World Peace," and "The Road to Women's Emancipation"), essays ("Going beyond Motherhood" was one), six poems—three *uta* in classical grammar and three *shi* in modern—and a score of *sashie* (original sketches or illustrations). The journal also carried an *obi* (promotional wrapper), which is usually reserved for books.

The literature in this inaugural issue—three short stories, one drama, and two translations—also departed strikingly from the commercial women's journals. "Aru tsuma" (A certain wife) by Masugi Shizue (1901–1955) chronicled the dilemmas of an abused wife who desperately desires to escape from her marriage but finds nowhere else to go as long as she continues to look after her children. Hirabayashi Taiko's "Seikatsu" (Livelihood) portrayed the cruel ironies and discrimination confronting women. The protagonist is the wife of a strikebreaker at a printing shop. She is fired from her job as a switchboard operator and, since her family's income is precarious, seeks to borrow from a moneylender who advertises, "We lend to women only." She discovers, however, that they have a policy of not lending to married women, since married women lack the legal standing that could ensure repayment of the debt (husbands could repudiate their wives' debts). Sasaki Fusa's "Enkin" (Perspective) presents one woman's musings about her suspicions of marital infidelity, and her conclusion about its inconsequentiality. Each of the stories presents women struggling with their subordinate, dependent position within the family and the public sphere. Moreover, each presents a female protagonist who not only suffers, but strategizes, scrutinizes, and interrogates her circumstances, even if effective solutions to her dilemmas remain nowhere in sight.

Hasegawa's play *Umashi hime* (Sweet princess) is set in the year 562 C.E., after the first introduction of Buddhism and takes place in a war-torn Japanese protectorate on the Asian mainland. It explores the position and the fate of the wife of the governor sent from the realm of "Yamato." Hasegawa begins with familiar themes of female fidelity in the face of long-absent males and the overcoming of women's inevitable suspicions and doubts. But her strong-willed protagonist declares—once she realizes how she has been duped in his power politics and payoff plots—that she will remain independent of her husband despite his pleas to reunite. The translations by women of European male authors—Liam O'Flaherty (1896–1984) and Alphonse Daudet (1840–1897)—underscored commonalties in women's dilemmas worldwide.

In 1930, *Nyonin geijutsu* moved closer to the themes and format of Proletarian literature. Men began to write for it. The cover art began to include portraits of women workers in the style of socialist realism. A large-format digest was added to each issue. The digest, described as "suitable for your younger sister or maid," included kana next to the kanji, short summaries of the articles and issues of the day, and lessons in Esperanto, which was seen as the lingua franca of the proletariat worldwide. The journal also began to include a column for letters from readers and to focus on the issues and experiences of women as workers.

The journal ceased publication in July 1932, after Hasegawa fell ill. In April 1933, she began a much more modest, inexpensive, four-page stenciled broadsheet, entitled *Kagayaku* (Radiant), which was published monthly until her death eight years later. The inaugural issue of *Kagayaku* begins with an explanation for *Nyonin geijutsu's* disappearance. Her illness was crucial, she noted, but beyond that, the audience for whom the journal was intended, and who avidly followed each issue, could no longer afford to buy it. She cited a letter from readers of *Nyonin geijutsu* that purported to be from a group of ten women who would pool their money for a single issue, and then circulate it among themselves. Though in appearance more like a movement newsletter, without any advertisements whatsoever, *Kagayaku* continued to carry many of the issues—and the writers—favored by *Nyonin geijutsu*. For its first two years, its masthead declared, in a manner reminiscent of Hiratsuka's invocation of Amaterasu in the inaugural issues of *Seitō*, but in tone far more optimistic: "The dawn is near—our destiny. We will stand in the midst of blazing brightness." Despite a continuing focus on women's experiences, by the late 1930s *Kagayaku* had adopted a decidedly more moderate tone, including accounts of the suffering of Japanese soldiers in China scarcely different from what appeared in major newspapers.

A Poet's Prose

Though Hayashi Fumiko's publication of *Diary of a Vagabond* in the *Nyonin geijutsu* brought her considerable recognition, she had begun her literary career as a poet. In 1921, under the name Akinuma Yōko, Hayashi published poems in the newspapers of Hiroshima prefecture, among them *Sanyō nichi nichi shimbun* and *Bingo jiji shimbun*.[27] In Tokyo, she continued to publish poems under her own name, starting in 1925 with "Zenma to akuma" (The good spirit and the devil) in *Bunshō kurabu* (Prose club), Shinchōsha's literary journal. Her first appearance in *Nyonin geijutsu* came in its second issue (August 1928), with her poem *Mugi batake* (A plot of millet). Throughout her career she continued to write poetry, although most later poems were embedded in or accompanied her prose. Hayashi also wrote many nursery tales and stories for children, which she appears to have viewed principally as a means to earn money. She did not discuss these pieces with her other adult fiction, and none were included in any editions of her collected works. Several do, however, appear in collections of modern nursery stories.

Hayashi began her first installment of *Hōrōki* in October 1928 with nine diary entries, each dated October, running a total of six pages. The title was "Fall Has Come," and only the subtitle was "Diary of a Vagabond." The first entry begins with a poem by Takuboku that sets the tone for the protagonist's predicament. She has moved to Tokyo from Onomichi and is working as a nursemaid at the home of the writer Chikamatsu Shūkō. She recalls Takuboku's poem while gazing at the falling snow from the toilet window during a break in her work, and it serves to distance her from the realities of her menial job.

> Alighting at a station at the end of nowhere,
> In bright snow
> I enter a lonely town.[28]

The installment was dated September 1928, though it is not clear if Hayashi wishes this to be perceived as the date of composition or the date when the piece was submitted. The next two installments, which ran in November and December 1928 and contained diary entries from October, November, and December, were both, somewhat inexplicably, dated December 1928. By her fourth installment, Hayashi seems to have decided to use the date at the end of the piece to alert the reader that the entries refer to events from several years before. Her January 1929 installment of January and February diary entries is dated 1926, and her February 1929 installment of April diary entries is dated 1923. After these, the years to which the diary entries refer can be inferred only from the text.

Hayashi would serialize the *Diary* in twenty-two installments that ran from October 1928 through October 1930. All installments except one begin with a title, usually a phrase taken from one of the entries: "Traveling Alone," "Raw Sake," "An Old Wound." Hayashi also contributed several articles to *Nyonin geijutsu* that were not part of *Hōrōki*. In March 1929, she published the short story "Ears," but nothing from the *Diary*. In January 1930, she offered a travelogue of a trip to Taiwan that she had taken at the invitation of the Japanese colonial governor-general of the island, joining a tour of "women writers" that included Ikuta Hanayo.[29] In November 1930, after the final installment of *Hōrōki*, she published another travelogue, this time of her trip to Shanghai and the Chinese mainland. During these two years there was only one month, October 1929, in which Hayashi made no contribution to *Nyonin geijutsu*. In that month she published what became the prologue to her book, in a non-diary format, in the mainstream journal *Kaizō*.

The closing entry of her first installment gives an example of what attracted Hayashi's audience. Her unnamed protagonist begins as a nursemaid, loses her job, and, preoccupied with basic necessities and concern for her distant mother, finds work as a waitress. There is the promise of an (ill-fated) love story, when she sees the name of her former lover emblazoned on the pennants in front of the theater in Asakusa. Her fellow waitresses bestow small kindnesses on her, but her aspiration to become a writer sets her apart.

> I hadn't eaten since morning. . . . Hunger made my head fuzzy, and even my ideas ended up growing mold. My head made no distinction of Proletarian or Bourgeois. I only wanted to cook and eat one handful of rice.
>
> "Please feed me."
>
> Should I throw myself into the middle of a stormy sea, awash in the troubles of others? When evening arrived, from downstairs I could hear the clatter of bowls from all the people assembled. A grumbling stomach set me pouting like a child. Suddenly I became envious of the women in the distant red-light district. I was starving. All my many books have now dwindled to a few. Kasai Zenzo's *With Children on My Hands,*[30] Artzybaschev's *Worker Seryov,* and Shiga Naoya's *Reconciliation* are rattling around in the beer crate.
>
> "Maybe I should try to earn some money at a restaurant again."
>
> Painfully resigned and strangely unsteady, like a tumbling toy Daruma, I roused myself. Placing my toothbrush, soap, and hand towels in my kimono sleeve, I went out into the windy evening streets. Like a stray dog, I inquired at cafes, one after the next, that were likely prospects for "help wanted." Above all else, my stomach craved solid food. No matter what, I had to eat. Wasn't the street enveloped in delicious aromas! It looked as though it might rain tomorrow. In blustery winds, fragrances of fresh autumn fruits stimulated my senses.

Hayashi's description of her circumstances were a mixture of anecdote, introspection—which included her own neurotic anxieties—and self-realized bits of wisdom, which she used throughout *Hōrōki.*

Apparently it was not Hayashi, but Mikami Otokichi, the husband of Hasegawa Shigure, who named it *Hōrōki.*[31] Hayashi later wrote that the title *Hōrōki* had not been used in the serialized version in *Nyonin geijutsu,* but this is a misleading assertion. *Hōrōki* appeared as the subtitle of each installment. For the first two installments, as well as four later entries, *Hōrōki* was not used in the table of contents. A few times it appeared there, but not on the opening page. It was, however, definitely used, and Hayashi's claim to the contrary indicates either a rather disingenuous attempt to distance her best known work from the journal in which it initially appeared or extreme forgetfulness.

During the serialization of *Hōrōki,* Hayashi published two bizarre letters in *Nyonin geijutsu.* In August 1929, eight women, nearly all of whom had made formative contributions to the journal—Kubokawa (née Sata) Ineko, Hasegawa Shigure, Mochizuki Yuriko (b. 1900), Ikuta Hanayo, Yagi Akiko (1895–1983), Masugi Shizue, Wakayama Kishiko (1888–1968), and Hayashi Fumiko–were asked for vignettes of their most destitute moments under the title "A Record of My Penniless Days."

Hayashi's entry, "Abunōmaru na tegami nitsū" (Two abnormal letters), were desperate pleas that she had supposedly written to Mikami Otokichi and the painter Yoshida Genkichi:

> Mikami Otokichi,
>
> Please forgive such an impolite letter. It's the consequence of two days without food.
>
> I really want to eat.
>
> I have three volumes of an insignificant diary. Would you like to buy them?
>
> I would be overjoyed to receive ¥100 for the diary. But even ¥10 or ¥5 would be fine. I haven't eaten for two days, so even though you are so far removed from me, I thought I would take the chance of sending this letter to you.
>
> Your name appears time and again in the magazine advertisements found in the newspaper scattered next to my futon.
>
> I suppose I could have written this letter to anyone, but dreamer that I am, the letters in your name scattered across the newspaper sent me into raptures.
>
> Since I don't have a yen to my name, I am not affixing a stamp. Please forgive me.

> Yoshida Genkichi,
>
> I have heard that you are an emotional person.
>
> I have suffered two days without food, and how I would like to eat! If you learn of an unfortunate weeping girl, will you save her?
>
> I live in a small garret room, like out of the pages of a novel.
>
> Around me there are women who enjoy the cafe life, who spread all kinds of malicious gossip, and are devoid of compassion; while I enjoy the cafe life, I don't even own the proper kimono for the job.
>
> I am so hungry that I am daydreaming about becoming your lover . . . but won't you buy my manuscripts to use for your inspiration? When I eat my fill I can write good poetry. . . .

Hayashi claimed that she had written these letters four years earlier, had never sent the letter to Mikami, and had not received a reply from Yoshida. She went on to write, "the letter I wrote [to Mikami] has disappeared along with my wandering. When I think about it now I'm glad I didn't send it. Now I've sent a manuscript to Hasegawa, the wife of Mikami, and I'm at peace. Mikami greets me with a smile." Her letters top the other accounts of destitution by far as the most pathetic. The rest of the contributions read as plausible depictions of a bad patch in the lives of their authors. Hayashi's is almost surely a wild fabrication.

These letters are, in my view, tongue-in-cheek. The references to her diary or cafe life are meaningful particularly, if not only, to readers already familiar with *Hōrōki,* and the supposed date—four years earlier—is calculated to deceive. Hayashi appears to wish to flatter Mikami's fame and to suggest how it affects all those women who, like her, might be swooning in their beds over his very name. And despite her hunger and utter destitution, everything turned out all right. She didn't sell the diary and, as the readers would know, had even made something of a name for herself through it. To top it off, Mikami even graces her with a smile. It was not unknown for artists to pay others for accounts of their lives to serve as the basis for fiction. This is the case with Natsume Sōseki's *Kōfu* (The miner, 1908) and Ibuse Masuji's *Kuroi ame* (Black rain, 1966).[32] On the face of it, trying to sell unsolicited diaries, even at a steep discount, is not unimaginable. But the letter introduces a trope Hayashi used periodically throughout her career—"no food for two days "—whenever she wished to underscore the enormous distance between her experience and that of other literati.[33] And the thinly veiled suggestion of readily available sexual favors seems facetious, particularly when contrasted with *Hōrōki's* testimony of furious resistance to coerced encounters (not to be confused with the more common consensual ones). A flippant response to a commission to come up with an account of her most "destitute moments" was very much in character. Her public persona was that of a sometimes petulant but prolific reporter on the real life of the underclass, one whose first-person accounts provided verisimilitude to the lives of people whose sufferings most writers could only imagine.

Daring as they were, the editors of *Nyonin geijutsu* still practiced some self-censorship, employing *fuseiji* (marks, commonly xxx's or ooo's) to replace certain words or passages in *Hōrōki* for which they might come under censure from the Police Bureau. According to Rubin, this was a widespread practice in journals from the 1880s to the beginning of the Pacific war. It was seen as "a countermeasure to [state] censorship" that could avoid bringing down the ire of the authorities, with its concomitant prohibition of publication or imprisonment. But it still gave hints to readers about what had been excised.[34] Rather than edit or require revisions in texts (the practice later used during the Occupation), offending kanji would be cut from the galley proofs and replaced with marks that allowed the reader to infer what was missing. Perhaps the clearest example appeared in the September 1929 issue of *Nyonin geijutsu* when, in two places, references to *Chōsenjin* (Koreans) are deleted. The massacres of Koreans in the wake of the Great Kanto Quake are alluded to first in a conversation the protagonist has with a neighboring student. After acknowledging that she will have to walk all the way to Shinjuku since no trains are yet running and streets are still impassable for cars, the neighbor observes, "I hear the xxx are having real problems in the suburbs," and that they'd been purposely burned out. In the next entry, published in the same issue, Hayashi's stepfather reports that he had missed their rendezvous because he had been mistaken for an "xxx," implying that he had been detained or harassed. But this self-censorship was highly infrequent, and its justifications were not always apparent. For example, in the December 1929 installment, a reference to Hayashi's contemplating suicide is xxx'd out. Similarly, if rather mystifyingly, in a poem that appeared in an entry in May 1930, a "patrol boat" is transformed into an "xxx boat." The editors may have been responding to extralegal "consultations" or warnings, perhaps not even directly related to Hayashi's passages.[35]

In 1935, Hayashi recalled with some apparent bitterness how her *Diary* was "laughed at by the magnificent leftists [of *Nyonin geijutsu*] for being too *runpen* (lumpen)."[36] (One biographer characterized her as bristling at the charge of writing "lumpen sentimentalism" and "a poor girl's graffiti.")[37] She continued, "Proletarian literature was on the rise. I was isolated, without support," and implied that she was hounded from the pages of *Nyonin geijutsu.* In fact, she continued serialization even after *Hōrōki's* publication as a book. In *Hitori no shōgai* (One person's life, 1940) Hayashi described receiving, out of the blue, a special-delivery letter from Kaizōsha announcing that, after having held her manuscript for more than two years, they were agreeing to publish it after all, a tale duly taken up by scholars.[38] Hayashi failed to divulge in this account that the book had already been serialized, and she made no mention of *Nyonin geijutsu.* Similarly, in her 1949 "Afterword" to a reprint of *Hōrōki, Nyonin geijutsu* was completely absent from her version of the history of its publication.[39] On occasions when her memory improved—somewhat—she claimed to have published only "five or six" installments in *Nyonin geijutsu* (instead of the actual twenty), an assertion repeated by all her biographers, including Hirabayashi Taiko, who should have known better, since she had reviewed Hayashi's work after it had run for a year (although forty years before she wrote the biography)[40] Hayashi claimed that, after those few installments, she had taken *Hōrōki* to the more mainstream journal *Kaizō.* But the only portion that appeared in *Kaizō* was what became the prologue to the book—the only portion not written as a diary entry. Hayashi published many other items in *Kaizō,* and she did stop publishing in *Nyonin geijutsu,* so her claim corresponded to the general trajectory of her work and may have reflected how she wanted her literary entrée to be remembered. But however much she sought to obscure the record, *Hōrōki,* and much of its first sequel, were initially published in the relatively small, increasingly politicized, and always openly feminist *Nyonin geijutsu.*

Notes

1. Tokura, "Fujin katei tosho no shuppan kan"; Minemura, "Kigyō fujin zasshi keitai ron."

2. While this characterization derived from deep-rooted patriarchal practices, the formula *ryōsai kenbo* "good wife/wise mother" was popularized by the Education Ministry in the last decade of the 19th century, "exhort[ing] women to contribute to the nation through their hard work, their frugality, their efficient management, their care of the old, young and ill, and their responsible upbringing of children" (Nolte and Hastings, "The Meiji State Policy toward Women," 152). See also Garon, "Women's Groups and the Japanese State," 11–15.

3. See Brownstein, "*Jogaku Zasshi* and the Founding of *Bungakkai*."

4. *Asahi Shimbun* wrote of the attempted "love suicide" that "it is simply unprecedented for a gentleman and lady like this, who have received the ultimate education, to act like such fools. This bizarre event represents the climax of naturalism and sexual gratification-ism" (quoted in Rubin, *Injurious to Public Morals*, 89). The dean of Hiratsuka's college wrote "Had our educational policies taken their full effect, the present example of self-centered recklessness should never have happened. . . . On the other hand, it occurs to me that it was *after* she had graduated from here that . . . the popular literature she so relished began to work its evil and she was finally converted to the enveloping tide" (ibid., 90–91). During the journal's first year, press coverage of an overnight visit Hiratsuka made to the licensed quarters of Yoshiwara was so sensational that her house was stoned (Horiba, "Kaisetsu," 359–367).

5. Hiratsuka, "Genshi josei wa taiyō de atta," 14–15.

6. Inoue, "Hiratsuka Raichō," 182.

7. Sievers, *Flowers in Salt*, 181.

8. A succinct English summary of *Seitō* appears in Copeland, "Hiratsuka Raichō," 133–140. Cf. Horiba, *Seitō josei kaihō ronshū*, 242–357.

9. Cf. Setouchi, *Seitō*.

10. Hane, *Reflections on the Way to the Gallows,* 123. Cf. Niroko Mizuta Lippit, "*Seitō* and the Literary Roots of Japanese Feminism" and "Japan's Literary Feminists: The *Seitō* Group."

11. Cf. Copeland, "Hiratsuka Raichō," 135.

12. Nihon kindai bungakkan, ed., *Nihon kindai bungaku dai jiten* 5:125, 333, 176; Iwahashi, *Hyōden Hasegawa Shigure*, 147–148.

13. Mawatari, "Joryū bungei kenkyū," 40.

14. Maeda, "Taishō kōki tsūzoku shōsetsu no tenkai (ge)," 650.

15. Ōya, "Bundan girudo no kaitaiki." For a discussion of the *bundan* in this period, see Fowler, *The Rhetoric of Confession*, 128–145; Keene, *Dawn to the West*, 546–552.

16. Ōya, "Bundan girudo no kaitaiki," 80.

17. Maeda, "Taishō kōki tsūzoku shōsetsu no tenkai (ge)," 649. *Shōgi* is a Japanese game somewhat like chess.

18. Ōya, quoted in ibid., 650.

19. Even in the 1960s, though he was embarrassed about doing it, Mishima Yukio "devote[d] about one-third of his time each month to writing popular fic-

tion and essays in order to be able to live comfortably and to spend the remaining time on serious fiction and plays" (Keene, *Dawn to the West*, 1188–1189).

20. Muramatsu, " 'Onna de aru koto' ron," 175.

21. For a brief history of *Nyonin geijutsu*, see Kōno, "*Nyonin Geijutsu.*" A more extensive, definitive account of the journal is found in two volumes by Ogata, *Nyonin geijutsu no sekai* and Nyonin geijutsu *no hitobito*. Fuji shuppan issued a reprint of the collected issues of *Nyonin geijutsu* in 1987.

22. Setouchi, *Subarashiki onnatachi*, 10–11.

23. Ibid., 11.

24. Iwahashi, *Hyōden Hasegawa Shigure,* 146. Cf. Hasegawa and Kōno, *Hasegawa Shigure,* 45, and Ikuta Hanayo, quoted in Ogata, Nyonin geijutsu *no hitobito*, 29–30.

25. Mikami was a popular author who had reaped a windfall in profits from the success of the publishing industry's *enbon* (one-yen book) boom. In November 1926, responding to the post-earthquake slump, Kaizōsha initiated a sixty-three volume series, *Gendai nihon bungaku zenshū* (Collected works of modern Japanese literature), available only to subscribers. A new volume, priced at one yen, appeared each month. The *enbon* departed from industry practices in several ways: "Printed in triple columns in small type, they squeezed four books into the space of one and cost only half the price of a typical volume" and proved phenomenally popular. Within months, every major publisher had started its own *enbon* series, many with similar success. Scores of such series followed in the next several years, and the authors who were included became rich almost overnight. (Rubin, *Injurious to Public Morals*, 247).

26. Special issues focusing on women writers had been pioneered by *Bungei kurabu* (Literary club) in December 1895 and January 1897, but despite a favorable response from the public, women writers did not receive mainstream attention again for almost twenty years. The early deaths of several of the most prominent women undoubtedly contributed to this hiatus.

27. Kobayashi Masao, "Omoide." Kobayashi was a teacher of Hayashi's and claimed to have given her the pen name Akinuma Yōko; for a sampling of poems Hayashi published under this name, see pages 28–31. Kobayashi also claimed to have chosen the characters "cotton rose, beauty, child" to fit the name Fumiko, which before then had been written in katakana.

28. Hayashi, *Hōrōki*, 18.

29. Isome and Nakazawa, eds., *Hayashi Fumiko,* 36.

30. *Ko o tsurete* (With children on my hands, 1918), the work of fiction that made Kasai Zenzo (1887–1928) famous. Evicted from his rooms, the narrator wanders the streets with his children, homeless and penniless.

31. Itagaki, *Meiji, Taishō, Shōwa no joryū bungaku*, 219. Hayashi is reported to have observed, after the war, that her manuscript had been accepted at *Nyonin geijutsu* only because of Mikami's intervention, and that Hasegawa had initially rejected it (Kawase Yoshiko, quoted in Ogata, Nyonin geijutsu *no hitobito*, 272).

32. The nature of their collaboration with their informants varied. Shizuma Shigematsu's contribution to *Black Rain,* for example, was more like a co-author's. Cf. Treat, *Writing Ground Zero*, 261–300.

33. In a postwar roundtable discussion, Hayashi expressed astonishment at the ease with which male university coteries could publish impressive literary journals, when she had pawned her coat and gone without eating "for two days" to put out her first eight-page poetry journal *Futari* (Two people). Niwa, Hayashi, and Inoue, "Bundan ni deru kushin," 116.

34. Rubin, *Injurious to Public Morals*, 30.

35. Ibid., 27–28. Rubin describes the consultation system as an administrative practice of the Police Bureau that worked to the advantage of publishers in allowing them to avoid outright bans. But it was only one element in a far-reaching system of statutory and extralegal censorship of the press and the publishing industry. By the time that *Nyonin geijutsu* ceased publication in July 1932, the range of what was permitted was severely restricted. Cf. Mitchell, *Thought Control in Prewar Japan*.

36. Hayashi, "Bungakuteki jijoden," 17.

37. Hashizume, "Hayashi Fumiko Ashura," 212.

38. Fukuda and Endō, *Hayashi Fumiko*, 101–102.

39. Hayashi, "Atogaki," in *Hayashi Fumiko zenshū,* 2:291.

40. Hirabayashi, *Hayashi Fumiko,* 109; Fukuda and Endō, *Hayashi Fumiko*, 58 and 104. Itagaki Naoko also repeats Hayashi's assertions, but in the preface she warns the reader, "There are no objective records of her life. . . . and her own version is a mixture of truth and lies, made possible by her vivid imagination" (*Hayashi Fumiko no shōgai,* 7–9).

4

Reading a Woman's *Diary*

Hayashi's *Diary of a Vagabond* (July 1930) was an immediate and unexpected best-seller.[1] Other titles in the *Shinei bungaku sōsho* (Library of new literary faces) series by Kaizōsha were far more heavily advertised, but none, including the first work of Ibuse Masuji, generated the same kind of runaway success. Within the first two years, *Diary of a Vagabond,* often combined with its sequel (published in November 1930), sold 600,000 copies.[2] It was reprinted numerous times and regularly selected for inclusion in *zenshū* (collected works) of modern Japanese literature.[3] This fine first novel continues to be a well-known title, even, by some measures, the best known and most popular modern work by a woman.[4]

International recognition for Hayashi's *Diary* has been far more modest. It was published twice and apparently enthusiastically received in Chinese (1937, 1956) and Korean (1966, 1973), but in European languages, only a short four-page excerpt of the prologue in English (1951) and, curiously, an eight-page translation of the first diary entry into Esperanto (1965), have appeared to date.[5] Elisabeth Hanson's fine translation (1987) of excerpts from Hayashi's work, which appears in Tanaka's anthology *To Live and to Write,* misidentifies "Vagabond's Song" as coming from *Hōrōki* (1927 [*sic*]), when it is taken from the sequel published some twenty years later that employed far more sustained narration and a different literary style. Critical treatment of Hayashi in English has been scanty, and only Donald Keene, Yukiko Tanaka, and Victoria Vernon give her early efforts more than a passing reference.[6] Very few English-speaking readers are aware of the critical discourse on her work in Japanese or can appreciate the work's place in or relation to the modern canon.

Most Japanese commentary about Hayashi in general, and *Diary of a Vagabond* in particular, emphasizes her lyrical quality and sentimentality. In 1936, the critic Ōya Sōichi described lyricism as the basis for all her works.[7] Yoshida Seiichi wrote that Hayashi was able to attract a large male audience because of an unusual combination of content and style. She "carved out an image of a group living in a nihilistic, anarchistic environment, while describing it all with sweet lyricism and feminine sentimentality."[8] In addition to lyricism, Hayashi's work was often summarized as being *shominteki* (of the people). Obara Gen described her writing as "popular lyricism."[9] Kusabe Kazuko reiterated the prevailing view that the *Diary* was lyrical but added that it was a strange mixture of lyricism, humor, and narcissism. She marveled that through her poetic realism Hayashi could take a mundane, trite experience or idea and make it fascinating.[10]

Nakamura Mitsuo, who had characterized Hayashi as the quintessential feminine writer, had praised *Diary of a Vagabond* as being her best work. Yet for Nakamura, what made it superior was that it was better than what one might expect: "[Hayashi's] writing style and manner of looking at herself were already formulated by the time [of *Diary of a Vagabond*]. The literary style that seems unrestrained at first glance in reality has a rather correct style and meter, and if it is read even today, it does not seem antiquated. The natural humor sprinkled throughout also shows that she had room to be objective even in the depths of her misery."[11] In other words, a calculated style and capacity for objectivity—qualities presumed to be masculine—were what raised the *Diary* in his estimation.

However contradictory they may seem today, Nakamura's assumptions were widely shared in his time. Gender attributions to literary styles have a very long history in Japanese literary criticism. Contemporary readers need to remain alert to the complex array of gendered literary allusions, but also to the other affiliations that explain the deep chord Hayashi's struck with her readers. For example, Hayashi's notelike observations about her personal life did not share the sentimental pessimism of the I-novel. These seemingly unrestrained, evocative, sometimes despairing, sometimes playful notes about her life had a direct relation to such classical Japanese literary traditions as the *nikki* (diaries) and *uta monogatari* (poem tales) written by women. At the same time, there is an undeniable modernity in their subject matter and frequent reference to western writers and themes. In my view, the originality and power of her work are rooted not so much in the mixture of literary allusions as in the clarity and immediacy with which she was able to convey the humanity of those occupying the underside of Japanese society. She captured the resilience of people who existed on the margin and the ever-resurgent tenacity of those for whom modernity was an unrelenting catastrophe. This contribution merits recognition in Japanese literary history, and its place is obscured by categorizing the work as "women's literature."

Lineages of a Woman's Diary

In *Hōrōki,* Hayashi echoed the structure of classical *uta monogatari* through frequent inclusion of poetry and letters. Prior to its publication as a single volume, Hayashi referred to it as her "poetic diary" *(uta nikki).*[12] Atsuta Yuko said that Hirabayashi Taiko recalled having seen this title on the cover sheet of Hayashi's bundle of manuscripts before publication.[13] The poems (thirty in all) interspersed throughout the entries followed the pattern of the classical Japanese literary diary.[14] The poems were written by both Hayashi and other poets, notably Ishikawa Takuboku (1885–1912), but also Shimazaki Tōson (1872–1943), Murayama Kaita (1896–1919), Murō Saisei (1889–1962), Hirano Banri (1885–1947), and Emile Verhaeren (1855–1916).

Poems often introduce a new section, setting the tone. The prologue begins with an unattributed verse the protagonist purports to have learned in grammar school.

> In the deepening autumn night,
> A traveler distressed by desolate thoughts,
> Yearns for home, longs for family.[15]

These lines succinctly convey how Hayashi wanted to portray her protagonist/self: as the eternally sorrowful wanderer, pining for an emotional connection to a place or people that remain out of reach.

Hōrōki includes a variety of poetic forms, including several tanka and many poems in free verse. Among her best known poems was her openly erotic paean to the Buddha.

> I fell in love with the Buddha
> When I kissed his faintly cold lips.
> Oh, I am unworthy of your attention.
> *My heart begins to tingle.*
>
> I am unworthy of your attention,
> But my gently coursing blood
> *Flows backwards.*
>
> His aloofness and refinement,
> Irresistibly composed,
> Enticed my soul completely.
>
> Buddha!
> *How indifferent you are*
> To my heart

That is like a broken beehive.
Just giving me lessons on the transiency of
"Namu Amidabutsu"
Is not enough.
With your refined manner,
Please jump
Into my enflamed breast.
With the dust of the world still on me,
Embrace me tightly
Though I might die,
"Namu Amidabutsu."[16]

The poem's passion and abandonment to desire introduces an entry that chronicles the duplicity and deception of the protagonist's lover, as well as her own aching, angered analysis. The poem helps the reader understand how the narrator had allowed herself to be fooled so readily, and how her distress sends her reeling through a succession of emotions and inebriated fantasies, finally summoning her resolve and steadying herself in solitude. While her longer free-verse poems sometimes contain descriptions of significant incidents, their principal effect is to preview an emotional state. They allow the reader to glimpse the narrator's interior conflicts, which remain only partly expressed in the entries, so as better to understand the intentions and motivations behind the actions that follow.

Aside from the poetic evocation of classical literary diaries, the situations encountered by Hayashi's protagonist harked back to the classical canon by mirroring many well known incidents. Like the neglected secondary wife in *Kagerō nikki* (Kagerō diary; translation published as *The Gossamer Years*), who sends her husband's clothes back to him unmended,[17] the protagonist intentionally fails to mend the kimono her lover wears both at night and on stage: "This morning I noticed that about two inches along the seam had come undone, but I didn't mend it on purpose. I have had enough of this self-satisfied man."[18] As if to remind the reader of another world stretching as far back as the Heian period, the protagonist encounters women who still blacken their teeth: "I stared in fascination at the landlady, whose teeth were blackened as in the old days."[19] And the theme of a female protagonist who suffers from the loneliness of having been neglected and discarded by a succession of lovers is common in the classical diary literature.

Since *Hōrōki* does not present passages chronologically, at least not in a fashion that is coherent or convincing, the narrative is discontinuous and fragmented. Yet precisely because the entries have been reordered, and their arrangement seemingly calculated to emphasize specific themes, the result is more like *renga*, with implicit linkages between various sections. These linkages and the juxtaposition of sensory elements are reminiscent of Kawabata Yasunari's use of *renga*-style sequences in *Sound of the Mountain. Hōrōki* also clearly evokes other elements from the post-classical literary canon. The protagonist refers more than once to a difficult "floating world,"[20] but also lives for the day without calculating the effect of this behavior on the future. This is reminiscent of Saikaku's fiction, particularly of Oharu in *Kōshoku ichidai onna* (Life of an amorous woman), and has the aura of the Genroku era. *Hōrōki's* protagonist works at a number of shops on the border of the licensed quarters and associates with the men who are on their way to or from visiting there—the setting of much of Tokugawa literature, as well as of works by Higuchi Ichiyō.

Hayashi revised the sequence of the entries as they had appeared in *Nyonin geijutsu*. She also removed nearly all explicit references to her own name. As was common in classical diaries, Hayashi presented a protagonist who, for the most part, remains anonymous. A variant of Hayashi Fumiko does appear five times: "Fu" in the beginning narrative section when the mother is talking to the father about the child; "Hayashi" when the maid at the viscountess' house speaks to her; "Fumiko" in a poem written after her separation from Nakano; "Fumiko" in a passage where she dreams of becoming rich; "Hayashi" when a registered letter containing much-needed money arrives for her.[21] So while Hayashi still hinted that the work should be considered autobiographical, she did not make herself the center of the story. The diarist could have remained unnamed without affecting the tone or the power of the piece. Similarly, the author refers to each of the significant relationships in her life only as "he" or "that man" or "my husband," indicating an interest in the narrative and not in revelations about these particular men.

But the characters the protagonist encounters are not always anonymous. A dozen aquaintances, mostly anarchist poets or writers of Proletarian literature, whom readers were expected to be able to identify, appear, often only briefly, throughout the text. Her descriptions of these figures were rather deflating and appear to have angered some of those portrayed. For example, in a highly laudatory review of Hayashi's first volume of poetry, *I Saw a Pale Horse*, Hirabayashi Taiko caustically dismisses depictions of herself and her compatriots, and explicitly warns Hayashi to "stop treading upon this territory . . . trumpeting the weaknesses of women's character."[22] For the most part, her lovers are identified explicitly only if the protagonist uses them as brief diversions. She identifies her honorable, if ineffectual, suitor Matsuda by name,[23] and the painter Yoshida appears only during an evening's seduction.[24] Her long-term lovers—whom she referred to as "husbands"—such as the poet Nomura Yoshiya, remained unnamed. But she was not above implicating

Nomura Sawako, the woman who did marry him, in an extramarital affair, while portraying herself as the self-sacrificing injured party.

In the following passage depicting Hayashi as the wronged woman, the protagonist is living apart from her husband for financial reasons and returns to his rented room to do his laundry and give him money.

> When I returned to the room my husband was renting, I saw he had acquired several large bookcases. Here he was, making me, his wife, work as a waitress in a cafe, while he bought such extravagances for himself! As always, I placed twenty yen under his writing paper. Completely at home and indulging in the luxury of the solitary moment, I looked in his closet for dirty clothes.
>
> "Excuse me, a letter's just come," said the maid as she handed it to me. The envelope was fairly thick, with a six-sen stamp. It was from a woman. I bit my nails uneasily, and my heart pounded anxiously. Chiding myself for my stupidity, I found a substantial pile of this woman's letters hidden in the corner of the closet.
>
> "I prefer the hot springs."
>
> "From your Sawako."
>
> "Ever since staying that night, I have. . . ."
>
> I stood up unsteadily, chilled by the cloyingly sweet letters.
>
> The letter about the hot springs said, "I will get some money ready, but please get some yourself." I wanted to fling it across the room. I left after pocketing the twenty yen that I had placed under the writing paper.
>
> Wasn't he the one to berate me for my insensitivity whenever he saw me? Didn't he write all those poems and short stories for magazines just to slander me? And wasn't I reduced to singing to all the bar patrons, "For you alone I threw away myself and the world. . . ." just to support that morose, half-crazed, tubercular man? Walking down the streets of Wakamatsu with the cool evening wind on me, I did not feel like returning to the cafe in Shinjuku. *Now I knew why there was only a fraction of the money left.*
>
> "Won't you go with me to the hot springs?"
>
> That night I got so completely drunk Toki-chan pitied my sorry state.[25]

In the postwar sequel to *Hōrōki,* Hayashi identified the poet (by then deceased) and presented an increasingly damning portrait, claiming that he terrorized her, crammed her into the storage space under the kitchen floor,[26] and threw knives at her.[27] Others, however, challenged her account of their relationship.[28] Nomura Sawako, his widow, reportedly told the critic Hashizume that Nomura had kicked Hayashi out because she had infected him with gonorrhea.[29] In one of his poems from 1926, Nomura has a line about "that woman who foisted venereal disease on me and left."[30] Nomura Sawako published a detailed rebuttal of Hayashi's negative portrait of her husband. She had written to Hayashi asking her to refrain from writing lies about Nomura in what the public might assume to be a genuine autobiography.[31] Hayashi's response, included in Sawako's article, assured her: "If I don't write things like that, I can't make a living. Please do not think ill of me, and instead, glance through it with a smile."[32]

Literature from Below

Despite the classical trappings and irrespective of its veracity, Hayashi's *Diary of a Vagabond* should be viewed principally in the context of—and as a major contribution to—a perspective from below that, in this era, was categorized as *runpen bungaku* (lumpen literature). The term itself deserves some introduction, for it is no longer commonly understood even in Japan, at least among the younger generation. In early 1995, when I presented a lecture on Hayashi at Meiji University to a graduate seminar in Japanese literature, none of the dozen bright, perceptive graduate students in attendance was familiar with the term.

The classic western use of "lumpen" *(runpen)* comes from Karl Marx's condemnation of the "lumpen proletariat. . . thieves, criminals of all sorts, living off the garbage of society, people without a definite trace, vagabonds, *gens sans feu et sans aveu* [people without hearth or home]."[33] Marx's initial 1850 use of the term in "The Class Struggles in France" was meant to distinguish between the proletariat, which was progressive, and the underclass, which formed the shock troops of reaction. It was used specifically to indict those manning the Mobile Guards of the Revisionist Government of February 1848. In *Capital* (1867), Marx continued to use "lumpen proletariat" as an essentially derogatory reference to those who did not hold wage-earning jobs and were not a productive part of society—not simply paupers, but also "vagabonds, criminals, and prostitutes."[34] He also referred derisively to those members of the bourgeoisie who acted like criminals as "lumpen" speculators and plunderers.

The usage of the term in Japan in the 1920s and 1930s departed from that of Marx in muting its strong criminal connotation. Also, *runpen* covered a wider social terrain, including male day laborers. Such people existed on the margin, with only a tenuous hold on employment, residence, or relationships, and often found themselves scrambling for any means to survive. The Japanese usage reflected different assumptions about the composition of social forces and class alliances capable of contributing to a working-class revolution.[35] The lumpen proletariat were generally not condemned, as they had been by Marx, for their lack of organizational capacities or immediate interests in revolution. In part, this reflected the relative size of the industrial proletariat. In Japan, as in much of the world, such workers remained only a minority of the urban population. The majority, especially among women, labored in a variety of small shops, service, or "informal" sector jobs, far more than ever joined the so-called working class in large-scale factories. In addition, the political implications of waged employment, or the lack thereof, derived from the still-predominant weight of rural social relations (urban residents constituted just under a third of the population in 1930). The *runpen* were themselves most often migrants from the countryside, dispossessed, destitute, but still determined to piece together some sort of life in the big city of Tokyo.

This image of the irrepressible poor was captured in the comic hit song "Runpen bushi" of 1931, the title track of the movie *Runpen Kuma-kō*.

Dozing—a wad of banknotes falls from the blue sky,
Bouncing against my cheek.
Money, Money, Money,
My eyes open before I can spend it all.

Refrain: [A belly-laugh]; Stone broke, my wallet's clean empty.
But I'm a happy-go-lucky lumpen.

I'm sloshed on five cups of sake.
When I peer through my drunken eyes,
An ugly woman can seem beautiful.
I take a cheap cigarette, break it,
and suavely share the smoke with her.

Refrain

Proletarian heaven—cheap rickety rooms.
Curled up tight at night, only my knees receive my caresses.
Rolled up in a single futon,
When I listen to the winter rains, my dead wife comes back in my dreams.

Refrain

Don't worry if you don't have any money.
Even the wealthy get white hairs.
Even the wealthy get only one tomb.
Whether you laugh or cry,
You've got fifty years.

The song was characteristic of how the term *runpen* was adapted and used in Japan to mean "rubbish," "someone out of work," or "vagabond," but without the moral condemnation implicit in the German.[36] Hayashi Fumiko stood out in her portrayal of women in *runpen* circumstances, whose interests and experiences were neglected by contending political ideologies and ignored by male literati.[37]

Many earlier works of modern literature had dealt with the problems of poverty and dislocation. Irokawa Daikichi characterized farmers in the late Meiji Period as feeling a helpless resignation in the face of poverty and distress, and blaming themselves or their parents for their situation. They often had to resort to sending their children away from home to work: Daughters became factory workers or prostitutes, and sons fishermen, construction workers, or miners. "Meiji writers published works that responded—though unintentionally—to the stagnation and changed consciousness of the populace at the bottom of society."[38] Noted portraits of their plight are Shimazaki Tōson's *Hakai* (The broken commandment, 1906), Mayama Seika's *Minami Koizumi-mura* (Minami Koizumi village, 1907), Kunikida Doppo's *Kyūshi* (Death from suffering, 1907), Natsume Sōseki's *Kōfu* (The miner, 1908), Tayama Katai's *Inaka kyōshi* (The country teacher, 1909), Nagatsuka Takashi's *Tsuchi* (Earth, 1910), and Iwano Hōmei's *Hōrō* (Wandering, 1910).

These literary accounts of the underside of Japanese society were very different from Hayashi's *Diary of a Vagabond,* which depicts similar social strata but with a lighter touch. Hayashi wrote from bitter personal experience, yet was still able to put an optimistic face on otherwise depressing circumstances. Others often wrote from a distance, intellectually and physically. For example, Sōseki paid a young coal miner to recount the details of his personal hardships and used the information as the basis for *Kōfu*. Despite its setting, his ironic depiction of a would-be miner is principally a study of a youth's interior life, not an indictment of social conditions. Hayashi's portrayal of ghastly conditions in grimy mining communities came from her own experience. Yet her protagonist possesses a youthful resilience, remains animated even in the face of grinding destitution, and is undeterred by grim prospects.

The contrast between *Hōrōki* and Miyamoto Yuriko's first work, *Mazushiki hitobito no mure* (A flock of the poor, 1916), published in *Chūō kōron*, also illustrates the distinctiveness of Hayashi's voice. Miyamoto's story portrayed the misery of impoverished tenant farmers as viewed by a privileged, if well-meaning, schoolgirl from the city. The protagonist's initial revulsion when confronted with the coarse connivance and calculated cunning of those grasping to alleviate their own desperate circumstances prompts her to a far more searching, skeptical, and nuanced appraisal of her own motives for charity. The depiction of social conditions is far more analytical, the protagonist far more reflective, and the tone more cautionary than in *Diary of a Vagabond.* Hayashi's protagonist might adopt a cynical perspective after a crushing betrayal or reversal of fortune, but she also seeks out comforting delusions and readily embraces a succession of short-lived schemes that offer momentary gratification and the hope, however misplaced, of realizing her literary ambitions.

Hayashi's work did share certain characteristics with Ryūtanji Yū's *Hōrō jidai* (A vagabond era, 1928), the first book published in Kaizōsha's *Library of New Literary Faces.* Both works shared upbeat but frank first-person accounts of struggling young artists in abject destitution, and both included portraits of irrepressible, abrasive women. Yet Ryūtanji's protagonist, a male window-dresser, was not meant to be ostensibly autobiographical, and his story was written as a standard chronological narrative. Moreover, his protagonist is presented as having to choose between a career as a painter, which would be helped by the considerable support of his widowed mother, and the vagabondage of his friends who "live for the moment." Succeeding as an artist would require a degree of middle-class conformity, a message that was antithetical to Hayashi's *Diary,* if not her life.

Runpen came to be used in the late 1920s in popular discourse. In part its wider use reflected the increasing visibility of the unemployed homeless in Tokyo. Their numbers were estimated to have increased more than sixfold from 1922 to 1930.[39] In the winter of 1930–1931, some two thousand were housed by municipal authorities in seven barges, dubbed "Noah's Arks," that were docked in the Arakawa River below the Senjū Ōhashi bridge.[40] In 1931, Shimomura Chiaki asserted that the swelling legions of the unemployed had, by 1930, created a sizable stratum that, though lacking the (potential) consciousness of the proletariat, had developed a distinct identity.[41] But as a category of criticism and literary history, *runpen* was rooted not so much in the particular social experience of the dispossessed and destitute as in the collision between increasingly politicized art under the direction of the Communist Party and escalating state repression.[42] *Runpen* flourished as a perspective for only a few years. During that time it acted as a representation of the lives and aspirations of the most downtrodden, unencumbered by the baggage of party directives, and without explicitly assaulting the current political authority. This approach, however, faced increasing censorship. By the latter half of the 1930s, it was as effectively squelched as Proletarian literature. After the war, when freedom from both state repression and party dictates enabled writers to explore this terrain again, those who wrote from this perspective did so under a different name.[43]

The notion of a distinct *runpen bungaku* (lumpen literature) was popularized by Shimomura Chiaki (1893–1955). Beginning in 1928, he published fiction and investigative journalism about the experiences of vagrants in the journal *Chūō kōron.*[44] His exposé *Machi no hōrōsha* (Street vagrants), serialized for more than three years in *Asahi shimbun,* spotlighted the stark conditions in which the lumpen lived. Its long run shows how interested the general public was in such experiences. The term *runpen* was frequently used in newspaper coverage of the literary scene in the early 1930s.[45] In *Asahi shimbun* (July 17–18, 1931) Kobori Shinji reported that *runpen* had become a very popular word, applied not just to literature but also to movies *(runpen eiga)* and music—popular lyrics, for example, were advertised as *runpen no uta* (lumpen songs). It was, according to Kobori, a *runpen jidai* (a lumpen period), but he acknowledged that the meaning of the term was still in flux.[46] He did distinguish *runpen* from proletarian sensibilities in general and Proletarian literature in particular. That same year, the critic Arai Kaku criticized Shimomura's analytical distance and lack of empathy with those whose fate he chronicled, in contrast to Hayashi, to whom he referred approvingly as "our Apache in Paris."[47] Ōya Sōichi would observe about Hayashi that it was unusual for any writer—particularly a woman writer—to possess such a *runpen* spirit.[48]

The movie industry had also served as a wellspring of the *runpen* genre. From the 1920s, what were known as "tendency films" focused on characters who found themselves in desperate circumstances, lacking money or employment. This genre grew into the "*rumpen-mono.*"[49] "Instead of purposely or accidentally suggesting that their characters were part of the 'workers' world,' [*runpen* films] made them members of the 'lumpenproletariat.' "[50] Like the tendency film before it, the *runpen* film chose socially sensitive topics but maintained an unfocused political perspective. In 1931, popular films about "life in the lower depths" included Ikeda Yoshinobu's *Machi no runpen* (Village lumpen), based on a story by Shimomura and starring the actress Kurishina Sumiko, and Mizoguchi's *Shikamo karera wa iku* (And yet they go on), which focused on a mother and daughter who become prostitutes. Elements of this genre of film can still be seen today in highly formulaic, sanitized, and even wistfully nostalgic depictions of the ever-resilient "Tora-san."

Hayashi's *Diary* was among the first works sympathetically representing the struggles and illusions of those on the margins considered "authentic." The originality of the work was largely overshadowed both by its supposed success in reflecting a specific reality—not so much the desperation as the dogged determination of the *runpen*—and for its perceived failure to reflect calls for art to contribute to the political struggle. Hayashi had embraced the lifestyle of the anarchist authors she had met while working as a waitress in 1924.[51] But she exhibited only a scant interest in political ideology, and neither *Hōrōki* nor her poetry was consciously political. However much she was viewed then, and may still be seen today, as the most popular, best known, and most enduring author of the *runpen* genre, it was an appellation with which she remained uneasy.

Hayashi's discomfort with her categorization as a *runpen* writer may have reflected a reluctance to restrict either her ambitions or her literary imagination. But it is also clear that the originality and appeal of *Hōrōki* are overlooked if too much emphasis is put on the issue of impoverishment. Hayashi illustrated a strong affinity with works that were far more self-consciously feminist, and succeeded in presenting a protagonist who could claim, even in her destitution, to have secured the kind of autonomy that some of her contemporaries had identified as the preeminent feminist objective. For example, at the same time that Hayashi was beginning to serialize *Hōrōki,* on the same pages of *Nyonin geijutsu,* Kitamura Kaneko championed a place for women outside their roles as wives, mothers, or daughters, even if, struggling to survive on their own, they had been cast out of work, replaced by machines, or let go in the economic distress of the times. She observed, "Now that the era of the 'modern girl' [has] passed, the next will be that of the female rōnin (masterless samurai)," meaning that even unemployed women needed to have autonomy instead of "falling back into the hell of the family."[52] In this context, Hayashi's appeal came from demonstrating that, even destitute and out of work, women had the capacity to live independently, without having to fall back on the family. Hayashi's protagonist does take "husbands," but without either the formality or the legal restrictions of being placed in a man's family registry. She supports her parents in a variety of ways, often at considerable sacrifice, but she is bound by obligations of affection and has yoked herself to these burdens. She frequently leaves jobs and lovers, if not always graciously or by choice, and she goes some distance toward Kitamura's goal of "masterless female warriors."

The crackdown on *runpen* literary works was far less sweeping or systematic than that on Proletarian literature. But all works that contained unfavorable portraits of the Japanese society or cast aspersions on the state were increasingly prohibited by the mid-1930s. The extension of censorship was, from 1933 on, punctuated by a series of high-profile prosecutions and bans of liberal academics as "un-Japanese."[53] Lumpen literature was suspect as unpatriotic and unflattering. With the state's more active attempts to limit literature to positive and favorable assessments, lumpen literature had fewer outlets and received a more hostile reception by censors. In the face of an increasingly narrower range of permitted expression, *runpen's* most celebrated exponent, Shimomura, turned to pulp fiction in 1935.[54] But unlike Proletarian writers or organizations, *runpen* was, mostly, a post hoc attribution, rather than an author's self-imposed identity, and the suppression of this perspective was only partial before the war. Hayashi has been included in lists by American scholars of authors whose works were banned from the latter half of the 1930s,[55] but for her, as for others labeled as *runpen*, the restrictions applied only to specific works or projects, often unexpectedly—such as the post-production ban on a 1937 movie based on her 1935 novel *Nakimushi kozō* (Crybaby)[56]—and never kept her from publishing elsewhere. In 1940, censors cited the pessimism in *Crybaby*, as well as in the 1939 revision of *Diary of a Vagabond* and in *Joyū ki* (Diary of an actress, 1940), as justification for their ban, but only after each had had marked commercial success.[57] *Hatsu tabi* (First trip), a collection of short stories, was banned, seventeen days after its release in July 1941, for being deletorious to public morals. Its depiction of extramarital affairs was considered "incompatible with the national spirit."[58]

Revisiting a Diary

Once *Diary of a Vagabond* had made Hayashi a public figure, she wrote for an audience that wanted to learn more about her. The first sequel to the book (November 1930), over a third of which had already been published in *Nyonin geijutsu*, covered the same period and used roughly the same structure and language. It ended with a non-diary entry in which Hayashi specifically identified herself as the protagonist/diarist. She returned to many of the same incidents, but often with more graphic elaboration and incriminating detail. For example, Hayashi confessed that in going to see "the man," still unnamed and only later identified as Okano, in his hometown of Onomichi, she supposedly aborted his child by hitting her stomach repeatedly against a gravestone.[59] Later in those same sections, she indicated that his family paid her to leave.[60] This style was more similar to works by other confessional writers, who revealed their exploits to a well-informed audience and chose to put themselves under public scrutiny.

Hayashi not only revisited and revised the same incidents or events in successive sequels, but she also rewrote or revised the text for each new edition. Comparison of editions illustrates an evolution in style and use of language; a careful reading gives indications of Hayashi's aesthetic transformation, even in what is usually assumed to be the same book. Many of the changes involved the prologue, first published in *Kaizō* in 1929. The language of this section in the first 1930 Kaizōsha edition was more colloquial, spontaneous, and sometimes melodramatic, while that of the 1939 Shinchōsha edition was more standard, composed, and grammatically complex. In the later edition longer paragraphs made the text seem less staccato as well. Some passages were altered, some eliminated.

The later edition also eliminated subtitles to the diary entries. This served to present the work as a whole, instead of as random pieces.

One of the most striking emendations was the addition of some sixty passages in classical Japanese grammar—or more accurately pseudoclassical grammar, since only the ending of each phrase or sentence was cast in classical grammar, most often *nari*—providing a distinct perspective on the actions or judgments that they were used to emphasize. On one level they seem like a literary affectation, not only because the subject matter seems far removed from Heian Japan, but also because they hardly meet the standard of proper classical syntax. One can argue, however, that they function as an integral element in setting the tone by providing an unexpected atmosphere. Though topically *runpen*, the classical references distance the work and convey a sense of the mundane as elevated, even transcendent. For example, the first classical grammatical form comes at the beginning of an entry in which the protagonist had been working as a nursemaid in the home of the writer Chikamatsu Shūkō. The opening statement for the day in December, "*They have fired me,*"[61] highlights her surprise, but serves at the same time to soften the harsh reality of having no job and nowhere to go. The grammar encourages the reader to pause and reflect on the plight of the protagonist. It also serves to move the action from one location to another with a minimum of words.

Often classical grammar serves as an abbreviated seasonal introduction or stage setting to an entry, indicating the weather, for example, "*It's a serene summer morning.*"[62] At times the noticeably different grammar redirects our attention by briefly changing the focus of the sentence. "We were so poor, there weren't even any mice around. Leaning on my orange crate desk, I began to write a children's story. *Outside the sound of rain.* Off toward the Tama River there was a ceaseless succession of gunfire. Even in the middle of the night, it crackled. But how much longer could our insect-like existence endure?"[63]

This usage also highlights the protagonist's emotions. At times the mood is wistful, as when she declares, "*Composing poetry is my only solace.*"[64] At times it is wild, as when the protagonist suggests a remedy for a souring relationship with her second husband, the actor Tanabe. After watching his performance one evening, she writes: "I went outside into the warm air with a couple of poet friends. *I thought it would be great fun to strip naked and go running on such a wonderful night.*"[65] In addition, it underscores concrete concerns, particularly money. This incorporation of classical grammatical endings into a sentence full of modern vocabulary and modern sensibilities often jars. It emphasizes particular actions, elements, or twists in the story while introducing a contemplative perspective that distances both protagonist and reader from the often dire circumstances, and contributes to the lyrical quality of the work.

The use of classical grammar reminds the reader of the poetic roots of Hayashi's prose. She had incorporated such grammar into some of her poetry as first published in *Nyonin geijutsu* (1928–1929). She also used it in several more poems that were included in her first volume of poetry, *Aouma o mitari* (I saw a pale horse), published by Nansō shoin in 1929.

Hayashi's revisions were unusual even in the Japanese context. Publication of a serialized work conventionally reproduces, in order, the work as it first reached the public. When her *Diary of a Vagabond* first appeared as a book, Hayashi not only chose to select just a portion of what had already appeared in *Nyonin geijutsu.* She also reorganized the presentation, making slight emendations in the text, and she continued to rework the material through successive editions. Other authors might add chapters and revise the conclusion many years later, for example, Shiga Naoya, in *A Dark Night's Passing.* But I can think of no other such well known work where the text itself continued to change. This protean quality of Hayashi's *Diary of a Vagabond* was due in part to the fragmentation of the narrative, which left the account of the narrator's experiences incomplete, and in part to the assumption that the work was a reflection of the author's life, and that reconstituted memory would inevitably be recast in the telling. These characteristics also helped to make the sequels, however different they were in tone or style, seem more like parts of a whole, as discontinuities and unresolved incidents allowed the narrator to revisit specific events—or moments immediately adjacent to those already recounted—and retell the experiences in a new way. Nevertheless, our reading should discriminate between these successive versions, because Hayashi's revisions were tailored to meet her readers' expectations. The 1939 revisions were extremely successful with the public, and more than a hundred printings of *Hōrōki* (paired with its initial sequel) were issued in its first year on the market. This version, combined with the postwar sequel (1949) and sold as a single volume, became the canonical text of *Diary of a Vagabond* from the time of Hayashi's death.

Notes

1. Ōka, "Kaisetsu," 490.
2. Fukuda and Endō, *Hayashi Fumiko,* 61.
3. Hōrōki has appeared in *Shin Nihon bungaku zenshū* (Kaizōsha, 1941); *Gendai Nihon shōsetsu teikei* (Kawade, 1950); *Gendai nihon bungaku zenshū* (Chikuma shobō, 1954); *Nihon bungaku zenshū* (Shūeisha, 1966); *Nihon gendai bungaku zenshū* (Kōdansha, 1967); *Shinchō Nihon bungaku zenshū* (Shinchōsha, 1971); *Gendai Nihon bungaku taikei* (Chikuma shobō, 1972); and by at least a dozen others.

4. In 1988, at a literary exhibition of thirteen women writers (including Hayashi, Okamoto, Higuchi, Sata, Uno, Tsuboi, Enchi, Yosano, Tamura, and Miyamoto), a short poll of men indicated that Hayashi and, in particular, *Diary of a Vagabond* were the best known and most popular. Okuno et al., *Josei sakka jūsan nin ten*, 89.

5. The Esperanto translation by Masao Hukuta [Fukuda], "Putino Kaj Mangato," in *El Japana Literaturo*, edited by Miyamoto Masao and Ishiguro Teruhiko (Tokyo: Japana Esperanto Instituto, 1965), was originally completed in 1928, within months after the entry first appeared in *Nyonin geijutsu*. The sole English translation, by Brickley, "*Hōrōki* (the first section)," in *The Writing of Idiomatic English*, (Kenkyūsha, 1951) appeared in a textbook on translating into English. Full citations for East Asian language translations can be found in International House of Japan Library, *Modern Japanese Literature in Translation*, 61–62.

6. Keene, *Dawn to the West*, 1138–1146; Masao Miyoshi, *Off Center*, 207; Tanaka, *To Live and to Write*, 99–104; Vernon, *Daughters of the Moon*, 148–158. Non-Japanese critics publishing in Japanese have also focused exclusively on Hayashi's later works: cf. Ehrenburg, "Hayashi Fumiko no bungaku", and Seidensticker, "Hayashi Fumiko."

7. Ōya, "Hayashi Fumiko ron," 30–32.

8. Yoshida, "Kindai joryū no bungaku," 16.

9. "Minshūteki jojō" (Obara, "Hayashi Fumiko ron," 441).

10. Kusabe, "Miyamoto Yuriko to Hayashi Fumiko no buntai," 66–67.

11. Nakamura Mitsuo, "Hayashi Fumiko bungaku ron," 102–103.

12. Hayashi, *Hōrōki*, 468.

13. Atsuta Yūko, in Ogata, *Nyonin geijutsu sekai*, 73–74.

14. See Miner, trans., *Japanese Poetic Diaries*.

15. Hayashi, *Hōrōki*, 8.

16. Hayashi, *Hōrōki*, 57; the italicized passages are in pseudoclassical grammar, and I discuss the implications of this form in the last section of the chapter.

17. Michitsuna no Haha, *The Gossamer Years*, 95.

18. Hayashi, *Hōrōki*, 54.

19. Ibid., 150.

20. Ibid., 48, 68.

21. Ibid., 9, 76, 130, 151, 155.

22. Hirabayashi, "Sehyō to kanojo—Hayashi Fumiko no tame ni," 66–67.

23. Only in the sequel is Matusda portrayed in a more sinister light. He visits Hayashi with a razor, and she fears he is about to kill her. Hayashi, *Hōrōki*, 190–192.

24. Ibid., 61.

25. Ibid., 125–126.

26. Ibid., 369.

27. Ibid., 392.

28. Takemoto, "Ningen-Hayashi Fumiko (1): Tsuminokoshi—Nomura ron."

29. Hashizume, "Hayashi Fumiko Ashura," 214. Sawako complained that she contracted the disease as well.

30. Ibid. See also Hirabayashi, "Bungakuteki seishun den," 238.

31. Nomura, "Hayashi Fumiko den no shinjitsu no tame ni." The letter is on p. 86.

32. Ibid., 83–84.

33. Marx, "The Class Struggles in France, 1848–1850," 52.

34. Marx, *Capital*, 797.

35. Germaine Hoston, in *Marxism and the Crisis of Development in Prewar Japan,* presents an extended discussion of debates within the Japanese Communist Party and the various wings of the Comintern on the prospects for revolution and the basis for class alliances. She does not, however, discuss the *runpen,* and there is no evidence that party intellectuals perceived them as a significant factor.

36. Shigeki and Shōno, *Orijinaru genban ni yoru Nihon no ryūkōka shi,* 29.

37. Itagaki, *Meiji, Taishō, Shōwa no joryū bungaku*, 106. Miyoshi Yukio, the late Professor of Japanese Literature at Tokyo University, concurred with this assessment when I presented it to him in 1985.

38. Irokawa, "Meiji Conditions of Nonculture," 239.

39. Kusama, "Runpen monogatari," 9. The collapse of farm incomes during the latter half of the 1920s was behind the increase in destitute urban migrants. In 1929–1931, average household farm incomes dropped by more than half. Nakamura, *Lectures on Modern Japanese Economic History, 1926–1994*, 42.

40. Kusama, "Runpen monogatari," 10.

41. Shimomura, "Runpen—sono jittai, sono teigi, sono bungaku," 10.

42. Ten days after the March 15, 1928, nationwide roundup of communist activists, the *Zen Nihon musansha geijutsu renmei* (All-Japan federation of proletarian arts) known by its Esperanto acronyms as NAPF (Nippona proleta artista federatio) formed. It adopted a highly politicized perspective that closely followed the changing theses of the Communist Party and the Comintern.

43. The Proletarian literature movement revived immediately after the end of the war, but founders of such Marxist journals as *Kindai bungaku* (Modern literature) resisted the politicization of literature, and even *Shin Nihon bungaku* (New Japanese literature), which was openly supported by the Communist Party, remained more accepting of an array of perspectives under the rubric of *minshushugi bungaku* (democratic literature). See Keene, *Dawn to the West*, 970–974.

44. Examples of Shimomura's work from *Chūō kōron* include: "Furōji" (Waifs, August 1928), "Asakusa kōen shinya no gure kari" (Hunting for dropouts in Asakusa Park at midnight, December 1928), "Runpen bataya no seikatsu sensen" (Vagrants and ragpickers battle for life, April 1931), "Machi ura no ōkami mure" (Packs of wolves of the back alleys, March 1932). His *Bōfū tai* (Storm zone), serialized in *Asahi shimbun* (May–October 1932), was published as a separate volume by Chūō kōronsha later that year. During this same period, Shimomura also published journalistic exposés on the lives of streetwalkers.

45. The literary critic Ikuta Chōkō (1882–1936) heralded "Runpen no tetteiteki kakumei sei" (The sweeping revolutionary aspect of lumpen) in his four-part series in *Asahi shimbun* (July 23–26, 1930). The author Kawabata Yasunari, in his series "Runpen bungaku no sakuhin" (Works of lumpen literature) in "*Bungei jihyō*" (*Asahi shimbun,* April 29–May 1, 1931), discussed five articles published under the heading "Runpen no kenkyū" (Lumpen studies) in the magazine *Shinchō*, especially the entry by Ishihara Tomoyuki, who talked about going

to Russia to see a *runpen* village; a magazine devoted to *runpen bungaku* put out by Ibe Takateru and others; and articles by Tokuda Shūsei, Masamune Hakuchō, and Ō Hisamitsu, who had written on *Amerika runpen.*

46. Kobori, "Goruki jidai to gendai no runpen bungaku," 9.

47. Arai, "Runpen bungaku no shihyō." Hayashi had used "Apache" as a subtitle for a *Nyonin geijutsu* entry that appeared in her *Diary* sequel, and she had traveled to Paris on the royalties of her work.

48. Ōya, "Hayashi Fumiko ron," 30–32.

49. Anderson and Richie, *The Japanese Film,* 45.

50. Ibid., 70.

51. For further discussion of the anarchist group (prominent members included Hagiwara Kyōjirō, Okamoto Jun, Tsuboi Shigeji, and Tsuji Jun) that met in the French restaurant above the Nantendō book store in Hongō and their bohemian lifestyle, see Hirabayashi, "Bungakuteki seishun den," 234–238.

52. Kitamura, "Onna rōnin," 76–78. Quotations are from pp. 76 and 77. Cf. Silverberg's fine discussion of 'mo' ga' (modern girl) in "The Modern Girl as Militant."

53. Rubin, *Injurious to Public Morals,* 232.

54. Nihon kindai bungakkan, ed., *Nihon kindai bungaku dai jiten,* 194.

55. For example, Havens, *Valley of Darkness,* 23.

56. Fukuda and Endō, *Hayashi Fumiko,* 127.

57. Itagaki, *Fujin sakka hyōden,* 109; Fukuda and Endō, *Hayashi Fumiko,* 127–128. The chronology in *Hayashi Fumiko zenshū* (Bunsendō, 1977), 16:302, gives 1941 for the dates of censorship.

58. Jō, *Hakkinbon,* 109–111; Odagiri and Fukuoka, *Shōwa shoseki shimbun, zasshi hakkin nenpyō,* 782.

59. Hayashi, *Hōrōki,* 158–159; she again revisits the incident in the postwar sequel, *Hōrōki dai sanbu,* 223.

60. Hayashi, *Hōrōki,* 161–164; and again in *Hōrōki dai sanbu,* 224–225.

61. Hayashi, *Hōrōki,* 20.

62. Ibid., 84.

63. Ibid., 78.

64. Ibid., 74.

65. Ibid., 54.

5

Transformations

Hayashi Fumiko reached the peak of her popularity and productivity in the immediate postwar era. Her portrayals of struggle and perseverance among the dispossessed and disaffected struck a chord in a broad segment of the reading public. Hayashi's short fiction and serialized works were published in major newspapers, mainstream literary journals, and women's magazines, and her books and collected volumes sold exceptionally well. In the four years prior to her death in 1951, she published eleven serialized novels, twenty-two other volumes, principally novels, and more than thirty short stories, among them those considered her most sophisticated and successful works.[1] The literary prize *Joryū bungakushō* (Women's literary prize) awarded to her for "Bangiku" (Late chrysanthemum) in 1949, confirmed her status among the preeminent women writers of the era.[2] In the wake of her premature death at forty-eight, Hayashi was characterized as "the representative woman writer in our country."[3]

The persistent categorization of her as a "woman writer" *(joryū sakka)* of "women's literature" *(joryū bungaku),* however, assured that while she might be especially prominent, her work would also be considered marginal to the canon and would rarely receive sustained critical scrutiny. Even those who closely read and evaluated more than a smattering of her work were hobbled by the received wisdom about "women writers." For example, Fukuda Hirotoshi dismissed Hayashi's early works (including *Diary of a Vagabond*) as girlishly sentimental but characterized "Late Chrysanthemum"—the work that won the Women's Literary Prize—as more masculine or "androgynous" *(chūsei),* and therefore more mature and serious.[4] The irony of Fukuda's presumption that works by women writers merit critical attention and women's literary prizes to the extent that they distance themselves from those characteristics of their gender underscores the stigma attached to "women's literature." Other critics, however, failed even to observe this transformation of Hayashi's style, imposing the same "feminine" characterization on wholly dissimilar works. Moreover, categorization by gender obscured the relation of her work to more salient literary, social, and political trends.

Aesthetic Transformation

By the late Taishō era, notably in Nakamura Murao's 1925 essay in *Shinchō,* a clear distinction had crystallized between *kyakkan shōsetsu* (objective fiction) and autobiographical or confessional genres.[5] *Kyakkan shōsetsu,* also referred to as *honkaku shōsetsu* (authentic fiction), did not directly reflect the author's experiences or views. In contrast, *shinkyō shōsetsu* (mental attitude fiction), which projected the author's interior states, and *watakushi shōsetsu* (confessional fiction), which revealed largely self-destructive practices, were based on the writer's experiences.[6] Tokuda Shūsei, a novelist whom Edward Seidensticker regarded as having a decisive impact on Hayashi's aesthetic development, argued that a writer should begin with autobiography before attempting objective fiction, which he held to be the decidedly superior style.[7] While this assessment was hotly contested, Hayashi apparently adhered to it.

In the afterword to *Onna no nikki* (A woman's diary), first published in 1936, Hayashi described her calculated, self-conscious effort to change her style of writing from the ostensibly autobiographical *(Diary of a Vagabond)* to the avowedly fictional *(A Woman's Diary)* in order, in her words, "to separate myself from the retching [lit., throwing up bloody vomit] confusion of the autobiographical *Hōrōki.*"[8]

Kaki (Oyster), published in the September 1935 issue of *Chūō kōron,* was indicative of a decided shift in Hayashi's style. The story, told from a man's point of view, was no longer autobiographical or sentimental, but a rather unvarnished and straightforward depiction of an inept, possibly retarded man unable to adjust to transitions in his workplace or to resolve tensions in his family life. Due to ill-defined maladies, the protagonist, Morita Shūkichi, who sews tobacco pouches, is unable to produce the weekly quota or to adapt to machine production. He decides to take his wife from Tokyo back to his family home in Shikoku, which he had not seen in nine years. They plan to stay for a month or two but, when he arrives unexpectedly, his elder sister tells him that he has no right to his ancestral home, having left without ever aiding the remaining family after the parents had died. Back in Tokyo, he takes up sewing again but is given inferior goods and forced to work at a cheaper rate. Neurotic and suspicious, he accuses his wife of infidelity. His wife leaves him and their poverty-stricken existence, although within the week she sends him ¥40 in a letter from her earnings as a live-in waitress. He goes to Chiba to check up on her, certain that she has turned to prostitution but, unable to substantiate his accusation, returns to Tokyo alone.[9]

A month after the publication of *Kaki*—and also a volume of short stories with the same title by Kaizōsha—Hayashi flouted publishing industry conventions by organizing and paying for her own gala celebration in honor of these works.[10] The receipt from the banquet, held in the basement of the Marunouchi Meiji Insurance building, noted that one hundred two people attended. The total bill came to two hundred fifty-four yen and fifty sen. Among the literati in attendance were Uno Kōji, Hirotsu Kazuo, Satō Haruo, Hayashi Fusao, Hasegawa Shigure, Yoshiya Nobuko, Kubokawa Ineko, and Tokuda Shūsei.[11] Reportedly in high spirits, Hayashi danced the *dojō sukui* (a fisherman's folk dance imitating scooping loaches), much to the derision of some of the literary establishment.[12]

Hayashi had published fictional, as opposed to autobiographical, stories earlier that year—for example, *No mugi no uta* (A song of wild wheat), serialized in *Fujin kōron* from January through March 1935—but with *Kaki,* she appears to have wished to call attention to the new approach in her writing.[13] Even at the outset of her career, Hayashi had experimented with a non-autobiographical approach in *Senshun fu* (A record of a shallow spring), serialized in *Asahi shimbun* in January and February 1931.[14] When this fictional piece about an unhappy homeless young woman abandoned by her husband failed to secure either critical or popular success, however, Hayashi returned to writing in an autobiographical voice with two works, both published in *Kaizō: Fūkin to uo no machi* (A town of accordions and fish) in April and *Seihin no sho* (A record of honorable poverty), serialized beginning in November. Both were well received, but they remained out of step with a still vibrant Proletarian literary movement.[15]

Contrary to the usual depiction of Hayashi's writing trajectory, this change in style was additive rather than exclusive. In a number of later works, Hayashi returned to the self-referential lyrical approach that characterized *Diary of a Vagabond.* Several of these ostensibly autobiographical accounts might best be considered as a revision and elaboration, or continuation, of the personal odyssey that began with *Diary of a Vagabond.*[16] *Hitori no shōgai* (One person's life; serialized for one year in *Fujin no tomo* in 1940) began with a description of her recent trips to Kyoto and Peking. However, the bulk of *Hitori no shōgai* focuses on those few years in the mid-1920s recorded in *Diary of a Vagabond,* organized in a more cohesive prose narrative form. This narrative, perhaps in keeping with the times, downplays her poverty and generally adopts a positive, upbeat tone. As in *Diary of a Vagabond,* thirty free-verse poems were an integral part of the narrative. Hayashi also included an account of her trip to Europe. She had already recounted her 1930 European tour in *Santō ryokō no ki* (Record of a trip by third class, 1933), and further elaborated on these incidents in the 1947 publication of *Pari nikki* (Paris diary). *Hitori no shōgai* was one of a series of confessional diaries—*Yūshū nikki* (Melancholy diary, 1939), *Nikki* (Diary, 1941), *Nikki II* (Diary, part II, 1942), and *Den'en nikki* (Rural diary, 1942)—published in quick succession. Perhaps the most notable of her later autobiographical works was the serialization of *Hōrōki dai sanbu* (Diary of a vagabond, part three), beginning in May 1947. This third version of Hayashi's exploits from her 1920s diary was far more sensational than the first and explicitly identified all those who appeared in earlier installments.

Hayashi also suggested the revelation of personal experiences by using in the titles such terms as diary *(nikki),* chronicle *(ki),* record *(sho* or *fu),* scribbling *(rakugaki),* and biography *(den),* even though these works were clearly fictional. *Senshun fu* (1931) was the first of such titles, *Sazanami—Aru onna no techō* (Ripples—a certain woman's datebook, 1951) the last.[17]

Hayashi exhibited a particular penchant for taking an image, often only a title, from a prominent foreign work as the basis for a story. During her association with Tanabe, Hayashi attended a reading of August Strindberg's play *Ovader* (Thunder), translated into Japanese as *Inazuma* (Lightning). She wrote that it inspired her story *Inazuma* (1946), which was based largely on her mother's unhappy marriage.[18] Other examples of this pattern can be seen in the titles *Onna no nikki* (1935), taken from Octave Mirbeau's *Le Journal d'une femme de chambre* (1900), and *Omokage* (Vestiges, 1933), the same as Mori Ōgai's volume of translated European poetry (1889). Hayashi also took her titles from prominent works of Japanese fiction, such as *Ukigumo* (Drifting cloud, 1949–1951), from Futabatei Shimei's work (1887–1889), or *Gan* (Wild geese, 1947), from Mori Ōgai's novel (1911).

If Hayashi borrowed titles and imagery liberally, however, her stories were usually wholly unlike their namesake or inspiration, and while her habit may indicate an affectation, her work was not simply imitative. For example, Futabatei's *Ukigumo,* touted as Japan's first modern novel, focused on the life of Utsumi Bunzō, an ordinary man who finds his dreams of marriage crushed when he loses his low-level job in the government bureaucracy.[19] Hayashi's *Ukigumo* described the malaise and rootlessness of postwar Japanese society as seen through the ill-fated relationship of Yukiko and Tomioka after their repatriation from French Indochina.[20] Hayashi's story has a strong and more fully developed female protagonist whose plight and societal setting are much bleaker.

Hayashi's appropriations were often done in such a way that, without her own admissions, their origins would be undetectable. Reportedly inspired by the Joan Crawford movie *Rain* (1932), Hayashi published two works—the novel *Ame* (Rain, 1941) and a short story "Ame" (1946).[21] Neither of these stories has anything in common with the setting, plot, moral dilemmas, or dynamics of sex and religion that characterized Somerset Maugham's novel or the succession of its Hollywood productions, Crawford's version included.[22] Hayashi did, however, adopt the melancholic mood conveyed by a ceaseless downpour that exacerbates the sense of gloom and frays the emotions. In the 1941 novel, the inescapable, depressing rain in the background underlines the female protagonist's ambivalence toward marriage at the expense of a career. The 1946 "Rain" depicts a young soldier, Kōjirō, who returns home to Shinshū from war only to learn that there is no longer a place for him, since his family, mistakenly informed that he was dead, has married his wife to his younger brother. Urged by his father not to disrupt the new arrangement, he agrees to remain hidden and unsuccessfully seeks out a friend in the burned-out city of Sasebo. Throughout, the rain pelts this pathetic figure, condemned to wander without refuge.

Hayashi employed similar imagery in her *Ukigumo,* where the female protagonist dies in an unrelenting downpour on Yakushima, an island south of Kyushu.[23] Edward Seidensticker has suggested that Hayashi's persistent use of rain to set a dreary and depressing mood stemmed from her early years: "For peddlers like her parents, rain was disastrous . . . what appears to be a mannerism in her later works is essential to her *oeuvre;* it is not grotesque to have so much rain, it is part of wandering."[24]

War Reportage

Through the early and mid-1930s, state censorship increasingly restricted what kinds of publications were permissible. The 1925 Peace Preservation Law, enacted a month prior to universal male franchise, was initially used to target political activists. In a nationwide campaign, 1,600 suspected Communists and radicals were arrested on March 15, 1928, and 700 more on April 16, 1929. By 1932, large numbers of writers were being picked up in sweeps of the membership of the KOPF (*Nihon puroretaria bunka renmei,* Japan proletarian culture federation, known by its acronym in Esperanto, Federacio de proletaj kultur-organizoj) and the NALP (*Nihon puroretaria sakka dōmei,* Japan proletarian writers' league; in Esperanto, Nippona alianco literaturistoj proletaj).[25] Harassment of individual authors and banning of their works had long preceded this systematic crackdown. For example, Kobayashi Takiji had been arrested in May 1930 on suspicion of soliciting funds for the Communist Party, and he was rearrested on his release for the *lèse-majesté* of having had a character in his novel *Kani kōsen* (The factory ship, 1929) suggest mixing gravel with crab meat and serving it to the emperor.[26] Kobayashi achieved martyrdom after his initial evasion of another arrest in May 1932 and death in police custody in February 1933. His death, and the capitulation of other such previously prominent movement figures as Hayashi Fusao, proved to be a turning point for the Proletarian literature movement.[27]

In 1933 Hayashi Fumiko was arrested in Nakano and detained for nine days for having subscribed to the Communist Party's newspaper, *Akahata*.[28] Mitchell misleads, however, in equating her arrest with Kobayashi's in January 1931 (Keene dates it May 1930), even if both were ostensibly contributing funds to the Communists in violation of the Peace Preservation Law. Hayashi's interest and involvement in the party were slight, and of an altogether different character from Kobayashi's sacrifices.[29] There is no record of Hayashi's *tenkō* (political apostasy), or public confession of error, although the overwhelming majority of those arrested in this era wrote *tenkō*.[30] Honda Shūgo estimated that more than ninety-five percent of the 500 authors arrested underwent some kind of *tenkō*, much like political activists in general.[31] Making a *tenkō* was so common that suspicions about those few writers, such as Miyamoto Yuriko, who were not known to have done so lingered long after the war.[32] Perhaps because Hayashi had never firmly held any political ideology, had so enthusiastically participated in wartime propaganda, and had made no apologies for these efforts, the issue of her *tenkō* was moot.

Hayashi received considerable publicity in January 1938 when, on assignment for the *Tōkyō nichi nichi shimbun* (after January 1, 1943, *Mainichi shimbun*), she was the first Japanese woman to enter Nanking after it fell to Japanese troops.[33] But her articles not only failed to note atrocities. They hardly made any observations about Nanking at all. Her initial article, accompanying a story written by another reporter of her often repeated claims of being first into Nanking, recounted experiences in Taiwan in 1930.

In 1938, Hayashi was one of two women, along with Yoshiya Nobuko, that the Ministry of Information included in the first "Pen Squadron," as it came to be known—a group of twenty-two popular writers who were to tour the front and write about the circumstances and sacrifices of soldiers for readers back home.[34] Later that year, Hayashi was able to hitch a ride on the *Asahi shimbun* truck and again received front-page publicity for having been among the first Japanese to enter the city of Hankow.[35] Hayashi and the other Pen Squadron writers also toured extensively as speakers both in Japan and among military units and the Japanese community in Korea, Manchuria, and China.[36]

Hayashi's reportage of this tour—*Sensen* (Battlefront, 1938), *Hokugan butai* (Northern bank platoon, 1939), and *Hatō* (Rough seas, 1939)—included poetry and brief vignettes of individual soldiers and their difficulties and perseverance, but its overwhelming emphasis was on the minutiae of her own travels and travails. These works, essentially, daily entries in a diary format, detailed her escapades, usually at some considerable distance behind the front lines. There are no descriptions of battle per se, very few references to any Chinese, and what descriptions of the landscape there are most often focus on the muck she was forced to traverse. Despite the occasional inclusion of gruesome details, Hayashi's reputation for producing "graphic accounts" is unwarranted.[37] More typical of these works was her account, in *Hokugan butai,* on hearing of the lament of a soldier at the death of his beloved horse. Hayashi not only quoted passages from the soldier's plaintive letter home, which centered on his grief and enclosed an auburn lock of the horse's tail, but appended her own poem celebrating the sacrifices of this noble steed.[38] Several of the poems included in her reporting became the lyrics of popular patriotic songs, including an ode to Okumura Sayuko's tour—"ignited by patriotism"—of Japanese troops in China during the Boxer Rebellion.[39] On occasion, Hayashi's praise for the perserverance of ordinary Japanese echoed crude racial stereotypes, as in her reassurance to the soldiers that their women's chastity could be trusted for at least a year between conjugal visits, unlike wantonly indulgent Western women.[40] To her credit, however, Hayashi avoided the jingoistic slogans and clichés so common in the period, especially by those writing from the front, for example, *muteki kogun* (invincible imperial army) or *zen toa no kaiho* (liberation of all East Asia), and kept her observations highly personal and focused on the world that was immediately before her. Itagaki Naoko has noted that these articles received very little critical notice and are largely dismissed not only for their politics but also for Hayashi's rather uninspired obsession with her mundane experiences.[41]

Hayashi's reporting from China sharply contrasted with that of Ishikawa Tatsuzō (1905–1985), whose *Ikite iru heitai* (Living soldiers, 1938) included depictions of brutal massacres of civilians by ordinary soldiers during the occupation of Nanking. His work was first heavily censored, then stopped. Eventually it earned him a prison term. Though Hayashi was writing under official supervision or for major newspapers, and so was highly restricted in what she could write, her literary contributions to the war effort paled in comparison with those of, say, Hino Ashihei (1907–1960). His enormously popular *Mugi to heitai* (Wheat and soldiers, 1938) heralded the patriotic sacrifices of those serving in the ranks through rather gritty portraits of ordinary soldiers.[42] Hayashi also failed to express even a hint of skepticism about the war propaganda, although such skepticism could be seen in Ibuse Masuji's "Hana no machi" (City of flowers, 1943), which cast a critical eye on those in Singapore who were collaborating with the Greater East Asian Co-Prosperity Sphere.

Hayashi traveled behind the front lines repeatedly. In September 1940 she joined Kawakami Tetsutarō, Nii Itaru, Matsui Suisei, and Kobayashi Hideo on a lecture tour of Korea and Manchuria that was organized by the *Asahi Shimbun* company.[43] In 1941 she went to Manchuria with an *Asahi Shimbun*–sponsored group that included the writer Sata Ineko. In 1942 and 1943, Hayashi spent eight months as a reporter in South and Southeast Asia, spending time in the Andaman Islands, Singapore, Java, and Borneo.[44]

In 1944 Hayashi formally adopted an infant boy whom she named Tai and for whom she had cared since his birth the year before. Tai was said to have been the illegitimate child of a male journalist.[45] At this juncture she also entered Ryokubin's name in the Hayashi family register as her husband, and he took the Hayashi surname. Like many other residents of Tokyo, she fled to the Nagano countryside with her son and mother that same year to escape the bombings. From May through August 1944 she stayed at the Kambayashi hot springs near her husband's hometown in Nagano, returned briefly to Tokyo, and then moved her family to the Kadoma hot springs and other locations until October 1945.[46] During this time in the country, she wrote poetry and nursery tales in lieu of fiction.

Hayashi's collaboration with state-sponsored wartime propaganda was the focus of a good deal of postwar criticism. For example, *Akahata* singled her out in a 1946 editorial that condemned the wartime collaboration of writers. Sata Ineko, who had joined Hayashi on tours of Manchuria and, later, Southeast Asia, wrote successive accounts—*Kyogi* (Falsehood, 1948) and *Homatsu no kiroku* (A record of foam, 1948), agonizing over how her actions to participate in government-defined roles and try to maintain a personal commitment to her former political beliefs were yet condemned by former associates. Hayashi, in contrast, never apologized nor even rationalized her participation in the war effort.

Postwar Imagination

Shibaki Yoshiko observed after Hayashi's death that her "early works were full of poetic sentiment and feeling, and that lyricism eventually excessively sweetened her writing, but in her later years she was able to escape magnificently from this sphere. The war proved to be the opportunity for her literary style to face the shift in harsh reality directly and single-mindedly."[47] This shift in style does not appear to be rooted in any particular personal experience of war, nor is it marked by an adoption of fiction in lieu of autobiography. As we have seen, her "objective" fiction antedated the war, and her ostensibly autobiographical writing persisted until her death. Many of her postwar thematic concerns were readily apparent from the outset of her career. What did change in her writing, however, was her adoption of more standard, composed, and complex grammatical constructions and her abandonment of the fragmented, discontinuous narrative. Hayashi's poetic lyricism was eclipsed, but her mature style conveyed much of the friction, now internalized by characters, that the disjointed narrative previously achieved. The ability of her work to reflect the anxieties and harsh realities of the era and to strike a responsive chord among a broad section of the reading public also changed.

When the war was over, Hayashi returned to Tokyo. She had seemed to join the general enthusiasm of the war effort; now she raised her voice against the death and misery caused by war. Several of the short stories she wrote at the beginning of the occupation, such as "Rain" (1946) or "Uruwashiki sekizui" (Splendid carrion, 1947) were explicitly antiwar, although neither seems to draw on personal observations from her "battlefront tours." Both are set after the war and center on the dilemmas of repatriated soldiers, unwelcomed, rootless, and lost. *Uzushio* (Swirling eddies, 1947) serialized in *Mainichi Shimbun,* was the first long fiction to appear in postwar newspapers. It focused on the problems of the women widowed by the war often after only the most fleeting of relationships with their spouses and left to fend for themselves. Hayashi's themes of wandering, abandonment, and bare subsistence, as well as disillusioned intimacy, tempered by irrepressible resiliency, exhibit continuity with the best of her earlier works. This postwar fiction captured the imagination of a generation whose lives it mirrored.

In "Dauntaun" (The low city, 1949), Riyo, a young woman from the countryside, has come to Tokyo to peddle tea door-to-door to support herself and her son.[48] She has not heard from her husband, who has been stranded in Siberia, for six years. She is attracted to a kind and unpretentious laborer who had returned from the war, and Siberia, only to find his wife living with another man. Torn between a sense of obligation toward her absent husband, and the prospect of connecting with the generous and wonderfully sympathetic laborer, Riyo in turn stifles her desires, rejects his advances, regrets her resistance, hesitates, and then abandons herself to a new love. When she and her son arrive at his hut for their next visit, she is staggered to be informed of his death. In a typically selfless action, the laborer had volunteered to accompany an ill driver to help unload scrap metal, and the truck had plunged off a bridge. With her hungry, whining child in tow, Riyo sets off to wander the freezing, windswept low city, pathetically peddling her tea. The straps of her rucksack dig into her shoulder, and she welcomes the pain. She decides not to attend the laborer's funeral, not to call attention to their affair, but still to cherish his memory and stay forever in the streets where he had lived. The closing conveys the small comfort she finds through her resilience, when an old woman, dressed more shabbily than herself, roots around for money to make a purchase and invites her inside her hut for warmth and rest. The diligence of a handful of women sewing inside this tiny hut—"women like me"—reminds Riyo of how common her hardship must be, both resigning and steeling her in her determination to carry on.

Bangiku (A late chrysanthemum, 1948) depicts the sour end of a relationship between Kin, a remarkably well preserved former geisha in her fifties, and Tabe, a once dashing young officer who has returned from the war embittered and destitute.[49] Hardened by cruel experiences in her youth, including an assault by her stepmother's lover, and schooled through her adroit handling of many affairs, Kin has managed very well for herself, now as a kept woman, and has remained seemingly untouched by the war and preoccupied with preserving her still youthful appearance. Tabe, in contrast, is devastated by the war and is worn and disheveled. His desperate request to borrow money brings quick contempt and a refusal. The masterful depiction of weary disillusionment is effective because of the succession of false hopes that each character embraces: for Kin, rekindling an idealized romance to repossess not only the allure of Tabe's youth, but her own; for Tabe, receiving the largess from Kin that she so clearly could afford and, in rejection, entertaining the notion of killing her for it. Kin, stung by the contrast of Tabe with her photo of him in his glory, burns it when he is in the toilet. Tabe guzzles the whiskey he had brought as a present and, too drunk to leave, is allowed to stay overnight, but as an unwelcome guest, not as a lover. Both lovers are bitterly aware of the contrast with fairytale endings. Yet Hayashi suggests that even in their disgust for each other, they confront a welter of emotions that mixes and confuses illusions about themselves with memories they can no longer clearly recall. Rejection, when it comes, stems not simply from a cold calculus of self-interest or a steely rejection of sentimentality, but from the passage of time and distance that has inevitably so altered them.

Her last complete novel, *Drifting Cloud* (1949–1951), describes the relationship between Yukiko, a typist for a forestry survey, and Tomioka, a minor official with the Department of Agriculture and Forestry, who meet and have an affair in Dalat, in the highlands of Indochina, during the war.[50] After returning to Japan, Tomioka does not fulfill his earlier promise to leave his wife, but does not completely break off with Yukiko. She manages to support herself through secretly selling goods belonging to Iba, her brother-in-law's brother, with whom she had stayed for three years before going to Indochina, and who had raped her shortly upon her arrival from the countryside. With the money she made from the sales, she sets herself up in a room and takes on American G.I. lovers. Extremely unhappy with their current life, Tomioka and Yukiko plot to commit suicide together, but that plan aborts when Tomioka becomes involved with the wife of the innkeeper where they go to celebrate their last New Year. When Iba founds his own "new religion" and amasses a fortune in the process, Yukiko joins his staff. But after Tomioka's wife dies and he is assigned to work for the forestry department on remote Yakushima, an island south of Kyushu, Yukiko decides to run away with the sect's cashbox to join him, though she is still suffering the effects of an abortion. Amid Yakushima's ceaseless rains, Yukiko's health continues to deteriorate. After recalling once again her tangled web of encounters with Tomioka and others, she dies. Tomioka, finally, is deeply moved at her death, yet he also senses a profound relief now that he is free from the oppressive burden of a relationship that had dragged on beyond reason. But though free, he is now also rootless and has no direction. As Keene notes, "He will live like a drifting cloud, the traditional metaphor for an aimless life."[51]

Much of Hayashi's most successful postwar work had a dark tone—what Shibaki celebrated as reflecting the harsh realities of the era—and portrayed individuals, mostly women, confronting bleak circumstances and unpleasant choices. But, in contrast with other nihilistic authors who also explored the terrain of desperate poverty and disillusionment, Hayashi stood out in presenting the feints and false starts that occur within fractured personalities. Her characters internalized the ambiguities and conflict so characteristic of the uncertainties of the era. Still, there were echoes of the kind of resiliency that was such a hallmark of Hayashi's *Diary of a Vagabond.* Characters' interior monologues were the principal means of capturing conflicting, interacting desires. It is not so much what they did or how low they could go that arouses the reader's sympathy, but how they fought within themselves.

The unfinished novel *Meshi* (Food, 1950–1951) depicts the prosaic struggles of an unexceptional marriage. Hayashi admitted that the title was a bit enigmatic, but she appreciated the allusions to various meanings of the kanji in different compounds.[52] Taken alone the word meant cooked rice, a staple of the Japanese diet. But it could also imply a useless life *(meshi bukuro).* The prosaic title may be taken as a synecdoche for the unglamorous necessities of life. The character for *meshi* often appears on signs outside inexpensive eateries, as if to symbolize the simple tastes, if not sole concern, of working people.

In *Food,* a childless couple finds their marriage falling apart after five years. A salaryman of modest yet reasonably secure income, enters into a love marriage after the couple has lived together for a year until her family agreed to the union. The circumstances and the dilemmas are far more ordinary and conventional than those of most of Hayashi's previous characters. The wife tires of her predictable, uninspired relationship with her husband. Intending to leave him, she goes to Tokyo. Although the work is unfinished, there are indications that the couple may stay together to raise an adopted child.[53] Hayashi strove for a straightforward, accessible work: "I want calmly to write a plump story, like freshly boiled rice, for an unaffected audience."[54]

"Suisen" (Narcissus, 1949) was emblematic of her postwar fiction in demonstrating a growing sophistication in language use and in tightness of narrative. "Narcissus" portrays the irreconcilable differences and bitter recriminations between a mother and a son. Motherhood is characterized as a nightmare from which the protagonist is desperately attempting to awake. The unrelenting petty insults and bickering between two such selfish, vain, and irresponsible characters set a bleak tone and convey an especially dark, pessimistic assessment of human relations.

> "Saku, I can't tell if you're basically decent or bad."
> "I'm bad."
> "Don't be so sure. You're just twenty-two, and you haven't learned too many wily ways. Can't you seduce somebody like a rich man's young daughter? . . ."
> "Hmm, I don't much like young girls."
> "That's because you've never had one."
> "Mom, you're wicked. . . ."
> "I suppose so." Tamae felt that it didn't matter what sin she committed. In ten years she'd lose the taste for it. Everyone is led astray by hypocritical morality. Underneath the hypocrisy, people fight like ferocious lions for the prizes—control, power, and wealth. Peace and contentment escape like steam from the friction of human dynamics. For some, there may be laughter. But for Tamae and her son there was not even a single glimmer of hope. Not even in the bond between mother and child.[55]

The story chronicles the rift between Saku and Tamae, her growing detachment from her son, and her reaction to the eventual sundering of relations. From the outset, despite her transparently hollow denials, the mother broaches her desire for separation. Her shiftless twenty-two-year-old son finally lands an offer of a job in a coal mine in Hokkaido, and they prepare for what will be a final separation. She declares that she will not write and will not hear of him returning even if she becomes ill or dies. Unlike Hayashi's early work, this story lacks any hint of sentimentality. At the final parting, the mother thinks her son looks pathetic; he, for his part, quickly lets go of her hand. For her, the final parting is a liberation.

> Aware that now she was all alone, Tamae squared her shoulders and took a deep breath. At the end of the year, even the back streets were filled with people. Under the blue lights, a succession of store-

fronts—racks of silver salmon and mannequins draped with black velvet—streamed unperceived past her eyes. Downtown at this time of year seemed not to have changed a bit from years ago. For no particular reason, Tamae imagined she might breathe her last somewhere in this tempestuous city. That would surely be the only way to recapture the spirit of her youth. She nursed the notion that her life had been snuffed out like a candle in the wind. In the dark December streets, a girl with her hair up in the traditional style and several children were boisterously slapping a shuttlecock with decorated wooden paddles. The white feathers disappeared into the night, only to come streaking across the light of the lamp under the eaves.

Ambling out to the avenue, Tamae heard a salesman barking hoarsely in front of Morinaga's, mobbed with people. "Yes, here are the Morinaga Velvets you all remember. How about it?" Mixing with the crowd, Tamae swiped a shining cellophane bag and dropped it into her pocket. She felt extremely pleased with herself. At a china store, Tamae melted into the crowd and stole a pretty Kutani soy sauce container. More than the fact that no one caught her, the weight in her pocket was gratifying. She felt as if she were walking along wearing a mask. All of a sudden, she was happy to be alive. Her parting from her son made Tamae feel instantly much younger, and as she came to dim Sukiyabashi street, she took a Velvet from the cellophane bag and popped it into her mouth. The sweet melody of a popular song drifted in the air from an advertisement. The *Asahi Newspaper* electric news raced busily to the right, flashing the dissolution of the Diet onto the sky.[56]

Edward Seidensticker heralded this closing image from "Narcissus" as among the most memorable in immediate postwar literature.[57] Mishima Yukio considered "Narcissus" his favorite of Hayashi's later works; with it, she had reached "the level of mature art."[58] In sharp contrast to the rigid conformity of governmentally orchestrated "good wife wise mother" *(ryōsai kenbo)* perspectives or the didactic moralizing of household or domestic fiction *(katei shōsetsu),* "Narcissus" depicts a world from which righteousness has been ripped away. By centering on the most common and revered of personal relations, Hayashi reveals the dark underside of ordinary life, perhaps more widely experienced than the ideals, and she suggests that, however resilient the human spirit, the real exercise of free will is to choose between distasteful choices.

The continuities in Hayashi's work were striking. Her characters, predominantly women, embodied a dogged determination, perseverance, and resilience, despite the unrelenting ills from which they suffered. Most of Hayashi's work illuminated the lives of an underclass, a *runpen,* catch-as-catch-can world that was often drab, if not desperate. In her unfinished novel, *Food,* her "salaryman" family was more lower middle class, but their circumstances still resonated with the sense of powerlessness that had marked her earlier characters. Yet Hayashi infused a sense of humanity into all these situations and conveyed the unextinguished aspirations and inescapable anxieties of those who live among the debris of broken dreams. Hayashi's fictional world was "of the people" *(minshūteki),*[59] but not from a sense of ideological commitment or political correctness. Hayashi painted her portraits small: descriptive depictions of everyday life *(shomin no seikatsu).*[60] Her point of view was always particular, and cannot easily be generalized to a single stratum, class, or gender.

Notes

1. Itagaki, "Atogaki," 407.

2. The prize was first awarded in 1947 to Hirabayashi Taiko. Other early recipients were Amino Kiku (1948), Yoshiya Nobuko (1952), Ōtani Fujiko (1953), Enchi Fumiko (1954), Tsuboi Sakae (1955). No award was made in 1950 or 1951.

3. Tamiya, "Kaisetsu," 221.

4. Fukuda, "Hayashi Fumiko," 45.

5. Usui, *Kindai bungaku ronsō (Jō),* 195.

6. Keene, *Dawn to the West,* 506–517.

7. Tokuda Shūsei, cited in Usui, *Kindai bungaku ronsō (Jō),* 197.

8. Hayashi, "Chosha no kotoba," 248.

9. Hayashi Fumiko, "Kaki," *Hayashi Fumiko zenshū* 3 (Shinchōsha 1951).

10. Fukuda and Endō, *Hayashi Fumiko,* 77. See also Sakurada, ed., *Hayashi Fumiko,* 234; Isome and Nakazawa, *Hayashi Fumiko,* 67–69.

11. Isome and Nakazawa, *Hayashi Fumiko,* 69.

12. Ibid., 67.

13. *A Song of Wild Wheat* is rather melodramatic and sentimental: When Kazuko's husband falls in love with another woman, he summarily divorces his wife, telling her that she is as dangerous as a firecracker, and then promptly remarries. Kazuko is forced to earn a living as a waitress. She agrees to go to a hot spring with an older customer who turns out to be a famous Japanese-style painter. Later she decides to become a nude model for a young artist who, coincidentally, is the son of the older man. The story ends with the young man declaring his love for her despite her brief relationship with his father (*Hayashi Fumiko zenshū* [1952], 5:107–176).

14. Hayashi recognized this as an unsuccessful work (Sakurada, *Hayashi Fumiko,* 233).

15. The combined circulations of the Proletarian literature journals *Senki* and *Bungei sensen* (Literary battlefront) had peaked at close to 50,000 in 1929–1930. But a more telling measure of the impact of the movement comes from Yamada Seizaburō's 1954 study *Puroretaria bungaku* (quoted in Ruben, *Injurious to Public Morals,* 247) that in the influential mainstream journals *Kaizō* and *Chūō kōron,* Proletarian literature accounted for 29 percent of fiction in 1929–1930 (through March), and 44 percent in 1930–1931.

16. Hayashi discussed her return to this style in "Atogaki," *Hayashi Fumiko zenshū* (1952), 8:245–246. "Atogaki" was originally published in 1949 by Shinchōsha as the afterword to *Zoku Hōrōki* in *Hayashi Fumiko bunko.*

17. Other fictional works with ostensibly autobiographical titles were *Onna no nikki* (Diary of a woman, 1936), *Aijōden* (Biography of love, 1936), *Joyūki* (Record of an actress, 1940), *Maihime no ki* (Record of a dancing girl, 1947), *Onna no seishun* (A woman's youth, 1947), and *Yakushima kikō* (Travelogue to Yaku island, 1950).

18. Hayashi related that she attended a reading of this play at Tanabe's house (Hayashi, *Hitori no shōgai,* in *Hayashi Fumiko zenshū* [1952], 8:48).

19. See Ryan, *Japan's First Modern Novel.*

20. Hayashi, *Ukigumo* (*Hayashi Fumiko zenshū* 16 [Shinchōsha, 1952]. Translated by Yoshiyuki Koitabashi and Martin C. Collcott as *The Floating Clouds.* See also Keene, *Japanese Literature: An Introduction,* for a discussion of *Ukigumo.*

21. Itagaki Naoko recounted a conversation in which Hayashi indicated that the film *Rain* had inspired her. Itagaki, "Atogaki," 408.

22. In Maugham's and Hollywood's story, *Rain* is set on a tramp steamer quarantined in Pago Pago, where a zealous missionary attempts to reform and convert a prostitute. Gloria Swanson starred in the silent screen version, Crawford and Walter Huston in the 1932 film directed by Lewis Milestone, and Rita Hayworth and José Ferrer in the 1953 remake, *Miss Sadie Thompson.*

23. For a discussion of the rain metaphor in *Ukigumo,* see Imamura Junko, "Ame no hyōgen ni miru kanjō inyū ni tsuite." As a film, *Ukigumo* won the 1955 Kinema Jumpo "Best One" Award (Anderson and Richie, *The Japanese Film,* 280).

24. Seidensticker, "Hayashi Fumiko," 126.

25. By spring 1928, the precursor to the KOPF, the NAPF (Zen nihon musansha geijutsu renmei, or All-Japan federation of proletarian arts) had begun advocating explicitly politicized literature, art as an instrument of the Communist Party. The NAPF was superseded by the KOPF in late 1931 as part of a strategy to decentralize activities in response to police surveillance and repression (Iwamoto, "Aspects of the Proletarian Literary Movement in Japan," 164; cf. Arima, *The Failure of Freedom,* 199).

26. Keene, *Dawn to the West,* 621. *The Factory Ship* had been serialized in the journal *Battle Flag* (May and June 1929), but it was banned as a book. His earlier story *1928 nen 3 gatsu 15 nichi* (March 15, 1928) had led to the banning of *Battle Flag* (ibid., 617–620).

27. In one of only many instances of how the Peace Preservation Law worked, Sata Ineko's "Nigatsu hatsuka no ato" (After February twentieth), which chronicled the grief of a small circle of the KOPF at the news of Kobayashi's death and the suppression of their efforts to hold a wake, published in *Puroretaria bungaku* (Proletarian literature, April/May 1933), led to the banning of the journal for "supporting violent and revolutionary agitation" *(bōryoku kakumei sendō)* (Odagiri and Fukuoka, eds., *Shōwa shōseki zasshi, shimbun hakkin nenpyō,* 526).

28. Sakurada, ed., *Hayashi Fumiko,* 233; Hirabayashi, *Hayashi Fumiko,* 145–147.

29. Mitchell, *Thought Control in Prewar Japan,* 272.

30. For a discussion of *tenkō*, see Tsurumi, "Tenkō no kyōdō kenkyū ni tsuite," and Honda Shūgo, *Tenkō bungaku ron.*

Keene notes that "Writers of every political affiliation joined [the Japanese Literature Patriotic Association], including those of the left (like the poet Nakano Shigeharu and the woman novelist Miyamoto Yuriko) in the hopes that membership in this patriotic organization would shield them from charges that they had not truly renounced their former Communist beliefs" (Keene, "Japanese Writers and the Greater East Asian War").

31. Honda, *Tenkō bungaku ron,* 180.

32. For example, Hirabayashi Taiko would speculate that Miyamoto Yuriko probably made such a declaration to be released from prison. Hirabayashi, *Miyamoto Yuriko,* 236.

33. "Hayashi Fumiko shi, Nankyō ichiban nori" (Miss Hayashi Fumiko: The first into Nanking), *Tōkyō nichi nichi shimbun,* January 6, 1938, 2. The reporter notes that "swelling with pride, she claims 'You know, I'm the first Japanese woman in Nanking.' " Hayashi's exploits would continue to receive coverage even when she stumbled on an old friend and popular singer, now conscripted, for whom she had served as a go-between in marriage. "*Namida no ongaku gochō*—o Hayashi Fumuko joshi ga ginchu ni imon" (Miss Hayashi Fumiko visits in the field—staff sergeant "music of tears"), ibid., January 11, 1938, 2.

34. There is a captioned photograph of the dinner celebrating the departure of the "Pen Squadron" in the *Tōkyō nichi nichi shimbun,* September 7, 1938, 2. See also Kameyama Toshiko, "Yoshiya Nobuko to Hayashi Fumiko no jūgunki o yomu: Pen butai no kon'iten."

35. "Kankōsen jūgunki" (A Hankow war chronicle with the troops), *Asahi shimbun,* (evening edition), September 29, 1938, 1.

36. Accounts of Hayashi's stump speech in Japan in November 1938 suggest a flair for melodramatic accounts of personal suffering among the troops, as well as a reminder that she was in a position to judge—"I was the first in Hankow" ("Kyōhonsha shusai *bukan kōryaku kōenkai*" [Lectures on the attack and capture of Hankow], *Asahi shimbun,* November 2, 1938, 3).

37. The quotation is from Mitchell, *Thought Control in Prewar Japan,* 287, citing Keene; Keene observes that, in *Sensen,* Hayashi's description of her thirteen-kilometer march with the troops, during which she must forgo sharing the soldiers' canteens for lack of any appropriate toilet facilities, she includes such introspective queries as whether she had not been upset by the Chinese corpses along the route because they were of a different race. Keene, *Dawn to the West,* 910, 955.

38. Hayashi, *Hokugan butai,* 228–229.

39. Hayashi's poem "Hokugan butai" became the lyrics for a popular patriotic song in 1938 (Shigeki Nobuo and Shōno Masanori, eds., *Orijinaru genban ni yoru Nihon no ryūkōka shi,* 70). Her poem/lyrics "Hibana" (Spark) about Okumura Sayuko made its premiere in a radio broadcast on February 7, 1938, sung, coincidentally, by Tezuka Fumiko. (Tezuka was her "husband's" name, and had their marriage been registered, this would have been Hayashi's name as well; *Tōkyō nichi nichi shimbun* February 7, 1938, 5.)

40. *Hokugan butai,* 210–211.

41. Itagaki, *Hayashi Fumiko,* 189.

42. The 1939 English translation of *Wheat and Soldiers* by Baroness Shidzué Ishimoto fails to include the closing paragraphs, with their rather gruesome beheading of unrepentant Chinese prisoners and elimination of any doubt about the dehumanizing brutality of the campaign. Despite his unparalleled wartime popularity and unquestioned patriotism, Ishikawa's book of romantic, sentimental poetry, *Aogitsune* (Young fox) was banned by the censors in 1943 (Jō, *Hakkinbon*, 112–114).

43. According to Kawakami, unlike Kobayashi Hideo and himself, who would sneak away to see the sights, Hayashi was an enthusiastic participant in the official portions of the trip and attended every function. Kawakami, "Hayashi san to no Chōsen ryokō."

44. Sakurada, ed., *Hayashi Fumiko,* 235.

45. Itagaki, *Meiji, Taishō, Shōwa no joryū bungaku*, 223.

46. Sato Fumiko, ed., "Sokai no ki," 98.

47. Shibaki, "Kaisetsu," 218. Shibaki Yoshiko (1914–1991), was one of the two 1941 recipients of the Akutagawa literary prize. She also received the Women's Prize for Literature in 1961. Itagaki Naoko noted her resemblance to Hayashi Fumiko in background and focus on working-class women. According to Itagaki, Hayashi had a great influence on Shibaki's work. Itagaki, *Meiji, Taishō, Shōwa no joryū bungaku*, 339.

48. Hayashi, "Dauntaun," *Hayashi Fumiko zenshū* 17:21–32 (Shinchōsha, 1952). Translated into English by Ivan Morris as "Tokyo," in Keene, ed., *Modern Japanese Literature,* and also as "Downtown," in Morris, ed., *Modern Japanese Stories.* See my discussion of the translation in the preface.

49. Hayashi, "Bangiku," *Hayashi Fumiko zenshū* 13:37–52 (Shinchōsha, 1952). Translated into English by John Bester as "Late Chrysanthemum," and by Lane Dunlop in *A Late Chrysanthemum.*

50. Hayashi, *Ukigumo,* in *Hayashi Fumiko zenshū* 16 (Shinchōsha, 1951). Translated into English by Yoshiyuki Koitabashi and Martin C. Collcott as *The Floating Clouds.*

51. Keene, *Dawn to the West*, 1148.

52. The title *Meshi* was written in hiragana (phonetic syllabary); Hayashi had earlier written a short story with the title *Meshi* in kanji. See *Hayashi Fumiko zenshū* 7:59–84 (Shinchōsha, 1952).

53. Hayashi, *Meshi,* in *Hayashi Fumiko zenshū* 18:5–141 (Shinchōsha, 1952).

54. Hayashi, "Chosha no kotoba," *Hayashi Fumiko zenshū* 18:271 (Shinchōsha, 1952). First published March 29, 1951, in an *Asahi Shimbun* advertisement).

55. Hayashi Fumiko, "Suisen," *Hayashi Fumiki zenshū,* 13:63–64 (Shinchōsha, 1952).

56. Ibid., 65–66.

57. Seidensticker, "Hayashi Fumiko," 126.

58. Mishima, " 'Bangiku' kaisetsu," 46.

59. Kawamori, "Hayashi Fumiko no koto," 45.

60. Muramatsu, "Hayashi Fumiko no dansei henreki."

6
A Place in Literary History

The works of Hayashi Fumiko, like those of most modern women writers, were segregated and effectively stigmatized by their categorization as "women's literature." But the consequences of this categorization were complex, and the attribution was most often combined with other critical evaluations whose validity and relevance may continue to merit scrutiny. English-speaking readers should also recognize that sustained literary criticism in English on Hayashi or on almost any of the prominent modern women writers has so far been lacking.[1] Therefore, it is essential to situate my assessment within the extensive Japanese criticism of her work. Although the current wave of Japanese feminist criticism has done away with the term "women's literature," an alternative assessment must still scrutinize in what ways and to what extent Hayashi's writing can be considered feminine. But an alternative assessment can also consider whether, in her portraits of female relationships, she might be considered feminist, perhaps in spite of herself. And any assessment of her representation of women should enable, in our reading of specific texts, an appreciation of the dynamic nature of female identities.

As I completed this book, in the journal of the Modern Japanese Literature Association Yoshikawa Toyoko, professor of Japanese literature at Yamanashi Prefectural Women's Junior College and member of Shin feminizumu hihyō no kai, was writing with considerable skepticism about the lasting contributions of contemporary feminist criticism in Japan, reiterating Chida Hiroyuki's warning of the previous year about the risks of continuing to use unproductive gender stereotypes in discussing the representation of women and the female image.[2] Yet Yoshikawa's principal targets are those, including Chida, who adopt feminist criticism as a popular academic fashion without having a familiarity with or background in the history of literature written by women. Yoshikawa is surely correct in calling for more historically grounded appraisals of representations of the female and of works by women writers, and I believe that such an approach can more effectively demonstrate the multiple, fluid, and contested nature of female identity and suggest new ways of reading Hayashi's works and her contributions to Japanese literature.

Critical Reception

In 1947, Miyamoto Yuriko criticized Hayashi for having abandoned the natural volatility found in her *Diary of a Vagabond* in favor of excessive nihilism and sentimentality.[3] Miyamoto indicted both Hayashi and Uno Chiyo as women writers *(fujin sakka)* who embraced the progressive spirit only for personal advancement, not for larger political or aesthetic interests. Miyamoto saw their work both as too individualistic and as pandering to gender-based conventions. Both Hayashi and Uno, she argued, shamelessly postured as "women writers" for the sake of press coverage and to please consumers. "The success that they gained as a result served instead to create the boundaries of their literature."[4]

Miyamoto Yuriko's criticism coincided with the condemnation that Hayashi, among many others, faced in the politicized postwar environment for having participated too enthusiastically in state-orchestrated campaigns to herald the sacrifices of Japanese soldiers and generate civilian support for the war effort. While Hayashi had first surfaced in the company of Anarchist and Proletarian writers, she never exhibited any radical political commitment to or serious interest in Marxist ideology. Soon after achieving prominence as a writer, she had quickly distanced herself from the left. Her works were often dismissed, as she noted, for lacking a political vision.[5] After the war, Hayashi suffered no crisis of conscience for her active participation in propaganda efforts. She castigated wartime restrictions and censorship after the fact and bemoaned the lack of outlets for publication (and opportunities for income), but she never apologized for her support for the war. For Hayashi, the postwar dilemmas were personal: whether she would again have the confidence to write and the ability to look reality straight in the eye.[6]

Although Nakamura Mitsuo found Hayashi feminine, some critics thought she fell short on that score. At times, hostility toward her seemed wholly personal. For example, Mushanokōji Saneatsu went to great lengths to establish that his personal association with her was slight, always in public, and in the company of others, whom he lists (though using initials), as if to make clear that he was not and never had been involved with her in any way that could be misconstrued.[7] Mushanokōji granted that she was a pleasant, energetic, and hard-working writer, but he dismissed her for having done nothing more than mirror herself in her work. She lacked the beautiful, feminine, detailed emotion he sought in a woman writer. He admitted, however, that he had reached this judgment without having read much of Hayashi's work.[8]

Even for Nakamura Mitsuo, the suppposed femininity of Hayashi's writing was never the exclusive focus of his criticism. Consider how Nakamura elaborated his assessment of Hayashi through a comparison with Miyamoto Yuriko, both of whom died in 1951:

> Whereas Miyamoto professed fusion with "the people" on an ideological level, in reality she was not able to discard her genteel upbringing. In direct opposition, Hayashi Fumiko was born of common blood and made that the wellspring of her literature. For Miyamoto Yuriko, the masses were the destination to which she mentally aspired; Hayashi Fumiko, conversely, saw the masses as a morass through which one was forced to crawl. But at the same time, the common folk also constituted Hayashi's hometown, where one did not feel inhibited in one's actions.[9]

Nakamura saw in these two writers a yearning for something each lacked—a different class from the one into which they were born. Miyamoto, from a "good family," longed for the simplicity and authenticity of ordinary people, while Hayashi embodied the snobbish, social-climbing aspirations of the nouveau riche.[10] Nakamura observed that Hayashi's garish tastes and unsophisticated affectation were very much of the people. The contrast between Hayashi and Miyamoto was certainly striking, but this sort of assertion replicated the fundamental error of gender attribution in seeking to label writers. Evolution or maturation of style was ignored, and literary work was seen principally as a reflection of subconscious psychological motivations. The author's conscious choices were disregarded.

In 1957 a special issue of the influential journal *Bungei* devoted to Hayashi showed the range of critical assessments of her work. It included the results of a questionnaire given to seventy-three prominent writers and intellectuals who were asked: What is your opinion about Hayashi Fumiko's literature? Which of her works do you like the best? and What have you learned from Hayashi Fumiko?[11] Most respondents answered briefly. Many chose to answer selectively and enigmatically. Most often respondents mentioned only a favorite work, but their answers are nevertheless revealing. While some were adulatory—Kawabata Chōtarō "read [all] with great pleasure," and Itagaki Naoko, who became Hayashi's biographer, wrote that her "development from the first work to [the last] was very spectacular"—many indicated an undercurrent of, if not outright, condescension. The critic Odagiri Hideo noted that "from about the time of *Seishi no sho* [A record of honorable poverty, 1933], her self-conscious coquetry was impure; for the most part I stopped reading her works." Yoshida Seiichi, a professor of Japanese literature, was also critical: "I like her work. However, her core *(shin)* is weak, and she is not a first-rate writer." Several thought Hayashi was quintessentially female. The critic Takayama Takeshi wrote, "Of Japanese women writers, there are those who have become androgynous *(chūsei)*, but the term woman writer *(joryū sakka)* particularly fits Hayashi Fumiko." The writer Itō Einosuke thought "her works [were] full of feminine *(joseiteki)* sensitivity." But the pejorative traits of femininity were also cited. The poet Okamoto Jun described Hayashi's works as "of the people *(minshūteki)* . . . limited in intellect *(chisei)*." And Takayama said it "would have been better had she had more of an intellectual, contemplative aspect; lacking this, she has left only lovable jewels."

In 1963, in an article published in Japanese, Edward G. Seidensticker defended Hayashi's artistic achievements and criticized those who condemned her work for its lack of social or ideological content. Odagiri Hideo, Ōta Yōko, and others had criticized Hayashi for her lack of intellect and ideology, but Seidensticker believed that these charges obscured her artistry.

> Since she is not intellectual to begin with, it may be possible to say that she was not able to rise to the heights of first-rate art. But as in the case of Dickens, if one is too obsessed with this aspect, one is liable to overlook important matters. Hayashi Fumiko's vitality when compared with Miyamoto Yuriko is similar to a comparison of Dickens and George Eliot. Furthermore, as far as fiction is concerned, the presence of animation is a more important question than the existence of abstract social or moral ideas.[12]

For Seidensticker, "Hayashi Fumiko at her best had a dramatic imaginative power that was rare for modern Japan, even more so for modern women writers."[13] He accepted the judgment of Nakamura Mitsuo that, unlike Miyamoto Yuriko, Hayashi "had all the vices and virtues of a feminine *(onnarashii)* writer."[14] "An all-too-typical woman writer *(joryū sakka)* in her early career, Hayashi Fumiko abandoned her former feminine fixed outlook with the experience of Japan's defeat. . . . Hayashi wrote some of the best postwar short stories, probably the best by women."[15]

Itagaki Naoko observed that while Hayashi was immensely popular, she was neglected or dismissed by male critics.[16] Other critics agreed that Hayashi's work had yet to receive proper critical scrutiny. In 1964, Wada Yoshie noted, "Although there are commentaries about Hayashi the literary figure *(bungakusha)*, there is nothing as yet about Hayashi as a writer *(shōsetsuka)*."[17] He recommended further research on Hayashi, but his proposed approach belied his interest in her writing, as opposed to her life: "I think that the research lies in *Diary of a Vagabond.* To rearrange the three parts in chronological order is the first task."[18] Such an approach can help only to relate the entries to incidents in her own life and shows little interest in the works themselves. Muramatsu Sadataka advocated judging Hayashi by her works, not her life or actions, but in an article "Hayashi Fumiko's Love Life" that provides a considerable roster of lovers and spares few details.[19]

Biographies of Hayashi, including those by Itagaki Naoko, Hirabayashi Taiko, and that by Fukuda Kiyoto and Endō Mitsuhiko, as well as special issues or publications dedicated to Hayashi, such as that in the *Nihon bungaku arubamu* series, also share a relative disregard for an analytic appraisal of her work. The emphasis has been on organizing a coherent chronology of her life, with some discussion of her motivations and influences, and on comparison with other writers. Her biographers have tended to accept what she has written in *Diary of a Vagabond* and its sequels, or in such other works as "A Town of Accordions and Fish" and *A Record of Honorable Poverty,* as unreconstructed autobiography.[20] Incidents in these literary works are correlated with specific moments in her own life, and the passages are explained by references to her personal experiences. This is in keeping with literary-historical orthodoxy, where confessional fiction is "considered inherently referential . . . its meaning derives from the author's life . . . [and] the work is meaningful insofar as it illuminates the life."[21]

Much of the critical, as well as popular, interest in Hayashi has derived from a fascination with her as a sort of celebrity. She was a forceful and sometimes outrageous personality and went some distance to purvey sensational, if not salacious, intimacies to her reading public. Tsushima Yūko has described Taishō and Shōwa women writers as needing passion, vibrancy, or verve *(jōnetsu)* to be successful.[22] Hayashi had that quality, as well as considerable drive, showmanship, and a capacity for self-promotion. She could also sail close to the winds of bad taste and scandal while, for the most part, gauging correctly what was permissible and popular. Hayashi was somewhat reckless in her personal life, but much of what went into print was cut from whole cloth. She had a flair for the flamboyant and doggedly sought to preserve her slightly outré airs. At the same time she sought to maintain the image of an understanding wife and attentive mother.

Hayashi's legacy is largely as a "woman writer," the very categorization she sought, in her life, to transcend, even though she continued to exploit this identity for commercial success. A few of her most popular and best regarded works *(Diary of a Vagabond, Drifting Cloud, Food)* are still in print, in inexpensive paperbacks available in the mass-market section of most bookstores. Books about Hayashi and special editions of her work, however, are shelved in the "women's section." She is often included in issues of academic journals focusing on women writers, as well as in collections of works by women writers.[23] In such studies devoted to modern women writers as Itagaki Naoko's *Meiji, Taishō, Shōwa no joryū bungaku* (Women's literature of the Meiji, Taisho, and Showa periods, 1967) or Murō Saisei's *Ōgon no hari* (Golden needles, 1961), discussions of Hayashi's work occupy a full chapter. Whereas Hayashi is often selected in mainstream literary anthologies—for example, she was the only woman writer represented in the sixteen-volume set *Hito to bungaku* (Literary biographies), a series published by Gakushū Kenkyūsha in 1980—she is occasionally relegated almost to a footnote in literary histories.[24] New biographies continue to appear, with assiduously reconstructed details of Hayashi's life. These inject some realism into her heretofore romanticized early years, but they do not challenge prevailing interpretations of her work or her place in Japanese literature.[25]

Feminine, Feminist, Female

Hayashi died of a heart attack on June 28, 1951. She was forty-eight years old. At the time of her death, Hayashi left four serialized novels incomplete: *Food* for *Asahi Shimbun*, *Shinjubo* (Mother-of-pearl) for *Shufu no tomo, Sazanami* (Rippling waves) for *Chūō kōron,* and *Onna kazoku* (A family of women) for *Fujin kōron.* She had almost finished the manuscripts of short stories entitled "Raichō" (Snow grouse) for *Bungei shunjū,* and "Kiku obana" (Chrysanthemum pampas grass) and "Shin Hōjōki" (A new ten-foot-square hut) for a *Chūō kōron bungei* special collection.[26] Mushanokōji Saneatsu took it upon himself to dispel the rumors that Hayashi had been hounded to death by pressures from editors and the unrelenting demands of a publishing world eager to market a popular writer. He concluded that her own voracious appetite for ever more contracts, projects, and publications, necessary to finance, among other things, another trip to Paris, had prompted her to take on too much work and precipitated her death.[27] Hayashi's work schedule routinely involved writing through the night, but present-day observers would surely point to the contribution of her chain-smoking habit—up to two and a half packs a day—to her early death.[28]

Hayashi's funeral reflected her popularity. Two thousand people attended.[29] Kawabata Yasunari delivered a eulogy and commented that he would like a similar funeral where, after the official literary guests had finished offering incense, the ordinary people who had lined up for quite a distance outside the house were allowed to file by and pay their respects. Wada Yoshie described Hayashi's mourners as predominantly women from the low city *(shitamachi)* and apron-clad housewives with shopping baskets. It was this same audience that, in his view, Hayashi sought to address: "those who buy their rice by the cup."[30]

Hayashi received a number of posthumous marks of honor and recognition, both large and small. The literary world paid increased attention to her work, as is demonstrated by the 1957 *Bungei* special issue and inclusion of her writing in successive collected works of modern literature.[31] In 1957, her alma mater, which had banned her in 1931 because of rumored leftist tendencies, erected a monument in Hayashi's honor in front of the high school with an inscription in Kawabata's hand.[32]

In his eulogy at her funeral, Kawabata observed that finally, perhaps, the enmity between Hayashi and other women writers could be laid to rest, but this was wishful thinking. Alive or dead, Hayashi has often been on the receiving end of quite a bit of condemnation from other women writers, especially those who were her associates in one form or another. Enchi Fumiko has issued some of the sharpest indictments of Hayashi's character in recent years. According to Enchi:

> No matter how busy, no matter what the magazine, [Hayashi] would accept all requests for articles. And then she would extend the deadlines until the very last minute possible. In other words, she didn't want the work to go to anyone else [even if she couldn't complete the job]. And as if that weren't enough, she would readily agree to take someone else's manuscript and pretend to go about getting it published, only to return it claiming that all the magazines had turned it down, when it had really just been tucked away in her desk drawer all the time. She was not about to give up any of her own opportunities to anyone else. I understand that she betrayed the confidence of quite a few people.[33]

Enchi also asserted that Hayashi "really turned her back on Hasegawa [her editor and mentor at *Nyonin geijutsu*] after she became a popular writer."[34] Other women writers had made similar observations about Hayashi's treatment of Hasegawa. Atsuta Yūko criticized Hayashi for completely ignoring her mentor after returning from Paris in 1932. Hayashi was also said not to have attended her cremation, and she mocked Atsuta at a memorial service the following day for having cried at the crematorium.[35] According to Hirabayashi Taiko, Hayashi had even blocked Kaizōsha's publication of Hasegawa's work *Nihonbashi.*[36]

The truth of these allegations is difficult to judge. It would seem unlikely that Hayashi could have blackballed Hasegawa with a major publisher, and Hayashi had not severed ties with her. For example, when Hasegawa launched her journal *Kagayaku* in spring 1933, Hayashi attended the opening celebration. She contributed ten items to the journal, although most were only telegraphic notes from the field. Hayashi also sent a commemorative poem at Hasegawa's death in 1941, but this "Song of the Jade Lamp" had an oddly petulant, derogating tone that appears to have enraged other contributors.[37] If her biographers have emphasized her stormy relations with other women, particularly with any writers who might be perceived as rivals, then perhaps we should note that, unlike her life, her writing celebrated affectionate and altruistic relations among women that often sharply contrast with the cruelly exploitative nature of women's relations with men.

Hayashi left a massive body of work. Itagaki Naoko estimated that only a third of her published writing appeared in the twenty-three-volume *Collected Works of Hayashi Fumiko* produced by Shinchōsha between October 1951 and April 1953. In the special issue of *Bungei,* it was estimated that she had published 30,000 pages, an average of roughly thirty pages a week over the twenty years that she was actively publishing.[38] My own bibliography of her major works of long fiction (eighty-six books) and short stories (sixty-two in major periodicals)—not including her volumes of poetry or nursery tales and children's stories—published over twenty-one years demonstrates an extraordinary rate of productivity. I like to think that her place on the continuum of renowned prolific writers is well beyond, say, Anthony Trollope or even Victor Hugo, perhaps somewhere between Joyce Carol Oates and Isaac Asimov.

How can we assess her work as a whole and her place in Japanese literary history? The tendency among critics and enthusiasts alike has been to attempt to characterize her essence. Tamiya Torahiko, writing in 1954, was typical of Hayashi's supporters in summarizing her work as a reflection of "women's sorrow and pain." He elaborated that Hayashi had captured "a fragile, pathetic woman's life . . . caught in a quagmire the moment she tries to make it on her own, having been thrown out of the social order."[39] Others emphasized her "feminine sensitivity" (Itō Einosuke) or "overpowering feminine quality" (Nakamura Mitsuo). But many critics were more hostile: "lacking intellect" (Takayama Takeshi) or "impure coquetry" (Odagiri Hideo). Itagaki Naoko argued that male writers and critics tended to ignore her work, imposed preconceived notions, or rushed to premature judgments. In her view, they might read only part of an early work, such as *Diary of a Vagabond,* and assess her whole oeuvre, unread, as a variation on the same theme.[40] A review of her major publications dispels the notion that Hayashi published mostly, or was best known for, autobiographies and diaries that targeted a female readership.

Hayashi published seven longer works in women's journals that were later picked up by mainstream or parent journals or companies. All except *Diary of a Vagabond* were perceived as fiction. Two short stories and two novels written in the postwar period appeared only in women's journals. Aside from *Diary of a Vagabond,* the works published in women's journals were not included in the anthologies published by Kadokawa, Shūeisha, Shinchōsha, or in the special issue of *Bungei.* That is, they were not considered among her best, or her best known. And they constituted only a small fraction of her major publications: only nine of eighty-six novels, and only two of sixty-two short stories.

Hayashi also serialized seven of her novels in newspapers, which, many believed, catered to a female readership. Newspapers were often lumped with women's magazines as pandering to the lowest in popular tastes. Muramatsu Sadataka characterized their readership as housewives who, having seen their husbands off to work, avidly absorbed newspapers' daily installments of family-centered serials, spiced with the dilemmas of marital infidelity.[41] Some newspapers actively promoted their women authors. For example, after the war, *Mainichi Shimbun* sponsored a Joryū bungakusha kai (Literary women's group), extensively covering their activities and tours.[42] Even those who closely scrutinized newspapers' preconceptions and their intended audiences discounted them as appropriate for serious literature.[43] All of Hayashi's work that appeared in newspapers, except *A Record of a Shallow Spring,* was also republished in separate volumes, and all should be considered fiction. A few of these newspaper novels were included in single-volume anthologies. Kadokawa published *Uzushio* and *Meshi,* while both the Shinchōsha and *Bungei* collections included *Crybaby.* This might indicate that, aside from *Diary of a Vagabond,* the novels that Hayashi published in newspapers were somewhat better known and more highly regarded than those that appeared in women's journals. Note that serialized newspaper novels constituted only a small proportion of her longer works, seven of eighty-six.

The vast majority of Hayashi's novels—sixty-two of those eighty-six—were initially issued as separate volumes by major commercial presses. Hayashi also published fifty-eight short stories in mainstream literary journals, or nearly 94 percent of her published short stories. While there may be reasons to think that the publishers of her separate volumes were targeting a female readership, there is little evidence to view the short fiction she published in mainstream literary journals in such a light.

Women undoubtedly constituted a significant proportion of Hayashi's readership, but the evidence we have is either wholly impressionistic or derives from the presumption that she published principally in journals aimed at women. Descriptions of Hayashi's funeral indicated a devoted following among at least some of the *shitamachi* women who lined up, some with babies on their backs, five or six deep to file past the bier.[44] But Hayashi's simple, accessible style appealed to men as well. The critic Yoshida Seiichi claimed that it was precisely Hayashi's sweet, lyrical, feminine sentimentalism that attracted a male readership.[45] In the *Bungei* survey, the critic Kubota Masafumi related how, as a youth, he was attracted to her early works, particularly to her technique of using katakana for difficult kanji. He went on to observe that what he had taken to be a natural, uncalculated style was, in Itō Sei's opinion, entirely deliberate *(mokuteki ishiki)*.[46] Equating the sex of the readership with the type of publication should not be automatic. Shibaki characterized *Chairo no me* as "not necessarily written for women," despite its publication in a women's supplement to a newspaper.[47] As we have seen, Hayashi published most of her short fiction in mainstream literary journals and only a fraction of her novels in newspapers or women's journals. And the evolution of Hayashi's style, and her contribution to Japanese letters, cannot be reduced to where or how often she published.

Hayashi continued to publish works that purported to be autobiographical long after she began to write fictional stories and novels. Many of her ostensibly autobiographical works simply adopted the format of a diary or journal, but were clearly fictional. Those explicitly about Hayashi, in effect continuations of *Diary of a Vagabond,* were confessional in form but cannot be taken as an accurate reflection of her life. Written for an audience familiar with the incidents and personalities portrayed, these works sought to meet popular expectations about what a woman writer should write. When scrutinized closely, however, they demonstrate enough of a discrepancy with previous accounts of well-known incidents from her earlier work, in both tenor and detail, that one cannot help but view at least some of her later autobiographies as calculated to dissemble. She had a tendency to reinvent herself to fit the times.

The events surrounding her early years in Tokyo received strikingly different treatments in successive accounts. For example, in *Hitori no shōgai* (One person's life, 1940), she downplayed her poverty and, following the rules for permitted publications, adopted a generally positive and upbeat tone. She readily finds a succession of jobs that cover her basic expenses and is very circumspect about her private life. When she returns to these events in *Hōrōki dai sanbu* (Diary of a vagabond, part three, 1947–1948) in a postwar serialization, abject destitution has returned—in addition to sensational, salacious revelations. In *Pari nikki* (Paris diary, 1947), she similarly returns to the well-known escapades of her trip to Paris and London in 1930, emphasizing her hunger and poverty. But lest the reader presume she would include any sordid detail—imagined or not—that would pass the censors, she never exposed her love interests abroad even when it had become more permissible. She does not mentions that a principal motive for traveling to Paris was to follow the painter Sotoyama Gorō, that while there she also had an affair with the Yayoi archaeologist Morimoto Rokuji, or that Ryokubin did not anticipate her return to him.[48] *Pari nikki,* and later autobiographies in general, allowed readers a vicarious exposure to slightly offbeat, exotic, or artistic odysseys. But they did not derive their meaning—the orthodox approach to confessional fiction, as defined by Fowler—from illuminating Hayashi's life.

The inadequacies of the "woman writer" designation for Hayashi are twofold. First, it failed to capture what was specific to her distinct, somewhat idiosyncratic voice, and second, it failed to reflect what evolved in her work as she matured. Hayashi may have lacked a larger vision—she eschewed directly addressing societal contradictions and profound philosophical or existential questions—but her work merits continued scrutiny on several grounds. She chronicled a largely unilluminated world, and for many, her portraits of the everyday life of this stratum of society make her work memorable. For others, her imaginative fiction, especially in her postwar stories, not only succeeded in capturing a spirit of the era, the nihilistic disaffection against the backdrop of austerity and injustice, but in transcending the circumstances to present the personal exercise of choice and self-determination. Her writing offers a casebook in the multiple, contested nature of female identity and illustrates the complex and often contradictory attitudes of a female author toward gender conventions.

To consider Hayashi a feminist flies in the face of her overt affiliations. Yet as I noted above, in her writing, especially in *Diary of a Vagabond,* relations between women were often the principal locus of altruism and affection. The closing diary entries that focus on the relationship between the protagonist and Toki-chan present a portrait of intense emotional commitment, physical attraction, shared sacrifice, and domesticity, followed by betrayal, as well as a bitter denunciation of male sexual exploitation and manipulation of women's economic destitution. That the sexuality depicted in these passages has never received critical commentary should not be surprising. Only recently has Iwabuchi Hiroko sought to reinterpret the sexual awakening and emotional turmoil of Miyamoto Yuriko's story "One Flower" in a lesbian context, despite long-standing knowledge that it was written during her seven-year lesbian relationship with Yuasa Yoshiko.[49] The preeminent objective of Hayashi's protagonist—to preserve her autonomy and secure literary recognition despite the overwhelming obstacles of her class and gender—embodied the aspirations of many avowed feminists in her day and since. Despite the care with which Hayashi cultivated her postwar public persona as an attentive mother to her adopted son, her "Narcissus" skewered the most sacred of cows with its bitter depiction of motherhood, underscoring not only the thankless burdens even the most adored female roles come with but also the distinct individuality of all mothers.

In another recent essay of feminist criticism, Mizuta explored the significance of Hayashi's gender without the presumptions of a feminine style or feminist politics. Female identity constitutes both the focus of the analysis and the lens through which the writing is read. Mizuta's analysis of *Diary of a Vagabond* and *Drifting Cloud* perceptively underscores how vagabondage and wandering are a central experience in the works and lives of modern women writers. For Mizuta, Hayashi illustrated how freedom was possible for Japanese women only outside marriage and the family system. While Japanese men might traverse the boundaries of other countries and cultures, women, if they wanted to wander, had to move beyond the conventions of the Japanese social system. "Female wandering was, by definition, outside the norms of what it meant to 'be a woman.'"[50] Hayashi's singular achievement, through her success as a major writer, was in demonstrating the potential women from the masses had to speak in their own voice, and in illustrating how literary imagination was no longer the exclusive domain of university-educated males.

Yet if the revision of literary categories holds considerable promise for reinterpreting the works of modern female writers in ways that more effectively interrogate the significance of gender in Japanese literature, the risk remains that, in a rush to theorize in ways that conform to contemporary Western discourse, literary criticism will obscure the history of the now-obsolescent concept of "women's literature" and neglect the lived experience of writers who wrote under its reign. Recall the assumptions that underlay Setouchi Harumi's top ten stipulations for success as a "woman writer" in an earlier, less enlightened era: Hayashi, like other prominent writers labeled by gender, actively invoked and subverted stereotypes associated with female identity and simultaneously addressed a multiplicity of other identities, sometimes complementing, sometimes eclipsing, the significance of gender.

Gender and Literature

Modern Japanese women writers confronted a specific constellation of attitudes toward gender that shaped not only their prospects for publication and critical reception, but in some circumstances how the women themselves wrote. Attributes presumed to be natural in a woman's voice—sentimental lyricism and impressionistic, non-intellectual, detailed observations of daily life—were the result of a confluence of social and literary trends that, in the 1920s, crystallized in the notion of a distinct "women's style." However misguided the characterization "women's literature" was, it was historically bounded. By the 1980s, it no longer defined at least for most writers and critics, a distinct literary style.

Murō Saisei's *Golden Needles,* which surveys the work of nineteen Taishō- and Shōwa-era women writers, illustrates how these writers are segregated and subordinated even as they are rescued from relative obscurity. Murō depicts the essence of women writers, which in his view is fatally flawed, as their capacity to sew. Just as when women sew a kimono, he argues, when they write they leave nothing left over, resolving everything. In Murō's view, this resolution is inappropriate for fiction, which should leave some loose ends.[51] Murō also compares several women writers to fish: Nogami Yaeko and Kōda Aya (1904–1990) hide in deep recesses after making a name for themselves, whereas Hayashi Fumiko, flashy and highly visible, ascends to the surface of the pond.[52]

Murō's approach, arguing by means of analogy and relying on comparisons between authors, embodies a fundamental fallacy. In his sewing metaphor, he suggests that because some women sew, all women writers adopt habits appropriate to sewing, then transfer those specific skills to an entirely different arena. Of course, the presumption that sewing is somehow naturally feminine would be belied by any survey of such practices worldwide.[53] And the domestic imagery reveals a hostility toward boundary-crossing: Skills appropriate for the female domain are inappropriate in male spheres. But the basic fallacy is the logic of Murō's analogies. Since women are neat dressers (he might say), they cannot write as convincingly, given the disheveled state of everyday existence. Or since women are shorter, they cannot reach the literary heights of male authors. Such assertions are absurd. Murō's characterization of Hayashi as an eye-catching surface swimmer substitutes for the kind of contextual study and close scrutiny necessary to locate her work within modern Japanese literature.

"Women's literature" was a corollary and an outgrowth of the dominant literary movements and genres of the 1920s, naturalism and the I-novel. These naturalist-influenced confessional modes of expression enabled women, even those without much higher education, to represent their personal experiences in a way that captured the attention and imagination of a considerable portion of the reading public. But the capacity of women, as writers, to achieve prominence and economic independence through publication reflected broader changes in Japanese society, where the transformation of women's education and the increase of discretionary income had enabled them to become both producers and consumers of literary commodities. The growth of the women's market in the publishing industry, and of women's journals in particular, followed the rapid growth in women's literacy. By the 1910s, young women's literacy was virtually universal at the elementary level. A market niche that mirrored the sex-segregated world of higher education and gender-specific conventions of composition, employing, principally, a written-as-spoken rather than a self-consciously intellectual voice, came to be styled "women's literature." Such broad characterizations of style actually cut across the gender lines of both writers and readers. But the conventions were codified even as anomalies were allowed. Those women, or those works by women, that failed to meet these expectations were treated as "masculine" exceptions.

I point particularly to the mediating role of institutional structures, notably the publishing industry, in shaping the creation and reception of literary works by women. But I also underscore the crucial importance of each woman writer's intentions and affiliations, which confirm, subvert, or even reconstruct the norms associated with literary works. Women are now, or rather, are increasingly becoming recognized as, writing from a variety of perspectives and in a variety of voices that are not simply reducible to their gender. "Women's literature" may have been historically bounded, but its limited, transitory character remains only partially recognized by literary critics and even women writers themselves.

The stigma of "women's literature" continues to haunt women writers today. Tsushima Yūko claimed in 1991 that she was trying to eradicate sentimentality from her own writing style, as if to distance herself from the tradition, if not the derogatory label, "woman writer." And she distinguished contemporary women writers, such as Ariyoshi Sawako and Sono Ayako, from prominent women writers of the 1920s who relied on passion or verve to be successful. Ariyoshi and Sono, she argued, were brilliant, non-emotional, and intellectual.[54] Along with Kurahashi Yumiko and Kusaka Yōko, Ariyoshi and Sono have been described as representative of the first generation of postwar, college-educated women writers, and their work has been characterized as "intelligent, ironic, and [full of] black humor."[55] Such new approaches by women writers might suggest the complete passing of the term "women's literature" from the contemporary literary lexicon. On the other hand, an array of institutional sinews supportive of women writers—women's journals, prizes, lecture circuits, marketing networks—is well established and helps to present such writers and their works to the public. To refuse the label risks losing hard-won recognition and rewards. But there is no reason to presume that the connotations of the term must be fixed or frozen. The pace of change may be gradual, even glacial, but the process of reproducing literary conventions in successive generations inevitably requires an accommodation to the broader social context, as well as to the concerted efforts of the women writers themselves to recast how they are perceived and appreciated.

In an era when so much has been written on the issue of gender in literature, I hesitate to rush in with a sweeping summary of the relevance of the Japanese experience. On this side of the Pacific, gender has become one of the central concerns in literary studies. The institutional mechanisms that shape critical reception of women's writing have been transformed by the rapid growth of conferences, associations, publishing houses, and review journals dedicated to works by women. Equally important has been adoption of a more self-consciously inclusive policy by more mainstream literary institutions. Women's journals, in particular, celebrate a neglected tradition and offer an enthusiastic response to women's voices, if not to every woman writer, and feminist critics have proposed their own alternative canon, as illustrated by Gilbert and Gubar's *Norton Anthology of Literature by Women.* To adopt a separate feminist canon complete with its own hierarchy, however, risks anachronistically imposing criteria that for many women would be no less artificial or exclusive than the existing standards of conventional literary histories. But to enfold women wholly within the larger male-dominated tradition risks neglecting their specific experience and voice and replicating the same patterns that have subordinated women in the wider social sphere. The Japanese experience suggests a resolution to this conundrum.

One contribution that the long lineage of Japanese women writers and the varying reception to their works can make to the study of the role of gender in literature is to establish the inherent mutability of the substance and consequences of such terms as "women's literature." If we understand that the connotations and impact of the concept are not fixed but historically determined and subject to change, then we must approach the issue of gender as a heuristic problem. The goal cannot be to collate and codify what women have written. Instead it must be to reconsider the work of both men and women in light of a new set of questions and priorities. Such an approach must be historical, but it also requires greater attention to the institutional factors and the broader patterns and pace of social change that shape the context in which a work is created and received. To suggest that women constitute a separate and unbroken tradition grossly distorts their work and its relation to their times. But it would be a distortion also to neglect the significance of gender in shaping the content and quality of what is written and read.

Notes

1. Aside from Vernon's *Daughters of the Moon,* Tansman's *Writings of Kōda Aya, a Japanese Literary Daughter* presents the most notable exception, but his study does not mention gender.

2. Yoshikawa, " 'Feminizumu hihyō' wa seijutsu shita ka?" 182.

3. Miyamoto Yuriko, *Fujin to bungaku,* 177.

4. Ibid., 178.

5. "Proletarian literature was on the rise. I was isolated, without support" (Hayashi, "Bungakuteki jijoden," 17).

6. Hayashi, "Atogaki," *Fūkin to uo no machi,* 330.

7. Mushanokōji, "Hayashi Fumiko no shi,"18.

8. Ibid., 19. His daughter, he noted, was a great fan of Hayashi, as if to suggest that only an immature audience could read her with favor.

9. Nakamura Mitsuo, "Hayashi Fumiko ron," 96.

10. In 1950, Hayashi enrolled her adopted son in the first grade of the Peers School (Gakushūin), once reserved for children of the imperial family and nobility. The school became private only after the war. Generally it retained an exclusive character, appealing to those who had money or a good family name. Kawazoe Kunitomo asserted in his chronology of Hayashi's life that where she chose to enroll her son provides a telling insight into her personality (Kawazoe, "Nenpyō," 236).

11. *Hayashi Fumiko dokuhon, Bungei* (March 1957): 263–268.

12. Seidensticker, "Hayashi Fumiko," 124.

13. Ibid., 125.

14. Ibid., 127.

15. Ibid., 129.

16. Itagaki points to the experience of Shinchōsha, the publishing house that put out Hayashi's collected works after her death. This set enjoyed unexpectedly strong sales and, when the demand did not let up, the company hurriedly added another three volumes. Itagaki attributed this failure to anticipate the strong market to the denigration that a woman writer like Hayashi experienced at the hands of male literati (Itagaki, "Atogaki," 407).

17. Wada, "Hayashi Fumiko," 3.

18. Ibid.

19. Muramatsu, "Hayashi Fumiko no dansei henreki," 202.

20. Fukuda and Endō, *Hayashi Fumiko;* Itagaki, *Hayashi Fumiko no shōgai;* Hirabayashi, *Hayashi Fumiko.*

21. Fowler, *The Rhetoric of Confession,* xviii.

22. Interview with Tsushima Yūko, June 6, 1991, Tokyo.

23. For example, *Gendai joryū sakka no himitsu, Kokubungaku: Kaishaku to kanshō* 27/10 (September 1962); *Joryū no zensen: Higuchi Ichiyōkara hachijūnen dai no sakka made, Kokubungaku: Kaishaku to kyōzai no kenkyū* 25/15 (December 1980).

24. In one, Hayashi's name appears only in a list of writers who went to Southeast Asia with the Pen Squadron (Hirano, *Shōwa bungaku shi,* 223). More common is for *Diary of a Vagabond* to appear as a separate volume in multivolume collected works of modern Japanese literature.

25. Takemoto, *Ningen—Hayashi Fumiko,* and Isome and Nakazawa, *Hayashi Fumiko,* among others.

26. Kawabata, "Atogaki," 267.

27. Mushanokōji, "Hayashi Fumiko no shi," 18.

28. Yoshiya, "Juntokuin fuyo Kiyomi Oane," 62.

29. Kawazoe, "Hayashi Fumiko no 'Bangiku' ni tsuite," 9. Also see the photograph of the large crowd gathered outside the Hayashi residence on the day of the funeral in Isome and Nakazawa, *Hayashi Fumiko,* 95.

30. Wada, "Hayashi Fumiko," 3.

31. *Diary of a Vagabond,* in the revised 1939 edition, is included in all the editions of collected works of modern literature I have listed in note 3 of chapter 4. *Drifting Cloud* is included in *Chikuma gendai bungaku taikei* (Chikuma shobō, 1979).

32. Onomichi dokusho kai, ed., *Onomichi to Hayashi Fumiko,* 242.

33. Enchi, quoted in Ogata, *Nyonin geijutsu no hitobito,* 44–45.

34. Enchi, quoted in Setouchi, *Subarashiki onnatachi,* 11.

35. Atsuta, "Hasegawa sensei to no jūsannen," 17.

36. Hirabayashi, "Hayashi san," 91.

37. Iwahashi, *Hyōden Hasegawa Shigure,* 290; Kawase Yoshiko (one of the later members of the editorial staff of *Nyonin geijutsu*), quoted in Ogata, *Nyonin geijutsu no hitobito,* 272.

38. "Hayashi Fumiko ryaku nenpu," *Hayashi Fumiko dokuhon, Bungei* (March 1957): 266.

39. Tamiya, "Kaisetsu," 217.

40. Itagaki, "Atogaki," 407.

41. Muramatsu, " 'Onna de aru koto' ron," 175.

42. A photograph of the group, including Amino Kiku, Yoshiya Nobuko, Uno Chiyo, and Hayashi, during an excursion to Kisarazu in Chiba prefecture, appears in Isome and Nakazawa, *Hayashi Fumiko,* 93. See also Shibaki, "Ukigumo no hito," 66–67.

43. In 1931, Yasunari Jirō identified five views of female readers by newspaper editors, curiously employing the term "gender" written in kana, that explained the rationale for and means by which newspapers directed special columns or pages toward either the "working girl" or the housewife (Yasunari, "Shinbun to fujin," 1–5).

44. Shibaki, "Ukigumo no hito," 71.

45. Yoshida, "Kindai joryū no bungaku," 16.

46. *Hayashi Fumiko dokuhon, Bungei* (March 1957): 266.

47. Shibaki, " 'Seihin no sho' 'Chairo no me,' " *Hayashi Fumiko dokuhon, Bungei* (March 1957): 39.

48. Sakurada, ed., *Hayashi Fumiko,* 208. See also Isome and Nakazawa. *Hayashi Fumiko,* 46–47.

49. Iwabuchi, "Rezubianizumu no yuragi," 150–154.

50. Mizuta, "Hōrō suru onna no ikyō e no yume to tenraku," 308.

51. Murō, *Ōgon no hari,* 3.

52. Ibid., 89.

53. The small sweatshop that operated below my apartment during a year in Delhi in the mid-1980s was entirely male, and each step in the production process, from master cutter, to overseer, to sewer, to embroiderer, was performed by members of a separate religion or caste.

54. Interview with Tsushima Yūko, June 1991.

55. Okuno et al., *Josei sakka jyūsan nin ten,* 92–94.

The inaugural issue of *Nyonin geijutsu,* July 1, 1928. (Courtesy of Kindai bungakkan)

The first anniversary of the founding of *Nyonin geijutsu,* June 28, 1929, in the Koishikawa Botanical Garden. Hayashi Fumiko (squatting on stone path); Hasegawa Shigure (front row second from the right). Ueda (Enchi) Fumiko (standing third from the left); Itagaki Naoko (farthest to the right). (Courtesy of Kindai bungakkan)

Hayashi Fumiko's passport photo taken for her trip to France, 1931. (Courtesy of Hayashi Fukue)

Hayashi Fumiko en route to Paris through Manchuria on the Trans-Siberian train, 1931. She bought a one-way ticket with the royalties from *Diary of a Vagabond.* (Courtesy of Hayashi Fukue)

Hayashi Fumiko in Paris in front of her boarding house, 1931. She added the arrow pointing to her room. (Courtesy of Hayashi Fukue)

Hayashi Fumiko in 1933 in her Western-style house in Shimo Ochiai, where she lived from 1932 to 1941. (Courtesy of Hayashi Fukue)

A familiar pose of Hayashi Fumiko smoking, 1934. (Courtesy of Hayashi Fukue)

At Yoshiya Nobuko's house, 1936. From the left: Hayashi Fumiko, Uno Chiyo, Yoshiya Nobuko, and Sata Ineko. (Courtesy of Kindai bungakkan)

Hayashi Fumiko with Kawabata Yasunari on a trip to Nagasaki, April 17, 1950. They spoke at the *Bungei shunjū* readers convention. (Courtesy of Hayashi Fukue)

The last photo of Hayashi Fumiko before her death, taken June 28, 1951, in front of the eel restaurant Miyakawa in Asakawa. She died later that night at home. (Courtesy of Kindai bungakkan)

PART TWO

FICTION

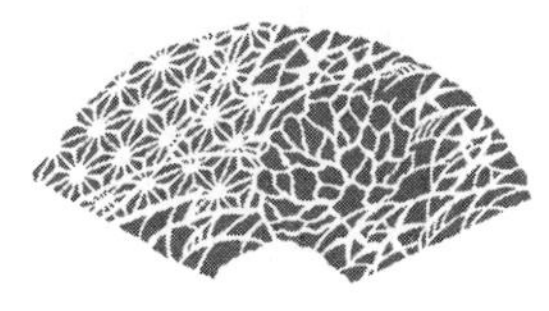

Diary of a Vagabond

Hōrōki

Translator's Introduction

Diary of a Vagabond (Hōrōki) was first serialized from October 1928 through October 1930 in the journal *Nyonin geijutsu* (Women's arts). What became the prologue to the book was published in the journal *Kaizō* (Reconstruction) in October 1929. The whole appeared as a separate volume in July 1930 issued by Kaizōsha and became an immediate best-seller. Hayashi made a number of small revisions in the text for *Hōrōki*'s publication as a book by Shinchōsha in 1939. This translation follows the Shinchōsha edition, 1979.

Hōrōki purports to be excerpts from a diary kept in the mid-1920s. Biographers and literary historians, Tanaka (1987) among many others, have treated these as "clearly autobiographical." An unsigned entry in Kōdansha's *Nihon kindai bungaku dai jiten* (Encyclopedia of Japanese literature) takes a more qualified stance in observing that the work was "half-autobiographical"; unfortunately, we don't know, and the entry doesn't tell us, which half. *Diary of a Vagabond* should be read as fiction, though many of the details, in the persons and places represented make this "confessional fiction" seem like a roman á clef.

My choice for the title, *Diary of a Vagabond,* is in part inspired by the structure of the work. But I also mean to underscore the work's fragmentary, discontinuous narrative. Hayashi wrote that, until its publication as a separate volume, she had referred to it as her *uta nikki* (poetic diary), and that the title *Hōrōki* had been suggested by Mikami Otokichi, the husband of her editor, Hasegawa Shigure, at *Nyonin geijutsu.* The tanka poet Takuboku also clearly inspired Hayashi, and a half dozen of his poems appear in *Hōrōki.* In 1910 Takuboku advised, "A poem should be a strict report of events taking place in one's emotional life (for the want of a better term)—a straightforward diary. This means it has to be fragmentary, it can't have unity or coherence" (Sesar 1966, 16). For Hayashi, a diary could aspire to be like such a poem.

Hayashi published two sequels *(zoku), Zoku Hōrōki* (November 1930), and *Hōrōki dai sanbu* (*Hōrōki,* part three; serialized in the journal *Nihon shosetsu* [Japanese literature, 1947–1948] and published as a separate volume in 1949). Elisabeth Hanson (1987) misidentified her fine translation of excerpts, *Vagabond's Song,* as coming from *Hōrōki* (1927 [*sic*]), when it is taken from the sequel published twenty years later. Although translations in Chinese and Korean have long been available, aside from a short four-page English translation (1951) of the prologue and an eight-page translation in Esperanto of one diary entry (1965), *Hōrōki* has not been translated into European languages.

In an earlier generation, translators often rendered items that might have been presumed exotic or unknown in terms more familiar to the English reader. But in order to retain the feel of the original, and in keeping with changing assumptions about readership, I have kept many terms that may already be common knowledge for the contemporary reader in romanized Japanese, such as "futon," "miso," "samisen," "tatami." But I have also left other terms, such as the ingredients to *oden,* like *chikuwa* and *kon'nyaku,* in Japanese, and have provided a glossary to all terms in appendix A. Brief notes on the people and titles mentioned in the text appear in appendix B, and other explanatory material is given in footnotes.

Prologue

I learned this verse at a grammar school in Kyushu.

> In the deepening autumn night,
> A traveler distressed by desolate thoughts
> Yearns for home, longs for family.

I was destined to be a wanderer. I have no home.

My father was an itinerant peddler of cotton and linen cloth. He came from Iyo on the island of Shikoku. My mother was the daughter of the owner of a hot springs inn on the island of Sakurajima in Kyushu. People say that since she took up with an outsider, they were run out of Sakurajima. They settled for a time in Shimonoseki in Yamaguchi prefecture, and that is where I was born.

Because my parents were cast out by their own families, travel is my only real home. Since I felt fated to wander, I memorized these lines about yearning for home with a sense of inescapable sorrow.

When I was still young, my life took a turn for the worse. After reaping a windfall at his kimono auctions in Wakamatsu, my father brought home a geisha. Her name was Hama. She had run away from Amakusa Island off Nagasaki. Mother left my father's house on a snowy New Year's Day, taking me with her. I was eight. I recall that you could get to Wakamatsu only by boat.

My present father, my stepfather, is from Okayama. Far too honest in nature and abnormally willing to take risks, he's spent his life in poverty, buried in debts. I hardly ever stayed anywhere you could call a home as I tagged along with my mother behind this man. We just made do with cheap rooming houses wherever we went.

"Papa, he doesn't like homes, doesn't like all the stuff it takes to set them up," my mother always explained to me. My mother and my stepfather dragged me along with them as they roamed Kyushu peddling their wares. As a result, I experienced only a life of low-rent rooms and remember nothing of the natural beauty of mountains or rivers. I first entered school in Nagasaki. Dressed in a discarded muslin frock altered to fit me, I would walk from our rooming house, the Zakkoku Inn, to the school near the Nankin precinct. From there, we moved on to Sasebo, Kurume, Shimonoseki, Moji, Tobata, and Orio, in that order. I did not have a single close friend, since I changed schools seven times in four years.

"Papa, I don't want to go to school no more." Discouraged, I quit. I hated it. That would have been when I was about twelve, when we were living in a coal-mining area in Nogata.

"How about having little Fu try her hand at hawking?" Since I was at an age when I was too useful to be allowed simply to play, I took up door-to-door peddling.

The sky in Nogata was dark and smoky day and night. It was the kind of town where the water curled your tongue, even though sand filters were supposed to remove the heavy iron. In July we settled into our lodgings, the Umaya in the Taisho neighborhood. My parents would just leave me behind, as usual, at the rooming house and rent a cart. Filling their large straw containers with knitted goods, socks, muslin, belly warmers, and whatnot, they would head off for the coal mines and the pottery works, my mother pushing the cart from behind.

To me, this was a new, unfamiliar place. I would wind up my three sen of spending money in my waistband and set off everyday for town. The streets were not alive as they had been in Moji, nor were they beautiful like those of Nagasaki. There were no pretty women as in Sasebo, either. In this neighborhood, sooty eaves yawned darkly, sandwiching alleys encrusted with coke. A cheap sweet shop, a noodle shop, a junk shop, a bedding rental—the random succession of shops made the town look almost like a freight train. Women with ferocious eyes strode past the shop entrances. Their unhealthy appearance was completely different from the women you would find strolling around a big city. The women passing by under the hot July sun wore only dirty belly bands and sleeveless under-kimonos. Come evening, small gangs of chattering women would return to the tenements, shovels on their shoulders and straw baskets dangling from their waists.

The folksong "Osayo, the Miller's Daughter" was popular.

My three sen disappeared on frozen sweets or miniature books like *The Beautiful Twins*. Instead of going to school, I soon started working at the millet-cake factory in the Susaki district for a daily wage of twenty-three sen. About that time my family paid eighteen sen for the day's rice we bought in our bamboo basket. At night I would rent books from the local lending library. I read a succession of romantic titles: *Skillful Kisaburo, Against-the-Grain Masanori of Fukushima, Nightingale, No Blood Relation,* and *Whirlpool.* Happily-ever-after selfish daydreams and sentimental heroics soaked into my head as into a sponge. I was surrounded from morning to night by talk of money. My highest ambition was to become rich. When it rained for days on end and drenched the cart my stepfather rented, we ate only squash and rice gruel for every meal. It was depressing even to pick up my bowl.

A lunatic lived in our cheap rooming house. He was a former miner who suffered from what was commonly called "nerves." The innkeeper said he had gone crazy after being shell-shocked by dynamite. He was mild-mannered for a madman. Early every morning he set off with the women of the neighborhood to push the coal cars. I often had Mr. Nerves pick out my lice. He later went on to make a career out of setting up tunnel beams in the mines. Besides him, there was a drifter from Shimane with a glass eye who sang ballads, two mining couples, a racketeer selling rotgut, and a prostitute missing a thumb. This group was more diverting than a circus.

"She says that the coal car took her thumb right off, but don't you go believing it for one minute. Somebody probably just cut it off . . . ," the wife of the Umaya innkeeper explained to my mother with a wink.

One day the thumbless prostitute and I went to the public bathhouse. The room was all dark and slimy with moss. A snake tattooed in a circle all around her belly was sticking a red tongue out at the navel. This was the first time that I had ever seen such an impressive sight. I viewed the light-blue snake tattoo with childlike solemnity. The prostitute usually did her own cooking. Even her friends who did not cook for themselves would buy rice and have her prepare it for them.

The billboards for the movie *Kachusha* appeared about the time that the street corners of Nogata blistered under the heat. The posters showed a young foreign woman pounding against a train window in a station, a blanket draped over her head in the falling snow. Before long, it became all the rage to have a Kachusha hairstyle with a part down the middle.

> My darling Kachusha, parting is such sweet sorrow.
> Let's offer our prayer up to God
> Before the melting of this powdery snow.

In no time at all the coal miners made this song popular. It still brings back such wonderful memories. I did not really understand the power of this Russian woman's love but, after seeing the movie, I turned into a very dreamy girl. I had been taken to a theater only once before, to listen to the old folk ballads sung to the music of the samisen. Yet now I slipped away every day to watch the *Kachusha* movie by myself. For quite a while

I was in a trance under her spell. As I passed the open square where the white oleanders blossomed, on my way to go buy oil, I would reenact *Kachusha,* or even "coal mining," with the neighborhood children. When we played "coal mining," the girls would pretend to push the coal cars, and the boys would pretend to dig while singing a miner's song.

At the time, I was a very healthy child.

I said good-bye to the twenty-three-sen salary from the millet-cake factory. I had worked there barely one month. Then I began a routine of crossing the Onga River and going through the tunnel to the mining quarters and huts. There I tried to sell the goods I had tied up in a gray cloth bundle on my back, things like fans and cosmetics my father stocked. Many peddlers went right into the mines.

"It's so hot. How're you holding up?" I would call out a cheery greeting to two of my friends. "Matsu-chan" was a cute fifteen-year-old sweet-shop girl who would walk all the way from Katsuki. But before long she was sold off to Tsingtao as a geisha. "Hiro-chan" was a popular salesboy at a dried fish shop and, though only thirteen, he put on the airs of a full-fledged miner. He could already drink sake and surprised people by the way he brandished his pickaxe high in the air. Besides, he got in to see plays and movies in town for free. I used to walk home along the edge of the Onga River after the moon had risen, listening to his stories.

"All for one price" was a popular sales gimmick. My fans all went for ten sen. They were decorated with drawings of carp, the seven Gods of Fortune, or Mount Fuji. There were exactly seven sturdy bamboo ribs on each fan. On an average day, I got rid of about twenty of them. The fans sold much better when I went round to the miners' hovels, rather than to the wives in company housing. And then there was the "harmonica tenement" where ten Korean families lived under one long roof. Naked as peeled onions, their children used to pile playfully on top of each other on the rough straw mats.

Under the blazing sky, you could hear the rumbling of coal cars, sounding like thunder far in the distance, coming from the gaping mouth of the torn earth. At lunchtime, I waited for the miners to spill out like foam from the dark tunnel entrance, with its scaffolding as intricate as an ant hill. Young as I was, I would walk among them, selling my fans. The miners' sweat was black and syrupy. They would flop down on the newly dug coal and sleep soundly, all the while gulping air like goldfish. They looked almost like a pack of motionless apes.

The only movement was the spinning of old-fashioned straw baskets dangling under the ridge poles. After lunch, the *Kachusha* song might float in from here and there. Then, as the piercing siren sounded, the lanterns—faint moonflower lights—would file back into the earth. "White skin when I left the country. . . ." It was not a particularly remarkable singing voice, but amid the smoky mountain of coal slag it conveyed something poignant even to a child.

When I could not sell any more fans, I began to peddle sweet bean-filled buns for one sen apiece. It was two and a half miles to the mine, and I used to make it with lots of rest stops, nibbling on the buns. My stepfather had gotten into a fight over business with a miner and was holed up in the rooming house with a towel around his head. Mother worked a banana stall near the Taga shrine. Countless gangs of miners would descend from the station. A pile of bananas sold for so little they went relatively fast. After selling the buns and leaving the basket next to my mother, I often went to play in the shrine. Mixing with the large crowds, I would pray at the bronze horse statue for my wishes to come true. "May I be blessed." It always rained on the shrine festival. With an eye on the drenching sky, stall operators would shuttle back and forth between the eaves of the station and the shrine grounds.

In October there was a miners' strike. The streets were deserted, as if everything, even noses, had been pinched shut. Only the strikebreaking miners brought any life or excitement. "A strike is a bitter thing, God knows." I learned this song, too. They said that because of the strike, the miners would just have to move on to other mines. The tradespeople would rarely credit any miner's account, since transactions between the two might abruptly come to an end. But even with the risks involved, those who traded with the miners said it was an easy and enjoyable business.

"You're past forty, so you've just got to try harder, there's no way round it."

I was immersed in a French detective novel, reading by the light of a tiny lamp. Lying at the opposite end of my futon, my mother kept grumbling about my stepfather. Outside the interminable rains continued.

"You know, we've got to have a place to settle down so we don't have these problems."

"Stop complaining, will you!"

After his rebuke, the sound of the rain returned. Only the thumbless prostitute was in good spirits, always drinking sake.

"I hope there's a war."

This prostitute's pet theory was on the benefits of war. She said it would be good if this world turned upside down. It would be great. Tons of money would flow into the mines. "You must have been born under a lucky star," my mother would tell her. "How can you even imagine that?"

the thumbless prostitute would reply, smiling sadly and tossing something out of the window. She claimed to be twenty-five, but had the freshness of a new recruit.

Signs of November were in the air.

My parents and I felt free to talk loudly on the return home from Kurozaki as we pulled a light cart along the bank of the dark Onga.

"You two get into the cart. We've got a ways to go yet and the walking's hard . . . ."

My mother and I got in, and my stepfather pulled us along, singing heartily.

Every autumn there are countless shooting stars. "Hey, mister!" a voice called out behind us as we were almost to the shopping street entrance. It seemed to be coming from a couple of miners who had been dogging us. My stepfather stopped. "What?" Whcn they said they hadn't eaten in two days, he asked whether they had run away. They were both Koreans. They were going to Orio and wanted to borrow money. They begged incessantly. Silently, he pulled out two fifty sen coins and let them each grab one. A cold wind blew on top of the embankment, and stars twinkled in the vast sky above the Koreans. Mother and I shivered. Once they had the money, the two silently pushed our cart into town from behind.

Some time later, when his father died, my stepfather returned to Okayama to sell the rice fields. His principal objective was to get his hands on some capital and try his luck at auctioning Karatsu pottery. But everybody knows that in a mining marketplace, the fastest-selling items are food. With my mother's bananas and my sweet bean buns, as long as it didn't rain we could sell enough to feed two people. We paid the Umaya inn two yen twenty sen each month. My mother claimed it was easier than renting our own house. But no matter what we tried, we were extremely unlucky. That fall, my mother suffered from arthritis and stayed away from her stall for several days. My stepfather returned with just forty yen from selling the land. He laid in a stock of pottery and took off alone to try his luck in Sasebo.

"I'll send for both of you soon."

With these words, my stepfather boarded the train, wearing his one sun-bleached set of thick cotton work clothes. I was left to sell the sweet buns day in and day out. Even when it rained, I did my rounds, not skipping a single house along the Nogata streets.

I will never forget this period. Sales were not all that difficult for me. As I plodded along from house to house, the cash in my homemade wallet grew a few sen at a time. I loved it when my mother praised my abilities. I lived with her and sold sweet buns for two months. I returned one day to find my mother stitching a beautiful skin-colored waistband.

"Where'd that come from?"

I looked on in wonder. My mother said that my real father over on Shikoku had sent it. I became wondrously elated. Before long we cleared out of Nōgata, accompanied by my stepfather, who had come to fetch us, and boarded a train bound for Orio. As the train crossed the steel bridge over the Onga River, I saw the street I used to walk down every day. The road along the embankment was awash in the pale sunset. Its sadness reflected in my eyes. The memory of a single white sail heading upriver even now overwhelms me with a longing for home. Peddlers hawking gold chains, rings, balloons, and picturebooks chattered nonstop in the train. My stepfather bought me a ring with a red glass stone.

December

Alighting at a station at the end of nowhere,
In bright snow
I enter a lonely town.

The snow was falling. This poem by Takuboku left me rather homesick. I opened the window in the toilet, and could make out dimly lit evening lights. They burned like the red rhododendrons I had seen long ago in the mountains of Shinshu. The lights were extraordinarily beautiful.

"Maid, come and take the little miss!"

It was the wife's voice.

Oh, but the baby Yuriko was such a bother. Like the professor, she was high-strung and cried a lot. It was just like trying to hold a fireball on your back. At least when I escaped to the toilet like this, it felt like I had a life of my own.

(Bananas and eel, pork cutlet and oranges—these are things I would really like to eat.)

For some strange reason, when I feel miserable, I get the urge to scribble graffiti. I traced "pork cutlet and bananas" on the wall with my finger.

I paced up and down the hall with the baby on my back until dinner was ready. Though it was only a week since I had come to Chikamatsu Shūkō's house, it did not look as if there was any future in this. The professor here scurried up and down the steps many times a day, almost like a mouse. I would never be able to survive his neurotic condition.

"Peek-a-boo! Sleeping well?"

Reassured by peering at his infant daughter over my shoulder, the professor tucked up his kimono and climbed up to the second floor.

Today I pulled Chekhov out of the bookcase in the hall. My soul was at home with Chekhov. His emotions and characters all came alive, whispering things to my heart in the darkness. The book was soft to the touch. After scanning the professor's collection, I couldn't help but think that it wouldn't hurt him to read his Chekhov again. Stories about Kyoto geisha were about a world too far removed.

Night.

I became delighted when I saw Kiku, the housekeeper, in the kitchen preparing delicious-looking sushi.

By the time I had given the baby a bath and she had calmed down, it was already eleven o'clock. I detested babies, but strangely enough, whenever they were put on my back, they fell right asleep, much to the amazement of the household.

Thanks to this, I was able to read lots of books. When you got older and had kids, you might be so worried about them that you wouldn't be able to do any work. Whenever I saw the professor fretting over the baby, however, I began to feel real animosity toward him. I wasn't going to be a maid all my life.

I wondered if the professor even knew about the lovely white flowers blooming amid the burr clover. Of all the members of this house, I liked his wife best, although she was so quiet she was almost asleep. You'd expect her to have had a bit more life in her, having been raised in the countryside.

December

They fired me.

I had nowhere in particular to go. Standing on the overpass above the train tracks and lugging a large cloth bundle, I opened the white paper envelope I had received. It contained only two yen. For more than two weeks, exactly two yen. Cold blood curdled up from the tips of my toes.

As I walked along with the large bundle dangling from my hand, I wanted to just chuck everything away and pick a fight with the first person to come along. I decided to take a look at the modern house for rent along the way, with its blue tiled roof. The garden was large, and the glass windows glistened in the cold as if polished by the December wind.

Tired and sleepy, I thought about taking a rest. When I opened the back door, I saw empty rusted tin cans scattered about, and mud-caked straw matting in the sitting room. A deserted house at midday was indescribably bleak. The faint shadows of former residents seemed to have remained behind in certain places. The cold penetrated deeply. I had nowhere to go. I couldn't do much with two yen. When I came out of the toilet, a doe-eyed dog stared at me from the side of the dilapidated porch.

"It's okay—nothing to worry about."

I only intended to reassure the dog while I asserted my claim on the porch.

(What should I do . . . there's nothing I can do.)

Night.

I stayed overnight at a rooming house in the Asahi area of Shinjuku. It cost thirty sen to stay in that inn—it faced out onto the mire of pasty slush covering the wall-lined road. I was able to rest my mud-caked body there. I had no guarantee of seeing the next light of dawn in the three-mat room with a tiny oil lamp that must have antedated the Meiji era. Although uncertain of any response, I wrote a long letter to the man on the island who had abandoned me.

The world, nothing but lies.
The last train bound for Kōshū runs across my head
As I stretch my veins across the futon of the cheap rooming house.
I abandon my existence, lonely as the rooftop entertainment of a
 department store.
I try embracing my own corpse shattered by the train
Pretending it was another man.
At midnight, opening the shoji dark with soot,
Even here I find a playful moon and sky.

Good-bye everyone!
I return to being a warped die
Here in the attic of the cheap rooming house.
Blown about by the wind
I grasp the layered loneliness of the journey.

People were coming and going, making quite a racket even in the middle of the night.

"Excuse me . . . ."

With this warning, a woman with big sweeping hair suddenly slid the shoji open and shut with a terrible clatter. She flung herself under my quilt. Heavy steps followed right behind her, and a weaselly-looking man, without even a hat on his head, cracked open the door.

"Hey! You! Get up!" he yelled.

Mumbling under her breath, the woman went out into the hallway. Then I could hear the sound of a cheek being slapped repeatedly. Soon it became eerily still, like the slow oozing of sewage. Disturbed by the woman's abrupt departure, the air of the room did not settle.

"What do you do? Address? Where you headed? Age? Parents? . . ."

The weaselly man had returned to my room and stood by my pillow, all the while wetting the tip of the pencil with his tongue.

"Are you a friend of that woman?"

"No, she just came barging in."

Even Knut Hamsun could not have been in such a predicament. After the detective left, I stretched out my arms and legs and checked on the wallet hidden under the pillow. *There was only one yen sixty sen left.* The moon was buffeted about in the wind. Through the distorted transom panes I saw the colors of the rainbow.

Pierrot the clown was skilled at leaping from precipitous heights, but it was no easy feat to leap back up. Yet somehow it should work out. I should be able to find some way to eat.

December

In the morning I went to the eatery at the entrance to Ome Road. As I was drinking hot tea, a muddy laborer rushed in.

"Miss! Can you give me something to eat for ten sen? I've only got ten sen," he asked in a booming unpretentious voice.

"Would the house tofu and rice special be all right?" replied a young girl of fifteen or sixteen.

The laborer broke out in a broad grin and seated himself on a bench.

A huge bowl. Onions and meat and tofu all finely chopped up. Murky miso soup. All of this nourishing food cost just ten sen. Preoccupied with his meal, the laborer opened his large mouth and shoveled it in. The whole scene brought tears to my eyes. A sign on the wall close to the ceiling clearly stated "Meals from ten sen and up." But with only a thin ten sen coin to his name, this middle-aged laborer was unabashedly making sure. He had gotten more rice than I would, but I wondered if it would be enough for him. He was an incredibly cheerful man. The waitress brought out rice, mixed stew, and pickles and placed them in front of me. It was certainly a poor rendition of "delicacies from the mountain and sea." I paid the total of twelve sen, and the waitress called out a thank you as I went out through the noren curtain in the doorway. Twelve sen for my fill and a morning greeting. This dead-end world is certainly a cheery place, but with not much distance between hope and despair. For that laborer back there, could it be that a single ten-sen coin was the only thing that came between him and deepest sorrow?

If only my mother would come to Tokyo, we could figure out some way of making a go of it. Like a ship fast taking on water, I was really a wreck that was sinking as far as it could. I was way past the point of just getting a bit wet. My thinking did not differ greatly from that of the prostitute I had encountered last night. She might have been well past thirty. Had I been a man, I might have indulged myself straight away, and in the morning we'd already be talking of a double suicide.

At noon I left my luggage at the inn and went to check out the job agencies in Kanda.

No matter where I went, I felt alone, deserted. My heart was in turmoil.

(I wouldn't even think of working for you.)

Moron!

Bitch!

Fool!

What a cold, stuck-up female. . . .

I handed over the pink card of blotting paper.

"You want about thirty yen a month?" muttered the female receptionist, laughing at my audacity. "Won't you settle for being a maid? There are oodles of female high school graduates who want to work in offices, and you won't be able to get that kind of job. But there are lots of openings for maids."

Younger and more beautiful women threatened to bury me like an avalanche. What you said was certainly true. There might be no work for me at all.

There were three possible openings—at an india-ink company, as a gas-pump attendant, and as a maid for the Italian Embassy. I had only about ninety sen to my name. On my return to my room in the evening, I encountered geisha lined up before mirrors, smearing on thick grayish makeup and looking a bit like clay flowerpots.

"I only sold two minutes last night."

"No one wants a squint-eye!"

"Is that so? I'll have you know that some men like this look."

"That's big of them."

The young women who were bantering with each other were fourteen or fifteen years old.

December

Waves of self-pity swelled up within me. Haunting hallucinations drove me crazy. I struck a match and lit an eyebrow pencil.

Ten A.M. I went to the Italian Embassy in Kōjimachi, sannen chō.

Laugh and live. A motto belied by my crooked smile.

A foreign child riding a horse came out the front gate. Next to the gate was what looked like a ramshackle gatekeeper's hut, and stretching far beyond it up to the front door was a beautiful pebble walkway. This was not the place for a woman like me. I was shown into a large red-carpeted room with a map on the wall. I thought that the foreigner's wife in her black-and-white dress was very beautiful, even more so when viewed from afar. The horse-riding boy returned home whinnying. Then a foreign man appeared. It turned out that he was not an ambassador after all, only a secretary. Both husband and wife were tall and overpowering. The woman dressed in black and white showed me the cook's room. Onions lay scattered in a concrete bin; two charcoal braziers served as the helpers' own cooking stoves. The room had the feel of a deserted house, with closed black Venetian blinds. It smelled foreign, like soap.

In the end, I left through the gate without reaching any conclusion. I escaped the opulent residences and descended the slope. The red shop flags flapping in the December wind reflected my turbulent thoughts. Different nations cannot understand each other. Shall I look elsewhere for work? Deciding not to board the streetcar, I walked along the edge of the moat. I wanted to go home. I knew that nothing would come of hanging on in Tokyo without a specific purpose. *When I looked at an electric streetcar I thought of dying.*

I went to the house in Hongō where I had previously stayed. *The landlady seemed distant.* A letter from Professor Chikamatsu was waiting for me. When I left, the professor had said he might just help me out since they needed a maid over at the Yoshii in Jyūnisō. But this was a rejection of my request, written in pale ink. Maybe writers were coldhearted.

As I made my way home down the evening streets of Shinjuku, my inexplicable reaction to my dilemma was to yearn for male company. (Wasn't there anyone to rescue me now?) As I stared at a purplish signal light flashing and swaying on a pedestrian overpass in front of Shinjuku station, my eyelids swelled with tears, and I began to hiccup like a child.

I'd take a chance on anything. I went and had a frank talk with my landlady. She agreed to let me live downstairs with her until I found work.

"Say, why don't you become a conductor on the Blue Line Bus? If you can cut it, they say you can bring in about seventy yen."

Someone must have been grilling a sandfish somewhere. Its terrible odor came wafting in. How wonderful if you could bring in as much as seventy yen. But I had to find a place to stay. Sitting at the landlady's office kotatsu under a ten-watt ceiling bulb, I wrote a letter to my mother.

"Am sick, in trouble, please raise three yen and send it to me."

The prostitute from the other day came in, shoving some sushi into her mouth.

"Two days ago you really put us through a horrible experience. You're pretty inconsiderate, you know," grumbled the landlady.

"Was the old man angry?" asked the prostitute.

Under the light I could see that she was already past forty, with a dried out, sagging body.

"I call that owlish, the way you bring all kinds of men back in the middle of the night. You're not the most welcome tenant. The police really gave my husband a dressing-down just now, and he's fighting mad." The usually good-natured, prematurely aged landlady complained as she poured tea.

That night she treated me to a bowl of noodles. Tomorrow I would go on the recommendation of the landlord to the Blue Line Bus depot to take an exam. With the end of the year almost at hand, it was sad not to have someplace to settle down, but this world was not the kind of place where it did you any good to fret. I would rely completely on my healthy body. Outside the wind moaned dreadfully between the power lines. I threw myself onto a dirty futon in a corner of the cheap room. Gazing at the face of the good-luck god Daikoku plastered to the wall, I daydreamed that I was lord above the clouds, though I was really quite small.

(Should I go home and get married?)

April

Today, with the introduction from Yasu at the knitted-goods shop, I took one large bottle of sake to the boss who was to give me a stall.

After I passed under the sign for a building contractor at the entrance to the alley, next to the pickle shop in Dōgenzaka, I opened the sliding glass doors. They had only been halfheartedly cleaned. The old man who gave out the daytime spaces was seated by the side of the charcoal brazier sipping tea.

"If you're going to start tonight to tend a night stall on top of your daytime one, you'll be able to build a bank pretty soon," he laughed amiably and in good spirits took the bottle of sake I had brought.

I didn't know anyone in Tokyo, so it didn't matter if I was embarrassed. You could find whatever you needed here in this city. Since I was stripped down to the bare essentials as it was, I would have to work as hard as I could. I told myself that this was nothing; my job at the sweets factory was much worse. I felt somewhat relieved.

Night.

I was given the spot between a woman selling fountain pens and the name-plate stall. The man there was churning out name plates without waiting for specific orders. I lined up men's knitted underwear on a shutter, which I had borrowed from the noodle shop, and hung a "20 sen sale" sign. Then I read *Lande's Death* by the bulb of the fountain-pen display. When I took a deep breath, it already felt like spring. It was as if the wind carried faraway memories. The pavement, a river of light, was thick with people.

"Ladies and gentlemen! How much is 89,503 plus 275,460? No one knows? There sure are a lot of fools here." In front of the china shop, a shabby university student was selling calculators. His high-handed way of doing business, disparaging the crowds, was most entertaining.

A refined, married woman fiddled with the underwear for twenty minutes but left after buying only one pair. Mother brought me my dinner. As it got warmer, it was strange how kimono stains stood out more and more. Mother's kimono had also lost its shape. I decided to buy her a bolt of cotton material for a new one.

"I'll take over for you for a bit, so you go ahead and eat."

The ceramic tiered lunchbox contained pickles and stewed chikuwa. I turned my back on the paved street and ate without tea or hot water.

"You can't get them just anywhere. Try them and see for yourself," yelled the young woman with the fountain pens.

Salty tears fell from my eyes. Mother was softly singing an old song, content with her somewhat less hectic routine. If only my stepfather, gone off somewhere in Kyushu, were more successful, then life would be as carefree as my mother's song: dum da da dum dum, dum dum.

April

The young women walked down the streets in thin flowing shawls. I wanted one of those. *I was blinded by the April window decorations of the Western-goods store, by the gold, the silver, and the cherry blossoms.*

As the limbs of the cherry spread out across the sky
Turn faintly to the color of blood,
Colored blossoming threads dangle off the tip of the flowering
  branches.
Pull to win the passion lottery.

To make ends meet
A nude dancer plunges into a cabaret,
But that is not the cherry blossom's fault.

There is one chance of love
For every two of duty.
Cherry blossoms blooming
Luxuriantly under an azure dome,

The enticing threads smoothly reel in
Every single woman's
Bare lips.

They say that, at night,
Impoverished maidens
Throw their lips like fruit
To the wide sky.

The light-pink cherry blossoms tinge the heavens.
But these "lovely" women's
Kisses of obligation
Leave traces without emotion.

I considered saving up money to buy a shawl, but decided not to bother. Instead, I went to see a cut-rate movie. White Rose of the Railroad *was not the least bit interesting.*

It had begun to rain during the movie, so I scurried out of the small theater back to the stall. Mother had already gathered up the straw mats. When we went to the station, carrying our things on our backs as usual, we found it teeming with young women returning from flower-viewing parties, as gaudy as goldfish. Gentlemen floated about here and there like algae. It was teeming with life.

We pushed our way onto the train. It was pouring rain. I was feeling fine. Rain harder, and harder, and make the cherry blossoms all drop off. I rested my cheek against the dark window and looked outside. I could see my mother's reflection in the window, as she stood unsteadily, like a crestfallen child.

Even inside the train there is a feeling of unease.

We received no news from Kyushu.

April

Mother came down with a cold because of the rain, so I went alone to set up the stall. I passed the front of a bookstore lined with many volumes fresh off the press, and wished I could buy them. The muddy roads were bad. Dōgenzaka Street looked as if it had been flooded with sweet bean paste. We would run into problems if I took a day off now, and there were sure to be several rainy days later, so I decided to bear with it and set up shop. It was just me and the man selling rubber shoes set up along the road thick in blurred colors. Women passing by tittered when they saw my face. Did I have on too much rouge? Was my hair funny? I glared back at them. Women offer the least sympathy.

Though the weather turned fine, the street was bad for business. At noon, the hairpiece seller who set up next to me grumbled about the rent going up two sen. I ate two bowls of noodles for lunch. *(Sixteen sen.)* A student bought five pairs of underwear. I thought about closing early today and going to Shiba to get more goods. On the way home I bought ten sen worth of sweet bean cakes in the shape of fish.

"Yasu was run over by a tram. It doesn't look good," my mother informed me. She was lying down when I returned home. I stared at her blankly, without removing the pack from my back. Just after noon, someone from Yasu's family had come with this news. Mother searched for the paper on which she had written the name of the hospital.

That night I went to Yasu's house in Shiba. His young wife, her eyes swollen from weeping, had just come back from the hospital. I took what few articles of underwear were ready and left some money. I pondered how the universe could dare be so full of cracks like this. *I imagined Yasu and his wife, just yesterday in full health, pressing down on the pedal of their sewing machine.* It was supposed to be spring, and the cherry trees had blossomed, but the season seemed out of place. I leaned against the window of the streetcar and studied the lights of the moat in Asakusa all the way home.

April

A long letter arrived from my stepfather. He wrote that he lived on the border of starvation because of the long rains. Mother asked that I send all of the fourteen yen we had saved in the flower vase, so I bought a money order and quickly posted it. A new wind would probably blow tomorrow. After Yasu died, they couldn't even continue to make simple underwear. Completely exhausted, even the most ordinary things became too much of a bother for them.

We sent fourteen yen to my stepfather in Kyushu.

"We can make do with a three-mat room, so how about renting the adjoining six-mat room out?" Mother asked me.

"Room for rent. Room for rent. Room for rent." I became quite optimistic, and childishly covered sheets of paper with these words. Then I went out to the road in Narukozaka to post them. Our conversation inevitably turned to death. Damn it! I laughed thinking about how nice it would be to afford a large sackful of rice once in a while. Mother talked about working in the neighborhood washing and blocking kimono. These days "help wanted" signs for waitresses and geisha caught my attention. A mayfly rises lazily from the black earth, while we sit on the veranda basking in the sun. Soon it will be May, the month of my birth.

"Next year should be a lucky one for you. This year there's no lucky direction for you or your dad," Mother blurted out.[1] She was slapping pieces of cloth she had just washed onto the uneven glass door to smooth them out.

1. Directional taboos were one of the many superstitious beliefs operating since the Heian period. During prescribed periods, it was considered unlucky to travel in certain directions.

How will I face tomorrow? I won't give in. It was just a string of back luck, wasn't it, Mama?

I wanted to buy an underskirt for my kimono.

May

Our room was so dirty that no one had come to rent it yet. Mother brought home a huge cabbage, claiming that the vegetable storekeeper had given it to her on credit. Seeing that cabbage made me want to bite into a plump steamy pork cutlet. As I lay gazing up at the ceiling of the bare room, I think how much fun it would be to become as small as a mouse, and to run around tearing into all kinds of things to eat. That night Mother discussed my becoming a temporary housekeeper, an idea she claimed to have overheard at the public bathhouse. That might be worth a try, but I naturally hated authority. It was more oppressive to kowtow to the traditions of a wealthy family than to commit hara-kiri. I wept at the sight of Mother's forlorn face.

You could not deny your hunger when your belly was empty. We would be starving tomorrow. We were starving today. I wondered if that fourteen yen had arrived in Kyushu. I was sick of Tokyo. It would be great if my stepfather could get rich quickly. Kyushu was nice, Shikoku too. I watched Mother persistently licking the lead pencil with her tongue as she wrote a letter to Father late at night. I wondered if anyone would buy a body like mine.

May

When I awoke in the morning, mother had already washed our wooden geta.

Dear Mother! I set out for the Temporary Housekeeper Association in Hyakunin chō in Ōkubo. Two middle-aged women were sewing inside the shop. Perhaps because there were not enough people to fill all the requests, the boss gave me a letter of introduction and a map. The job was as a helper to a pharmacology student.

I was the happiest when I ambled along the boulevards. Covered with the dust of May, I crossed the pedestrian overpass in Shinjuku. Boarding the streetcar, I saw scenes that might as well have included banners declaring, "All the world is at peace." The sight of these gracious thoroughfares wiped away my painful experiences. All the things I wanted to buy hung in the shop windows. Tilting my head, I fixed my hair in the glass window of the streetcar. I alighted at Honmura chō and discovered the house on a quiet lane of an exclusive residential section.

It was really a large house. Could I work in such a place? I stood by the front door dazed, wondering whether to go home.

"Hello!"

"Housekeeper! We had a telephone call a while ago from the agency that you had set out. The master's quite upset that you're so late."

I was shown into a small western-style living room. A faded magazine frontispiece of Millet's *Angelus* hung on the wall. It was an uninteresting room. I couldn't tell what kind of stuffing was in the chair, but it was unexpectedly bulgy and soft.

"Sorry to have kept you waiting."

It was a little unclear, but it seemed that this man's father ran a pharmacy in Nihonbashi and that I had the simple task of putting the medicine samples in order.

"But soon, when my work gets busy, I'll have you write out clean drafts for me. And in a week I'll be going to Cape Miura for research. Will you come with me?"

He was tall, and looked to be about twenty-five, but I couldn't tell the age of young men. I just gazed up at his face.

"Why not give up being a temporary and come here every day?"

I agreed, for thirty-five yen a month. It was a much better option than working for an employment agency that made you feel like a piece of merchandise. The black tea and Western sweets they served brought back youthful memories of church on Sunday.

"How old are you?" he asked.

"I'm twenty-one."

"Then you should let down the folds in your kimono. You're not a child anymore, you know."

I blushed.

I couldn't believe my luck. I hoped I could keep getting thirty-five yen a month.

When I returned home, I found Mother holding a telegram with news of my Okayama grandmother's serious condition. She was not a blood relation—she was my stepfather's mother. This grandmother had still been commuting to work to a factory in the country where they made thickly woven Sanada obi. It was depressing to think that she was already on the verge of death. Someone had to go. We had just sent money to my father in Kyushu several days earlier, and it would have been too audacious to ask to borrow money at the place where I had been today. So Mother and I went to talk to the landlord, though we still owed four months back rent. We borrowed ten yen. I promised we would repay it with lots of interest. I put together a box lunch of leftovers and wrapped it up in a cloth.

Traveling on a night train by oneself was a lonely prospect. But since

Mother looked old and pitiful, it was even more so. I didn't want to send her back by herself to my stepfather's home, but we were in desperate economic straits. Both of us knew that there was nothing for her to do but silently board the train. I bought her a ticket for Okayama. Under the pale light, the Shimonoseki express swallowed up many well-wishers as well as passengers.

"In the next few days, I'll get an advance and send it to you. Don't fall apart. It doesn't make any sense to break down like this."

Mother was sobbing like a child.

"You're so silly. I'll send you the train money no matter what. Don't worry and go take care of Grandmother."

After the train left, I began to feel dizzy. What had seemed like nothing—Grandmother's illness and scrambling for money—suddenly seized and distressed me. I left the National Railway platform and walked out to the open plaza in front of Tokyo station. I hadn't applied cream to my cheeks for some time, and my face smarted. I cried.

I could hear a faraway Salvation Army brass band playing, "Come to me, all ye who believe, to your Savior." What was this "ye who believe" stuff? If you couldn't believe in yourself, you couldn't believe in Jesus or Buddha. Poor people didn't have time to believe. What was this religion that they even advertised with a brass band? They didn't have to worry about making ends meet. So it was "Come to me, all ye who believe," huh? I'd had enough of such dour music. *I wanted a spring song.* I'd rather be retching my guts out, crushed by a nobleman's car on the beautiful streets of the Ginza, than listening to this.

Dear Mother, where were you now? Had the train reached Totsuka or Fujisawa? What were you thinking about in that corner of the third-class carriage? I imagined the scenery from the speeding train.

It would be great if my thirty-five-yen job continued. The moat reflected the lights of the Imperial Theater. Stillness surrounded me. All the world was at peace.

November

"Leaving the world behind, I live in the deep mountains." This vulgar ballad from Tateyama resounded around me as I commuted daily to paint at the celluloid doll factory. It had now been four months since I had become a factory girl earning the daily wage of seventy-five sen. The butterfly barrettes I painted seemed like such sentimental souvenirs. I wondered where they had scattered to by now. Ochiyo, from Kanasugi in Nippori, claimed she had a father who worked as a samisen player in a cheap theater. Her family, with its six children, lived in the back alley.

"Dad and me, if we don't work no one eats . . . ." She tilted her pale face wistfully as she slapped red paint on the butterflies.

Twenty women and fifteen men worked in this small factory. Kewpie dolls poured out on the world from our lethargic, leaden hands. Celluloid butterflies and kewpies that would begin the color of boiled squid filled our world from seven in the morning until five in the evening. Buried in stinking plastic scraps, we rarely had time to lift our heads up to look out the window.

"If you slack off there'll be real trouble to pay." The factory owner's wife, in charge of the office accounts, would notice our fatigue, and comment sarcastically.

This was the last thing we needed. She used to be a factory girl just like the rest of us.

"We ain't machines, you know!" The men in the shipping department used to laugh and stick out their tongues at her.

At five o'clock, we threw in an extra twenty minutes of our labor. When the bamboo basket containing envelopes of our day's wages came around, we rummaged frantically to find our own.

In the evening, Ochiyo followed behind me as I left through the factory gate with my kimono sleeves still tied back with a sash to keep them out of the way.

"Hey, aren't you going past the market this evening? I have to go buy food for dinner tonight."

Ochiyo and I clutched the saury fish in both hands. The fish, floating in its blue glistening oil, had cost only eight sen per plate. Its aroma regaled our stomachs.

"Doesn't it make you feel happy to walk down this road?"

"Sure, I feel so relieved."

"But I envy you your independence."

Beautiful Ochiyo's braided hair was dusted white from the factory. I began to feel an exhilaration, as if I could set all the showy goods along the street ablaze.

November

Why was it? Why?

Did we have to put up with the stinking celluloid forever? Was ours a celluloid life? Morning to night we daubed on primary colors, wriggling like earthworms in a warped factory hidden away from the sun. Slowly but surely, without respite, they squeezed from us long hours, youth, and health. Pity overwhelmed me whenever I looked at the faces of all the young women.

But wait. Just think of how the kewpie dolls and butterfly barrettes we made festively decorated the heads of poor children. It was probably all right to smile a little bit beneath that window.

In my two-mat room the earthen pot, the rice bowls, the cardboard rice bin, and the wicker clothesbasket, together with the small desk all stood firm, as if my lifetime debt. The morning sun sparkled through the transom and streamed above my futon laid out diagonally, dividing the room. The dust danced in stripes over my head. Where exactly blew the wind of revolution? You Japanese radicals certainly knew many clever words. I wondered exactly what kind of fairy tales the socialists were inventing. Exactly how much longer did we have to separate newborn babies by class, babies puffier than brown rice buns, by choosing for them a silk or a cotton diaper?

"Do you have the day off from the factory?" called out the woman as she rapped on the shoji to my room. I clicked my tongue and slipped both hands under my head. It had become strangely leaden. At such times I usually mulled over important matters, but all I could do was whimper.

A letter from my mother.

> Send me anything, even fifty sen. I'm having problems with arthritis. I'm really looking forward to seeing you and your father soon. I've heard from your father that things aren't going like he wanted. It makes me sad to hear that you're having problems too.

The letter was written in katakana in a halting hand. At the end she had written "To the Honorable Lady, from your humble servant, Mother." She was so precious, yet so exasperating. I wished she were near so I could nudge her with playful affection.

"Aren't you feeling well?"

Matsuda, a printer who was also renting a room from the tailor, opened the shoji door to my room without hesitation and entered. He was short, like a young teenager, with hair down to his shoulders. He epitomized all that I despised: a man generous to a fault. I had been gazing at the ceiling while thinking, but I turned my back on him and covered myself with the futon cover. He was so kind I couldn't help but feel grateful. But the more time I spent with him, the more obsequious he seemed. He made me disenchanted.

"Are you okay!"

"I ache all over."

I could hear the sewing machine grinding away down in the shop below. The tailor was probably sewing overalls.

"If we just had sixty yen I think we could live together quite comfortably. You've turned cold, keeping all to yourself."

Matsuda sat by my pillow like a rock and bent his dark face toward me. Hearing his heavy sighs, I muffled a cry. Up until now, there hadn't been even a single man who tried to comfort me with such solicitous attention. Hadn't they all made me their slave and then thrown me to the wind? I was almost ready to marry him and set up housekeeping in some small tenement. But it was too bleak a proposition. I knew I'd get sick of Matsuda if I were with him for ten minutes.

"I'm sorry, but I don't feel well. It takes a lot out of me just to talk. So please go away."

"Won't you take some time off from the factory? I'll take care of things in the meantime. I'd be content, even if you didn't marry me."

It was certainly an odd world.

Night.

I went out to buy a paltry measure of rice. As long as I was out, I decided to walk by the evening stalls of Aizome Bridge, my bundle dangling from my arm. The shops sold cut flowers, Russian bread, sweet bean-filled cakes, dried fish, vegetables, used books—I hadn't been in the area for some time.

December

The roads were all very Christmassy. The shop windows displayed turkeys and even Salvation Army alms pots. Newspapers and magazines inundated the streets, along with frantic flyers and advertising banners.

The express train passed by at dusk. We were still at work. The wind was buffeting the nearby window. In an efficiency campaign, the owner had begun to post the number of pieces we completed. Names of the twenty factory women appeared on the blackboard by the dirty wall, like the daily weather report. It began to intimidate us. When any of us fell below the prescribed quota of three hundred fifty, a flapping chit with the notation "five sen deducted" or "ten sen deducted," would be attached to our wage envelope.

"I really hate this. Don't you?"

Factory girls were like whisks—with a minimal shake they could whip up a great deal. We were all artists, but our collective portrait was like a Daumier caricature.

"It's like they think people are trash."

Even when the clock sounds five, there was no relief from the work. It didn't look as if the wage envelopes would be coming around. Work halted abruptly when little Ohikari announced that she had watched from the toilet window as the owner's wife had taken her children with her by car at about four-thirty. The place erupted. Some of us speculated that they must have gone off to the theater. Some held that they had probably gone to buy a New Year's kimono.

Seven-thirty.

After putting in a full day at work, I returned with sixty sen. I placed the earthen pot on the brazier and lined up my rice bowl and chopsticks on my desk. I wondered whether this was all life was about. I felt like slapping the first one to gripe and complain. While waiting for the rice to boil, I slipped five pink fifty-sen bills into a letter to my mother and sealed it. They had taken me so long to save. I fantasized about how happy I would be if, at this very moment, everything I had disappeared. Then the absurdity of my five-yen rent dawned on me—five yen for a two-mat room. A day's work averaged sixty sen, just enough to buy two measly measures of rice. I considered going back to working in the cafe. My faded silk kimono, dull from so many washings, hung on the wall. I felt as washed out as my kimono. I lost any taste for living. Nothing existed for me anymore.

Watch Out! I'm Danger! Because I was dangerously slack. If you had slipped me a bomb, I would gladly have thrown it. I preferred to burst apart and die in an instant rather than live like a mouse. I laid last night's leftover saury fish in an attack position atop some hot rice and took a huge mouthful. I was not wholly tired of living after all. In the old newspaper in which the pickle was wrapped, an article said that in Hokkaido there were still thousands of acres of pristine wilderness. *What luck! We could create a utopia in such a primitive land.* Maybe we could sing about cooing doves. "Come gentle people, let's all be friends" might become a hit song.

As I was coming home from the bathhouse, I passed Matsuda at the alley entrance. I slipped by in silence.

December

"Don't think you'll be forced into an awkward situation. Matsuda says he'll lend it to you, so why don't you go ahead and borrow it? My family's really counting on your rent, you know."

Facing the old, thin-haired landlady, I began to get so furious that I felt like just packing up and leaving. After fighting this battle, I hurried out to Nezu Road. Matsuda was waiting for me next to the postbox by the liquor store. He mailed a postcard. Even though he was a really good-natured guy and smiling patiently, I don't know why, but I was sick to my stomach.

"Just borrow it. You don't have to say anything. I could just pay it for you, but I know you wouldn't accept that." Matsuda started to put the small tissue-wrapped packet of money between the folds of my sash. I became acutely self-conscious about my kimono jacket, with the tuck still intact at the shoulder to accommodate a growing child. I broke loose from Matsuda and jumped on the streetcar.

I didn't have a destination in mind. I then hopped on the streetcar going in the opposite direction, and regretted stepping on my own shadow when I alighted in the cold at Ueno.

The towering frantic neon advertisement of the service employment agency swayed in the wind like the signal lights of a buoy.

"And how may I help you?" The clerk looked like a pimp. I looked up breathless at the help-wanted ads as if they were baubles for sale.

"Miss, you'd better think twice about it. Whatever you decide will have its consequences." He started to scrutinize my appearance—the scruffy woman before him who didn't even have a shawl. I asked for an introduction for a maid's position at a sushi shop in Shitaya, and got him to knock down the commission from one yen to fifty sen. Then I went to the park. The vagrants snored serenely, fast asleep on the benches, even though it looked as if it would snow at any minute. The statue of Saigo commemorated the hero of the Rōnin War. You and me, we were from the same place in Kyushu. Did you ever become homesick for Kagoshima or visiting Mount Kirishima, Sakurajima Island, and Mount Shiro? It was the season there for delicious yam sweets cut with hot tea, wasn't it?

We both looked cold.

We were both poor.

I went to work at the factory at noon. *Life was a bitch.*

December

Last night I found the money, which Matsuda had slipped in my desk drawer. Should I go ahead and keep it? I would be sure to pay him back. Oh frailty, woman's name was poverty.

> Quitting time
> Is all I wait for.
> I work again today.

Takuboku wrote this poem about the delight of going home. But when I got home from the factory, all I did was stretch out my legs like sticks across the two mats of my room and yawn widely. That was my only pleasure. I sneaked out a two-inch kewpie doll from work. Setting it on the shelf with the rice bowls, I scrutinized it. I had painted the eyes and the wings. I had given birth to this kewpie. I poured miso soup over cold day-old rice, and shoveled down a lonely evening meal.

I thought Matsuda had given an unusually loud cough as he had passed below the window. "Eating your dinner already?" he called up from the kitchen. "Wait a bit. I just bought some meat."

Matsuda cooked for himself, as I did. He seemed to be a rather thrifty sort. The aroma of meat simmering on the kerosene stove made my watering mouth ache.

"Excuse me, but could you cut these onions for me?"

Just last night he had pried open my desk drawer to slip in a packet of money. Now he presumed that ten yen clinched a friendship, and wanted me to chop his onions. I couldn't stand it when even his sort was so forward with me. In the distance I could hear the high-spirited pounding of rice cakes. I quietly nibbled on salted radish pickles. Off in the kitchen he was chopping the onion all alone. "Well, I'll chop them for you." The disgusting silence overcame me, and I opened the shoji. I took the knife from Matsuda.

"Thanks for last night. I paid the landlady five yen. There's five yen left over, so I'll return that to you, okay?"

Matsuda was silently taking the pieces of dripping red meat from the bamboo leaf wrapping and putting them into the pot. A single small tear glistened on his grimacing face when he suddenly looked up. The landlady's regular histrionics penetrated the room. They had probably started playing their flower card game. Without uttering a word, Matsuda began to wash the rice.

"What? Haven't you cooked the rice yet?"

"No. You were already eating, so I thought I'd quick give you some meat."

Could you imagine my thoughts as I swallowed the cooked meat he had sliced? I visualized many other men and rejected them all as less than worthy. Maybe it might be okay to marry this Matsuda. After dinner I went for the first time to visit him in his room.

Matsuda was shuffling pieces of New Year's rice cakes around on an outspread newspaper, and then arranging them in a bamboo basket. Such a superbly serene moment self-destructed in excruciating awkwardness. I turned around and went back to my own room.

"The sushi shop is pretty boring, too . . . ." I mumbled to myself.

A storm was blowing outside. Kewpie doll, I hope our utopia of cooing doves comes soon. Rage and roar, oh storm and driving snow.

April

Let the earth split open exactly in two, I screamed. But I was just a small bird. Looking askance, the world told me to be quiet, shush. *As usual, I faced another lonely morning rising.* The more I stared at the black parasol hung on the narrow wall, the more it appeared to take on many shapes. Again today he would probably take the young actress's hand down the cheerful cherry-blossomed path, and exchange with her the scripted vows, "We're in this together, comrade." Facing his back, I quietly inspected his hair while he slept. What if the futon were fastened shut just as it was, and he couldn't get out? If I pulled a pistol on him, would he squirm around squeaking like a mouse? Why, at best, you were once an actor. You've become the jester for the intelligentsia. It was ridiculous to say "We're in this together, comrade." I'd already fallen out of love with you. Your bank book with two thousand yen, and those love letters from another woman, were just dying to slip out of that black bag of yours.

"I'm so broke, soon I won't be able to even eat. I wish I could join a commercial theatrical group and make some money, but I have my own reputation to think about."

I would believe anything a man told me.

When I heard words like that, I would dissolve in tears and offer to go to town and try to scrounge up some work. So these past four or five days I had been out looking for work, coming home exhausted, a sticky, slippery mess, like fish guts, while this lying fool of a man . . . ! Last night I took a peek into the bag you always kept so carefully locked. Those two thousand yen belied your "we proletariat" talk. I felt humiliated to have shed such beautiful tears for you. If I had two thousand yen and a young actress, I'd be able to live a long life, too.

(Ah, this floating world was a bitter place.)

Sleeping like this you'd think we were the perfect, harmonious couple. But I'd had it with your cold kisses. Your body gave off the scent of your wife of seven years, and now this young actress. You'd had your arms around my neck taking care of business, yet your passionate embrace was meant for those others.

I wondered how much better it might have been, how much less of a mental strain it would have been, just to have become a prostitute. I jumped up and gave his pillow a kick. Liar! In my mind he crumbled apart like a briquette. Oh bright April night, when cherry blossoms appeared in all their wild glory. A rustling hot wind seethed outside our realm. "Hey, spread your wings!" an unseen voice burst out into the April sky. "Let's work somewhere no one knows us." I saw God's hands in the vast mist. I saw God's pitch-black arms.

April

Once is solace, twice a lie,
Thrice touched by the delusion . . .
Oh spiteful carnal desire, I am a woman. I can't help but drown in painful tears.

From the liver of a living chicken
Fireworks scatter, bringing the night.[2]
Attention! Attention!
The finale with him gradually came to pass.
In his entrails, cut in two with a single stroke of the sword,
Swim darting minnows.

On a smelly, stinking night,
If no one's home, I'll break in!
I was so poor that even my man ran away.

Now, it's a pitch-black good-for-robbers night.

Loneliness overcame me as I walked along peering down at the ground. I began to shake like a sick dog. Shit! This wasn't the way it was supposed to be. Today I again roamed the pavement like a stray. I would sell myself. Didn't anyone want to buy me?

Even if I didn't want to break off with him, it seems that he did, so I thought I might just as well beat him to it. Small white butterflies clustered on the enormous tree, bowed down with blossoming white flowers, outside the window. I'd forgotten its name, but its wonderful scent spilled through the window. On the moonlit verandah, I listened to him practicing his lines for the play. Suddenly memories of my youth mingled like the scent of the flowers. "Isn't there a good man somewhere?" I howled at the moon. He was famous for his role in *Razor,* in which he had starred with Sumako. When I was a young girl I saw him perform it in a small theater in Kyushu. Sumako's Kachusha was great, too. Ages had passed since then. He was already nearing forty. "An actor really needs an actress for a wife," I thought. Watching the shadows he cast in the light as he practiced solo, I couldn't help but feel pity. When he read the script beneath the purple lampshade, his profile shrank and he disappeared from sight.

"On our tour with the traveling theater, we stayed at the same inn and I even took care of her baggage. But, after making sure I wasn't looking, she sneaked off in just her nightclothes to some other man's inn.

"I got my kicks out of making her cry. When I hit her, she bounced back like rubber. It was great to watch how she put everything she had into crying."

The two of us stretched out our legs on the veranda. He turned out

2. Hayashi is girding herself by invoking ritual sacrifice before her confrontation with her lover.

the light and kept on talking about his former wife. I was forgotten, outside the conversation. It was a one-man show. Gazing at the sky in a daze, I could hear a voice tell me that things would not work out with this man, either. A devil was laughing somewhere. The bottoms of my feet itched the more upset I became. Seated next to a man absorbed in his soliloquy, I quietly tilted my mirror to the moon. My face, with its thickly drawn eyebrows, spiraled like a whirlpool. My sole wish was that all over the world it could be as bright as a moonlit evening.

"It's just that I want to be alone . . . I don't care what happens, I just want to live alone." As if he had returned to me, he heaved a big sigh and brushed aside a tear. Crying as if distraught by the idea of separation, he tried to embrace me. Was he doing this for my sake? Things might get out of control. I just wanted to shake hands. Leaving him behind on the second floor, I took off towards Dōzaka.

I poked my head into a stall selling wonton soup. Concentrating on some Chinese wine, I cleansed myself of any reminder of his wayward travels.

April

Our separation that morning at the intersection was colder than if we had been strangers. He had formed a small amateur troupe called The People's Theater, and he commuted daily to the Takinokawa rehearsal studio.

From that day, I commuted to work. To be supported by a man is worse than eating mud. Rather than look for a good job, I took the first one to come along as a waitress in a sukiyaki restaurant. "An order of roast, please." Scrambling up and down the stairs, lugging the heavily laden platters, I could scarcely contain my elation. In the large hall, the clusters of fascinating faces seemed like characters from a film. The space inside the front of my obi gradually swelled with tips. What could go wrong here? The room was full of the sweet aroma of bubbling beef. But all at once the constant trips up and down the stairs exhausted me. "You'll get used to it in a couple of days," sympathized Osugi, the head waitress, as she came upon me massaging my back out of sight of the customers. Her hair was done up in a maid's style.

Even at midnight the shop was bustling, and I became anxious about going home. Everyone lived on the premises except for Oman and myself. Unconcerned about the hour, they stayed behind to flutter over the clamoring customers.

"I'll have the fruit, Ta."

"What? Mine's the noodle soup with duck."

They were like a gathering of wild animals, laughing and chewing nonstop, oblivious of the time. I couldn't help but be impatient. When I finally left, it was almost one. Maybe the restaurant clock was slow; the streetcars had long since stopped running. Given the distance between Kanda and Tabata, I was so disheartened that I just felt like collapsing. Lights disappeared one by one like will-o'-the-wisps. Those remaining reflected cheerlessly in my eyes. Faced with no other alternative, I started to walk. I reached the bottom of Ueno Park but couldn't for the life of me move any farther. The dark slope was intimidating, and I stood still, straight as a rod. The wind carried hints of rain, and both sides of my traditional hairdo flapped like the wings of a bird. I studied the flickering neon signs advertising Jintan, the mouth freshener. Wasn't there someone I could walk with? It didn't matter who. I found myself looking for a large street.

Embittered, I wondered if I would have to devote myself entirely to him. A man in a happi coat on a bicycle unexpectedly whirled past me like smoke.

"Are you going toward Yaegakichō?" Throwing all caution to the wind, I raced after him, pleading.

"Yes, I am."

"I'm on my way home to Tabata. Could I go with you as far as you're going?" I entreated him as I ran along like a dog wagging its tail. I was all in earnest.

"I got delayed at work, too. If you'd like, hop on the bicycle."

I was up for anything. Clutching my wooden geta in one hand, I tucked up the hem of my kimono and hopped on the back. I firmly planted my hand on the shoulder of his happi coat. Suddenly, I found it so pathetic—the comical sight of a woman balancing precipitously on the back of a bicycle in the middle of the night—that I began to sob. I couldn't help praying that I'd get home safely.

I regained my composure as I stared at the glowing white characters for "dyed goods." I almost burst out laughing in relief. We parted in Nezu. I hurried along the road buoyantly, with a song on my lips, heading to that man as cold as merchandise.

April

They sent my futon from home. You could catch the scent of salt spray from the ocean. I was moved to sing out an ode to my parents as I hung the bedding out over the sunny veranda.

Tonight was The People's Theater performance. He left early with the makeup box and kimono. I watched his blithe figure from the second-floor window. Like a potted plant left unwatered, my ardor had completely dried up. In the evening I went to have a look at the Mitsuwa Hall in Yotsuya. It was already full of people. As usual, the play was *Razor.* His sharp-eyed younger brother sought me out and, winking, asked me why I didn't go to the dressing room. A carpenter by trade, this brother was such a good guy. It was almost as if he came from a different planet from my man.

On stage the couple had a rowdy fight. Hey, that's the woman. His leading lady spoke with the self-assurance of a favorite. For the first time I was overwhelmed by jealousy of another woman. He was wearing the kimono he usually wore when we slept together. This morning I had noticed that about two inches along the seam had come undone, but I purposely didn't mend it. I'd had enough of the smug man.

Sneezing more than once, I decided to head home. I went outside into the warm air with a few poet friends. *It would be great fun to strip naked and run wild on such a wonderful night.*

April

"When I send a telegram, come back right away," he told me. He was still telling lies. I was humiliated, but after he gave me fifteen yen, I hurried out to the regular streetcar stop.

I was going back to my parents' home, the one soaked with ocean salt. We sat down at a white table in the Seiyōken restaurant, he and I, for a modest parting banquet.

"I'm going to have a really good time back there."

"We both know we're not exactly parting on the best of terms. But I'm sure I'll really miss you. Even right now I can't stop feeling utterly lost."

I needed a smoke once I got on the train. At the kiosk in the station I bought six blue packs of Bat cigarettes. We shook hands mechanically through the window of the train.

"Good-bye. Take care, okay?"

"Thanks. . . . Bye. . . ."

I opened my tightly closed eyes, releasing the flood I had held back. I stretched out my legs as far as they would go and let the tears fall, sitting in a corner of the third-class car bound for Akashi without even a shred of luggage. I considered getting off before I reached my destination if there was someplace interesting. Staring up at the railway map hanging above my head, I went through the names of stations one by one. *Maybe I'd get off at a new place.* Should I make it Shizuoka? Nagoya? But I couldn't decide. Leaning against the dark window, I looked at the lights of the houses rushing by. I could see my face clearly, mirrored in the dark window.

It's over with that man!
In my heart, the children wave the red flag.
Are you rejoicing so much for me?
I won't go anywhere anymore,
I'll live here and wave the flag with everyone.
And then won't you all jump out of my heart,
And then pile the stones up for me,
And throw me up in the air,
And place me on top of the stone castle.

It's over with that man, no tears here!
Wave the flag securely, firmly.
It's the return of the impoverished queen.

It was pitch-black outside. As jumbled scenery rushed by the glass window, I pressed my eyes, nose, and mouth against it and cried, sticking to it like an too-salty pickle.

Where exactly did I think I was going? Each time I heard the vendors calling at one station after another, I opened my eyes in panic. If this life was so impossibly difficult, I preferred to be a beggar and wander about from place to place. That would be more interesting. I laughed, cried, and joked as I indulged in this childish daydream. I caught my strangely shifting countenance—my hundred comic faces—in the window. This was one way to keep amused. I shifted myself on the hard seat cushion. Without missing a beat, I returned to a pitiful encore of the hundred faces.

May

I fell in love with the Buddha

When I kissed his faintly cold lips.
Oh, I am unworthy of your attention.
My heart begins to tingle.

I am unworthy of your attention,
But my gently coursing blood
Flows backwards.

His aloofness and refinement,
Irresistibly composed,
Enticed my soul completely.

Buddha!
How indifferent you are
To my heart
That is like a broken beehive.
Just giving me lessons on the transiency of
"Namu Amidabutsu"
Is not enough.
With your refined manner,
Please jump
Into my enflamed breast.
With the dust of the world still on me,
Embrace me tightly
Though I might die,
"Namu Amidabutsu."

It was a strangely dark day. I might go crazy on account of the weather. The rain persisted from the morning, and wind came with the night, drenching both body and soul. I wrote this poem and pasted it up on the wall, but it did not ease my heart.

"Come immediately do you need money"

It was strange how the pale blue flimsy telegram paper had fluttered in the air and floated around me.

I wanted to shout "you fool, fool, fool, fool" a thousand or ten thousand times. When I received his telegram at an inn in Takamatsu, I had actually been so happy that I had cried. Then, cradling a bag bursting with presents, I had come home to Tabata. But why had he moved out to another new place in the less than two weeks I had been away? He had paid two months' rent for me, but kept the room in his name. He had moved effortlessly to a boardinghouse in Hongō, like a goldfish with a flick of its tail. The day before, carrying a pile of his freshly washed clothes, I had climbed the wide stairs of his rooming house with heightened anticipation, as if arriving for an affair. At that moment I had wished I could fly up to his joyful room. But when the lights went on I found them entwined, he and that actress. And to think how he had cried on my breast and clung like a child to get me to stay. I retreated to a dark corridor, eyes brimming with tears. My whole face, no, my whole body stiffened like a wire doll's. It was too much for me.

"Ha . . . ," I blurted out simply but forcibly, like an obnoxious child. I kept my swollen face facing the floor. My galloping around a crazy mixed up world began in earnest.

"A kiss for fifteen sen!" My petulant offers at all those bars haunted my memory.

It was obvious that all men were worthless! Consumed with anger, I wanted to torture him. I was a pitiful sight, blindly drinking whiskey, sake, and whatever I could get my hands on. Now motionless in bed, I listened quietly to the sound of the rain. He was probably cradling the actress's head, inside the mosquito netting billowing in the breeze. The more I dwelled on it, the more I wished I could fly over and bomb them.

I had a hangover and an empty stomach. I stood unsteadily, put the remaining uncooked rice in the cooking pot, and went out to wash it at the well. Everybody from downstairs was off to the public bath, so I made a lot of noise washing the rice. I was drenched from the rain, but enjoyed draining the white rinse water off the rice in solitude.

June

Morning.

It was clear, good weather. When I opened the rain shutters, I saw white butterflies swarming like snow. I was taken aback by the masculine scent of the season, the way the brilliant white clouds floated in a blue sky. I really needed to do some good writing. I threw out all of the cigarette butts stuffed into the brazier and thought about how nice it was for a woman to live all alone in an attic room. Boundless energy replaced my gloom as I inhaled the fresh air of the bright morning. But despite my best expectations, I was quite disgusted by the mail. The notice from the pawn shop just made me want to throw up my hands—interest due on the four yen forty sen. I put on a striped kimono and a yellow obi and set off for town, twirling my parasol, looking for all the world like a happy, carefree young woman. It was my daily visit to the used-book store.

"Buy it for a bit more than usual today, okay? I have to go somewhere far away. . . ." As always, the owner of this store in Dōzaka hid his friendly smile in his wrinkles, took the book I offered, and quietly examined it in both hands.

"This is the current best-seller. It's sold out elsewhere."

"Hmm . . . Steiner's *On the Self.* I'll take it off your hands for one yen."

He placed two fifty sen coins on my palm. I put one in each sleeve of my kimono and went out into the blinding sun. Then I went as usual to eat.

I wondered when I would be able to sit at a cozy dinner table like everyone else and blithely consume my meals. I could not fill my stomach enough by writing a few children's stories, and working at the cafe made me feel seedy and callous. It was distressing to be supported by a man. Selling books from time to time was all I had left. That night Yoshida, the art student, came alone to visit. I was cutting my nails after returning home from the public bath. He'd taken to painting scenes from nature,

and brought along several small landscapes. The scent of the oils wafted from the canvas. I had met him through the poet Aikawa. I didn't particularly like or dislike him, but his frequent visits were beginning to irritate me. Claiming to be tired, Yoshida had thrown himself down by the purple lampshade. He sat up abruptly.

> One eyelid, then another, he pierces the thin closed lids,
> And suddenly wrenches out both eyes.
> The Nagasaki,
> The Nagasaki Doll making is a frightening thing!

"Do you know this? It's a poem by Hakushū. You remind me of it."

The wind chime was quietly playing with my heart. I positioned myself next to the lamp, my feet out on the cool veranda and my head resting against his chest. The throbbing seemed mournful. I was spellbound by the melancholy, mournful, pitifully throbbing heartbeat. It was distressing to think that a woman's presence could bring this about. My own pulse surged like the spray of a fountain. Yoshida had fallen silent and was trembling. I considered for the first time how sad oil paints smelled. For quite some time, we made love. Then the tall Yoshida disappeared through the gate, and I burst into tears, still clutching the mosquito netting to my chest. My more vivid thoughts were of the other man from whom I was separated. I called out his name, and wailed like an uncontrollably selfish child.

June

Today, Isori, a friend of the man from whom I had separated, was going to move into the eight-mat room next door to mine. For some reason I was uncomfortable with the idea. It might be a plot my ex had concocted.

I bought a stick of incense for the Jizo statue along the road to the eatery. When I returned home, I washed my hair. Feeling refreshed, I set out for Shizue's boardinghouse in Dangōzaka. I dashed up the slope full of energy, since our poetry journal, *Two People,* was about to come out. Pushing aside the blue curtain, I talked with Shizue through the window, leaning against it as usual. She always looked young. She tilted her bushy bobbed hair, and her moist eyes sparkled. In the evening I went with Shizue to the printers to pick up the issues. It was only eight pages long, but it was as welcome as fresh fruit. On the way home we stopped by Nantendō and gave everyone a copy. I was determined to keep this journal going for a long time. Tsuji tapped me on the shoulder as I was drinking my cold coffee.

"You've put out something really great. I hope you keep it going." He loosened his headband and sang our praises. Shizue and I left feeling elated, buoyed by his enthusiasm.

June

This time the people who put together *The Sower* were going to put out a magazine called *Literary Front.*[3] I wrote up my experiences from working at the small celluloid toy factory as a poem called "Song of a Factory Girl" and submitted it. Today's *Capital* newspaper[4] printed the poem I had written to my ex-lover. I knew I should stop writing such poetry. It was preposterous. I resolved to try harder to write something exquisite. In the evening I went to the Pine Moon cafe on the Ginza, where they were holding an exhibit of John Donne's poetry. My pathetic scrawl adorned the top of the exhibition guest book. I met Hashizume.

June

A thin patter of rain fell.

> With a sunny early spring,
> Blossoms bloom together on the weeping willow.
>
> One night a spring wind sweeps into the women's quarters,
> Willow flowers fly down on the southern house.
>
> Consumed with love I step outside, but my feet have no strength.
> I pick up the willow blossoms, tears touch my heart.
>
> Autumn passed and spring came again, the swallow
> Wants to take the willow flowers into its nest.

Slouched under the lamp, reading of Empress Rei's poetic love for White Flower, I could not help but feel a wanderlust. *Since Isori's arrival, he had rolled in past one o'clock every night.* Working people lived downstairs, so they went to bed about nine. All one could hear was the rumble of the electric and steam trains that passed through Tabata station from time to time. Otherwise, the residential neighborhood was shrouded in a wilderness peace. All by myself, I became quite lonely. I yearned for some-

3. *Tane maku hito* (The sower, 1921) and *Bungei sensen* (Literary front, 1924) were short-lived literary journals that contributed to Japanese socialism and the Proletarian literary movement.
4. *Miyako Shimbun.*

one beautiful like White Flower. Laying the book open on its spine, I grew impatient and went downstairs.

"Where're you going at this time of night?" the woman from below asked. She rested her hands from her sewing and stared at me.

"Late-night discounts at the movie house."

"Well, you're certainly full of energy . . . ."

Opening the paper umbrella, I went to see what was playing at Dōzaka. The billboard touted something called *Young Maharaja*. I felt aroused by this cut-rate pubescent prince. Both the Oriental orchestra on the flat-bottomed barge and the rain pleased me. *Yet, no matter where I wandered, I was sad and lonely.* I slunk out of the closing movie house like a sewer rat, and returned to my room.

"I think you have a guest . . . ." the downstairs woman murmured drowsily. I climbed up, tired. Yoshida was rolling a piece of paper up into a ball and stuffing it into his pocket. He was so tall that he couldn't stand in the door frame.

"Sorry to come up so late."

"It's okay. I went off to see a movie."

"It was getting so late that I was writing a note to leave for you."

Here was a practical stranger who never had anything to talk about, trying to seduce me. I was flabbergasted.

"Rains a lot, doesn't it?"

I had to pretend I didn't know his intent. Leaning his back against the wall, he began to stare at my face. I was in a quandary. I couldn't bear the thought of falling madly for this man. But I really had had enough. Quietly, resting both hands on the desktop, I ran my eyes above the light of the lamp. The tips of my fingers were trembling. It felt as if two people were pushing as hard as they could against each other.

"You're not teasing me, are you?"

"What do you mean?"

What a dim-witted reply. Hadn't I just come to terms with my romantic desires? Yet they still caused those murmurings in the back of my throat. I hesitated to make him stop coming here again. Yes, I wanted a friend. I wanted someone with this kind of gentleness, yet. . . . Without my realizing it, my eyes brimmed with tears.

I thought of doing away with myself once and for all. This man might stare me to death. My mouth went sour. I couldn't help but feel sorry for myself. Countless memories still flooded this room, where for several months I had lived with my former lover. It was suffocating to stay here. As I bent over my desk, I imagined the fresh summer scenery of the outskirts of the city. The intensity of the rain increased. The anguish was unbearable.

"Please love me. Don't say anything. Just love me," he pleaded.

"Well, I'm not saying anything, am I? Aren't I loving you?" If all it took to soothe this young man's heart was to take his hand in mine. . . . Yet I was afraid of falling victim again. Even though I was no innocent when it came to men, still I could not dismiss the notion that somewhere, someplace, someone might appear to whom I would be able to entrust my whole life. Yoshida had a freshness, with a broad chest, fair brows, and eyes like the sun. I cried with the passion of a raging torrent.

June

I was lonely. Worthless. I wanted money.

I wished to walk all alone along one of the fragrant acacia-lined avenues of Hokkaido.

"Are you already up?"

It was unusual for Isori to be calling to me from the other side of the shoji.

"Yes, I am."

It was Sunday. Isori, Shizue, and I had planned a rare visit to Miyazaki Mitsuo's "American Chocolate House" in Kichijōji. Uenoyama, a western-style painter, stopped by while we were playing on the porch with the dog that evening. I had met him once before when I was younger and working as a maid for the Chikamatsu household. He had shown up all scruffy and unkempt, trying to sell a painting of a cow. I remembered that the children had been down with diphtheria, and Uenoyama had looked terribly disheveled. While I had arranged his shoes in the entryway, I had noticed that in one shoe the sole was separating from the upper section, yawning like the mouth of a hippopotamus. Without telling anyone I had plugged the gap with a small nail. Perhaps he had never realized this. Uenoyama drank copiously and talked a lot. That night, he went home alone.

Seating myself on the revolving stool of the earth,
I take a dramatic go-round.
One of the red slippers I scuff along
Flies away.

I'm lonely. . .
"Hey," I cry out, but
No one gets my slipper for me.
Plucking up my courage,
Shall I leap down off the revolving stool and
Go get the far-flung slipper?

My timid hands tightly
Clutch the stool.
"Hey, somebody,
Whack the side of my face
With all your might, won't you,
And send the other slipper I'm wearing flying."
I want to sleep peacefully.

I composed this poem in my head as I lay restless in bed. Downstairs, the cuckoo clock struck three.

June

The world consists of stars and people. I discovered this while reading Emile Verhaeren. But mine was only a boring world. I decided to disdain this deceiving poet.

O man, though that tall mountain be difficult to scale,
Do not diminish your desire to soar,
Fear not the impossible,
Attack the swift golden stallion.

This poem might be insignificant, but it certainly commanded impressive imagery. Attack the swift golden stallion?

A red balloon sailed by my window. Astonishing, amazing, bewildering. Living was truly unmasterable in this fleeting world.

A letter arrived from home.

> I wish you'd be more realistic about money. At least don't count on me to keep food on your table. You mustn't get too conceited about your own capabilities. I don't like your aimless wanderings. Mother is getting weaker, too. Come back soon.

My stepfather had enclosed a five-yen money order. I placed it on my lap. I bowed. Thank you ever so much. Shamelessly, I stuck out my tongue in the direction of their distant home.

June

A blue light shone tonight in the mortuary across from the rooming house. Another soldier had probably died. Shadows of two soldiers at the wake were dimly cast across the window.

"Hey, a firefly!"

By the wellside, Kuroshima's wife gazed vacantly up into the sky.

"No kidding?"

I got up from my sprawled position to go out onto the veranda, but I couldn't see even a single one.

Night. The Tsuboi couple next door and the Kuroshimas came for a visit.

"It was really quite a stroke of luck today. When Denji and I went to the market to buy a wash basin, before I even paid for it, they gave me about three yen's worth of change. Boy, was I surprised." Tsuboi blathered on.

"I wish that would happen to me. I think Knut Hamsun had the hero of *Hunger* go buy candles, and he too got change for a five Kroner and the candles for free."

Both my husband and I were a bit envious of Tsuboi's luck. We lived in such a miserable dark tenement in Taishidō, a veritable raft floating in a morass. I was sick and tired of our surroundings—a barrack mortuary, a cemetery, a hospital, and cheap cafes.

"By the way, how about having bamboo shoots with rice tomorrow?"

"Shall we go steal some shoots?"

The three men, Kuroshima, Tsuboi, and my husband approached Iida, who lived above the barbershop across the road. The barbershop had a back door leading onto the bamboo grove, and they set off for the hill behind to steal some bamboo shoots. We women really wanted to see the city lights, but we gave up and went walking around the neighborhood festival instead. The cheap metal lamps on the stalls set up along the paths of the park filled the air like a fountain.

June

We hadn't been on a walk for quite a while, so, poor as we were, we decided to go see the greenery on the hill under the exquisitely transparent sky.

I locked up and set out after my husband, though I didn't know which way he had gone. I couldn't even catch a trace of him. I traipsed up and down the paths on the dry, scorching hill, but as luck would have it, he returned while I was still out looking for him. Fuming at having been kept waiting, he pushed me down from behind when I returned and then went inside. He was furious yet again. I tried to sneak in through the back door like a thief, but he started throwing scrub-brushes and bowls at me. Why did you rage at me so? I was just careless. I stood by the well, watching the pale clouds. Just because I mistook the path to the right for the one to the left, wouldn't it have been enough just to say "You're stupid"? Watching my lonely shadow, I recalled a trick from elementary school. I'd stare at my shadow and then glance at the sky, and see that shadow mirrored in the clouds. Tirelessly, I peered from the shadows to the sky. Sobbing like a child, I crouched on the ground, longing to belt out old songs like a water-seller in Cairo.

The whole world was full of loving parents. Too preoccupied with my own problems, I had forgotten their importance and their love. Still wearing my white apron, I passed by a bamboo grove, a stream, and a western-style house, and then descended the hill at a leisurely pace. The steamboat whistle of a factory nearby reminded me of the sea at Onomichi. Carried back in time, I raced down the hill like a child, to find only a deserted open field, with the hum of a factory motor coming from next to a police box. Dizzy and hungry, I stood for a while at the Mishuku train station pretending to wait for a train.

"You've been standing here for some time now. Is something wrong?"

Two old women had been staring at me. They approached in a friendly way, then looked me up and down. When they took me in tow, you couldn't tell if I was laughing or crying. Starting out together at a leisurely pace, these kind ladies talked about the Tenrikyō religion, about how a cripple learned to walk because of his faith, and how the afflicted could live cheerfully as children of God.

Within the religious compound along the river, the cool garden had been sprinkled with water. New green leaves of a maple branch spilled refreshingly over the fence. The two women first bowed low before the altar and then spread their arms to begin a peculiar dance.

"Where are you from?" asked the middle-aged priest clothed all in white. Appraising my sorry state, he offered me green tea and a roll filled with sweet beans.

"I'm not really from anywhere. Officially, I'm registered in East Sakurajima in Kagoshima."

"That's pretty far away."

Unable to hold back any longer, I picked up the roll. It was rather hard, and crumbs dropped onto my lap.

Nothing. I didn't have to think about anything. I stood up abruptly, bowed to the altar, put on my geta and just kept on going. I didn't care if my cavities throbbed from the sweet, as long as the flavor lingered in my mouth.

When I passed by our place, I saw that it was shut as tightly as his pinched mouth. I made myself at home at the Tsubois', slowly stretching out my legs and then lying down.

"Do you have any rice to spare?"

Sakae kindly brought a bowl containing a handful of rice and sat down beside me. She began to talk despondently about how tired she was of living.

"I hear that Taiko's relatives have sent her some rice from Shinshū. Let's go see her," she suddenly remembered.

"Sounds great to me."

Kuroshima's wife, seated next to me, clapped her hands like a gleeful child. What a simple soul.

June

I hadn't been into the center of Tokyo for a while, so I decided to set off today. I met Katō Takeo at the Shinchōsha publishing company. He paid me six yen for my poem, which had appeared in the magazine *Literary Club*. I usually passed the streets along Kagurazaka with my eyes closed, but today they were a spectacle of delight. I poked my head into each store with great relish.

Neighbors and
Relatives and
Lovers.
What are they?
If not satisfied with life's fare,
The image of a charming flower would wither away.
I want to work cheerfully.
Among all the malicious gossip
I crouch down ever so tightly, ever so pathetically.
I try holding both hands up high for all to see,
But are there people who would betray my trust?
Am I not the one to keep silent forever, cradling such innocence?
My belly may be empty,
There may be no work,
But I must not wail,
For those living in comfort will object.

Though I die in agony, mopping up the blood,
The earth will not be moved an inch.
In the showcase
Lie buns hot from the steamer.
The world unknown to me must seem,
Ah, how light and airy like a piano minuet.

Then, for the first time,
I feel like screaming, "Motherfucking fate!"

Having been jolted along on the train for what seemed like hours, I faced the daunting prospect of returning to my comfortless room. *Com-*

posing poetry was my only solace. That night, Iida and Taiko came to visit me, singing this silly ditty.

That lovely feathered one
Singing "Kekko, kekko"
In my yard.
You probably want her, don't you?

I got rice cooked with green peas from Tsuboi.

June

It was the big evening of the Taishidō festival. Since I had something of a view of the sumo-wrestling grounds from my front veranda, everyone gathered there. "And in the Western Division! We have Maedagawaa!" the referee bellowed, sending us into gales of laughter. It was quite a sight with all of us on tiptoe on the narrow balcony, craning our necks. We just couldn't contain ourselves when we heard the familiar name Maedagawa being announced. When you're poor, you tend to open yourself up to everyone with more than just polite social graces. You become filled with bonhomie and one with the group.

Everyone carried on. When the conversation turned to ghost stories, even Taiko told a yarn of having seen a ghost on the beach at Chiba. Taiko had extremely beautiful skin, perhaps because she was born in a mountain village. *Men certainly have brought her untold grief.* We played the hanafuda flower card game until after one in the morning.

June

Hagiwara came for a visit.

I wanted a drink, but was broke, so I sold a futon to the junk man for one yen fifty sen and bought some cheap shōchū. As there wasn't enough rice to go round, I bought noodles for all of us to share.

With outstretched palm
My friend wiped my face drenched with the driving snow.
He made Communism his personal philosophy.

Drink sake and become blue as a storybook demon.
My immense face,
Filled with sadness.

Wasn't it great! Here we were, young poetic illiterates belting out verses by Takuboku, nibbling at the noodles, and swizzling cheap sake. That night, we all saw Hagiwara off at the station. On returning home, my man insisted that we close all the doors and windows of our place, since we did not have a mosquito net. We lit repellent coils and went to bed.

"Get up, get up!" Just then a flurry of footsteps rattled our slumber. We felt like barley shoots coaxed deeper into the soil by farmers stamping the surrounding earth.

"Hey, don't pretend to be asleep. . . ."

"You're awake, aren't you?"

"If you don't get up, we'll set fire to your place!"

"Hey! We've pulled up a radish. It's good. Aren't you going to get up?"

We could hear both Iida and Hagiwara spouting away. Smiling to myself, I kept still.

July

In the morning I read a wonderful story in the newspaper as I lounged on my futon. The Viscountess Motono was going to rescue delinquent boys and girls. A feature photo of her, trimmed to a circle, accompanied the article. If I could but some way, somehow, catch a piece of that charity, then surely a bright future would be guaranteed. I was, after all, a bit delinquent, and still twenty-three. So I screwed up my courage and jumped out of bed. I clipped the Motonos' address from the newspaper and set off for their residence in Azabu.

A yukata may have a proper crease in the shoulders and back, but it is still just casual and common. So attired, I ambled along with my heart filled with dreams.

"Are you the Miss Hayashi who bakes bread?" the maid quizzed me. On the contrary, I'm the Hayashi who's come to collect my bread and butter, I muttered to myself.

"I've come to see Madam Motono about something," I tried aloud.

"Is that so? She has gone out to the Women's Patriotic Association, but should be home shortly."

The maid ushered me in. I sat down on the divan next to the bay window and gazed out onto a beautifully cultivated garden. The cool breeze swelled the blue curtains as it entered the room.

"And what is the purpose. . . ."

Before long, a pudgy woman entered the sitting room. She wore a black, gossamer-thin short jacket over her kimono.

"Wouldn't you like to have a bath first?" the maid was asking her mistress.

I got tired of being a delinquent. I tried explaining that as my husband was suffering from consumption, I would like anything left over from the aid to delinquent boys and girls.

"It seems that there was something like that written up in the newspaper, but we've just helped out a bit in that project. If you have a problem, why don't you go to the women's group in Kudan and work there?"

Given this tepid reception, I was then brushed outside like dust. The brows of the Viscountess would no doubt have furrowed as she scolded the maid for letting someone like me into the house. I felt like spitting on her. "Philanthropy"? "Public works"?

My man and I wrote aimlessly, sitting morosely in a darkened room. By evening we were famished, having eaten nothing since morning.

"How about some western take-out?"

"What!?"

"Curried rice, or a cutlet, or a steak?"

"Got any money?"

" 'Need knows no law.' If we order western food tonight, no one will collect until tomorrow morning, right?"

So we ordered. I was overjoyed with the aroma, and savored the beef's slippery juices. It wouldn't have been strange if we had left a little on the plate, as if to ask for seconds. With stomach content, nay, reborn, we looked to a brighter future. What else could we do? We were so poor, there weren't even any mice around.

Leaning on my orange-crate desk, I began to write a children's story. *Outside the sound of rain.* There was a ceaseless succession of gunfire off toward the Tama River. Even in the middle of the night it crackled. But how much longer would our insect-like existence endure? My head began to fill with tears.

What a team—a man with warped sensibilities and a woman with poor judgment—it didn't look as if we would eat white rice again as long as we lived.

July

"I was off to buy me a prostitute, but I've taken a liking to you, so how about it?" a balding man propositioned me this evening. Rolling my apron into a ball, I choked back tears of heartwrenching loneliness.

I cried out "Mama!" sick of it all. I threw myself down in a corner of the maid's room on the second floor. The mice were roving about in packs. As my eyes became accustomed to the light, I could make out magazines and cloth bundles scattered about like pebbles. Nightclothes and sashes hung in disarray on the wall like seaweed. The clamorous cacophony downstairs had come to a brisk boil. Upstairs, the maid's room was so deserted it would not have been surprising to see a ghost.

A steady stream of tears had released a flood of swirling sorrow. All I wanted was a normal life. Calming myself, I picked a book to read.

No matter how much I try,
Only hardship at home
With an alcoholic lover who's sleeping around and gambling,
That's the sum of my labors.
Ah . . .

Cut them up,
Jump out of the way, send them flying.
How many times have I screamed from the pain?
Let's dance like a dervish and purge ourselves of talent along with
our bloody vomit.

So Kaita continued to howl. Such a pathetic muse. I wanted to plumb the depths of my soul with Chekhov, Artzybaschev, or Schnitzler. I had never before thought of working as an ordeal, but today I really would have appreciated some relief. It all seemed make-believe.

In the dimly lit room I recalled Shiga Naoya's *Reconciliation.* Surrounded by the din of this cafe, it was trying even to write a line in a diary.

First of all, a place where sparrows chirp, where bright morning sun shines with tranquil rays, and where the green foliage basks in the sun, its sound and color giving out the scent of rain. I longed crazily for such a place to live all by myself, just like Kaita did.

It was a monumental self-deception. Because it was dark, I just kept my eyes shut.

"Hey! Where'd Yumi go?"[5] the owner's wife was calling out downstairs.

"Yumi, are you around? The boss's wife's looking for you."

"Can you tell her I'm taking a rest because my tooth hurts?"

Yae descended the stairs with a great commotion. "I wish I could die," I moaned fearfully. By and by, Mephistopheles came out dancing.

"What's life? What's this organism called life?" asked Lunacharskii, once someone of importance. I wanted to repeat these questions. A fallen Mary Magdalene, my instinct for self-preservation was destroyed. Putting both hands under my head, I fantasized suicide. I fantasized I was drinking poison. "Instead of going out to buy a prostitute, I've gotten to like you." Life was certainly absurdly cheery. I was without a home, but still found it distressing to think about my mother. Should I become a thief? A mounted female bandit? The face of my former lover seared my eyelids.

The owner's wife sharpened the edge in her voice and climbed up the ladder. "Hey! Yumi, you know good and well that we don't have enough

5. Hayashi's bar name.

help. How about putting up with the pain for a little bit and coming downstairs and working?"

Every single thing was smoke, sand, mud. Retying my apron strings, I descended to the churning, surging sea, with a merry song on my lips.

July

It had rained since morning.

The woman who borrowed my new coat ended up never coming back. Begging a spot to stay for the night and the use of my coat, the woman had flitted off like a mosquito to another job.

"You're so kindhearted. Isn't there an old adage about needing to watch out for the thief in everyone?" Yae ridiculed me as she scratched her ashen ankle.

"Really!? Is there a saying like that? Well then, how would it be if I stole your umbrella and made a run for it?"

"If the world were only full of thieves, how thrilling it would be!" chimed in Yoshi, who had been lying down. She was nineteen and claimed to have been born in Sakhalin. Her pride was her pale complexion. The shadows of the raindrops, filtered through the green windowglass, showed clearly against Yae's chestnut skin. She had dropped her kimono off her shoulders, and it hung at her waist while she readied her toilet.

"People are such bores."

"But trees are much more boring."

"Even if there was a fire or a flood, a tree couldn't run away . . . ."

"Don't be so preposterous!!"

"Everybody's preposterous, isn't that right . . ."

Women's chatter was as sunny as a blue sky in summer. How fine if I had only been born a bird. Someone turned on the light. We all drew lots to see who would pay what for the snacks. Mine was four sen. The women looked like blanched asparagus, still in their pasty-white pancake makeup. They lay around slovenly, nibbling mitsumame. The rain cleared, and a cool breeze blew in through the window.

"Yumi, do you have a sweetheart? I've suspected as much."

"I had one, but he left me and went far away."

"How marvelous!"

"Why do you say that?"

"Even though I want out, my guy won't let me be."

Licking the now-empty spoon, Yae claimed she wanted to split up with her present boyfriend. I suggested she'd probably feel the same no matter who she was with.

"That's not the way it should be," she retorted. "Why take even soap.

There's a world of difference between the ten sen kind and the fifty sen kind, you know."

Evening. I gave myself up completely to drinking sake. I had earned two yen and forty sen. Thank you, thank you most graciously.

July

A preoccupied heart brought with it its share of setbacks. The car glided along the streets of Hachioji in the pouring rain.

Faster!

Faster!

It was great to ride in a car once in a while. Headlights pierced the night and colored the drizzly town.

"Where to?"

"Anywhere. Just drive until we run out of gas."

The driver, Matsu, was balding a bit—a little prematurely, I suspected.

I had nothing to do on the afternoon of my day off, and Matsu, who owned his own cab, offered me a ride. We got as far as Tanashi, where the car got stuck in the red clay. We came to a sudden stop by a stand of oaks, just as it started to rain. The only light was at the foot of the distant mountain. Not only did it pour, but thunder rumbled like the earth was growling, and lightning began to strike. The thunder refreshed me. When the rain hit the windshield, it would spray into this old Chevy. Only one car passed us on that narrow back road in the shadow of the oak grove. We were alone with the howl of the rain, the thunder, and the lightning.

"With it like this, there's no way we can get out to the main road, is there?"

Matsu smoked his cigarette in silence. Beneath his virtuous facade, I very much suspected he was up to something. The cold rain felt good. The thunder and lightning railed as if they would tear everything apart. The car was stranded in the oak-grove twilight, bombarded by rain.

I felt cornered. His stinking oil-stained overalls prompted a mirthless laugh. No longer an innocent young girl, I was well aware of the avenues of escape.

I put up a solid front. "You haven't even said you loved me yet. I hate men who think they can use brute force. If you're attracted, you have to be better behaved, or I won't stand for it!"

I left tooth marks on his predator arm. My throat choked with tears. Who said I'd submit? When the dawn began to break the dark night's drizzle, he was asleep, his face still dirty, but relaxed.

A distant rooster announced the blue skies of day. *It was a serene summer morning.* The breeze flowed like rustling silk, washing out the night's sordid struggle. If only he had been that other one. . . . Leaving the fool in the car, I eased myself onto the muddy road and walked away. The wind on my swollen eyelids swept away the fatigue from last night's endless vigilance. I found myself strolling lighthearted into the outskirts of town. I am worthy of contempt! I knew I was completely wild. As I ran out of the oak grove, I decided that Matsu was pitifully unfortunate. Thinking of him back in the car, just a tired guy in the sleep of innocence, I even entertained the notion of running back to wake him. But he might be embarrassed. *The memory of him at the wheel nonchalantly smoking made me decide he was despicable after all. I felt immensely relieved.* Someone, anyone, wasn't there anybody who would love me. . . . I recalled the man who left me. . . . Wandering clouds drifted far away in the July sky. That's what I looked like. How about singing a song from Provence while picking wildflowers.

August

I wrote letters for the maids.

Omiki, fresh from Akita, was lying down on the tatami, licking the tip of a pencil. The owner's wife was turning a profit in the bar by diluting the bottles of King of Kings whiskey sevenfold. Such dust, such stifling humidity. They said that if you sucked on a lot of ice, your hair would fall out. But even Yoshi, who rarely took any ice, stole a lump from the freezer and crunched away all by herself.

"What's a good way to start a love letter. . . ?"

Yae mouthed these words with her red lips and flashed her jet-black eyes. Country girls from Akita, Sakhalin, Kagoshima, and Chiba sat around a table in the shop writing letters to distant destinations.

Today I went to town and bought a muslin obi sash. I asked for eight feet—one yen two-sen. I always glanced at the classifieds to see if there wasn't a steady job that I could settle into, but there were no good leads. The usual medical student crowd came in. The scent of animated males flowed into the room like the tide. Yae, who liked students, put away her unfinished love letter and pressed both hands to her chest, playing the coquette.

Yoshi blamed everything on the karma from her days in Sakhalin. She was embarrassed when I caught her applying some pungent medicine, so she put it away and sprawled out on the second floor.

"It's pretty boring, isn't it."

"Yeah. . . ."

When I gazed at Yoshi's luminous skin, I found myself strangely attracted to her.

"You may not believe it, but I've had two children."

Yoshi had lived all over after her own birth in the basement of a hotel in Harbin. Entrusting the children to her mother in Korea, she had drifted into Tokyo with another man, not the father of her children, and lived the bar life in order to support him. It was the usual story.

"After I buy a few kimono, I'm thinking of working in a cafe in the Ginza."

"This line of work isn't something you can do forever. It really wears you down."

"As if it were all a dream" was one gentle affectionate phrase that caught my eye, reading Sato Haruo's story "Eastern moon in the morning sky." "*As if it were all a dream . . . ,*" *I'd like to try settling down.*

"Yumi! No matter where you go, be sure to write, okay. . . ." Yoshi tearfully implored me while wiping her lavender collar with benzene cleaner.

You knew it was all a dream.

"Is that book interesting?"

"Not at all."

"But it's supposed to be a good book. . . . I read a novel about Takahashi Oden."

"This kind of book just makes me depressed."

August

There were days when I thought about going out and finding a job in another cafe. I was depressed about being irresistibly addicted to this work, as if I were smoking opium. Every day it rained.

> Here we discover two paths of art, two kinds of understanding. Along which path will people progress? Dream on! Of course, whether it will be the path in pursuit of a small oasis of beauty, or the path in pursuit of active creation, depends partly on how high your ideals are. The lower the ideals, the more concrete people are. The lower the ideals, the less desperate the abyss between ideal and real appears. Chiefly, however, the path is determined by the degree of human resilience, the reserves of energy, and the tensile force of the nourishment that one consumes. A life of tension naturally consists of creation, the strain of struggle, and hope.

I found this passage in Lunacharskii's *Foundations of Positive Aesthetics* when I was reading in the waitress room one day after the girls had left for the public bath. *Alas, my current bogged-down existence and my unsettled emotions troubled me.* I became somber. No sooner did I think I wanted to study than an uncontrollable depraved wildness coursed through my body. I had no idea what my life would be, no idea which of these two roads I would follow—to live or to die. When night fell, I found myself singing a nonsensical song with the feeling of desperation of slaves on the white man's block. My muslin kimono easily ripped when it clung to my perspiring legs. There was nothing I could do in this relentless heat but wait until it cooled down and keep on going.

I figured that I could fulfill my dreams if there were someone who would give me thirty yen a month with no strings attached.

October

Gazing through the foot-square skylight, it was the first time I had ever seen the sky so clear. A lavender sky. Autumn had come. Eating in the cook's quarters, I yearned, pined, for autumn at home far away. The season was magical. A new woman had arrived. *She looks a rather curious, marshmallow white.* I tired for no reason and missed familiar faces. Every customer's face looked like merchandise. Every face seemed exhausted. I pretended to read a magazine, quietly meditating, oblivious to it all. I couldn't go on. Not doing anything would be just the same as letting myself rot.

October

I cleaned up the large hall, and felt for the first time that I could be my own woman. Every day and night, as I returned to my room, I carried the notion that I really must do something to change my situation. But I was on my feet all day long. I was so tired I would end up collapsing, asleep without even dreaming. I was lonely and bored. It was hard to live on the premises. I kept thinking that any day now I would go look for a room somewhere else, but I couldn't afford to leave this place. The night was too precious to spend on sleep, so I lay still with open eyes. The insects were buzzing off in the gutter.

Even though I tried to hold them back, cold tears flowed pathetically. There was nothing I could do to stop them. I felt left out at the sight of the three pillows in a row under the old mosquito net. The pillows belonging to the women from Sakhalin and Kanazawa looked like eggplants left out in the sun in front of a small shop.

"The insects are buzzing," I murmured softly to Aki beside me.

"On a night like this I could really go for some sake before bed," came her reply.

"Are you thinking about him?" asked Toshi from her futon at the foot of the stairs.

We were all as lonely as sad mountain cuckoos. A chilly autumn wind blew at the hem of the mosquito net. It was midnight.

October

I had saved a little spending money, so I had my hair put up in the traditional style. I hadn't had it done for awhile. It was great. When I had the paper cords tied squeaky tight, my eyebrows bristled. When the hairdresser combed my bangs with a long dripping comb, they fell lushly across my forehead. I was remade into a beautiful new me. If I were to make eyes at the mirror, it would simply swoon. With such beautiful hair, I felt I should be going somewhere. I wanted to board a train and go far, far away.

At the neighboring bookstore, I exchanged coins for a one-yen note and enclosed it in a letter home. I thought they would appreciate it. I knew I was pleased when someone sent me money.

I bought some sweet bean cakes and ate them with the other girls.

Today there was a horrible storm. Such rainy days were depressing. My feet froze as hard as ice.

October

A quiet night.

"Where're you from?"

The owner, who slept in front of the safe, was quizzing the newcomer, Toshi. It was kind of fun to eavesdrop on other people's conversation while you were lying in bed.

"You mean me? From Sakhalin. And from Toyohara. Do you know the place?"

"From Sakhalin? Did you come all alone?"

"Yes. . . ."

"Boy, you're a plucky one, aren't you?"

"I was in the Aoyagi district of Hakodate for a long time, too."

"That's a nice neighborhood, isn't it. I'm from Hokkaido, too."

"I thought as much. You've got a bit of the accent."

I recalled a fine, sad poem by Takuboku about the Aoyagi district and a weak, long-stemmed cornflower, and knew I would take a liking to Toshi.[6]

Wasn't living something to rejoice? I'd come to believe that life was somehow truly joyful. I was surrounded by good people.

It was the beginning of fall. A rather cool wind was blowing. *Though lonely, I still felt a passion for life ablaze within me.*

6. This poem is from Takuboku's *Ichi aku no suna* (Handful of sand, 1910).

October

Word came from my mother that her rheumatism was bad. I wasn't getting any tips.

I wrote fairy tales during lulls in business. Eleven pages under the title "A Tale of a Child Who Became a Fish." I would send what I got for it back home. It must be wretched to be old, penniless, and cast out on your own. Poor mother. I was all the more worried since she hadn't tapped me for money for a while.

"One of these days, why don't you come visit my home? The country is real fine," Okei invited me in her gruff male way of talking. She had been a waitress here for three years.

"Sure . . . I'll go. Can you put me up?"

I decided to save a bit of money for the trip. The women who worked at places like this were much kinder and more compassionate than others.

" 'Never leave me, okay?' or 'I've fallen for you.' You know, I've had enough of foolish things like love and endearments. These promises don't mean a thing. The man who did this to me is even a member of the Diet. As soon as he got me pregnant, he was out the door. If you bear an illegitimate child, everybody says that you're a modern girl, but it's still shameless. . . . It's an asinine, fleeting world. The world today wouldn't swallow sincerity even if you could bottle it. I've been working like this for the past three years because my child is so precious. . . ."

My irritation vanished as I listened to Okei go on. She was an extraordinary woman.

October

Staring out the window, I saw the rain pass like a streetcar. I pulled in a bit today. Toshi was griping about how difficult the times are. She was sitting on the electric fan stand, telling us her life story in such a dejected manner. I could feel her honesty. She had worked in a large cafe in Asakusa, but left after being abused by her fellow workers. A fortuneteller in Asakusa told her she would be all right in the Koishikawa neighborhood of Kanda, so she came here.

"But this is Nishikimachi," Okei said.

"That can't be right!" Toshi was startled. She was the most beautiful and honest woman in the shop, and by far the one with the most interesting stories.

October

A bath after work revived me. While we were cleaning up the big dining room, the cook and the dishwasher bathed and then fell asleep in the large communal tatami room upstairs. This left us the opportunity to soak in the hot bath at our leisure. Not having been able to sit down once since morning, we were all so tired we could have fallen into a trance.

"I gave up everything for just you, I'm a withered flower of first love," Aki started to sing. I sprawled out on the mat in the dressing area and listened until everyone got out of the bath. I really wanted someone to take care of me. But there were certainly a lot of dishonest men. I would save up my money and take a devil-may-care holiday.

There was an interesting story about Aki.

She spoke so beautifully that the thirty-sen set-lunch noon crowd of university students greeted her like a Paris daisy. Aki was nineteen and liked the students. From my vantage point I watched Aki's observant eyes, but could also see dark circles under them and creases around her neck that were certainly not those of a youth. These were sure signs of a jaded life.

That night, when everyone was in the bath, Aki waited self-consciously for some time in a corner of the hallway.

"Hey! Aki, your body'll rot to pieces if you don't get in the bath and wash off your sweat," Okei called out while brushing her teeth.

Eventually Aki slipped into the communal tub, covering her breasts with a hand towel.

"You've had a baby, haven't you?"

> The whole orchard is pure white! You haven't forgotten, have you my love? Lyuba? You remember that long tree-lined avenue endlessly stretching on, straight as an arrow, glistening in the moonlit, don't you, dear? You couldn't have forgotten, could you?
>
> That's right. Even this cherry orchard is being sold off to the moneylenders, unlikely as it may sound, but it can't be helped. . . .

My ex-lover often used to repeat Gayev's soliloquy in the cherry orchard.[7] Lost in salty reminiscences, I eyed the big moon through the warped window panes.

Okei was quizzing her in a high-pitched voice.

"Yes, I have a boy who will soon be two."

She uncovered her nipples and sat down in the thickly steaming bath.

"And you claimed you were a virgin. Ha! I suspected as much ever since you got here. There's probably a tragic tale of how you ended up here, too. What happened to your man?"

"He's got tuberculosis and is home with the baby."

There was no shortage of suffering women.

7. From Anton Chekhov's *Cherry Orchard,* written in 1903–1904.

"I was pregnant once," Toshi shrieked. We could see her hands and legs were as shapely and supple as a model's.

"I aborted mine at three months. Everyone in the city of Toyohara knew about my splendid life. I had married into a landowning family that was actually very modern. They even let me take piano lessons. The teacher was someone who had drifted in from Tokyo. I was completely fooled by that character and got pregnant. I knew it was his child all right, so I told him.

"Just make it your husband's child," was the line he gave me. I was furious. I figured having that guy's child would be horrid, so I dissolved a teacup full of hot mustard and drank it. Ha, ha, ha . . . I mean to follow him no matter where he runs, and spit on him in front of everybody."

"Incredible. . . ."

"You're really remarkable. . . ."

Compliments and encouragement continued for awhile. Okei jumped up and poured bathwater down Toshi's back again and again. Choked and at a loss for words, I was deeply impressed. I was weak. . . . I was thinking about the face of the man who had betrayed me, the one I should spit on. I was the biggest fool, beneath contempt. It didn't put my mind at ease to hear everyone's reassurances.

October

When I opened my eyes, Toshi was already getting ready.

"You overslept, we have to get out of here right now."

I felt relieved as we carried our luggage to the bath. I tied my stiff Hakata obi sash so that it wouldn't make any noise, tidied my hair, and then got two pairs of wooden geta from the dirt shop floor. It was already seven in the morning, but mice were still scurrying around in the quiet kitchen. The kind owner's snores were undisturbed. Okei was gone, returned home to Chiba the previous night on account of her child's illness. Toshi and I had secretly discussed how we really wanted to quit, that we didn't know what to do with just the student and set-lunch customers frequenting the place. Given the already small number of overworked waitresses, both of us had initially caved in after all and decided to bear with it. Yet, with no tips coming in, we couldn't keep it up just for fun. We had no other choice but to run away. The spacious deserted dining hall was fearfully hushed in the morning. Red goldfish swam in the cement pool. A dirty gray air had already blanketed the room. Opening the window facing onto the alley, Toshi jumped down effortlessly like a man, and went to get the cloth bags we had thrown out of the high window of the bath. I had only a small bundle of books and cosmetics.

"Oh, you've got a lot. . . ."

Toshi brought a bamboo umbrella and a sky-blue parasol. She also carried a cylindrical rucksack, making her a near caricature of the country bumpkin just arrived in the big city. As we waited near the Ogawa area stop, four or five streetcars went by completely filled with students. It was almost time for school. People laughed. No doubt we looked like vagabonds, with our unwashed faces basking in the invigorating morning sun. Unable to bear it any longer, we dove into a noodle shop and stretched out our stiff legs. The noodle shop's delivery boy did us a favor by getting us a one-yen taxi, but riding in the taxi, I had absolutely no confidence. I was completely exhausted and in desperate need of a drink of water. We moved into the second floor of a grocery store in Shinjuku where we had already made arrangements.

"It's all right. It's better to get out of that kind of shop. If my plan works out, things will be just great."

"I'll get myself together and work, okay. You can put yourself into studying."

With my eyes downcast, I couldn't do anything about the tears. Even if Toshi was only mouthing a girlish sentimental dream, in my hopeless situation, her words made me inexplicably happy. I would go back to my mother's home . . . I would run home to my mother's breast. . . . Through the window of the car, I looked up at buildings in the bright morning sky. I watched the roofs race by and the sparrows in the dark rust-reddish treetops fly along the road.

> Even if I become a ragged beggar in a distant place
> From far away I recall my home.[8]

This poem touched me in a special way.

October

The Autumn winds had begun to blow. Toshi was taken away by her ex-husband to Sakhalin.

"Because it'll get cold . . ." she said when she gave me a quilted twill jacket as a keepsake, and then left Tokyo. I hadn't eaten since morning. Selling several children's stories and poems didn't mean I'd be eating high off the hog. Hunger made my head fuzzy, and even my ideas ended up growing mold. My head made no distinction of Proletarian or Bourgeois. I only wanted to cook and eat one handful of rice.

"Please feed me."

8. One verse of the poem "Shokei ijo" (A beautiful scene of wonderful passion) in Murō Saisei's (1889–1962) anthology *Jojo shōkyoku shū* (Lyrical short musical pieces, 1918).

Should I throw myself into the middle of a stormy sea, awash in the troubles of others? When evening arrived, from downstairs I could hear the clatter of bowls from all the people assembled. A grumbling stomach set me pouting like a child. Suddenly I became envious of the women in the distant red-light district. I was starving. All my many books have now dwindled to a few. Kasai Zenzo's *With Children on My Hands,* Artzybaschev's *The Worker Seryov,* and Shiga Naoya's *Reconciliation* are rattling around in the beer crate.

"Maybe I should try to earn some money at a restaurant again."

Painfully resigned and strangely unsteady like a tumbling toy Daruma, I roused myself. Putting my toothbrush, soap, and hand towels into my kimono sleeve, I went out into the windy evening streets. Like a stray dog, I inquired at cafes, one after the next, that were likely prospects for "help wanted." Above all else, my stomach craved solid food. No matter what, I had to eat. Wasn't the street enveloped in delicious aromas! It looked as though it might rain tomorrow. In the blustery winds, fragrances of fresh autumn fruits stimulated my senses.

October

The chestnut roaster's familiar bellow came with the season. At the sound of his sluggish voice, which drifted into the licensed quarters, I became unexpectedly disheartened. I stared out the window of the dark room, motionless and alone. Ever since I was little, my teeth had hurt at the onset of winter. Spoiled by my mother, I would roll around howling on the tatami mat floor. I would get my entire mouth daubed with the all-purpose pickled plum, a home remedy that would leave me hiccuping and crying. Here I was on the second story of a lonely bar, nursing a toothache. My life nearly half spent, I could recall so much—the fields, mountains, and ocean of Onomichi, and the faces of those from whom I had parted.

I turned my watery eyes and spoke to God, but saw only the wandering moon beyond the distorting window panes.

"Does it still hurt?"

Okimi had come upstairs quietly. In the moonlight, the shadow of her wide sweeping pompadour loomed over me. She placed a plate of sushi near my pillow, and the scent of seaweed wafted toward me. I had eaten nothing since morning. Silently, with a tender concern, she watched me. I cried for no apparent reason.

"Don't be so foolish!" Okimi scolded me when I pulled my coin purse from beneath the thin futon. She slapped my hand with a rolled-up newspaper. Then, after smoothing down and tucking under the edges of the futon, she quietly descended the back stairs. Ah, what a wonderful world it was after all.

October

The wind was blowing.

Near dawn, I dreamt about a light-blue snake slithering into the ground. It was tied to a yellowish pink waist cord. From the time I awakened I couldn't shake a strange sense of anticipation that something delightfully splendid would happen. After finishing the morning's cleaning, I quietly stared into the mirror at my pale, swollen face, weathered and worn. I heaved a long sigh. I wanted to crawl into a hole in the wall. Breakfast was likely to be murky miso soup and leftover rice. I would have preferred Chinese noodles. Gazing at my own listless, unadorned face, I suddenly became irritated, and tried smearing on some bright red lips. I wondered what he was doing. I tried to grab hold of that broken cord, but he remained motionless like a row of trees in the landscape. . . . Maybe I was having a nervous breakdown? I was afraid to carry several plates at once.

I watched a crowd of female students kick the mound of purifying salt that was by the entrance, just under the short noren curtain. The mountain suddenly crumbled and the salt scattered. It was exactly two weeks since I had come to this shop. I had earned quite a bit. I had two co-workers. Ohatsu was unsophisticated, just as her name, "new," implied. She was truly a cute girl who looked good with her hair swept up in the "butterfly."

"I was born in Yotsuya. But when I was twelve, an older man kidnapped me and took me away to Manchuria. Pretty soon after that I was sold to a geisha house, so I quickly forgot what that man looked like. . . . I used to slide back and forth on a wide slippery hallway with a girl named Momochiyo. It was shiny like a mirror. When theater troupes would come from back home, I used to throw a blanket over my head, put on galoshes, and go see them. When the ground froze, you could walk just wearing geta. When you came out of the bath, it was real funny to see the hairs on your head freeze straight up. I was there about six years, but got a newspaper man in Manchuria to bring me back home."

After the customers had drunk, eaten, and left, winsome petite Ohatsu talked candidly as she traced letters on the table with spilled sake. The other girl, Okimi, who had started work there one day before me, was tall, motherly, and good-natured. Despite its location at the exit of the red-light district, this shop was surprisingly quiet. I was able to become friends with the other waitresses right away. No matter how ill-natured or hard-boiled they might be at first, no matter how guarded and without the least inclination to be friendly or altruistic, at some point women working in a place like this open up to reveal their true selves. They suddenly lower this guard, and, as if they'd been fast friends for years, they're closer than sisters. When the customers had gone, we would often curl up like snails in a circle and talk.

November

The sky was overcast. I smelled the fragrance of a flower from my youth as I sat quietly across from Kimi. In the evening, I returned from the bathhouse along the streetcar line. Mizuno, a perpetually inebriated university student, was having his usual libations. This time Ohatsu was pouring the sake for him.

"He says he finally saw you naked!" Ohatsu announced with a laugh. She peered over the mirror to see my face as I inserted combs into both sides of my traditional coiffure.

"Mizuno came and asked about you just after you went off to the bath. So I told him where you had gone."

The drunk university student waved his hand in feeble protest, and then tapped his head.

"That's a lie!"

"What! But that's what you just said! Mizuno, I wondered why you hurried off to the boulevard. When you came back, you said you'd opened the door to the women's side. Then the bathhouse attendant told him it was the women's side, but he said he thought it was the hospital and didn't move. You had just gotten naked, he said. Mizuno's really ecstatic about it. . . ."

"Really! How shameless!" I savagely applied some rouge.

"Are you mad at me? Please forgive me!" The university student put his suppliant hands together, pleading. What's he talking about? If he really wants to see me naked, I'll get stark naked out in the sunlight and show him! I wanted to scold him roundly. All evening it weighed on me. I cracked open more than a half dozen eggs, each time with a good whack against the table.

November

The aroma of grilling saury hailed the autumn season. Again today, when evening fell, the smell of saury fish escaped the licensed quarters. The prostitutes probably had scales floating around their insides from their daily diet of saury fish. The evening mist was white. Thin shadows of the light poles stretched out like needles. I ducked under the noren curtains in the open doorway, and once outside gazed at the moving streetcars. I became suddenly envious of the passengers, and felt as if I would cry. I was truly tired of this living. Working at a place like this had hardened me so much that I wanted to steal something. I wanted to become a female warrior.

Young woman, why do you weep?

I yearn for a cold-hearted man. . .

Everybody and anybody was laughing at me.

"Try drinking ten glasses of King of Kings, I'll bet you ten yen you can't!"

An easy-going man from who knows where laid an iridescent ten yen note on the table. His pomaded hair glistened horribly.

"That's nothing." I downed ten glasses of that whiskey with feigned indifference under the white light of the bar. The man with the glistening head stared at me in amazement. Then laughing, unwilling to admit defeat, he disappeared outside. Only the bar owner was happy. " You know, that young woman drank ten King of Kings at one yen a glass. . . ."

I felt like heaving it all up. My eyes were aflame. *I despised everyone.* Ah, I was an unchaste woman. Should I show you a naked dance, you refined people? You would knit your brows, preferring the stars, the moon, and the flowers! I shuddered merely at the thought of roughing it in the wilds on my own. But having a man support me would be ten times harder. Even my friends laughed at me derisively.

> If you listen to singing, oh it's Umekawa.
> You can throw troubles away for a time,
> Here and there love abounds,
> That's Chūbei's dream tale.[9]

Reciting this poem put me in a good mood as I opened the window and inhaled the evening mist. To think that I'd get drunk on ten glasses of such cheap watered-down whiskey. . . Ah, please raise your eyes to the brilliant rainbow under the mantle of the evening sky.

"Are you okay? It doesn't hurt, does it, your chest, or your heart?" Okimi questioned me wide-eyed, then got her best grip on me and led me upstairs.

9. One verse of the poem "Kasa no uchi" (Under the umbrella) from the poetic anthology *Wakana shū* (Young herbs, 1897) by Shimazaki Tōson (1872–1943). It refers to the story of Umekawa and Chūbei, from the play *Meido no hikyaku* (Courier of Hades) by Chikamatsu Monzaemon (1653–1724).

How sweet are the young
In the innocence of first love.
You two who go hand in hand,
Why are you hiding?[10]

This was one of my favorite poems. Bewitched, drowning in tears, my body and soul began fleeing to the ends of the earth. Then around the time the clock unwound, those cheeky *kowairo* children, trained to spout poetic passages like "White fish in the misty moonlight" came begging.[11] "Hey, mister! Anything you please . . . hey, mister, anything you can spare. . . ."

Go ahead and throw out your washed-out and disabled actors. The children's pitiful faces, pasted with thick white dried-up makeup, made me want to seek comfort in someone's arms.

November

The boss got bent out of shape if I ate all my meals in the kitchen, but I hated having the customers buy me food. Even though the shop closed at two, when those on their way home from the pleasure quarter crowded the place, the boss pretended not to notice the time up until dawn. He didn't even try to take down the noren curtain in the open doorway to signal closing time. The jarring clip-clop from wooden geta on the concrete floor gave me chills and made my blood run cold. The smell of sour sake was disgustingly rank.

"I've had it. . . ."

Ohatsu stood blankly, wringing her beer-soaked kimono sleeve.

"Give me a beer!"

It was already past four, and I heard a rooster's familiar crow from far off. Toward the end of the night, as the train whistle blew from Shinjuku station, it was my turn to wait on a flashy latecomer.

"Beer!"

Since there was nothing else I could do, I opened a bottle and filled a glass. The man sulked, just staring up at the ceiling, and then tossed off the beer, feigning indignation. "What! Ebisu beer? I can't stand the stuff." With that parting shot, he left for the misty pavement, just like that, without paying. Stunned at first, I suddenly grew angry and rushed

10. One verse of "Kusa makua" (Grass pillow) from Shimazaki Tōson's *Young Herbs* (1897).
11. *Kowairo* were itinerant bards who recited dialogue from popular plays. This line is from the play *Sannin kichiza kuruiwa no hatsugai* by Kawatake Mokuami (1816–1893).

off after him, taking the half-empty beer bottle with me. Just as he was about to turn at the bank, I hurled the bottle with a vengeance at his black shadow.

"If you want beer, I'll give you some."

The bottle smashed to smithereens, shooting up a spray.

"Hey!"

"You fool!"

"Watch it. I'm an Anarchist!"

"What, such people really exist? I don't believe it! What a puny terrorist."

Okimi was worried and ran after me. As several taxis pulled up, the pathetic anarchist quickly ducked into the alley. I felt like quitting this line of work . . . but then, the letter from my stepfather had arrived from Hokkaido. He said he didn't have the fare for a trip home now. The gist of the long letter was that he wanted me to send whatever little I could spare. I was determined to send something, maybe even forty or fifty yen. He couldn't bear the cold. When I had saved a little, I would go up to Hokkaido too. I wondered if, together with my parents, I couldn't try my hand again at peddling rather than continue as I was. I spied Ohatsu when I poked my head into an oden stall. She had turned off the light in the stall, skewered dumplings onto chopsticks, and was gulping rice and tea with all her might. To calm my nerves after all the excitement, I had Okimi undo my apron and heat up a bottle of sake to go with the oden.

December

Asakusa was a great place.

It was always a great place no matter the occasion. I was a wandering Kachusha twirling around in this quickly flashing light. Having gone without face cream for ages, my skin had become hard and brittle as crockery. Nobody frightened me, drunk as I was on cheap sake. Behold, one inebriated woman. Once drunk, I turned maudlin. The absurdity of this feeling, as if my numb hands and feet would fall off. . . . If I didn't drink sake, the world would be too crazy for me to pass through without cracking up. He said he had another woman. What in the world was that supposed to mean? I wanted to grieve, but the sake said it would have nothing more to do with worldly matters. The street lights suddenly went out. I stared at ripped, distorted faces plastered on the wall of the movie house. The band in the movie house sounded ethereal, as if it were emanating from a dream. Maybe I was too immature. I despised myself. In my anger, I resolved to start writing again tomorrow.

Growing old quickly . . . was not so bad after all. Dead drunk on sake, I had a momentary sober reflection. I would just tie on a kerchief like a monkey in a street show and go for a stroll.

Asakusa was a good place to drink. It was a good place even when you were sober. Sweet sake for five sen a cup, sweet bean soup for five sen, a skewer of grilled chicken for two sen, what a feast! And you didn't have to mind your manners. I gazed at the banners blowing in the wind over the theater. I saw the name of the man who once loved me. I could hear him still ridiculing me, in that same old voice of his. So long, everybody! It was the coldest winter sky I'd seen in many years. Wouldn't you know it, my shawl was only a cheap synthetic blend. The wind stealthily penetrated through to my skin as if someone were laying an icy hand on my shoulder.

December

There was no greater consolation for a girl who didn't like to be awake alone than to smoke a cigarette in bed first thing in the morning. Blowing wavering rings, I found the wafting purple smoke pleasurable. As I reclined, basking in the sun . . . I prayed for something good to happen today. Worn-out kimonos of various shades lay where they had been dropped, cluttering the tiny three-mat room. Half awake, like a sunning baby turtle, a lone woman alone in a comfy spot. Rather than find a troublesome job at a cafe or sukiyaki restaurant, I wondered whether I should set up my own food stall and make oden. Let them laugh, let them mock me, with my kimono tucked up out of the way, exposing my red slip like a monkey's ass! I'd like to try setting up a stall and become my own boss this year. My spirits soared at the thought of each ingredient: kon'nyaku, ganmodoki, chikuwa, and dumplings. You dipped them in burning hot mustard and ate them with bright green spinach in soy sauce and sake. I savored each morsel. When I reached a certain point, I fell back to reality. Though they might be silly, these daydreams brought me childish delight.

I couldn't mooch off my poverty-stricken parents. After working so many odd jobs, what could I buy but a couple of books a month? Before I knew it, all my earnings would go to food and drink. Even though I was living a bare-bones existence in a three-mat tatami room, what savings I once had had been eaten away. When I was in a fix and the future became dark, I seriously entertained the idea of burglary. But I knew I'd be caught on my first try since I was so nearsighted. My absurd new career choice suddenly seemed hilarious. A self-mocking laugh echoed off the cold walls of the room. I wanted money. Then dark fantasies invaded my dreams, and I slept soundly until evening.

December

Okimi came to get me. With renewed hopes of finding good jobs, and armed with a small newspaper clipping. we boarded the National Railway for Yokohama. The bar where she had been working had gone downhill, and Okimi had quit at the same time as I had quit my job. She had returned home to her husband in Itabashi in the northern part of Tokyo. He was more than thirty years her senior. When I had first gone to visit her house, I had mistaken him for Okimi's father. The chaos of the household with Okimi's children and stepmother around was a little hard to take. I didn't like to be bothered with such things. Okimi was quiet about her personal life and didn't especially like to talk about her family. It made my heart ache to listen to her stories when she did open up. We quietly alighted from the train, and went out to the bluff, gazing at the blue sea all the while.

"It's been a long time since I've seen the ocean. . . ."

"It's cold, but the sea's so nice. . . ."

"Yes, like a lover. I feel like stripping and jumping right in. It's like the color blue is melting right there in front of us."

"You're right! It's scary. . . ."

Two Westerners with neckties flapping in the wind were sitting on the steps of the pier, staring at the rough waves.

"The hotel's over there!"

What Okimi's quick eyes had discovered was a small drinking establishment—whose ad had billed itself as a hotel—that looked like a blind for hunting ducks. Stained blankets aired in the sun, draped from the crooked windows of the second floor.

"So this is it. . . ."

"Let's go home!"

A winsome girl in a vermilion kimono was petting a black dog on the porch of the hotel, all the while laughing shrilly to herself.

"How disappointing. . . ."

We stared silently at the vast cold ocean before us. I wanted to become a bird. I thought about how nice it would be to travel, unencumbered, with nothing but the smallest of bags. Kimi's traditionally styled hair was blown askew by the wind, as poignant a sight as a willow tree on a snowy day.

December X

A white sky, the sound of the wind,
Such a wonderfully cold winter sea!
The ocean so blue arouses you from sleep.

A crazy man may whirl like a dervish,
But it's straight ahead to Shikoku.

Blankets are twenty sen, sweets ten.
The third-class passenger room is like a pan of loaches
Brought to a deadly boil.

With sprays of water sprinkling like rain,
Gazing upon the overarching white sky,
I clutched a purse containing eleven sen.

Ah, I'd like to smoke a good cigarette.
"Hey!" I shout,
But you see the wind swept it away.

In the vast tumbling sky,
The face of the man who gave me a hard time
Appeared, large, gigantic.
Ah, ours is a solitary journey after all.

Far off, the sound of the steamship whistle pierced me to the core. Here and there, small lead-gray ocean eddies disappeared one by one. The cold moaning December wind blew, trying to plaster my tangled butterfly tresses onto my cheeks. Inserting both hands into the underarm openings at the sides of my kimono, I gently pressed against my soft breasts. My cold nipples elicited unintended bittersweet emotions. I had lost at everything. Removing myself far away from Tokyo, racing above the sea, I saw hazy faces of lovers peeping through the gaps in the clouds.

Yesterday's blue sky had made me nostalgic, so I had forced myself to set off for my mother's home. This morning I was already on a ship in the open sea off Naruto.

"Passengers! How about breakfast!"

On the empty deck at daybreak, it was not surprising when my scattered daydreams turned their back on those small towns of my youth and scurried off to the capital. Since travel was my home, there was no special need to amass anecdotes of success for the home crowd. Yet I was full of remorse. I sat upon my blanket in the dark cellar-like third-class cabin. Unappetizing stewed seaweed, miso soup, and the like were lined up on the peeling lacquer of a small, low vermilion table. I mingled with the groups of touring actors, temple pilgrims off to Shikoku, and fishermen's wives with children in tow. Under the dim lantern light, I felt the poignancy of travel.

"Where're you from?" asked some of the old women, since I had my hair up in the more urban butterfly style. "Where're you off to?" inquired the young men. A young mother lying next to her two-year-old softly sang a lullaby I had heard before in my travels.

> Hush-a-bye little one,
> Go to sleep and
> Wake up early in the morning.
> The beach wind tonight will give you such a chill,
> So sleep early in the evening.

Freely breathing the exhilarating air of such a refreshing sea made it great to be alive, after all. It was far better than exhaustion in a corner of that impure city.

December

I opened the sooty canary-yellow paper windows and stared mesmerized at the swirling snow, soon to melt as it hit the ground.

"Mama! The snow's really early this year, isn't it."

"Uh huh."

"Papa must be having it rough because of the cold."

"I've come too far north, and the business isn't going like I planned, so I'll be back in Shikoku in the spring," he had written in a recent letter. It had been more than four months since he had gone off to Hokkaido. It had gotten really cold here, too. The aroma of boiling noodle soup stock pervaded the town of Tokushima in winter. The cascading river that ran through the town's rows of low buildings spewed a light vaporous mist. As the number of hotel guests diminished, my mother was reluctant to light the lanterns in front of her shop.

"When it's cold, nobody travels, you know. . . ."

Lacking real roots, my parents had recently settled in Tokushima. I had helped them open a weather-beaten inn amid the lovely women and beautiful water of the city. I was excited by my first seasons in Tokushima when I was younger, but now this run-down inn earned nothing but a little extra pocket change for my mother. I turned over shy love letters and large photographs of big, sweeping hair I had found in the depths of a worn chest of drawers. Sweet, ancient memories gradually flooded back. Living in Tokyo can wear out even someone like me. I had left my parents behind, but now yearned to return to their home. I found memories in the yellow noodles of Nagasaki, the Senkoji cherry blossoms of Onomichi, and the song of Joga Island I had learned at Niyu River. Several of my early, awkward sketches had faded brown. When they had appeared out of the storage room, it was as if I was viewing myself from a completely different planet. I heard a duet of a four-stringed "pipa" and a plaintively sung lonesome lament while I warmed myself at the kotatsu at night. The music resonated beyond their room at the inn. Outside, the sleet fell softly.

December

Beach-combing weather had finally arrived. The ballad-singing couple who had been staying at the inn for a few days set out early in the morning, each with a black muffler flung around the neck. My mother and I stayed behind, grilling sardines in the large sooty kitchen. I was already bored with the country.

"You know, enough is enough. How about giving up, leaving Tokyo, and settling down here? There's somebody who says he'd like to marry you. . . ."

"Really? What kind of person is he?"

"His family runs a sembei cracker store near Shogoin Temple in Kyoto, and he's in line to take over the family business. But now he's here working for the city hall. . . . He's a good man."

". . . ."

"What do you think?"

"I wonder if I shouldn't meet him. It sounds like fun. . . ."

It was all so childishly delightful. So I was to become a country maiden, my innocent face ablush as I offered up tea. My heart began to leap like a virgin's as I raised and lowered the bucket in the well. I felt like a voracious caterpillar gobbling passion. Or like a leech sucking all the blood out of a man. With the cold weather, a man's skin would be as welcome as a coverlet.

I would return to Tokyo. During my evening walk my feet took me unconsciously in the direction of the station road. As I read the station timetable I couldn't stop the tears from streaming down my cheeks.

December

He stepped up into the parlor after untying his red shoes. I felt ill. I frowned as I looked him directly in the face.

"How old are you?" I asked.

"Who, me? Twenty-two."

"Hmm . . . then I'm older."

His thick eyebrows and thick lips were somehow familiar, but I couldn't place him. Suddenly, I brightened and felt like whistling.

There was a good moon that night. The stars twinkled at the top of the sky.

"Shall I see you off part way. . . ?"

Strangely enough, he seemed the picture of composure. We passed under a banner that someone had forgotten to take in. When we came out onto the brightly moonlit street I was able momentarily to breathe a loud sigh of relief. We covered one block, then two, but we both kept silent. I don't know why the river saddened me the way it did. I wanted to start a fire and burn up all men. Maybe I would fall in love with Buddha. Buddha to whom we pray—"Namu amidabutsu"—had unusually erotic eyes, and had been stealing into my dreams lately.

"Well then, good-bye. You get yourself a good wife now."

"What?"

Darling man, you country people were simple and good. Whether he understood my words or not, he went back to the next town dragging the long shadow of the moon behind him. Tomorrow for certain I resolved to pack my bags and set out on a trip. . . . It had been a long time since I had looked at the paper oil lantern in front of the inn. The fact that my mother was so dear to me suddenly struck home. I stared at the lantern, which listed like an owl's eye.

"Boy, it's cold. Do you feel like drinking some sake?"

Sitting face to face with my mother in the living room, I felt pretty good after one large glass of sake. I realized how wonderful it was to have family, to be able to gaze on my mother's face with uninterrupted tranquillity. To leave my mother behind again under this sooty ceiling where the mice run rampant filled me with remorse.

"I really don't like his type."

"But he seemed so good-natured. . . ."

It was a lonesome comedy. I decided to write a bunch of letters that would make all my Tokyo friends miss me.

January

The pure white sea
That day I was Tokyo bound,
Filling a basket full of the first green tangerines,
I boarded the vessel *Tenjin* from the shores of Shikoku.

Though the seas were fretfully rough,
The skies sparkled mirrorlike.
The light from the carrot-shaped lighthouse was so red it pierced my eyes.
To throw away with no regrets
Sorrow on the island,
I bear the cold briny wind.

Watching the sailing boats in the distance,
The white sea of January and
The fragrance of the first tangerines
Made me on that day as disconsolate as a woman about to be sold.

January

A dark snowy sky. Lined up on the morning tray were white miso soup, kōya dōfu, and black beans. Everything seemed somewhat watered down. *I had nothing but sorrowful memories of Tokyo.* I suddenly considered the possibility of living in Kyoto or Osaka. . . . From the second floor of the cheap inn Tenbōzan, I sprawled out absent-mindedly, listening to the incessant caterwauling of the cats outside. Why was it so difficult to be alive? My body and soul alike were already worn out. The bedding reeked of the sea, dank and dirty, like the entrails of a fish. The wind beat against the sea, and the sea replied with the deafening crash of the waves.

I was a shell of a woman. Without the means to go on living, there was no beauty in life. All I had left was my drive. When bored, I would bend one knee up and twirl in a circle like a crane. My eyes, grown unaccustomed to reading, just kept skipping over the sign on the wall listing the rates, which started at one yen a night.

Snow began to fall from evening. *I traveled alone, no matter what direction I chose.* I even wondered if I should retrace my steps back to my mother on Shikoku. I was in a terribly lonely inn. *This was the kind of night that made me want to stay put and enjoy myself.*

To soothe my old wounds,
We steal a cup of sake, just you and me,
Under the mantle of love.

I scribbled off this haiku that I learned long ago. I gazed at the postcard in my hand and recalled my many friends in Tokyo. Each was self-preoccupied.

The train whistle blew. I slid open the window and looked out over the quiet bay. Several boats lay asleep, blue lights blazing. You and me, we're vagabonds. Snow falls. Suddenly I yearned for my faraway first love. I have not thought of him for a long time. It has been this kind of evening. He was singing "Rain at Joga Island" as well as "Silent Bell." The sea off Onomichi did not have waves as rough. Under the cape covering us both, we gazed into each other's eyes by the light of a match. Our parting came all too quickly. "Oh woman, how far you have fallen!" was the last I heard from you, now already seven years ago. You used to discuss Picasso's paintings and admire Kaita's poems.[12] I hit my head brusquely with my hands until it hurt. I sat down in a daze. I continued whistling steadily. The strains of a samisen sounded from somewhere around me.

January

Well! Empty-handed, I had to start all over again. Exiting through the gate of the city employment agency, I boarded the train bound for Tenma in Osaka. I had been directed to a blanket wholesaler and, as a graduate of a girl's high school, I was to be an office worker. The train raced by overcast streets. I considered Osaka an interesting place, too. It would probably be good to work somewhere where no one knew me. The withered willow trees along the river banks swayed gracefully at the waist in the strong wind.

The blanket wholesaler's store was relatively large. With a wide frontage and a deep interior, it was as dark as a seashell. The seven or eight sickly, pale-faced shop assistants scurried about. There was an extremely long hallway. I sat facing the elderly female head of the house in the neat sitting room arranged to suit Osaka tastes. Everything shone from being so well kept.

"Why did you come here from Tokyo?"

Having fabricated my permanent address as Tokyo, I was slightly at a loss as to what I should say.

"Because my older sister is here. . . ."

Now that I had gone and said this, I felt my usual resignation. It was just a matter of time until I would be turned away. The maid brought in a beautiful plate of sweets and tea. It had been a long time since I had drunk good tea, and longer since I had eaten such sweets. *So there are still hospitable households in the world.*

"Ichirō," the female head of the house called out gently. From the next room entered a quiet and composed man in his mid-twenties, probably her son, his back as straight as a rod.

"She's here. . . ."

The young master, his features as delicate as an actor's, looked at me with sparkling eyes.

I felt sure I had made the trip out here only to humiliate myself. I was convinced my hands and feet were going numb. This world was too far removed from mine. I wanted to flee. When I returned to Tenbōzan, the harbor inn, the sun had already set. Many ships were in.

"Why are you dawdling? Come quickly. I have an interesting job,"

12. Murayama Kaita. See appendix B.

Okimi had written on her postcard from Tokyo. No matter how desperate her straits, she's always in good spirits. Reading her card revived me.

January

I had thought it wasn't going to happen, but I finally went to work in the blanket wholesaler's shop.

I moved out of the cheap Tenbōzan inn where I had stayed for five days. I still didn't feel any stability, with my fate blown by the wind. I went to live in the blanket shop, like a puppy who has just found a new home.

Even at noon, the gaslights in the back rooms were lit and hissing. As I sat in the large office, I addressed many envelopes and often had inexplicable daydreams. I would hit my face each time I made a mess of things. When I put both hands under the blue gaslight, each fingernail turned yellow, and my ten fingers looked as transparent as silkworms. I seemed to have become a specter. At three, someone would bring tea and a pile of cinnamon crackers out to the shop. All told, there were nine assistants, six of them shop boys. Since they usually went out on errands, I didn't yet know who was who. There were only two maids, Okuni, the kitchen help, and Oito, the parlor maid. Oito, like a lady-in-waiting with an impenetrable expression, appeared to be asleep. Kansai women had a gentle mien, and I couldn't at all tell what they were thinking.

"Coming from such a distance, you probably think this place is boring, don't you?"

Tilting her tightened hairstyle, one characteristic of unmarried young women, Oito pulled the weft tightly as she wove an exquisite cloth pattern, the likes of which I had never seen. Oito had told me that the young master, Ichirō, had a wife who was almost nineteen. She was at the other house in Ichioka for the birth of a child, and the house was silent as the grave.

At eight o'clock at night the main door was already closed, and the nine assistants had all disappeared one by one for the night. I stretched both legs out gingerly under the stiffly starched futon and gazed up at the ceiling, becoming all too aware of how hopeless my situation was. Oito and Okuni's box-shaped black pillows were lined up at the head of their futon, just like high geta. Oito had thrown her long red kimono slip over her quilt. I kept eyeing that slip as if I were a man. The two young women were splashing around silently in the remaining bathwater. I wanted to touch Oito's beautiful white downy hands. Aroused, overwhelmed, I was in love with Oito in her red kimono slip. The silent woman gave off a gentle fragrance like a flower. I closed my tear-blurred eyes and turned away from the brightly lit lantern.

January

I had become accustomed by now to the daily breakfast of rice porridge with sweet potatoes, but still longed for the red miso soup of Tokyo. It was so fine, cooked with thinly sliced mountain potatoes and cabbage. I liked to peel off and savor salted salmon flake by flake. I wanted to eat a salty delicacy together with delicious tea over rice. The Osaka sun, like the round cut end of a long radish, was all I could see. My daydreams all seemed a little childish to me while I worked.

In winter I ran into trouble with persistent frostbite on my toes. Every evening I would hide from the rest in the shadows of the high stacks of boxes and scratch my itching feet with all my might. My toes were flushed and puffed up, and I couldn't help wishing I could puncture them with a needle.

"Wow, you've really got a case of frostbite there," Kenkichi, the head clerk, peered over with amazement. "If it's frostbite, you should massage it with a lit pipe."

He enthusiastically popped open a tobacco can and filled the pipe. After giving it a number of puffs, he massaged my red blistering toes with the head of the long metal pipe. You can find kindness even among people who speak of nothing but accounts.

February

"You were born under the sign of gold, but it's the gold of the gold-leaf screen, so you've got to go for delicate work," my mother used to tell me.

I've gotten tired of this type of refined work. Easily bored, quickly exhausted, and timid, I despised my inability to make friends. *I wanted to cry and vent my impatience somewhere alone.*

I enjoyed reading my copy of Oscar Wilde's De Profundis.

> I was caught up by the mob jeering in the gray November rain. Tears are a part of daily experience for people in jail. The day that people in jail don't cry is when their heart has hardened, not when they're happy.

It pained my heart to see such words. What friends? What family? What neighbors? I even yearned for someone who would be concerned enough to jeer at me. There may also be a blessing in Oito's love. I could see many stars scattered across the sky at night as I soaked in the bath and stared out the ceiling window. I gazed up at the stars unmoving, oblivious, as if dredging up a distant memory.

My heart was worn out in inverse proportion to my youthful body. I extended my reddened arms and stretched out in the bath. I suddenly felt feminine and decided then and there to get married.

I could smell the wedding makeup. I trimmed my eyebrows and painted my lips thickly, trying to attach an innocent face to the body reflected in the mirror attached to the pillar. I next wanted to tie up my hair with a mother-of-pearl comb and a peach-colored chignon band.

"Frailty, thy name is woman." After all, who was the one sullied by the world? Was there no handsome groom. . . ? Should I sing a sweet old song from Provence? With a smoldering heart, I turned and rolled through the water like a minnow in a bucket.

February

The streets were filled with the flapping red flags signifying spring sales.

After I had received a letter from Onatsu, a high school friend, I wanted to throw everything over and head off to Kyoto.

"You've probably had a hard time of it . . ." Not at all, I responded while reading her letter. You don't have to be a man to appreciate a letter from a nice girl. There was a vaguely pleasant childlike scent to it. I had graduated with her. During the last eight years, there had to have been hundreds of miles separating the two of us, but here was a splendid letter, a real tearjerker. She had opted not to marry and instead was the dutiful daughter helping her father with his traditional Japanese-style painting. I felt like going to see her, if even for a short time, to talk things over with this dear woman.

I went to Kyoto on my one day off from work in a cold blowing wind. I arrived at the station in the early evening. Onatsu had come to meet my train. Her pale face was buried in a black fluffy shawl.

"You remembered me?"

"Of course."

We silently gripped each other's cold hands.

Onatsu presented a strange sight. She was dressed completely in black, like a widow. Only her lips signaled to me.

They were wonderful lips, like the petals of a camellia flower. Securely holding hands, we walked childlike down the misty streets of Kyoto, confiding in each other whatever came to mind. The Kyōgoku area had not changed. Beautiful paper envelopes, which had previously enthralled us, were displayed in the window of a familiar shop. We discovered a noodle shop called Kikusui in a side alley during our leisurely stroll of the area. We hadn't looked at each other by such bright lantern light for some time. I was poor and on my own, and, of course, Onatsu didn't get much spending money from her father. After comparing the meager resources in our purses, we ate simply, fried tofu on noodles in broth. But carefree, like students again, we loosened our obi sashes and ordered seconds.

"There's no one who moves as much as you, you know. You're the only one who messes up my address book."

Onatsu gazed at me with her big black unblinking eyes. *I want someone to take care of me.*

We walked together just like lovers by the fountain at Maruyama park.

"Mount Toribe in autumn was great, wasn't it? With the fallen leaves . . . remember when the two of us visited the graves of Oshun and Denbei?"

"Shall we go there again?"

"That's the kind of thing that gets you in trouble." Onatsu gave me a startled, guarded look.

Kyoto is a fine town. A nightbird cried out from the trees across the way. The streets were filled with evening mist.

There was a small police station with a red light lit across from Onatsu's house in Shimogamo. Ducking under the hanging stone lantern at the front gate, we quietly went upstairs. The slowly tolling bell of a faraway temple echoed in the room.

"Instead of spinning stories, let's be quiet. . . ." Onatsu went downstairs to get some charcoal, and I leaned out the window, yawning widely.

July

A lone hilltop pine
At its base
I silently gaze skyward.

In the pure pale blue sky, the aged bough
Sparkles like pins.
Oh, how difficult it is to live,
To survive.

Then,
Drawing my ragged sleeves across my chest,
I tap the trunk of the pine
With that unguarded innocence beloved
From days of my childhood.

A sadness fell over me. I wandered aimlessly in the dark green stand of trees.

It had been a long time since I had worked as a waitress. I wore only light touches of makeup. I thought of my home as I twirled my parasol. That old pine on the hill haunted my memories.

When I returned to the room my lover was renting, I saw he had acquired several large bookcases. Here he was, making me, his beloved, work as a cafe waitress, while he bought such extravagances for himself. As always, I placed twenty yen under his writing paper. Completely at home and indulging in the luxury of the solitary moment, I looked in his closet for dirty clothes.

"Excuse me, a letter's just come," said the maid as she handed it to me. The envelope was fairly thick, with a six-sen stamp. It was from a woman. I bit my nails uneasily, and my heart pounded anxiously. Chiding myself for my stupidity, I found a substantial pile of this woman's letters hidden in the corner of the closet.

"I prefer the hot springs."

"From your Sawako."

"Ever since staying that night, I have. . . ."

I stood up unsteadily, chilled by the cloyingly sweet letters.

The letter about the hot springs said, "I will get some money ready, but please get some yourself." I wanted to fling it across the room. I left after pocketing the twenty yen that I had placed under the writing paper.

Wasn't he the one to berate me for my insensitivity whenever he saw me? Didn't he write all those poems and short stories for magazines just to slander me? And wasn't I reduced to singing to all the bar patrons, "For you alone I threw away myself and the world. . . ." just to support that morose, half-crazed, tubercular man? Walking down the streets of Wakamatsu with the cool evening wind on me, I did not feel like returning to the cafe in Shinjuku. *Now I knew why there was only a fraction of the money left.*

"Won't you go with me to the hot springs?"

That night I got so completely drunk Toki-chan pitied my sorry state.

July

"Every dark cloud has a silver lining," read his letter of apology.

Night.

Toki-chan's mother came to the back door of the cafe. *I lent Toki-chan five yen.* Everything in this flavorless world is as insubstantial as chewing gum, and tastes like cigarette butts. Maybe I should save my money and go see my mother. On my way to the kitchen I swiped some whiskey and drank it.

July

I woke feeling displaced, like a fish out of water. Four soundly sleeping women were a mass of thick white goo. I smoked a cigarette and looked at Toki-chan's arm flung out above the bed. She was still seventeen and had light, pink-colored skin.

Her mother ran a shaved-ice shop in Zoshiki. Since her dad had gotten sick, every few days she came to visit Toki-chan at the back door to get money. Gazing through uncurtained windows, I felt almost as if I were advertising myself like the red flag of the Chinese restaurant, flapping in the wind. When I worked in a cafe, the illusions I held about men disappeared into smoke. It seemed as though the value of things dropped, as if I were buying in bulk at a discount. Since I didn't need to earn money for that man any more, I contemplated going off to feel the salty wind of my youth. He was really such a sorry creature.

It was a muddy road.
Like a broken-down car, I stood still.
This time for sure I'll sell myself and make money.
I wanted to please everyone.
Hadn't I returned to Tokyo this morning after such a long journey?

No matter where I look there is no one to buy me.
"If I could watch a film and eat a hearty dinner of grilled eel over rice, then I wouldn't mind dying."
Recalling the words he spoke this morning,
I wept bitterly.

My man stays in a rooming house.
If I lived with him, the rent would go up.
Like a pig I smell my way
Walking from cafe to cafe.

Love or family or society or a husband,
With my brain beginning to rot
All appear so far away.

Not having enough courage to call out,
I don't even have the strength to die.
Whatever happened to the frisky kitten *Otekusan* toying at my hem?
I considered casing the clock shop show window like a female burglar.
There are only impostors loitering about.

They say that drinking horse piss will cure tuberculosis.
What would it be like,
To have my sick man drink it?
To go through with a lover's double suicide?
Money, money, money is indispensable!
They say that the wheel of fortune may come your way, but
I work and work and it doesn't come round.

How about a miracle round about now?
Isn't it somehow, some way possible?
Where does the money I work for run off to?

And in the end I become a coldhearted person,
The pale shadow of a woman.
Until the day I die I will only remain a bar hostess or a maid, amid the dregs of society.
Do I have to work myself to death?
A man prejudiced by disease
Calls me a red pig.

Just try to attack me with arrows and guns.
In front of those disgusting men and women,
I'll show you Miss Fumiko's guts.

You were so hard on me that I wrote this poem for a magazine to get even with you. I was a big fool. I had the good faith to think that you would be irritated at how easily I could make money in this trade, and object to our way of life. I had enough to go back to my mother's, so I took the train. The spray of the fast ship would have been quite nice, too. The blue sea would whiz along by the cinnabar color of the carrot-shaped lighthouse. But I took the night train. With no one to see me off, and with a funereal air, I boarded the Tōkaidō line as I had done countless times before whenever things had gone wrong.

July

"Maybe I'll get down at Kobe. I bet there's some interesting work there. . . ," I thought to myself.

The third-class train car bound for Akashi was full of people getting off at Kobe. I also took down my wicker basket, carefully put away the leftovers from my box lunch, and alighted at Kobe station with some trepidation.

"If I can't get work again and eat, it'll be just as Hinkelmann said, it's the dirty world's fault."

The sun beat down. But I couldn't buy any ice cream or shaved ice. I felt refreshed after washing my face at the sink on the station platform. I drank a bellyful of lukewarm water. The dirty yellowed mirror reflected my sorry state. So, give it your best shot, I told my reflection. I tucked my layover ticket in a safe place, and, without any particular destination, ambled toward Kusunoki Park.[13]

One ratty basket.

A broken parasol.

A woman paler than cigarette ash.

This is all combat preparation for my desperate fight.

In the dusty precincts of the shrine to General Kusunoki there were the usual pigeons and picture-postcard stand. I seated myself on the stone edge of the dry hexagonal fountain and invited the wind with my parasol. I gazed up at the clear blue sky. The bright sun exposed everything limply.

How many years would it be now—maybe it was when I was about fifteen. I was a maid at a music shop run by a Turk. I looked after his two-year-old girl, Nina. After putting her in the baby carriage with the black rubber wheels and high wainscoting, I would walk in the direction of the American pier. The pigeons would come close to my feet. *Men should be born pigeons.* I cried when I thought of my disappointments in Tokyo.

Even with the passing of a lifetime, exactly when would I be able to send several thousand yen, several hundred yen, or several dozen yen to my mother? When would I be able to console my poor stepfather? He was still supporting my mother through peddling, and had tried his best to take good care of me. Yet I couldn't do anything successfully. My head hurt when I thought about it.

"Hey, you there! Aren't you getting hot? Why don't you come in here?" yelled an old woman. She sold beans for pigeon feed from her hovel of a shop next to the fountain. Her friendly smile and kindness merited a reward. Fearful of hitting my head, I entered the shop encased in rush mats. Just as I imagined, it was like a pigsty. I placed my basket on my lap. The hut reeked of beans, but still it was cool. Swollen soybeans were soaking in an oil can. Amulets and hard pieces of seaweed lay under the glass covers of two boxes. All the goods were covered with dust.

"Ma'am, please give me a plate of those beans."

As I put down my five-sen coin, the shop woman's wrinkled hand brushed mine aside.

"Forget the coin."

In response to my asking, she told me she was seventy-six. She was just like a once-elegant doll, moth-eaten and forgotten.

"Is Tokyo all recovered from the earthquake?" she asked.

13. Named for Kusunoki Masashige (1294–1336), a military commander of the Namboku Period.

The toothless woman's mouth looked like the tightened drawstring of a money pouch. She eyed me kindly.

"You have some too, ma'am."

When I removed the box lunch from my basket, she beamed. Her cheeks soon bulged with my omelet.

"It's pretty hot, isn't it, Granny." A frightening-looking old woman who appeared to be a friend of the shopkeeper crouched in front of the stall, her back still straight.

"You know of any work, anything at all? If I just hang around too much the neighborhood rep will get after me, so I was wondering. . . ."

"Well, you might try the inn over in Sakae. They were saying they had some bedding to be washed. It would probably pay up to twenty sen."

"That's great! If I wash two of them I could get something to eat. . . ."

These two women were willing to take on any job for the money. It saddened me to think that even at their age they had to worry about where the next meal came from.

Finally night fell. By the time the harbor lights began to go on, I still had no place to go. I had worn my sweat-drenched kimono since morning. Feeling totally powerless, I was at the point of bursting out in tears. I wouldn't let this get me down! Not even this! It felt as if something were pressing against my head. Damned if I was going to let this get to me, I whispered. Walking aimlessly from house to house, I was more of a sight than a traveling snake-oil salesman with his accordion.

I soon found the Tradesman's Inn the old woman had told me about, guided by its paper lanterns. It wouldn't make any difference wherever I went. I entered, and, embarrassed, asked the rates. The innkeeper glanced in her register and told me that it was sixty sen for the night. "Please come in." Her kind words reassured me. The blue-tinged walls of the three-mat room created a peculiar and lonely atmosphere.

When I inquired, the innkeeper said they were indeed looking for a kitchen maid if that kind of work interested me. On the road along the beach, I ran across groups of boatmen who clucked their tongues in an attempt to catch my attention. Boatmen were certainly unrestrained and transparent.

After changing into a light cotton kimono—I had been wearing my regular kimono since morning—I got directions from the innkeeper and set off for the local public bath. Travel may seem frighteningly unpredictable, but it really doesn't have to wear you down. Women bathers encircled the small bathtub like lotus flowers in a pond. They spoke strangely, in dialect. As I soaked my travels and cares away in the tub, my face revived. But when I anticipated the dreams I would have, surrounded by those blue walls, I became apprehensive.

July

The mosquito netting billowed up like a wave in the refreshing morning breeze, creating a truly pleasurable start to the day.

"The priest said he'd buy a hair ornament for his love . . . ." Below the window laborers passed by singing this Tosa ballad. Listening to the sentimental lyrics, I began to yearn for that harbor in Takamatsu, Shikoku, and the pristine places of my memories. I'd like to go back after all. . . . Nothing would come of my becoming a kitchen maid. With all my might I bounced the abusive language of the man I just left off the ceiling. Then I took a deep breath.

"Heigh-ho," the boatmen yelled at each other below the window. As a favor, the innkeeper arranged to sell my layover ticket for Okayama to a mothball broker for one yen. From Hyogo I decided to take the boat to Takamatsu.

I must gird myself and not let down my defenses no matter what the circumstances. After buying a box of the local crackers made in the shape of roof tiles, I bought a ticket for the Takamatsu boat at the run-down riverside inn. I would go back after all.

"Come home right away." My mother's enthusiasm telegraphed across the transparent blue sky. I was a selfish daughter. I would probably go through life irresponsibly, like a perpetual child. Wrapping bits of chipped ice in a dirty handkerchief, I pressed it against my throbbing cheek.

October

I stared blankly at the dirty map over the stairs. Above the map, a dreary autumn picture was lit up by the rays of the evening sun. My eyes blurred with inexplicable tears while I smoked a cigarette lying down. I was despondent. My poor mother probably thought about me day and night. She lived simply along on the beachfront in Shikoku. It covered only two or three inches at the top of the map. I could hear the downstairs clamor of women perhaps just returned from the public bath. My head hurt most peculiarly. I had time on my hands.

> If you're lonely, let's go resplendently into the sea.
> If we plunge in, the sea will constrict us.
> If we swim, we will be carried along.
> Stand firm with all your might, man on the rock.

The blueness of the autumn air brought to mind this poem by Hakushū. Is this all the joy that exists in this world? One, two. . . . I counted with my fingers and pondered the insignificance of my years.

"Oyumi! Please turn on the light," the innkeeper called out shrilly. So I was Oyumi. *Oyumi was a good name.* Then my mother was the jōruri puppet character Tokushima Jūrōbei from the island of Awaji.

The evening meal consisted of the usual stewed cuttlefish and kon'nyaku. Some other special catered trays pretentiously featured a deep-fried golden pork cutlet. My appetite was already on automatic. Without my chewing the cuttlefish, it would slide down my throat with a gulp of water. That evening, a fancy gramophone, the twenty-five-yen kind, played the popular children's ditty "Zuizui zukkoro bashi."[14] Tōko returned to the cafe after having been out and about since morning on her day off.

"It was so much fun. Four men were waiting for me in the Shinjuku station waiting room and I stiffed them all. . . ."

It was a common practice among waitresses to promise to spend their day off with a number of different male customers, have them all wait in the same place, and then snub them.

"I took my younger sister to see a movie. It came out of my pocket, so I'm flat broke. I can't even pay for a bath until I save up some more money."

After she put on her dirty apron, Toko treated everyone to sugar-coated beans.

Today I had my monthly cramps. I could barely keep standing with the pain.

October

The women were lying this way and that like broken pencils. I made a stab at writing letters in the margins of a notebook.

> I have tried to live to the fullest. It's been a long time since I've seen you, hasn't it? Not since we parted at Kanda. . . . I'm desperately lonely. When I realize that I don't have anyone in this whole world to care for me, I want to cry. Though I'm always alone, I want to hear kind words. And if someone is even a little bit considerate toward me, I cry for joy. I go so far as to sing in a loud voice, waltzing down the road in the dead of night. With the coming of autumn, I wanted to work but wasn't able to due to my usual poor health. Of course, putting food on the table became a major problem. I want money. If I could eat white rice with radish pickles crisp to the bite, I couldn't

14. "Zuizui zukkoro bashi," a children's song from Tokyo that became popular from the middle of the Meiji period. It accompanied a hand game for choosing the person who would be "It" similar to "eenie, meenie, minie, moe." Although there is one theory that this song is about the transport of tea containers from Kyoto to Edo in the Tokugawa period, the words are, for the most part, nonsensical.

ask for anything more. When you're poor you get down to basics. Tomorrow I'll be very happy. Some payment for a manuscript did come in, only a little, but I'm thinking about traveling as far as I can on it. All I do is look at maps. There is no joy to be found in the waitresses' common room on the second floor of this bar. It is only the soiled map above the stairs that makes me a daydreamer. Maybe I'll just go to a place called Ichiburi on the Japan Sea. Either to live or not to live. . . . Anyway, I just want to set out on a trip.

I can accept the words "Frailty, thy name is woman." They fit me exactly. But I am also untamed, and that's fine. There's nothing I can do but throw myself back into the wild. As things stand now, the fact is that I can't send any money back home. I've done unforgivable things to him. I've put up with a lot, smiling. If I set out on a journey, I plan to work a while until the country sky and earth gradually bring me back to health. Nothing worries me more than my weakened condition. Besides that, he is sick too. I don't like it. I want money. I negotiated to go to Ikaho hot springs to become a maid, but they claimed that an advance of one hundred yen was too much. You may wonder why I want to travel, but in my present situation I'll just explode. I've lived this long with all kinds of thoughtless, malicious gossip, and I don't care what people say. I'm completely exhausted. When winter comes, I'll meet you with the strength of ten people. I'll go where I can. Carrying only my bright yellow poetry manuscripts, which are my sun and moon, I will go to the Japan Sea.

Please take good care of yourself.

Goodbye. . . .

I am sorry that I have not written to you in such a long time. Are you keeping well? To send such a letter to someone as scornful as you will no doubt make you laugh at me. I actually shed tears over you. Even though we've separated, when I think of your illness I wish I were with you. I recall both hard and joyful times. But your cruel treatment made me miserable, embittered.

I have enclosed two one-yen bills. Please do not get angry, but use them for something. They say you are not with that woman any more. Was I making too much out of nothing? Autumn has come. My lips are freezing in the cold. Since we parted. . . .

Tai is working back in the kitchen too.

Dear Mother,

I'm sorry I'm late with the money. But I've had many expenses since the beginning of fall.

I hope you are well. I am okay. Could you please send me at your convenience a little more of the herb medicine you sent recently? My dizziness stopped when I made tea with it. I like its fragrance, too.

As usual, since I have already stamped the money order with your name, all you have to do is take it as is to the post office.

Have you heard from Father? Just take it easy until your luck changes. I'm lying low since this is a bad year for me.

I pray for your health. I'll enclose a return envelope, so please answer.

My whole face was drenched with tears. I sobbed convulsively. No matter how I tried, I couldn't stop crying. Alone, writing letters on the second floor of such a rowdy place, my heart filled with thoughts of my elderly mother. I hoped she wouldn't die before I could do something. It would be too pathetic if she passed away alone in the oceanfront inn. I'll go to the post office and send it off first thing tomorrow morning. I had stashed six or seven one-yen bills in the padding of my obi sash. The money had been in and out of my bank account and didn't amount to much. Resting my head on the wooden pillow, I heard the two A.M. clacking of wooden clappers by the night watchman from the licensed quarters.

October

A gloomy autumn landscape loomed outside the window. Entrusting all of my possessions to my one basket, I boarded the train bound for Okitsu. Beyond Toke there was a small tunnel.

> Long ago pilgrims to Rome
> Exited out of Simplon, an unknown hole, and went south.

I really liked this poem by Banri. I had heard that Simplon, in the Alps, was the longest tunnel in the world. A tunnel on a solitary journey without a destination evoked depressing emotions, and I feared going to the sea. Memories of my former lover's face and thoughts of my mother sustained me.

I alighted at Mikado. Lights had started to turn on, illuminating the mulberry fields in front of the station. Here and there, thatched roofs caught my eye. I stood absent-mindedly in the station holding onto my basket.

"Is there an inn here?"

"There's one if you go on ahead to Chōja."

I cut through Hiari Beach. Here in Chiba, the awesome fury of the swelling tides of October aroused me. There was nothing but sea and sky and beach. Dusk fell. *This wide expanse of nature underscored the insig-*

nificance of human efforts. A dog howled from afar. A girl in a short quilted ikat jacket was walking a black dog as she hurried toward me singing. With each surging wave the dog stiffened its neck in fear and howled at the ocean. The howling and rumbling created an ominous combination.

"Is there an inn around here?" I called out to the pretty maiden. She was the only other person on the beach.

"Our house isn't an inn, but you can stay there if you like."

Without a sign of fear, she took me home. She lit the way back to her house, all the while skillfully blowing on a purple Chinese lantern plant.

Looking like a shipwreck at the edge of Hiari Beach, the small teahouse was adjacent to the town of Chōja. The elderly couple who ran it kindly heated the bath and took care of me. How amazing to discover a world so carefree and natural. Recollections of the fearsome atmosphere of the rough city bar were enough to frighten me. I couldn't identify the dried tails of fish pasted on the ceiling.

The electric light in my room was dim, as was my wandering soul. Although I wasn't able to tour the Japan Sea coast as I had really yearned to do, I found the scenery in Chiba to be even more stirring. The roofs of the houses from Ichifuri to the neighboring Oyashirazu were covered with what looked like heavy pickling stones. The salt spray blanketed everything as far as the train tracks. Stinging thistle bloomed atop a crumbled bluff. I remembered all this from many years before. Snuggling into the futon that reeked of the sea, I took out a bottle of chloroform from my basket and applied a few drops to my handkerchief. It was more than I could bear. Quietly smothered by memories and moved by a present urge to vanish, I pressed the horrible chloroform flat against my nose, like a pressed flower.

November

It was about ten o'clock in the morning when I awoke dreamily to the sound of the rumbling of distant thunder, followed by the heavy rain beating against the window. I quietly opened a window, since the vinegary chloroform odor still pervaded the room. Pale, rainy fog painted the beach in the inlet. It was a subdued morning. I could smell sardines grilling in the main house.

My head hurt so much at noon that I went with the girl to take the black dog for a walk. We set off in the direction of Hiari Beach. Women and children were gathered in small groups in a fisherman's house near the beach, spearing fresh sardines on bamboo skewers. The skewered sardines lining the straw mats were speckled with silver from the faint sunlight that seeped through the rain. After getting a bucketful of fresh sardines, the girl pulled up weeds from around the area and covered the fish.

"This is ten sen worth," she said on the way home, thrusting the heavy bucket out in front of me.

That night we feasted on sardines in soy sauce, sake, and vinegar, along with stewed seaweed and raw eggs. The girl, Onobu, said she would walk from Chiba to Kisarazu in good weather selling dried fish. While I sipped tea and chatted with the old couple and Onobu, a pale blue crab scurried across the threshold. I became quite envious from my glimpse of these people's lives that were as unchanging as a rock. I was worn out by my vagabond existence. The shutters creaked like a ship at sea, as if the wind had caught its sails. *The old-fashioned seashore inn could have leapt from the pages of Chekhov.* Around here, with the coming of November, the soles of my feet were already frozen.

November

I saw Fuji.
I saw Mount Fuji.
As long as red snow doesn't fall,
Fuji doesn't deserve to be praised as much of a mountain.

I'm not going to let that mountain defeat me,
I thought countless times from a train window.
Threatening my disconnected life,
The heart of that peaked mountain
Looks coldly down at my eyes.

I saw Fuji.
I saw Mount Fuji.
O raven
Fly over that mountain from the ridge to the summit,
Sneer with your scarlet beak, if you please.

O wind!
Fuji is a palace of sorrow for snow.
Blow to your heart's content.
Fujiyama is the image of Japan,
The Sphinx,
Nostalgia steeped in dream,
A palace of sorrow where lives the demon.

See Fuji.
See Mount Fuji.
In your image sketched long ago by Hokusai,
I saw your youthful spark, but
Now you're an old decayed mud pie,
Always rolling your eyes skyward.
Why do you hide yourself in snow?

O raven, o wind,
Hit that exceedingly clear white
Shoulder of Mount Fuji.
That is not a silver citadel,
But a snowy palace of sorrow that unhappiness haunts.

O Mount Fuji!
Here stands one woman unwilling to bow,
One woman sneering at you.

O Mount Fuji, O Fuji
Until your plain but fiery passion
Whirls and groans,
And strikes this stubborn woman's head,
I'll wait gaily whistling.

I was no better off than before. Wearing an apron, I went to open a window on the second floor, and could just faintly make out Mount Fuji far in the distance. I have passed by the foot of that mountain numerous unhappy times in my travels by train. But even though my recent trip was short, the lonely scenery of those two days in Chiba cleansed and beautified my body and soul. Like a solitary cedar standing alone in the field, I require this kind of respite and joy.

We were to celebrate autumn leaf day tomorrow, and we would have to dress up like lunatics in matching scarlet kimonos. How could city people think up such comic ideas without a hint of embarrassment? Another new woman had arrived. So again this evening I would apply my mask of makeup and fool them with a duplicitous smile. They called it the floating world, which was right on the mark. My mother had sent me two white cotton camisoles while I was away.

January

A ring I unexpectedly received from a drunk customer at the cafe came in handy. I hocked it for thirteen yen and went shopping with Toki-chan along the streets of Sendagi. At a used-furniture store I bought a box brazier and a small, low dining table. After getting together an assortment of pickle and tea bowls, and even a tea set, the rest could barely cover half a month's rent. The absurdity of thirteen yen.

It was close to ten o'clock when we arrived home. Each of us grasping one side of our heavy loot, we dragged it upstairs. We could see our breath in the cold air.

"Hey! There's a ballad teacher in the place across from ours . . . Look, isn't that great!"

> Umbrella outfurled.
> Hold aloft the flower storm of the licensed quarters!
> About the time that this samurai's sickness passes,
> It's spring in Edo, purple with haze.

From the second floor of the building a stone's throw across the way, I could hear this melancholy samisen melody. Through our slightly open window shutters, I could see the delicate frame of their latticed shoji by the light that shone brightly next door.

"Let's just go to sleep now and take a bath tomorrow. Did you borrow the top futon?"

Toki-chan slammed our shoji shut. The bottom futon was left over from when Taiko and I had shared a room. She had left it behind when she went to marry Kobori, along with pots and knives. I recalled the most wonderful and, at the same time, most oppressive memories from the second floor of the bar in Hongō where we had lived. Our neighbors on the second floor were a nice couple—the man was just out of the army, and his wife washed diapers. When I've taken care of business, I'll take out my diary from that period and read it.

"I wonder what's happened to Taiko?"

"She's probably finally found happiness. Kobori seems like such a strong man that nobody could beat him up. . . ."

"Please take me along with you on your next visit, okay?"

Covering ourselves with the quilt we borrowed from the lady downstairs, we went to bed. I made an entry in my diary.

First of all, out of thirteen yen:

Low dining table	1 yen	
Box brazier	1 yen	
One flower in a pot	35 sen	
Rice bowls	20 sen	Two
Soup bowls	10 sen	Two
Horseradish pickle	5 sen	

Radish pickle	11 sen	
Chopsticks	5 sen	Five sets
Tea set with tray	1 yen 10 sen	
Momotarō container	15 sen	
Plates	20 sen	Two
Rent (3–mat room)	6 yen	(2/3rds of a month)
Metal brazier chopsticks	10 sen	
Mochi grill	14 sen	
Aluminum soup ladle	10 sen	
Rice paddle	3 sen	
One packet of tissue paper	20 sen	
Astringent	28 sen	
Ritual sake for the altar	25 sen	One measure
Moving-in noodles	30 sen	For the people downstairs
Remainder, 1 yen 16 sen		

"I can't believe that's all that's left. . . ."

As I prodded my cheek with the tip of my pencil and wrote in my diary, I caused Toki-chan, high nose and all, to glance my way.

"Do we have any charcoal?"

"The lady downstairs said she'd get the charcoal from the usual shop and arrange it so that we would pay at the end of the month."

Looking relieved, Toki-chan lifted up the sidelocks of her butterfly tresses with her slender fingers as she leaned against my back.

"I'm telling you everything's okay. From tomorrow I'll work really hard, so lift up your spirits and study, okay? I'll quit my job in Asakusa. I think it would be good to work at one of the cafes around Hibiya and commute, they say that there are lots of drinkers in that area. . . ."

"If I commute, that'll be fun for both of us. Food doesn't taste good if you eat alone, you know."

I contemplated what had been a complicated day. I had received two measures of uncooked rice from Setsu-chan at the Hagiwaras. The painter Mizoguchi had wrapped up some of the mochi for me, which he said someone had sent from Hokkaido. He had taken my ring to the pawn shop.

"Let's both of us work really hard for a while, okay?"

"It'll be fine if I can send thirty yen a month to my mother back in Zōshiki," Toki-chan responded.

"I'll be getting a little bit from my manuscripts, so we'll get by if we just stop worrying and work."

I wondered if it was snow. There was a muffled sound of something hitting the window.

"Cyclamen flowers smell horrible." Gently pushing away the flowerpot from the head of the bed, Toki-chan removed her hair ornaments and combs. "Now let's really go to sleep," she said. In the dark room, the scent of the red cyclamens was the only unpleasantness.

February

> Though you see the swirling light snowfall drift,
> It disappears, without a trace, an evanescence.
> Willows may sway gently
> In the spring, the dawn of the heart.

Hearing Toki-chan singing this song, I woke up to find bare white ankles astride my pillow.

"Hey, are you up already?"

"It's snowing."

When I got up I saw that the water was boiling. Atop the plank outside the window where we had rigged up a stove, the simmering rice was bubbling over, frothy white.

"Have they already brought the charcoal?"

"I borrowed some from the lady downstairs."

Toki-chan had never before done kitchen work. She was wiping rice bowls with wonder. *I drank my tea at the minuscule low table with contentment.*

"For now, let's not tell the people at the Yamato Inn where we are, okay?"

Toki-chan nodded and warmed her hands on the small brazier.

"Are you going out even in this snow?"

"Sure."

"Well, then, I'll go meet Shiroki at the Jiji Newspaper. I've sent them a children's story."

"If you get any money, please cook something hot. I'll be looking around here and there, so I'll be late."

I made my introductory greeting to the couple in the six-mat room next door. They ran a used-clothing store. I also met the husband of the landlady who supposedly was head of a scaffolding team. Everyone was boisterous, like shitamachi types.

"This house used to face the road. But there was a fire and now it stands back from the road like this. . . . In the front is someone's mistress, at the end of the alley is a male ballad singer. It can be really noisy, you'll see. . . ."

I stared in fascination at the landlady, whose teeth were blackened like in the old days.

"Is she somebody's mistress? I got a glimpse of her on the street, and she seemed to have a fine, upstanding appearance."

"The woman downstairs was saying that you're quite a nice girl, not the usual type we get around here."

The two of us set out for the snowy town, both with our hair done up in tresses. Like lifeless foam, the snow fell haphazardly, yet it seemed as if it were trying to search out my nose and eyes.

"It's tough to make any money, isn't it?" Snow, fall as much as you like, until you bury me. I obstinately twirled the umbrella while walking. All the windows along the wide street in Yaesu were lit. Women in purple or red coats were returning home from work, walking against the snow. Since I was not wearing a coat, my sleeves were soaking, as wet as a wretched toad.

Shiraki had already gone home. Served me right! This kind of run-around made me want to go back to working at a cafe. But Toki-chan told me to keep to my writing. I left my standard message at the large receptionist's desk of the newspaper company, about my having trouble making ends meet. I wrote it by hand in linking blurred letters.

The door of the Jiji Company was interesting. It revolved just like a water wheel. When I pushed on it twice, it went back to right where it started. The mailman was laughing at me. What petty people. It was as if the towering building was telling me that it didn't matter if an insignificant nobody like myself lived or died. If I could own that building and sell it, I could buy a lifetime's supply of all my necessities, besides sending a long telegram back home. If I told all my hard-hearted relatives and cold friends that I was going to strike it rich, they would dismiss me out of hand. "Shameless Fumiko, just get out of here."

Toki-chan was probably shuffling numbly in the snow like a stray dog.

February

Tonight again I waited in vain. Heating the tea at the brazier, I ate dinner alone, later than usual. It was already past one o'clock. . . . Last night was two o'clock, the night before one-thirty. She had always returned home exactly at twelve-thirty. I couldn't imagine what was happening to Toki-chan. A couple of half-finished manuscripts were scattered on the low table. There was only eleven sen left in the house.

Last night I missed the chance to ask about the ten yen that Toki-chan had had me put aside. She had taken it without telling me. I wondered what she had done with it.

The rice in the steamer had gotten soggy from being repeatedly reheated. The clam miso stew had gotten too thick. I couldn't write any more. I thrust my desk next to the vanity and, with resignation, sadly spread out the futon. I wished I could afford to go to the hairdresser. It had been more than ten days since I had last had my hair done up. My scalp itched like crazy. It would be too lonely for her to come home to total darkness, so I turned on the light and dimmed it with a purple cloth covering the shade.

Three o'clock.

I awoke at the sound of the landlady downstairs making a fuss. Then came the heavy footsteps that indicated that Toki-chan was drunk. And it appeared that she was.

"I'm sorry!"

Her hair was disheveled, her face pale. Wearing a purple coat, Toki-chan crumpled at the foot of the futon. Just like a spoiled child, she burst out in tears. Even though I had readied a speech, I was silent, unable to utter a single word.

"Good-bye, Toki-chan!" A man's voice disappeared from beneath the window, and at the entrance of the alley sounded the silly honking of a car horn.

February

We ate the meal without looking at each other.

"These days we've been slacking off, so you wipe the stairs, okay, and I'll wash clothes . . . ," I suggested to Toki-chan.

"No, I'll do it, so just leave everything as it is, okay?"

Her eyelids were swollen from lack of sleep. She was such a touching sight that I could hardly stand it.

"Toki-chan, where'd you get the ring?"

On her slender ring finger sparkled a white stone in a platinum setting.

"And that purple coat?"

". . . ."

"Toki-chan, have you gotten tired of being poor?"

It pained me to come face to face with the landlady downstairs.

"Hey, Sister! Something's gotten into Toki."

He spoke while the water ran from the faucet, and his words pained my heart.

"Right over there, you know, with a car horn going off like that in the middle of the night . . . I'm the area representative. Even a little indiscretion really causes problems. . . ."

He was right. The words pressed on my heart as I washed.

February

It has been five days since Toki-chan last came home. I awaited news desperately. She was lost to that ring and coat. What has she gotten herself into? I kept telling her that poverty wasn't disgraceful . . . but an eighteen-year-old probably wants both red lipstick and purple coats. I bought five cheap sweets with the few pennies I had, and ate them in bed reading old magazines. Despite past declarations about the honor in poverty, those last five cheap sweets failed to convince my stomach. *Nibbling on leftover cabbage, I fantasized about the texture of white rice.*

I swung open the closet with my outstretched hand. I had nothing. Tears began to blur my sight. I could turn on the light. . . . As though cheated by cheap sweets, my stomach growled. The penetrating aroma of grilled saury fish emanated from the used-clothes dealer next door.

Hunger and sex! Could I get a bowl of rice by doing what Toki-chan did?

Hunger and sex! Wanting to cry, I chewed on these words.

February

> Please read this and don't be angry with me. I've been forced to work at a house of assignation in Asakusa by the man who gave me the ring. He has a wife, but he says he'll divorce her. Please don't laugh, will you? He's a contractor, and he's forty-two. He had lots of kimono made up for me, and when I told him about you, he said he'd send you about forty yen each month. So I'm happy.

Tears burned like fire as I struggled through her letter, unable to read straight. This wasn't the way it was supposed to be. My teeth grated like metal. When had I ever asked her for anything like this! Fool, what a fool to be so, so . . . was she so fragile? With eyes completely swollen, blubbering until I was blinded, I turned toward my memory of her and cried out my soul.

You didn't tell me where you are. What did you mean by a house of assignation?

And not such an old man . . . forty-two!

Kimono, kimono.

What was it with the ring and the kimono? Were you so lacking in willpower?

Ah, with that lovely figure, like a wild lily, soft, light-pink skin, and jet-black hair, still she had been a virgin. That worm from the floating world probably stole her first kiss. . . . She used to tilt her lovely neck and sing to me about spring. Damn you, you middle-aged lech!

"Miss Hayashi, there's a registered letter for you!"

The woman from downstairs sounded unusually good-natured. I picked up the envelope she had placed on the stairs. It was a registered letter from Shiraki at the Jiji Newspaper. Twenty-three yen! It was payment for the manuscripts of the children's stories. I wouldn't have to starve, not for a while. My spirits rose until I was almost ecstatic. But then, God, maybe it was this bit of luck, but now I felt so terribly alone. God, the friend who should share my joy was in the arms of a forty-two-year-old man . . . how could this have happened?

"As usual, I'm praying for your hard work and diligence." Shiraki had enclosed one of his kind, solicitous letters.

I opened the window wide and heard the temple bells of Ueno. I would eat some fine sushi that night.

Appendix A

Terms

chikuwa. Fish paste formed into a tube along a stick, steamed, and then grilled.

Daruma. Rounded, papier-mâché doll representing a legless, armless Buddha.

futon. Japanese bedding, much like thickly padded quilts, spread on the floor at night, and put away in closets during the day. The term refers to both the mattress and the coverlet.

ganmodoki. deep-fried tofu patty.

geta. Wooden zori, or sandals, with thongs and two ridges on the soles that significantly raise the foot from the floor.

jōruri. A ballad drama acted out by very large puppets manipulated by several people.

katakana. one of two syllabic scripts used in Japanese. In this era, katakana was the first script taught to students, and women's names were most often officially registered in it.

kon'nyaku. A jelly-like food made from the root of the arum plant.

kotatsu. A low table with a heating unit under it. One sits at the table covered by a quilt to keep the heat in.

kōya dofu. Dried tofu softened by simmering in a sweet broth.

miso. Soybean paste. Used most often as the basis for the soup that commonly accompanies meals.

mitsumame. A sweet mixture of gelatin, fruit, and small black beans.

mochi. Pounded, steamed rice formed into a thick pancake shape.

Momotarō. "Peach Boy" (from the legend of the little boy born out of a peach). The reference could indicate either the shape of the container or a design painted on the container.

Namu Amidabutsu. Literally, "Buddha, I implore you." The opening line to the Lotus Sutra, commonly recited as a mantra or prayer.

noren. Short curtain that hangs in the entry of shops.

obi. The wide stiff sash worn with a kimono.

ochazuke. A simple meal of green tea over cooked rice.

oden. A stew made of vegetables, fish products, tofu, and kon'nyaku and eaten with hot mustard.

onnagata. A kabuki actor who specializes in playing female roles.

samisen. A three-stringed musical instrument that accompanies folk ballads. The samisen is also used in performances of kabuki and bunraku theater.

sembei. A cracker made of pounded rice. Sembei are formed into various shapes and are grilled over coals.

sen. One-hundredth of a yen.

shitamachi. The geographically low-lying parts of Tokyo, known as an artisans' and entertainment district. People from this area are often stereotyped as friendly, jovial, and straightforward.

shō. A measure containing about two quarts.

shōchū. Inexpensive distilled spirits made from sweet potatoes.

shōji. A translucent paper sliding door separating a room from a corridor or an exterior veranda.

tanka. A thirty-one syllable poem written in 5–7–5–7–7 meter.

tatami. Thick, woven-rush matting that is recessed into the whole floor of a room. It comes in 3′ × 6′ sections.

yukata. An unlined cotton kimono worn in summer, usually in the evening.

Appendix B

Names

Artzybaschev. Russian Modernist Mikhail Petrovich Artzybaschev (1879–1927), who wrote about the aspirations and self-indulgence of the intelligentsia during the last years of the Russian Empire. His work had achieved prominence in Japan through a series of translations in the 1910s. Hayashi's protagonist refers to his novel *Lande's Death,* translated in 1919.

Banri. Hirano Banri (1855–1947), tanka poet.

Chikamatsu. Chikamatsu Shūkō (1876–1944), novelist generally categorized with the Naturalist movement. Chikamatsu's wide-ranging personal confessions, for example, in "Kurokami" (Black hair, 1922), helped foster the I-novel tradition.

Daikoku. One of the seven gods of good fortune, Daikoku brings food and drink.

Hagiwara. Hagiwara Kyōjirō (1899–1938), the cofounder (with Tsuboi Shigei) of *Aka to kuro* (Red and black, 1923–1924) and *Bungei Kaihō* (Literary liberation, 1927). His major work is the poetic anthology *Shikei senkoku* (Death sentence, 1925).

Hakushū. Kitahara Hakushū (1885–1942), Symbolist poet.

Hamsun. Knut Hamsun (1859–1952), Norwegian writer and recipient of the Nobel Prize for Literature in 1920, who influenced modern literature through his emphasis on psychological states, fragmented writing, use of flashbacks, and lyricism. Hayashi wrote that after she had read his novel *Hunger,* she was convinced that she too could become a writer.

Hashizume. Hashizume Ken (1900–1964), poet, critic, and fiction writer. He was an Anarchist and Dadaist.

Hinkelmann. Protagonist of a 1923 play of the same name by Ernst Toller (1893–1939), German playwright and poet.

Iida. Iida Tokutarō (1903–1933), Anarchist critic and writer. He was Hirabayashi Taiko's husband.

Kachusha. A character in the play *Fukkatsu,* a translation of Henri Bataille's dramatization of Tolstoy's *Resurrection,* which was first performed in March 1914 by Matsui Sumako. Her Kachusha song became an instant hit. In October 1914, a silent movie of this name was released. The role of Kachusha was played by the *onnagata* Tachibana Shinjiro.

Kaita. Murayama Kaita (1896–1919), a poet and painter, and author of a poetic anthology *Kaita no utaeru* (Kaita's song; published posthumously).

Katō. Katō Takeo (1888–1956), an employee of the Shinchōsha publishing company and a fiction writer.

Kasai. Kasai Zenzō (1887–1928), writer best known for *Ko o tsurete* (With children on my hands, 1918) in which, having been evicted from his rooms, the narrator wanders the streets with his children, homeless and penniless.

Kuroshima. Kuroshima Denji (1898–1943), a Proletarian writer who wrote antiwar novels based on his experience as a soldier in Siberia.

Lunacharskii. Anatolii Vasilievich Lunacharskii (1875–1933), Russian literary critic and playwright.

Maedagawa. Maedagawa Hiroichirō (1888–1957), a Proletarian writer affiliated with the journals *Tane maku hito* (The sower, 1921), and *Bungei sensen* (Literary front, 1924).

Murō. Murō Saisei (1889–1962), poet heralded as a major literary figure from the late 1910s. Murō later turned successfully to short stories and novels.

Oshun and Denbei. The courtesan Oshun is the central character in a kabuki play about double suicide, *Chikagoro kawara no tatehiki* (Recent riverbed rivalry) by Tamekawa Shūsuke, most active as a kabuki and kyōgen playwright between 1751 and 1763.

Saigo. Saigo Takamori (1827–1877), a Satsuma leader of the Meiji Restoration who opposed the foreign policy of the new Meiji government. In 1877 he led a major rebellion.

Sakae. Tsuboi Sakae (1900–1967), a well-known writer of "women's literature" and children's stories. Perhaps her best known novel, *Nijūshi no hitomi* (Twenty-four eyes, 1952), chronicled the lives and bittersweet reunion of students of a young female teacher in a remote village. She was the wife of Tsuboi Shigei (1898–1975).

Satō. Satō Haruo (1892–1964), Japanese Modernist writer and poet best remembered for the novel *Yameru sōbi* (The sick rose, 1917), a work also known by the title *Rural Melancholy.*

Schnitzler. Arthur Schnitzler (1862–1931), Austrian playwright and novelist.

Shiga. Shiga Naoya (1883–1971), author. His novella *Wakai* (Reconciliation, 1917), told of his own reconciliation with his father. His only full-length novel, *An'ya kōro* (A dark night's passing, 1921–1923, 1938) has often been heralded as the quintessential I-novel.

Shimazaki. Shimazaki Tōson, (1872–1943), poet who made an enormously influential contribution to modern poetry in his early years. He later became one of the preeminent Naturalist novelists.

Shizue. Tomotani Shizue, a poet with whom Hayashi published four issues of a small poetry journal *Futari* (Two people) from 1924.

Steiner. Max Steiner (1806–1856), German philosopher. Tsuji Jun translated *On the Self* into Japanese.

Sumako. Matsui Sumako (stage name of Kobayashi Masako [1886–1919]), actress best known for her leading roles in the Bungei kyōkai (Literary Association) productions of modern western dramas in the early 1910s, and then for those with the Geijutsuza (Arts theater) that she formed with her lover Shimamura Hōgetsu. She played the role of Kachusha.

Taiko. Hirabayashi Taiko (1905–1972) began as a Proletarian writer but achieved her greatest prominence through her postwar autobiographical accounts of her hardships and frustrations as a "woman writer," as well as by her portraits of gangsters in *Chitei no uta* (Song from the bowels of the earth, 1948). She and Hayashi were close compatriots in the mid-1920s, and Hirabayashi wrote several biographical sketches of Hayashi after her death.

Takahashi. Takahashi Oden, the wicked female protagonist of a series of historical novels. Kanagaki Robun's (1829–1894) version is the most famous account of her life.

Takuboku. Ishikawa Takuboku (1885–1912), tanka poet and essayist, whose critical perspectives on social conditions served as a precursor to the Proletarian literature of the 1920s.

Tsuboi. Tsuboi Shigei (1898–1975), poet and co-founder (with Hagiwara Kyōjirō) of the Dadaist-Anarchist poetry journal *Aka to kuro* (Red and black, 1923–1924) and *Bungei kaihō* (Literary liberation, 1927). Tsuboi later played a prominent role in Proletarian literature. Tsuboi Sakae (1900–1967), a well-known writer of "women's literature," was his wife.

Tsuji. Tsuji Jun (1884–1944), critic who spurred the New-Dadaist movement in Japan.

Verhaeren. Emile Verhaeren (1855–1916), Belgian playwright and poet.

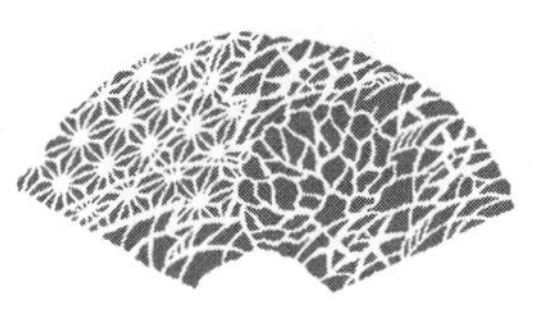

Narcissus

Suisen

Simply by standing at the head of her futon with a cigarette in his mouth, he forced her to take her eyes away from the magazine and ask, "How'd it go?" Sakuo was scarcely the considerate sort to volunteer, "Mother, this is what happened today." "How'd it go?" Even as she asked, he smirked and drew the cushion toward him with the tip of his toe. "No good, buddy, since you're such a parental delinquent." He blew smoke rings around his protruding red tongue.

"What do you mean, 'parental delinquent'? Don't go calling your mother 'buddy.' Did you introduce yourself to Mr. Tsuda?"

"I met him, all right. He said to give you his regards, buddy."

Tamae got up and stared at Sakuo for a moment. "What do you mean by 'parental delinquent'?"

"There's the expression 'juvenile delinquent,' right? It's the opposite of that. I'm saying that Queen Mama is a parental delinquent."

This was her son, but Tamae began to seethe at his spite.

"There's no reason for you to call me that. Your father left us when you were so tiny. I've raised you all on my own, haven't I? You look just like him. You mistreat me just the way he did. And you're almost twenty-two already. Can't you go get a job and straighten out? Nothing works out because of your attitude. Mr. Kamiyama said that, too. When you went to ask for a job, smug and smoking a cigarette, you were disqualified at once . . ."

"Hmmm. So you're saying that to get a job, all you need is a proper attitude? You mean even a fool or a dunce can make it if he just has the right demeanor?

Sakuo's long sideburns made him look like a Spanish matador. Yet to Tamae, the down below his nose made it difficult to say that he had completely grown up.

Tamae could not believe that this was the child who had been in grade school such a short time ago. She began to feel that some other person was sitting by her bed.

"Why can't you have some humility? No one can stand you."

"That's the way you raised me. I can't do anything about it. You raised me to be an ideal son, so you shouldn't have any complaints . . ." With tears in her eyes, Tamae examined her son, now sitting cross-legged against the wall, scornful and remote.

"Why do I always have to quarrel with you like this—mother against child? What did Mr. Tsuda say?"

"Nothing. Only that I wasn't quite right and I should take a test, so I did. That's all."

"And how do you think you did?"

"Terrible. They were all stupid questions, and I didn't feel like answering."

With a slight grin, Sakuo ground the butt of his cigarette in the dirty ashtray.

"At least if you do all right on the exam . . ."

Tamae felt forlorn. From now on, and for the rest of his life, her dull-witted son had no hope of succeeding.

"Your attitude is crummy. If you've completely messed up on the exam, there's no way Mr. Tsuda can do you a favor, is there?"

"Yeah, that's about the way it is."

Tamae didn't want to talk any more. Long ago, she had wanted to abandon this child. Had she really left him then, she wouldn't be so plagued now.

"What kind of test was it?"

"It was really boring. Things like 'How did France escape catastrophe?' and 'How old is Truman?' I've never even thought about things like that."

Disgusted, Tamae threw a short soiled silk dressing gown over her dirty worn-out terry-cloth nightgown and staggered to her feet. She went to the washroom and drew water in a kettle, and then returned to find Sakuo rummaging through her handbag. "What are you looking for?"

"I want some money."

"You won't find any no matter how hard you look. You've really become an awful pest, haven't you? Don't do anything more to torment me, please. Why do you have to bother me so much? That's what I want to know."

Sakuo found a nail file in the handbag and roughly edged his nails.

"You're kidding, aren't you? I'm not tormenting you. I've got a date to go to Sakurai's place this evening. A real man can't go with just tram fare."

Tamae kept silent. After setting the kettle on the electric hot plate, she stood in front of the wall mirror and gazed at her face with a frozen stare.

Without her realizing it, old age had crept up on her. Forty-three was somehow regrettable. She felt that she had aged carelessly. It wasn't that she had been totally absorbed in her child's life. But had she not had the child, she'd have been free and, now, might be surprisingly happy. Now, no matter how much she might try, there was little hope that happiness would again be hers. She combed out her unkempt, lusterless hair. Her hairline had receded. She wondered if it might be due to her carrying on in her youth. Tamae applied hair oil and tried brushing her bangs down across her forehead. With its gaunt cheekbones, her angular face made her seem somewhat youthful. Then, like a surgeon, she combed it back decisively. Strangely, it suddenly aged her. As the water in the kettle boiled, she emptied it into the sink, soaking a towel. As she pressed it to her face, her eyelids twitched under the hot towel.

"Mom, are you going out?"

"Yes. I have to go round up some money."

"Do you have someplace in mind?"

"No, but I have to go anyway . . ."

Tamae removed the towel and peered into the mirror. Her ruddy complexion had come alive. Wishing her skin were always this color, she smeared on a thick layer of oily cream that reeked like kerosene.

Her bony fingers repeatedly massaged the corners of her eyes. Her face glistened. Makeup complete, she again arranged her hair in a full fashion, daubed rouge on her crow's-feet, and looked into the mirror from a distance. Tamae did not like to look at the muddied lukewarm water from the washbasin. It reflected poverty. Maybe because she had not been to the public bath in five days, her face, despite the makeup, was not very elegant. Her lips were so chapped her lipstick would not spread at all. The protruding lower lip looked like a badly colored piece of raw tuna.

"You know, I don't have the strength any more to help you as you expect. How about leaving me and getting Sakurai to let you live at his place? I'm really exhausted. It's as if you and I were born enemies, from something in a previous life. You're a grown-up man now. Don't you want to be free of your mother? I won't complain no matter what you do, and I don't want to have you complain about anything I do. I worry about your poor health, but if you get sick, I'll deal with things when that time comes. Okay? Can't you support yourself? I think it would do you good if you did."

"I've become a nuisance to Queen Mama, right? . . . We don't have to part. If you like, I'll call you sister like I used to . . ."

Tamae looked in the mirror, desperately stroked on her lipstick, and flashed a sweet smile. She did not answer.

"I don't like it . . . ." he continued.

"I don't have the patience to live in the same room with you. I'm not young any more, either." Tamae answered bitterly as she looked at her own reflection. "You know, I feel you'll kill me. I'm not exactly like that woman in Maupassant's 'A Woman's Life,' but you too must've read it."

"Don't be silly. You're too full of self-importance. What son would kill his mother? I don't care about you enough. . . . Like Jesus Christ, I just borrowed your belly."

"So that's it. Then you should grow wings and just fly up to Mary. There's nothing that says I have to support a grown man like you forever, you know." Tamae put on a threadbare green jacket and black slacks. Her legs were so spindly it was comic. After she put on wool socks, she sat sideways in front of the electric burner. Holding her dirty hand above the whirling rings of the burner, she daubed red polish on her nails. Sakuo inspected Tamae's hand with detachment. It had to belong to a demon. His heart was full of malice; he resented the lack of small kindnesses from his mother's lips. Suddenly rebellious, he felt like tormenting her.

"What filthy hands. You're old, Mom."

"That's none of your concern. What got them get so dirty? These are the hands that hauled firewood and fed you after coming home from work."

"Oh? Is that how they got so dirty?"

After finishing painting her nails red, she buffed them to a high gloss with an old rag and dunked them in the scuzzy lukewarm water. She tried washing her hands with the soap, but it did not lather well. Then she wiped her hands and again examined them at arm's length.

"You know, I'm not kidding. Please just take off anywhere. I'm completely fed up with you."

Sakuo closed his eyes for a bit and lightly tapped his head against the wall, as if knocking at someone's door. Tamae flung her overcoat off her shoulders, poured out the remaining hot water from the kettle into a cup, mixed in some brown sugar rations, and drank it.

"Mom, you've never loved me, have you?"

She suddenly drew the cup back from her lips. Tamae gazed at her son. His was a very tired face. There was a faint resemblance to her ex-husband when he was young.

"Of course there were times I loved you. But when I'm caught up in making a living, sometimes I can't think only of you. Of course, you're my child. I labored to give birth to you. And I think fondly of you, after all. But the time has come for us to part. That's what I think. The Saku I loved was a little boy. Now you've grown up, and your grown-up eyes look at your mother as if we were strangers. Our relationship was like that, I guess. I don't want to go on like this until I'm dead and buried. I still feel a lot like working. I'll be ruined if I have to deal with your spite. You're a heavy burden on me, too . . . ."

Sakuo took out a cigarette case from a pocket of his frayed overcoat and offered it to her. She took one and held it to her lips. Sakuo lit his own, then hers.

"Okay. I'll have to go to Eiko's place then. Is that all right with you?"

Upon hearing the name, Tamae said, "So that's your only alternative? Then go ahead and do it. When your mother can't feed you any more, you sponge off Eiko? Why can't you work like an adult, instead of always relying on a woman? Eiko may be crazy about you, but she's not reliable, and anyway, she's so much older than you, isn't she . . . People have told me that, and it embarrasses me."

Tamae was born in Taipei, Taiwan. Her father worked for the railroad and, as the daughter of a government official, she received a strict upbringing. She met Ibe Naoki, a graduate from a theological seminary in Amoy, while he was staying for a month at Tamae's friend's home in Taipei. The two had come to Tokyo, pretty much eloping. It was the spring following her graduation from girls' high school. Tamae was nineteen. In Oimatsu-chō, Zōshigaya, the two had rented a modest fifteen-yen house, and there Tamae gave birth to Sakuo. Ibe had ambitions to go to America, but such a voyage was beyond their very slender means. Ibe was barely able to eke out a living to support his family by helping the editor of a theological journal. Tamae's high school friend Ōkawa Tatsuko came to Tokyo to study for the entrance exam for a music school. While she rented the second floor of Tamae's house, Tatsuko and Ibe developed a relationship, right under Tamae's nose. She discovered their affair after about two months. Half-crazed, Tamae tormented Tatsuko daily. Tatsuko bore her wrath stoically. After her affair with Ibe had begun, Tatsuko grew more discouraged every day. She became disenchanted with going to music school and fell into idleness. Unable to bear living in the same place, Tatsuko found a little house with only three rooms in Dōzaka, Hongō, and moved there. Even though it was far out by the Jizo shrine in Tabata, many wholesale workers commuted from this area to downtown. She moved while Tamae was out, but in no time Tamae sniffed out the house in Dōzaka, barged in, and created a scene, dragging Tatsuko around by the hair. Within half a year of moving, Tatsuko had committed suicide by gassing herself. Ibe immediately quit work and left abruptly for Amoy and then Malaya. She heard that he might be in Kuala Lumpur. That was in 1928. Tamae hated Ibe and hated Tatsuko even in death. Whenever she recalled Tatsuko's fair, freckled face, Tamae was haunted by the image of her dying with a rubber gas pipe in her mouth. Seeing the light freckles under Sakuo's eyes, Tamae was repulsed. She projected her antipathy for Tatsuko onto her son.

Through a friend of Ibe's Tamae got a job helping with the editing of a religious magazine, but it was hard to maintain herself, her child, and the help of a housekeeper on her income. Having severed relations with her family in Taipei, Tamae walked a dangerous tightrope between one man and the next.

As he grew from childhood to adolescence and came to judge things for himself, Sakuo viewed his mother's life as an enigma. From the standpoint of unsullied youth, he found it distasteful. From junior high school on, Tamae had him call her sister. When the two of them started living without a housekeeper, Sakuo would curse his mother for staying out overnight. For a long time, the two were constantly at loggerheads. Disappointed with family life, Sakuo was too timid to socialize with groups at school and tended to neglect his studies. Finally graduating, he enrolled in a college and idly sponged off Tamae. Judged too weak for military service even during wartime, he avoided the draft for labor gangs. Skillfully evading the regulations, he and Tamae had changed residences any number of times. After the war, Tamae rented a room from a friend in Kōenji and lived there with Sakuo. Through a newspaper ad she found a job as a kind of head maid at a love hotel in Ikebukuro and commuted from home. Befriending the black marketeers who came to the hotel, she became adept at dealing foreign drugs. Gradually she would save a bit of money, but just when it looked as if she could breathe a bit easier, Sakuo would take the money and spend it all. Their relationship deteriorated from one day to the next. Sometimes Tamae felt like killing Sakuo. She didn't know whether Ibe was dead or alive. There had been no news from him for twenty years.

About this time, Sakuo took up with a woman. He brazenly boasted to his mother about his married dancer. When Tamae unexpectedly arrived home early one day, she found Sakuo sleeping with the woman. Tamae assailed her as she had Tatsuko, yanking her hair and flaying her with abuse. The woman was terrified by Tamae and did not return. But Sakuo taunted his mother. He said his lover had separated from her husband and was urging him to move in with her. It wasn't particularly out of love that Sakuo had taken up with her. She was simply a convenient meal ticket. Raised by an eccentric mother, Sakuo did not know what real love was. From early on he had a cantankerous disposition, and he had turned out to be so lazy he expected everything he needed to come from women. "If you want us to split up, that's okay with me, Mom. But I can't do it right away today, you know. I have to go to Eiko's place to talk it over. It's not as simple as all that."

Tamae had begun to scheme that, if only she could get away from Sakuo, she could have her own way. She would not have to pay out so much for a rented room in order to have a tryst with Tomita. And she wanted to redecorate to make this room a bit more bearable. What she swept off the veranda onto the narrow yard had piled up. Stray cats poked about in the rubbish, scattering it. The cypress fence at the front of the yard was still broken. Once a robber got in through the break in the fence and ran off with her one pair of shoes. She was so sloppy that she wasn't allowed to use the landlord's kitchen. Tamae had been in bed these past few days with a cold. Showing her age, perhaps, she didn't have the energy to do anything but stay where she was. It would soon be New Year's, but this was the only place where there wasn't any sign of that holiday. Tamae didn't even feel like celebrating with a bit of rice cake.

Getting ready to go out, Tamae felt reluctant to venture into town in wooden clogs after yesterday's rain. "Saku, don't you really feel like working?" Sakuo shimmied his shoulders back and forth to a tune he was whistling.

"I don't feel like it. I'm sick of everything. I'm bored with living like this, too. But, you know, if I don't have you or Eiko fluttering around me, I'm real lonely. It's better to have someone to fight with than no one at all," he snickered.

"If you have an itch to get into the black market, I'll ask Mr. Tomita for you. Don't you want to try it?"

Sakuo kept his shoulders and knees shaking. "Sakurai's older brother helped me out once. He set me up selling fountain pens in front of Shibuya with Sakurai, and I tried, but I couldn't even sell one of the buggers. It was really crazy. I just don't have the knack for business. I asked Eiko, and she sold six of them. It just goes to show that it takes a pretty woman to make a sale."

Tamae thought it was rather funny that Sakuo had the nerve to boast about his lover, whom he obviously considered to be attractive. "Whoa! You think Eiko's good-looking? What's so great about that fatty? She's so bloated. . . ."

"She's beautiful to me, and that's all that counts. Beautiful soft and white skin and a sleek belly."

"I bet you're saying all that because she's your first woman."

"Well, you were never that beautiful when you were young. . . ."

Disgusted, Tamae opened the sliding side doors. The sky had cleared. It was so sweltering that the humidity seemed to waft up from the farmland, dancing out of the black soil. The red slip that Tamae had hung under the eaves dangled like persimmon peel. It had been left out for days and looked pretty grimy.

Toward dusk, Tamae and Sakuo went out. Tamae went to Kichijōji, the opposite direction from Sakuo. She took the broad boulevard and then a shortcut through the park to Yuki's house. She immediately had the attendant phone Tomita's house for her, but was told that he had left a few days earlier on business and would not return before January third.

She thought it strange, since they had definitely agreed to meet once more at Yuki's place before the year was out, so she called his office in Kayabachō herself. A woman at the office informed her that Mr. Tomita had been out with a cold all the last week. She didn't know which one to believe, but Tamae couldn't bear to be stood up like this at the end of the year. Venturing near Tomita's house in Shimorenjaku, she waited until dark, hovering next to the wall at the corner, watching for anyone to come out of the house. When a young helper wearing loose work trousers came out, Tamae pretended to be a messenger from the office. "Excuse me. I've been sent from the office with a message for Mr. Tomita. Is he at home?" she asked the young woman.

"Oh? The boss is away on a business trip and will be returning around the second of January. . . ."

"I see. Then I don't know what to do. I've been sent from the office with an urgent message. I wonder if his trip is really company business."

"Perhaps you're right. It does seem unusual. I'll go ask Mrs. Tomita. . . . " The maid headed back toward the gate. Tamae immediately retraced her steps and scurried back to the station. She could smell the water from a dark stream along the road.

When she got off the train at Kōenji station, she changed her mind. She suddenly hit upon the alternative of stopping by Kamiyama's place. He was at the dinner table, his face bright from the bath. Kamiyama was drinking sake and eating herring roe. "Hey, how about a drink?" he offered Tamae. Fresh from the beauty parlor, his wife had her hair swept up in a perm that looked cool on her neck.

"Whenever I come here, it's so pleasant, it makes me envious. You're really fortunate, aren't you, Atsuko!" Kamiyama's wife, Atsuko, had been Tamae's classmate in the girls' high school in Taipei, and after the war they had grown close living in the same neighborhood in Kōenji. Kamiyama worked for an economic journal in Marunouchi. He had once tried to help Sakuo but, astounded by his unmitigated impudence, had never volunteered to help him again. Knowing that Tamae had driven their classmate Tatsuko to gas herself, Atsuko always kept the overbearing Tamae at something of a distance. But she could not bear to coldly watch her friend fall to pieces before her very eyes. Since Atsuko looked like the Empress, her family called her "Your Highness." Taking the sake cup offered by Kamiyama, Tamae had several refills.

"Tamae, it's too soon to grow old. Why didn't you remarry earlier?"

"Because I have this child."

"So what difference does it make if you have a child?"

"My boy Saku is really malicious. He's always keeping an eye on what I do and then ruining everything."

"Don't be absurd, a child naturally wants his mother to be happy."

"Maybe so, but my boy is different, I'm telling you. He's a real delinquent."

Tamae didn't feel like returning to her cold, dark home. Only when she was in bed daydreaming could she think momentarily of cheerful things. But when forced to confront reality, she found nothing whatsoever of interest in her life. Whenever she passed a vivacious young woman accompanying a man, Tamae swelled with the jealousy she usually reserved for rivals. No matter what she might do, she had lost that kind of youth. She did not even know herself why she had aged and decayed so quickly. She only raged at how Sakuo had ruined her life. People think about many things, but in the end, they all just pursue selfish greed. Sitting around the lively table at Kamiyama's place, Tamae imagined that if things went well, the Kamiyamas would invite her to stay for dinner. If she ate here, all that remained was to go home and sleep. Still, now that she hadn't been able to see him tonight, she really missed Tomita. It might be all over between them. Tomita had once told her she looked emaciated. If she pinched really hard on the flabby skin on her arm, it did not spring right back anymore; the skin at that spot stayed wrinkled, like weathered rubber. She knew she should get her body into shape somehow, yet she would get caught up in everyday events and embroiled in inadvertent arguments with Sakuo. Invited to stay for dinner, Tamae finally left their house around nine. Perhaps because she had been so pushy, the Kamiyamas hadn't bothered to see her to the door. Tamae strolled down the broad boulevard that continued past the houses and through the cedar grove. The frost-chilled wind blew fiercely, and countless tiny stars glittered in the clear sky. A tall, vigorous man followed Tamae. Her hopes rose. She vainly entertained the notion that he would call to her. As if deep in thought, she slowed. In front of the post office, the man passed by Tamae, glanced at her face under the street lights, and briskly walked off. He was young, and Tamae couldn't help but feel betrayed.

Upon returning home, Tamae went in through the back entry and opened the glass door. The electric burner glowed in the dark like a one-eyed goblin. Sakuo seemed to have crawled into the futon. "Saku, is that you?"

"Yeah."

"Why'd you come back?"

"Eiko said not today." Switching on the light, Tamae noticed that Sakuo's eyes looked swollen from crying.

"Don't you know this is really dangerous? You should put a kettle or something on it."

"Mom, do you have any cigarettes?"

"None. You should be the last one to bum cigarettes—you don't even work." Since it was cold, Tamae took her overcoat off, threw it over the futon she always left out unmade, and crawled under the covers just as she was.

"On the way home I stopped at Sakurai's, and he wanted to know if I didn't want to go to Hokkaido. He says there's a job in the coal mine office, with company housing, and the pay's good, too."

"Really? Sounds encouraging, doesn't it? You should go. What about your school record?"

"I could just claim any old thing probably. . . ."

"You should go to that kind of place and toughen up your body. Where is it?"

"Bihoro."

"Hmm, it's going to be cold up there from now on, hard for people with bad lungs, I bet."

"You'd probably be happy if I went off somewhere like that, wouldn't you, Mom? You'd be rid of me, wouldn't you. . . ."

"That's right, you just go on thinking exactly what you're thinking . . . I'm a terrible woman, and without you I'll probably start to really live again." Tamae was getting irritated by the noise of the mah-jongg game from the apartment in the back of the house.

"Going to Bihoro is like going to my death."

"That's not true. It might be better than living in Tokyo, and if you're onto something good, be sure to send for me, okay? . . . I'm completely fed up with Tokyo."

A fire engine siren screamed by beyond the vegetable field, shaking the ground.

"Say, Saku."

"What is it?"

"I'm very lonely. You probably won't understand this loneliness . . . but today I really felt awful. Since I'm so bullheaded, I've suffered a lot, but I'm just sick of living . . . I just keep decaying, and I don't have my old energy. You're a man, Saku, so you can understand a man's feelings. Men really are cruel, aren't they."

"You've finally realized that?"

"Yeah, I've realized it. Is it only when they're young that men and women click? Is that how it is? Even your dad—he just up and left, heading off where he wanted to go. He fell for women easily and was irresponsible. I'm thoroughly disgusted with life."

"It's okay as long as you have money. God made humans devise this wonderful thing. No matter what your problem, you can fix it as long as you have money. Even Eiko said she'd leave her husband in a minute if she had the money."

Tamae spread her fingers like a fan and inspected her polished nails intently. Her grimy weathered hands were a picture she could show to no man. "Saku, I can't tell if you're basically decent or bad."

"I'm bad."

"Don't be so sure. You're just twenty-two, and you haven't learned too many wily ways. Can't you trick somebody like a rich man's young daughter? . . ."

"Hmm, I don't much like young girls."

"That's because you've never had one."

"Mom, you're wicked. . . ."

"I suppose so." Tamae felt that it didn't matter what sin she committed. In ten years she'd lose the taste for it. Everyone is led astray by hypocritical morality. Underneath the hypocrisy, people fight ferociously, like lions, for the prizes—control, power, and wealth. Peace and contentment escape like steam from the friction of human dynamics. For some, there may be laughter. But for Tamae and her son there was not even a single glimmer of hope. Not even in the bond between mother and child. . . .

"Do you feel like going?"

Sakuo didn't answer. He looked up at the ceiling in silence. Tamae tried to remember until what age she had slept in the same bed with her child. She had not even intentionally touched him since he was six. He had always slept quietly by himself. He knew neither ordinary happiness nor common manners. She had never taken him on an outing. Yet he was precocious, and she knew that he had enjoyed masturbating as a child. Tamae ignored it, assuming that if someone had no other pleasures in life, it was only natural. Tonight she didn't even ask Sakuo where he had eaten dinner.

Two days later, Sakuo actually began to prepare to go to Hokkaido. He brought home ¥3,000 from Eiko as a kind of parting gift.

"When are you going?"

"On the thirtieth, by the night train. I'm going with Sakurai. I won't be coming home again."

"Yeah, well let's both stay well, okay. . . . " For the first time, Tamae's eyes brimmed and overflowed. She didn't mean to stop him, but in spite of herself she was moved to tears.

The night of his departure, they walked down the streets of the Ginza, bustling with the year-end crowd.

"The women are incredibly beautiful, aren't they."

"There're a lot of beauties in Hokkaido, too."

"City women are really nice, and that's that. They all have men, too, probably. . . ."

As Tamae walked alongside Sakuo, shoulder to shoulder, they talked like friends.

"Hokkaido's probably already cold with snow, isn't it?"

"Hmm, I'll have to go see for myself . . . but I'll be able to warm myself by a coal-burning stove. Now won't that be a treat."

"I was born in Taiwan and don't know anywhere that's colder than Tokyo, but deep snow sounds a bit romantic, don't you think?"

"Romantic? If you live there I don't suppose so. . . . What are you going to do now, Mom?"

"I'll probably get older and older. It won't be like old times, will it? During the long winters, I'll suffer from asthma, and then I may just up and die."

At a tobacco shop, Sakuo bought two packs and slipped one into Tamae's hand. "You won't have any more men, will you, Mom?"

"I don't suppose there's much hope. Nothing will ever bloom for me again. Do you still have time?" Sakuo peered into a Western-goods store to look at the clock.

"It's still okay. Two hours."

"I won't go to see you off, if that's okay with you."

"Yeah, it'd be better that way. Eiko's coming to see me off, so you'd better not."

"Didn't you already say good-bye to Eiko?"

"Yeah, I went by this morning. She's supposed to wait at the Columbin store over there." Tamae stopped short. She didn't feel like seeing Eiko.

"You know, if anything should happen to me, you don't have to come back, okay . . . I may want to just up and die, you know me. Even if that happens, you don't have to come, Saku." He nodded with his chin.

Even though this was her own son, he looked pathetic wearing his dusty, moth-eaten beret. Perhaps it's a good thing, she thought—at least Sakuo has a lover in Tokyo to see him off, even if she is someone else's wife. Tamae grasped his hand. Sakuo had a rather weak grip, and let go of hers right away.

"I won't see you for a while, so take care, okay? I'm not the greatest letter writer, so I won't write." On a tree-lined avenue in front of a coffeehouse whose aroma permeated the air, Sakuo quickly disappeared into the darkness, carrying his bundle of belongings. Tamae looked back once or twice but lost sight of him in the night fog.

Aware that now she was all alone, Tamae squared her shoulders and took a deep breath. At the end of the year, even the back streets were filled with people. Under the blue lights, a succession of storefronts—racks of silver salmon and mannequins draped with black velvet—streamed unperceived past her eyes. Downtown at this time of year seemed not to have changed a bit from years ago. For no particular reason, Tamae entertained the idea that she might breathe her last somewhere in this tempestuous city. That would surely be the only way to recapture the spirit of her youth. She nursed the notion that her life had been snuffed out like a candle in the wind. In the dark December streets, a girl with her hair up in the traditional style and several other children were boisterously slapping a shuttlecock with decorated wooden paddles. The white feathers disappeared into the night, only to come streaking across the light of the lamp under the eaves.

Ambling out to the avenue, Tamae heard a salesman barking hoarsely in front of Morinaga's, mobbed with people. "Yes, here are the Morinaga Velvets you all remember. How about it?" Mixing with the crowd, Tamae lifted a shining cellophane bag and dropped it into her pocket. She felt extremely pleased with herself. At a china store, Tamae melted into the crowd and stole a pretty Kutani soy sauce container. More than the fact that no one caught her, the weight in her pocket was gratifying. She felt as if she were walking along wearing a mask. All of a sudden, she was happy to be alive. Her parting from her son made Tamae feel instantly much younger, and as she came to dim Sukiyabashi street, she took a Velvet from the cellophane bag and popped it into her mouth. The sweet melody of a popular song drifted in the air from an advertisement. The *Asahi Newspaper* electric news raced busily to the right, flashing the dissolution of the Diet onto the sky.

Bibliography

The place of publication is Tokyo unless otherwise noted.

Works by Hayashi Fumiko

Books

Aouma o mitari [I saw a pale horse]. Nansōshoin, 1929.

Hōrōki [Diary of a vagabond]. Serialized in *Nyonin geijutsu* October 1928–October 1930; published by Kaizōsha, 1930; revised edition published by Shinchōsha, 1939.

Zoku Hōrōki [Diary of a vagabond, part 2]. Kaizōsha, 1930.

Seihin no sho [A record of honorable poverty]. Kaizōsha, 1933.

Watashi no rakugaki [My scribbling]. Keishōdō, 1933.

Omokage [Vestiges]. Bungaku kuōtarisha, 1933.

Chūjo zakki [Miscellaneous notes of a kitchen maid]. Okakura shobō, 1934.

Sanbunka no nikki [Diary of a prose writer]. Kaizōsha, 1934.

Tabi dayori [Tidings from the road]. Kaizōsha, 1934.

Inaka gaeri [Returning to the countryside]. Kaizōsha, 1934.

Nakimushi kozō [Crybaby]. Serialized in *Asahi Shimbun* November–December 1934; published by Kaizōsha, 1935.

Ningyō seisho [The doll's Bible]. Uedaya, 1935.

Nomugi no uta [A song of wild wheat]. Serialized in *Fujin kōron* January–March 1935; published by Chūō kōronsha, 1936.

Kaki [Oyster] (short stories). Kaizōsha, 1935.

Tanpen shū (short stories). Kaizōsha, 1935.

Bungakuteki danshō [Literary fragments]. Kawade shobō, 1936.

Aijōden [Biography of love]. Miwa shobō, 1936.

Aijō [Love]. Kaizōsha, 1936.

Onna no nikki [The diary of a woman]. Serialized in *Fujin kōron* from January 1936; published by Dai ichi shobō, 1937.

Inazuma [Lightning]. Serialized in *Bungei* (from January 1936); published by Yūkōsha, 1937.

Suppon [Snapping turtle]. Kaizōsha, 1937.

Hana no ichi [The location of flowers]. Takemura shobō, 1937.
Kōyō no zange [The confession of the fall colors]. Hangasha, 1937.
Hyōga [Glacier]. Takemura shobō, 1938.
Watashi no konchūki [Entomological souvenirs]. Kaizōsha, 1938.
Kawa [River]. Ōru yomimono, 1938.
Tsukiyo [A moonlit night]. Takemura shobō, 1938.
Sensen [Battlefront]. Asahi shimbunsha, 1938.
Yūshū nikki [Melancholy diary]. Chūō kōronsha, 1939.
Mippō [Secret bee]. Sōgensha, 1939.
Shinkyō to fūkaku [Mental state and character]. Sōgensha, 1939.
Jūnenkan [Ten years]. Serialized in *Fujin kōron* January–December 1940; published by Shinchōsha, 1941.
Hitori no shōgai [One person's life]. Sōgensha, 1940.
Seishun [Youth]. Jitsugyō no Nihonsha, 1940.
Akutō [Bad fight]. Chūō kōronsha, 1940.
Joyū ki [Diary of an actress]. Shinchōsha, 1940.
Rekisei [Successive generations]. Serialized in *Bungei shunjū* from September 1940; published by Kanchō shorin, 1941.
Budō no kishi [Shore of grapes]. Jitsugyō no Nihonsha, 1940.
Shokujo [Woman weaver]. Jitsugyō no Nihonsha, 1940.
Gyokai [Seafood]. Kaizōsha, 1940.
Nanatsu no tomoshibi [Seven lights]. Murasaki shuppansha, 1940.
Zuihitsu [Random jottings]. Chippu shobō, 1941.
Bara [Rose]. Rikon shobō, 1941.
Ame [Rain]. Serialized in *Shin nyoen* March 1941–March 1942; published by Jitsugyō no Nihonsha, 1942.
Senka [River song]. Serialized in *Miyako shimbun* from July 1941; published by Shinchōsha, 1941.
Hatsu tabi [First trip]. Jitsugyō no Nihonsha, 1941.
Keikichi no gakkō [Keikichi's school]. Kigensha, 1941.
Shūka [Autumn fruit]. Kaizōsha, 1941.
Nikki I [Diary, part 1]. Tōhō shobō, 1941.
Nikki II [Diary, part 2]. Tōhō shobō, 1942.
Den'en nikki [Rural diary]. Shinchōsha, 1942.
Onna no fukkatsu [A woman's revival]. Hakubunkan, 1943.
Ryojō no umi [The sea of travel weariness]. Shinchōsha, 1946.
Ukigusa [Floating grass]. Tankō shobō, 1946.
Ryokan no baiburu [The Bible at the inn]. Ōsaka shimbunsha, 1947.
Ningen sekai [The world of people]. Eikōsha, 1947.
Rinraku [Depravity]. Kantō shoin, 1947.
Onna no seishun [A woman's youth]. Kawabata shoten, 1947.
Uzushio [Swirling eddies]. Serialized in *Mainichi Shimbun* July–November 1947; published by Shinchōsha, 1948.
Sōsaku nōto [Writing notes]. Kantōsha, 1947.
Kagi [The key]. Shin bungeisha, 1947.
Hitotsubu no budō[One grape]. Nanboku shoin, 1947.
Maihime no ki [Record of a dancing girl]. Ozaki shobō, 1947.

Yume hitoya [One night's dream]. Sekai bungakusha, 1947.
Gan [Wild geese]. Fusōsha, 1947.
Kitsune monogatari [Tale of a fox]. Kokuritsu shoin, 1947.
Ochibo hiroi [The gleaners]. Asahi shimbunsha, 1947.
Pari nikki [Paris diary]. Tōhō shobō, 1947.
Otōsan [Father]. Kigensha, 1947.
Shukumei o tou onna [The woman who questions fate]. Ozaki shobō, 1948.
Minamikaze [South winds]. Rokugatsusha, 1948.
Aru onna no hansei [Half of a certain woman's life]. Miwa shobō, 1948.
Kurai yoru [A dark night]. Bungei shunjūsha, 1948.
Jinsei no kawa [The river of life]. Mainichi shimbunsha, 1948.
Hōrōki dai sanbu [Diary of a vagabond, part 3]. Serialized in *Nihon shōsetsu* May 1947–October 1948; published by Ryūjo shobō, 1949.
Dai ni no kekkon [The second marriage]. Shufu to seikatsusha, 1949.
Chairo no me [Brown eyes]. Serialized in *Fujin asahi* from January 1948; published by Asahi shimbunsha, 1950.
Shin Yodogimi [New Yodogimi]. Yomiuri shimbunsha, 1950.
Kinka [Rose of Sharon]. Serialized in *Chūbu Nihon shimbun* from January 1949; published by Jitsugyō no Nihonsha, 1950.
Ukigumo [The drifting clouds]. Serialized in *Fūsetsu* from November 1949 to August 1950 and then in *Bungakkai* from September 1950 to April 1951; published by Rokkō shuppansha, 1951.
Ehon Sarutobi Sasuke [Picturebook Sarutobi Sasuke]. Serialized in *Chūgai shimbun* June–December 1950; published by Shinchōsha, 1951.
Ore ashi [Bent reed] (short stories). Shinchōsha, 1951.
Aware hitozuma [The sorrowful married woman]. Rokkō shuppansha, 1950.
Sazanami—Aru onna no techō [Ripples—a certain woman's datebook]. Serialized in *Chūō kōron* January–June 1951; published by Chūō kōronsha, 1951.
Shinjubo [Mother-of-pearl]. Serialized in *Shufu no tomo* January–June 1951.
Onna kazoku [A family of women]. Serialized in *Fujin kōron* January–June 1951.
Meshi [Meal]. Serialized in *Asahi Shimbun* April–June 1951; published by Asahi shimbunsha, 1951.

Short Stories:

"Fūkin to uo no machi" [A town of accordions and fish]. *Kaizō*. (April 1931).
"Shōku" [Shoku]. *Chūō kōron* (March 1932).
"Yaneura no isu" [The chair on the roof]. *Kaizō* (August 1932).
"Santō ryokō no ki" [Record of a trip by third class]. *Kaizō*. (May 1933).
"Uguisu" [Bush warbler]. *Kaizō* (January 1934).
"Chiridame" [Dustbin]. *Bungei* (April 1934).
"Yamanaka uta awase" [Poetry contest in the mountains]. *Kaizō* (November 1934).
"Asayū" [Morning and evening]. *Bungei shunjū* (March 1935).
"Hinkei" [Hen]. *Kaizō* (May 1935).
"Jinsei fu" [Ode to life]. *Shinchō* (July 1935).

"Taikō made" [As far as the wide zone]. *Bungei shunjū* (July 1935).
"Bungakuteki jijoden" [A literary autobiography]. *Shinchō* (August 1935).
"Kaki" [Oyster]. *Chūō kōron* (September 1935).
"Irezumi" [Tattoo]. *Bungei* (December 1935).
"Kareha" [Withered leaf]. *Chūō kōron* (April 1936).
"Tsuioku" [Reminiscence]. *Shinchō* (May 1936).
"Kōgan" [Departing wild geese]. *Chūō kōron* (February 1937).
"Hototogisu" [Cuckoo]. *Chūō kōron* (June 1938).
"Hokugan butai" [Northern bank unit]. *Chūō kōron* (January 1939).
"Hatō"[Rough seas]. *Asahi Shimbun* (January 1939).
"Gyokai" [Seafood]. *Kaizō* (December 1940).
"Fubuki" [Snowstorm]. *Ningen* (January 1946).
"Ame" [Rain]. *Shinchō* (February 1946).
"Hōboku" [Pasturage]. *Bekkan bungei shunjū* (May 1946).
"Boruneo diaiaya" [Borneo diamond]. *Kaizō* (June 1946).
"Aibiki" [Assignation]. *Bekkan bungei shunjū* (December 1946).
"Kawa haze" [River goby fish]. *Ningen* (January 1947).
"Yubi" [Finger]. *Josei kaizō* (January 1947).
"Uruwashiki sekizui" [Splendid skeleton]. *Bekkan bungei shunjū* (June 1947).
"Hōrō teishujin" [The wandering husband]. *Shōsetsu shinchō* (October 1947).
"Yo no kōmorigasa" [The night umbrella]. *Shinchō* (January 1948).
"Arano no niji" [Rainbow of the wilderness]. *Kaizō bungei* (March 1948).
"Mōmoku no shi" [Blind poetry]. *Sandee mainichi* (April 1948).
"Ajisai" [Hydrangea]. *Bekkan bungei shunjū* (April 1948).
"Nobi no hate" [The bounds of the brushfire]. *Ningen* (September 1948).
"Taikutsu na shimo" [Wearisome frost]. *Shinchō* (October 1948).
"Bangiku" [Late chrysanthemum]. *Bekkan bungei shunjū* (November 1948).
"Hashiba Hideyoshi" [Hashiba Hideyoshi (Toyotomi Hideyoshi)]. *Bungei shunjū* (January 1949).
"Bon gū bon tōn" [Bon goût bon temps (Good taste good times). *Bungei jidai* (January 1949).
"Suisen" [Narcissus]. *Shōsetsu shinchō* (February 1949).
"Hone" [Bones]. *Chūō kōron* (February 1949).
"Dauntaun" [Downtown]. *Bekkan shōsetsu shinchō* (April 1949).
"Shirasagi" [White heron]. *Bungei kikan* (April 1949).
"Toranku" [Trunk]. *Bungakkai* (May 1949).
"Nioi sumire" [Fragrant violet]. *Bungei shunjū* (December 1949).
"Yaen" [Night monkey]. *Kaizō* (January 1950).
"Fuyu no ringo" [Winter apples]. *Shōsetsu shinchō* (serialized January–December 1950).
"Ueda Akinari" [Ueda Akinari]. *Bungei shinchō* (March 1950).
"Mekakushi hōō" [Blind phoenix]. *Ningen* (March 1950).
"Zanshō" [Afterglow]. *Bungei shunjū* (March 1950).
"Amakusa nada" [The Amakusa open sea]. *Bekkan bungei shunjū* (May 1950).
"Yakushima kikō" [Travelogue to Yaku Island]. *Shufu no tomo* (July 1950).

"Ore ashi" [Bent reed]. *Shinchō* (October 1950).
"Kinshi jaku" [Canary]. *Bekkan bungei shunjū* (October 1950).
"Fuyu no umi" [Winter sea]. *Kaizō* (December 1950).
"Jidōsha no kyaku" [The fare]. *Bekkan bungei shunjū* (December 1950).
"Ukisu" [The green sandbar]. *Bungei shunjū* (January 1951).
"Dōwa" [A fairy tale]. *Shinchō* (February 1951).
"Onshitsu no sakuragi" [The cherry tree in the room]. *Bekkan bungei shunjū* (May 1951).
"Kiku obana" [Chrysanthemum pampas grass]. *Chūō kōron bungei tokushū* (June 1951).
"Shin Hōjōki" [A new "Record of a ten-foot-square hut"]. *Chūō kōron bungei tokushū* (June 1951).
"Raichō" [Snow grouse]. *Bekkan bungei shunjū* (July 1951).

Collected Works

Hayashi Fumiko zenshū [The collected works of Hayashi Fumiko]. 7 vols. Kaizōsha, 1937.
Hayashi Fumiko chōhen shōsetsu zenshū [The collected long fiction of Hayashi Fumiko]. 8 vols. Chūō kōronsha, July 1938–February 1940.
Hayashi Fumiko bunko [Hayashi Fumiko library]. 10 vols. Shinchōsha, December 1948–October 1950.
Hayashi Fumiko zenshū [The collected works of Hayashi Fumiko]. 23 vols. Shinchōsha, October 1951–April 1953.
Hayashi Fumiko zenshū [The collected works of Hayashi Fumiko]. 16 vols. Bunsendō, 1977.

Sources in Japanese

Adachi Ken'ichi. "Hyōdenteki kaisetsu: Hayashi Fumiko" [Hayashi Fumiko: A critical biographical commentary]. In *Gendai Nihon no bungaku* (Gakushū kenkyūsha, 1971) 23: 449–464.
Aeba Takao. "Kaigai bungaku to sengō joryū no bungaku" [Literature abroad and postwar women's literature]. *Kokubungaku: Kaishaku to kanshō* (March 1972): 79–84.
Akiyama Shun. "Ima joryū bungaku to wa nani ka: sengo shi to no kanren de." *Kokubungaku: Kaishaku to kyōzai no kenkyū* 25, no. 15 (December 1980): 124–127.
Araki Jūichi. *Takuboku to Fumiko shō* [A summary of Takuboku and Fumiko]. Hondo Shi, Kyūshū: Kaichōsha, 1986.
Arai Kōichirō. "Hayashi Fumiko: hōrō to jojō no keishū sakka" [Hayashi Fumiko: A woman writer, wandering and lyrical]. In *Monogatari: Kindai Nihon bungaku shi* (Shin dokushosha, 1970), 177–184.
Arai Tadashi. "Runpen bungaku no shihyō" [An index of lumpen literature]. *Shinchō* (May 1931): 12–17.
Ariga Chieko. "Kafu chōseika no Nihon josei bungaku: Amino Kiku wa doko e" [Japanese women's literature under patriarchy: Whither Amino Kiku?]. In *Nichibei josei jānaru* [Japan-American Women's Journal] 8 (1990): 83–100.

Asami Fukashi. "Amino Kiku san no sakuhin" [The works of Amino Kiku]. In *Gendai Nihon bungaku taikei,* vol. 48, *Takii Kōsaku, Amino Kiku, Fujieda Shizuo shū* (Chikuma shobō, 1980): 386–390.

———. "Joryū sakuhin no shinshutsu ni tsuite" [Concerning the advancement of writing by women]. In *Asami Fukashi chosaku shū,* 1 (Kawade shobō shinsha, 1974): 282–284.

———. "Shimomura Chiaki shi no koto" [About Shimomura Chiaki]. In *Asami Fukashi chosaku shū,* 1 (Kawade shobō shinsha, 1974): 263–267.

Atsuta Yūko. "Hasegawa sensei to no jūsannen" [My thirteen years with Hasegawa]. *Nyōninzō* (March 1959): 16–17.

Baba Akiko. "Sengōno kaihōto joryū bungaku" [Postwar liberation and women's literature]. *Kokubungaku: Kaishaku to kanshō* (March 1972): 68–72.

Chiba Kameo. "Bungaku no ichinen" [The literary year in review]. *Kaizō* (December 1921): 183–189.

Dan Kazuo. "Shōsetsu: Hayashi Fumiko" [Fiction: Hayashi Fumiko]. *Shinchō* (November 1951): 118–129.

Eguchi Kan. "Fujin sakka ni nozomu" [What I ask of women writers]. *Bungaku annai* (March 1936): 16–20.

Egusa Mitsuko and Urushida Kayo, eds. *Onna ga yomu Nihon kindai bungaku: Feminizu hihyō no kokoromi* [Readings by women of modern Japanese literature: Venturing into feminist criticism]. Shinyōsha 1992.

Egusa Mitsuko et al. *Dansei sakka o yomu: Feminizumu hihyō no seijuku e* [Women reading male Japanese writers: Toward a maturation of feminist criticism]. Shinyōsha 1994.

Ehara Yumiko. *Feminizu ronsō: Nanajū nendai kara kyūjū nen e* [Debates of feminism: From the 1970s to 1990]. Keisō shobō, 1990.

———. *Feminizu to kenryoku sayū* [Feminism and the use of power]. Keisō shobō, 1988.

Ehrenburg, Ilya. "Hayashi Fumiko no bungaku" [The literature of Hayashi Fumiko]. Translated by Yamamura Fusaji. *Takiji to Yuriko* 8/11 (November 1960): 23–25.

Enchi Fumiko. "Hirabayashi Taiko dansō" [Fragmentary thoughts on Hirabayashi Taiko]. In *Kindai joryū bungaku: Nihon bungaku kenkyū shiryō sōsho,* edited by Nihon bungaku kenkyū shiryō kankō kai (Yūseidō, 1983), 175–176.

Endō Orie. "Kotoba to josei" [Words and women]. *Kokubungaku: Kaishaku to kyōzai no kenkyū* Special issue, "Feminizumu no kotoba—josei bungaku" [The vocabulary of feminism—female literature]. 37/13 (November 1992): 28–37.

Endō Yu. " 'Shirakaba ha' to joryū bungaku" [The Shirakaba group and women's literature]. *Kokubungaku: Kaishaku to kanshō* (March 1972): 28–33.

Endō Yu and Sofue Shōji. "Kaidai" [Explanatory notes]. In *Kindai bungaku hyōron taikei,* vol. 5, *Taishō ki II* (Kadokawa Shoten, 1972): 480–507.

Enoki Takashi. "Shizenshugi to joryū bungaku" [Naturalism and women's literature]. *Kokubungaku: Kaishaku to kanshō* (March 1972): 23–27.

Fujii Sadakazu. "Tsukurimono no jukusei" [The maturation of fictional tales]. *Kokubungaku: Kaishaku to kyōzai no kenkyū* 26/12 (September 1981): 82–89.

Fujikawa Tetsushi. "Hayashi Fumiko ron" [On Hayashi Fumiko]. *Bungakusha* 16 (October 1951): 94–100. Reprinted in *Kindai joryū bungaku: Nihon bungaku kenkyū shiryō sōsho,* edited by Nihon bungaku kenkyū shiryō kankō kai (Yūseidō, 1983), 90–95.

Fujioka Sakujirō. "Hayashi Fumiko san—eien no shi to hito to seikatsu" [Hayashi Fumiko—forever gone: The person and her life]. *Sakka* (August 1951): 91–95.

Fukagawa Kenro. "Hayashi Fumiko no Onomichi jidai (4)" [Hayashi Fumiko's Onomichi period, no. 4]. From Hiroshima kenritsu-shi kōkō kyōiku kenkyū nenpō, *Tetsujū* 17 (April 1977): 7–14.

Fukuda Hirotoshi. "Hayashi Fumiko." *Kokubungaku: Kaishaku to kanshō,* Special Issue. *Gendai joryū sakka no himitsu* [Secrets of the modern woman writer] 27/10 (September 1962): 43–48.

Fukuda Kiyoto and Endō Mitsuhiko. *Hayashi Fumiko: Hito to sakuhin (15)* [Hayashi Fumiko: The person and her works, no. 15]. Shimizu shōin, 1966.

"Fumiko o kataru" [Talking about Fumiko]. *Sanyō Shimbun* (May 30, 1983), p. 7.

Furubayashi Takashi. "Puroretaria bungaku undō to joryū sakka: Sata Ineko no baai" [Proletarian literature and women writers: The case of Sata Ineko]. *Kokubungaku: Kaishaku to kanshō* (March 1972): 41–47.

Furuya Tomoyoshi, ed. *Joryū bungaku zenshū* [Collected works of women's literature]. 4 vols. Tokyo bungei shoin, 1918–1919.

Furuya Tsunatake. "Kaisetsu" [Commentary]. In *Ukigumo* by Hayashi Fumiko (Shinchōsha, 1953), 378–381.

Hara Shirō. "Hayashi Fumiko." *Kokubungaku: Kaishaku to kyōzai no kenkyū* (January 1969): 160–161.

Harada Fusako. "Hageitō" [Amaranth]. In *Harada Fusako ikashū* [Posthumous poetic anthology of Harada Fusako] (August 1978), 36–39. Published privately by Harada's daughter, Okamoto Yukiko.

Hasegawa Masashi and Kōno Toshirō, eds. *Hasegawa Shigure: Hito to shōgai* [Hasegawa Shigure: The woman and her career]. Domesu shuppan, 1982.

Hashimoto Michio. "*Hōrōki*" [Diary of a vagabond]. *Kokubungaku: Kaishaku to kanshō* (November 1966): 196–197.

Hashizume Ken. "Hayashi Fumiko Ashura: Bundan zankoku monogatari" [Hayashi Fumiko Ashura: The story of brutality in literary circles]. *Shōsetsu shinchō* (November 1961): 206–218.

Hayashi Fumiko. "Atogaki" [Afterword]. In Hayashi Fumiko, *Fūkin to uo no machi* (Kamakura bunko, 1946), 329–332.

———. "Atogaki" [Afterword]. In Hayashi Fumiko, *Nakimushi kozō,* 131–132. Azumi shobō, 1946.

———. "Atogaki" [Afterword]. *Hayashi Fumiko zenshū,* 2 (Shinchōsha, 1953 [1949]), 289–293.

———. "Bungakuteki jijoden" [A literary autobiography]. *Bungei* Special Issue. *Hayashi Fumiko dokuhon* [Hayashi Fumiko reader, 1957]: 10–20. Originally published in *Shinchō* (August 1935).

———. "Chosha no kotoba" [Words from the author]. In Hayashi Fumiko, *Chairo no me,* 246–248. Kadokawa shoten, 1958. Originally published as "Atogaki" [Afterword] in *Chairo no Me* by Asahi shinbunsha (1950).

———. "Hatachi no koro" [When I was twenty]. *Shin jōen* (March 1953): 63.

———. *Hōrōki.* [Diary of a vagabond]. Tokyo: Shinchōsha, 1979.

———. "Sakuhin ni tsuite" [Concerning my works]. In *Shin Nihon bungaku zenshū,* vol. 11, *Hayashi Fumiko shū* (Kaizōsha, 1941): 463–464.

Hayashi Fumiko, Hasegawa Haruko, et al. "(Taidan) Ren-ai isetsu" [(Discussion) Divergent views of love]. *Nyonin geijutsu* (November 1928): 78–88.

Hayashi Fumiko, Nakajima Kenjo, Awatoku Saburō, and Koyama Eizō, eds. *Inochi aratani: Sengō seikatsu chōsa kai hen* [New life: Compiled by the postwar life research group]. Sakata shobō, 1950.

Hirabayashi Taiko. "Bungakuteki seishun den" [A literary biography of her youth]. *Gunzō* 6/26 (October 1951): 234–238.

———. "Fumiko san." *Ningen* (October 1951): 50–51.

———. *Hayashi Fumiko.* Shinchōsha, 1969.

———. "Hayashi Fumiko: Kaisetsu" [Commentary on Hayashi Fumiko]. In *Nihon no bungaku,* vol. 47 (Chūō kōronsha, 1967): 486–503.

———. "Hayashi san." *Bungakkai* (August 1951): 91.

———. "Kaisetsu: Hayashi san no omoide" [Commentary: Remembering Hayashi]. In *Bungakuteki jijoden* [Literary autobiography] by Hayashi Fumiko, 103–106. Kadokawa bunko, 1956.

———. *Miyamoto Yuriko.* Bungei shunjū, 1972.

———. "Sehyō to kanojo—Hayashi Fumiko no tame ni" [What the world is saying about Hayashi Fumiko]. *Nyonin geijutsu* 2/3 (September 1929): 66–67. Reprinted in *Kindai joryū bungaku: Nihon bungaku kenkyū shiryō sōsho* (Yūseidō, 1983), 75–76.

Hirabayashi Taiko and Ōhara Tomie. "Joryū bungaku no dōtei" [Identifying women's literature]. In *(Taidan) Nihon no bungaku* [(Discussions) About Japanese literature] (Chūō kōronsha, 1971), 345–352.

Hiraike Senkurō et al., eds. *Joryū bungaku sōsho* [A library of women's literature]. 2 vols. Tōyōsha, 1901, 1902.

Hirano Ken. "Fujieda Shizuo no koto" [Concerning Fujieda Shizuo]. In *Gendai Nihon bungaku taikei,* vol. 48, *Takii Kōsaku, Amino Kiku, Fujieda Shizuo shū* (Chikuma shobō, 1980): 391–393.

———. "Kaisetsu" [Commentary (on Nogami Yaeko and Amino Kiku)]. In *Nihon no bungaku* (Chūō kōronsha, 1965), 502–522.

———. "Keishikishugi bungaku ronsō no suketchi" [A sketch on the dispute over formalistic literature]. *Bungakkai* (August 1951): 92–99.

———. "Shōwa bungaku" [Showa period literature]. In *Shinchō Nihon bungaku shō jiten* (Shinchōsha, 1968), 608–612.

———. *Shōwa bungaku shi* [History of Showa literature]. Chikuma shobō, 1963.

———. "Sōsetsu" [General remarks]. In *Kindai bungaku hyōron taikei,* vol. 7, *Shōwa ki II,* edited by Takahashi Haruo and Hosaka Masao (Kadokawa shoten, 1972): 451–491.

———. "Watakushi shōsetsu" [The I-novel]. In *Shinchō Nihon bungaku shō jiten* (Shinchōsha, 1968), 1243–1248.

Hiratsuka Raichō. "Genshi josei wa taiyō de atta" [In the beginning, woman was the sun]. In *Seitō josei kaihō ronshū* [Bluestocking: A collection on female liberation], edited by Horiba Kiyoko (Iwanami bunko, 1991), 14–28. (Originally published in *Seitō* [September 1911])

Hirotsu Kazurō. "Sanbun geijutsu no ichi" [The position of prose art]. In *Kindai bungaku hyōron taikei,* edited by Miyoshi Yukio and Sofue Shōji (Kōdansha, 1973), 33–37. (Originally published in *Shinchō* [September 1924])

Honda Shūgo. *Tenkō bungaku ron* [On political apostasy]. Miraisha, 1964.

Horiba Kiyoko. "Kaisetsu" [Commentary]. In *Seitō josei kaihō ronshū* [Bluestocking: A collection on female liberation], edited by Horiba Kiyoko (Iwanami bunko, 1991), 359–367.

———, ed. *Seitō josei kaihō ronshū* [Bluestocking: A collection on female liberation]. Iwanami bunko, 1991.

"Ichinenkan hihan kai" [A gathering to critique the year]. *Nyonin geijutsu* 2/6 (June 1929): 4–18.

Ikari Akira. "Nihon no kazoku seido to joryū bungaku" [The Japanese family system and women's literature]. *Kokubungaku: Kaishaku to kanshō* (March 1972): 53–57.

Imai Kuniko, ed. *Nihon joryū bungaku hyōron (Chūsei/Kinsei hen)* [A critique of Japanese women's literature (Medieval/Tokugawa)]. Nagano: Asuka shobō, 1948.

Imai Tokusaburō. "Hayashi Fumiko yuku" [Hayashi Fumiko passed away]. In *Kashū seisen* [Crystal spring poetic anthology] (Hiroshima: Privately published by Ko Imai Tokusaburō sensei kashū kankōkai, 1956), 65–67.

Imai Yasuko. "Kaisetsu" [Commentary]. In *Tanpen josei bungaku gendai* [Contemporary women's short stories], edited by Imai Yasuko, Yabu Teiko, and Watanabe Sumiko (Ōfūsha, 1993), 20–26.

Imai Yasuko, Yabu Teiko, and Watanabe Sumiko, eds. *Tanpen josei bungaku gendai* [Contemporary women's short stories]. Ōfūsha, 1993.

———. *Tanpen josei bungaku kindai* [Modern women's short stories]. Ōfūsha, 1987.

Imamura Junko. "Ame no hyōgen ni miru kanjō in'yū ni tsuite: *Ukigumo* o chūshin ni" [Rain as a metaphor for emotion: Focusing on *The floating clouds*]. In *Kindai joryū bungaku: Nihon bungaku kenkyū shiryō sōsho* (Yūseidō, 1983), 123–130.

Inagaki Tatsurō. "Sōsetsu" [General remarks]. In *Kindai bungaku hyōron taikei,* vol. 5, *Taishō ki II,* edited by Endō Yu and Sofue Shōji (Kadokawa shoten, 1972): 473–479.

——— "Watakushi shōsetsu to shōsetsu janru" [The I-novel and fictional genres]. In *Kindai Nihon bungaku no fūbō* [Features of modern Japanese literature] (Miraisha, 1957), 156–163.

Inoue Yuriko. "Hayashi Fumiko to Akinari" [Hayashi Fumiko and Akinari]. *Kokubungaku: Kaishaku to kanshō* 41/9 (July 1976): 118–119.

———. "Hiratsuka Raichō." *Kokubungaku: Kaishaku to kyōzai no kenkyū* 24/4 (1979): 182–183.

Ishibashi Makio. *"Hōrōki"* [Diary of a vagabond]. *Kokubungaku: Kaishaku to kyōzai no kenkyū* (November 1966): 180–181.

Isome Hideo and Nakazawa Kei, eds. *Hayashi Fumiko: Shinchō Nihon bungaku arubamu (34)* [Hayashi Fumiko: Shinchō's album of Japanese literature, no. 34]. Shinchōsha, 1986.

Itagaki Naoko. "Atogaki" [Afterword]. In *Hayashi Fumiko shū. Shōwa bungaku zenshū* [Collected works of Shōwa literature], 19 (Kadokawa, 1953): 405–409.

———. "Genkon Nihon no joryū bundan" [The women's literary guild in Japan today]. *Bungaku* 1/9 (Sept. 1931).

———. "Hayashi Fumiko ni tsuite no bunken" [Documents about Hayashi Fumiko]. In *Gendai no esupuri: Hayashi Fumiko* [Hayashi Fumiko: A modern spirit] (Shibundō, 1965), 201–202.

———. *Hayashi Fumiko no shōgai: Uzushio no jinsei* [The career of Hayashi Fumiko: Life in a swirling eddy]. Raifusha, 1965.

———. "Kaisetsu" [Commentary]. In *Chairo no me* by Hayashi Fumiko (Kadokawa shoten, 1958), 249–254.

———. "Kaisetsu" [Commentary]. In *Ukigumo* by Hayashi Fumiko (Kadokawa shoten, 1963), 350–356.

———. "Kindai joryū sakka no shōzō: Hayashi Fumiko—sakufū no kōjō to hatten" [Portraits of modern women writers: Hayashi Fumiko—development of her literary style]. *Kokubungaku: Kaishaku to kanshō* (March 1972): 101–104.

———. *Meiji, Taishō, Shōwa no joryū bungaku* [Women's literature of the Meiji, Taisho, and Showa periods]. Ōfūsha, 1967.

———. " 'Dauntaun' kaisetsu" [Commentary on "The low city"]. In *Dauntaun* by Hayashi Fumiko (Kadokawa shoten, 1961), 104–110.

———. "Shōwa no joryū sakka" [Showa women writers]. *Kokubungaku: Kaishaku to kanshō* (September 1962): 29–33.

Itō Sei. "Geijutsu no shisō" [Art and thought]. In *Kindai bungaku hyōron taikei,* vol. 7, *Shōwa ki II,* edited by Takahashi Haruo and Hosaka Masao (Kadokawa shoten, 1972), 233–242. (Originally published in *Shinchō* [March 1937])

Iwabuchi Hiroko. "Kaisetsu" [Commentary]. In *Tanpen josei bungaku kindai* [Modern women's short stories], edited by Imai Yasuko, Yabu Teiko, and Watanabe Sumiko (Ōfūsha, 1987), 144–152.

———. "Rezubianizuma no yuragi—Miyamoto Yuriko 'Ippon no hana' " [Reverberations of lesbianism—Miyamoto Yuriko's "One Flower"]. In *Feminizumu hihyō e no shōtai: Kindai josei bungaku o yomu* [An invitation to feminist criticism: Reading modern literature by women], edited by Iwabuchi Hiroko, Kitada Sachie, and Kōra Rumiko (Gakugei shorin, 1995), 149–174.

Iwahashi Kunie. *Hyōden Hasegawa Shigure* [A biography of Hasegawa Shigure]. Kasama shobō, 1993.

Jō Ichirō. *Hakkinbon* [Banned books]. Tōgensha, 1965.

Joryū bungakusha kai, ed. *Nyonin geijutsu* [Women's arts] (January 1, 1949).

"Joryū o tsukihatarakasu mono" [Those who have exhausted women's style]. *Kokubungaku: Kaishaku to kyōzai no kenkyū* 25/15 (December 1980): 6–25.

Joseishi sogō kenkyū kai, ed. *Nihon josei shi* [History of Japanese women]. 5 vols. Tokyo daigaku shuppankai, 1982.

———. *Nihon joseishi kenkyū bunken mokuroku* [Catalogue of research materials on Japanese women's history]. Tokyo daigaku shuppankai, 1985.

"Josei ketten tekihatsu zadankai" [A round-table discussion to expose the deficiencies of women]. *Nyonin geijutsu* 2/4 (April 1929): 2–15.

Kagoshima shi, Kaishin shōgakkō. "*Hōrōki* ni egakareta Hayashi Fumiko" [Hayashi Fumiko as portrayed in *Diary of a vagabond*]. Booklet published by the Kaishin Elementary School, Kagoshima, 1981.

Kaigo Tokiomi, ed. "Tōkei" [Statistics]. In *Nihon kindai kyōikushi jiten* [Dictionary of the history of modern Japanese education] (Heibonsha, 1971), 77–93.

Kamei Katsuichirō. "Horobi no shitaku" [Preparation for ruin]. In *Kindai bungaku hyōron taikei*, vol. 7, *Shōwa ki II*, edited by Takahashi Haruo and Yasumasa Masao (Kadokawa shoten, 1972): 242–260. (Originally published in *Bungei* [April 1939])

———. "Inshō" [Impressions]. *Bungakkai* (August 1951): 86–88.

Kameyama Toshiko. "Yoshiya Nobuko to Hayashi Fumiko no jūgunki o yomu: Pen butai no kō ni ten" [Reading the war correspondence of Yoshiya Nobuko and Hayashi Fumiko: The pen squadron's two roses]. *Jūgōshi nōto* (July 1981), 78–89.

Kanai Shigefumi. *Heian joryū sakka no shinzō* [The image of Heian women writers]. Izumi sensho, 1987.

Kanda Mikio, ed. "Kashi no mi: Imai Tokusaburō sensei tsuitō shū" [Acorn: Collection of writings in memory of Imai Tokusaburo]. Hiroshima: Ko-Imai Tokusaburō sensei kashū kankō kai, September 1956.

Kaneko Sachiko. "Meiji ki ni okeru seiō josei kaiho ron no jūyō katei: John Stuart Mill 'The Subjection of Women' (Josei no reijū) o chūshin ni" [Ideas of western women's liberation in the Meiji period: Focusing on John Stuart Mill's 'The subjection of women']. *Shakai kagaku Jānaru* 23 (October 1984): 1–92.

———. "Taishō ki *Shufu no tomo* to Ishikawa Takemi no shisō" [*Housewife's friend* in the Taishō period and Ishikawa Takemi's thoughts]. *Rekishi hyōron* 42 (July 1984): 43–59.

Kano Takayo. "Wakamatsu Shizuko: Hazama ni tatta josei" [Wakamatsu Shizuko: A woman in transition]. *Gakutō* 82/7 (July 1961): 40–43.

Karatani Kōjin. *Nihon kindai bungaku no kigen* [Origins of modern Japanese literature]. Kōdansha, 1980.

Kawabata Yasunari. "Atogaki" [Afterword]. In Hayashi Fumiko's *Sazanami* (Chūō kōronsha, 1951), 267–274.

———. "Hayashi Fumiko san no tegami" [The letters of Hayashi Fumiko]. *Bungakkai* (August 1951): 82–85.

———. *Kawabata Yasunari zenshū* [Collected works of Kawabata Yasunari]. Edited by Sato Sōichi. Shinchōsha, 1977.

Kawakami Tetsutarō. "Hayashi san to no Chōsen ryokō" [Miss Hayashi's trip to Korea]. *Bungei,* Special Issue. *Hayashi Fumiko dokuhon* [A Hayashi Fumiko reader] 14/7 (June 1957): 79–80.

Kawamori Yoshizō. "Hayashi Fumiko no koto" [About Hayashi Fumiko]. *Tenbō* (August 1951): 45.

———. "Hayashi san no shōsetsu" [Hayashi's fiction]. *Bungei* (September 1951): 27–29.

Kawazoe Kunitomo. "Hayashi Fumiko no 'Bangiku' ni tsuite" [On "Late Chrysanthemum" by Hayashi Fumiko]. *Kokubungaku: Kaishaku to kanshō* (September 1951): 5–9. Reprinted in *Kindai joryū bungaku: Nihon bungaku kenkyū shiryō sōsho* (Yūseidō, 1983), 86–89.

———. "Nenpyō" [Chronology]. In *Hayashi Fumiko: Gendai Nihon bungaku arubamu (hito to bungaku shiriizu)* [Hayashi Fumiko: An album of modern Japanese literature (the person and his/her literature series)]. Gakushū kenkyūsha, 1980.

Kikuta Shigeo. "Nihon no koten bungaku to kindai joryū no bungaku" [Japanese classical literature and contemporary women's literature]. *Kokubungaku: Kaishaku to kanshō* (March 1972): 73–78.

Kishida Kunio. "Hitotsu no sōwa" [One episode]. *Bungei* (September 1951): 20–21.

Kitagawa Noriko. "Okamoto Kanoko no shōsetsu no buntai ni tsuite: Hayashi Fumiko to no hikaku" [On the fiction and writing style of Okamoto Kanoko: Comparisons with Hayashi Fumiko]. *Ōtani joshidai kokubun* 9 (March 1979): 240–244.

Kitamura Kaneko. "Onna rōnin" [Masterless female samurai]. *Nyonin geijutsu* 1/5 (1928): 76–78.

Kobayashi Hideo. "Hayashi Fumiko—no inshō" [Hayashi Fumiko—my impressions]. *Bungakkai* Special Issue. *Josei sakka no inshō* [Impressions of women writers] (April 1965): 111.

———. "Watakushi shōsetsu ron" [On the confessional novel]. In *Kindai bungaku hyōron taikei,* vol. 7, *Shōwa ki II,* edited by Takahashi Haruo and Hosaka Masao (Kadokawa shoten, September 1972): 181–202. (Originally published in *Keizai ōrai* [June and August 1935])

Kobayashi Jinsaku, et al., eds. *Joryū bungaku shi* [A history of women's literature]. 2 vols. Tōyōsha, 1901.

Kobayashi Masao. " 'Hayashi Fumiko' omoide no ki" [A record of memories of Hayashi Fumiko]. Privately published, n.d.

———. "Ko Hayashi Fumiko no tegami" [Letters of the late Hayashi Fumiko]. *Sanyō hibi shimbun* nos. 1–5 (January 5–9, 1965).

———. "Omoide" [Recollections]. In *Onomichi to Hayashi Fumiko* (Onomichi: Onomichi dokushō kai, 1974): 18–45.

Kobayashi Masaru. "Hayashi Fumiko 'Bangiku': sakuhin kaisetsu" [Commentary on Hayashi Fumiko's 'Late Chrysanthemum']. In *Nenkan daihyō shinario shū* [A yearbook of representative screenplays] (1954 ed.), 362. Mikasa shobō, 1955.

Kobayashi Tomie. *Hiratsuka Raichō: Hito to shisō* [Hiratsuka Raicho: The person and her thought]. Shimizu shōin, 1983.

Komatsu Shinroku. "Hito to bungaku" [The person and her literature]. In *Chikuma gendai bungaku taikei,* vol. 40. *Amino Kiku, Tsuboi Sakae, Kōda Aya shū* (Chikuma shobō, 1980): 477–494.

Kondo Yūko. "Okamoto Kanoko to Akinari" [Okamoto Kanoko and Akinari]. *Kokubungaku: Kaishaku to kanshō* 41/9 (July 1976): 120–121.

Kōno Toshirō. "Fujin bungeishi no ichi seikaku: *Hi no tori o* megutte" [Women's literary magazines and their position and character: Concerning *Firebird*]. *Kokubungaku: Kaishaku to kanshō* (March 1972): 34–41.

———. "Higuchi Ichiyo, Meiji joryū bungaku, Izumi Kyoka kenkyū annai" [Study guide to Higuchi Ichiyo, Meiji period women writers, and Izumi Kyoka]. In *Gendai nihon bungaku taikei,* vol. 5. *Higuchi Ichiyo, Meiji joryū bungaku, Izumi Kyoka shū* (Chikuma shobō, 1982): 6–7.

———. "*Nyonin Geijutsu:* Sono tenkai to shiteki igi" [The magazine *Women's Arts:* Its development and significance]. In *Nyonin geijutsu* (a reprint of the collected volumes, 1928–1932), 5–16. Fuji shuppan, 1987.

Kōra Rumiko. "Jiko to tō no shinwaka: Miyamoto Yuriko" [Mystification of herself and the party: Miyamoto Yuriko]. In Kōra Rumiko, *Onna no sentaku* [Women's choice's], 95–111. Rōdō sentā, 1984.

Kubota Yoshitarō. "Kindai joryū sakka no shōzō: Sata Ineko" [Portraits of modern women writers: Sata Ineko]. *Kokubungaku: Kaishaku to kanshō* (March 1972): 107–111.

Kumasaka Atsuko. "Kindai joryū sakka no shōzō: Okamoto Kanoko" [Portraits of modern women writers: Okamoto Kanoko]. *Kokubungaku: Kaishaku to kanshō* (March 1972): 94–97.

———. "Onna no seishun *Hōrōki*" [A woman's youth: *Diary of a vagabond]. Kokubungaku: Kaishaku to kyōzai no kenkyū* (April 1979): 90–91.

———. " 'Onnen to shite no joryū bungaku': Hayashi Fumiko to Okamoto Kanoko" [Malice in women's literature: Hayashi Fumiko and Okamoto Kanoko]. *Kokubungaku: Kaishaku to kyōzai no kenkyū,* Special Issue, *Joryū no zensen: Higuchi Ichiyo kara hachijūnen dai no sakka made* [The battle lines of women's literature: From Higuchi Ichiyo to the writers of the 1980s] 25/15 (December 1980): 79–83.

Kume Masao. " 'Watakushi' shōsetsu to 'shinkyō' shōsetsu" [The I-novel and "mental attitude" fiction]. In *Kindai bungaku hyōron taikei,* vol. 6, *Taishō ki IV, Shōwa ki I,* edited by Miyoshi Yukio and Sofue Shōji, (Kadokawa, 1973): 50–57. (Originally published in *Bungei kōza* [January and May 1925])

Kusabe Kazuko. "Miyamoto Yuriko to Hayashi Fumiko no buntai: Sono sanbunsei to jojōsei" [The literary style of Miyamoto Yuriko and Hayashi Fumiko: Their prose and lyricism]. *Kokubungaku: Kaishaku to kyōzai no kenkyū* (May 1960): 66–70. (Reprinted in *Kindai joryū bungaku: Nihon bungaku kenkyū shiryō sōsho,* 108–113 [Yūseidō, 1983])

Kusama Yasō. "Runpen monogatari" [Lumpen tales]. *Shinchō* (May 1931): 8–12.

Maeda Ai. "Taishō kōki tsūzoku shōsetsu no tenkai (ge): Fujin zasshi no dokusha sō" [The evolution of late Taishō popular fiction (parts 1 and 2): About the readers of women's magazines]. *Bungaku* (June and July 1968): 649–662, 808–822.

Maruyama Noboru. "Rō Jin to Hayashi Fumiko, Yokomitsu Riichi" [Lu Xun, Hayashi Fumiko, and Yokomitsu Riichi]. *Tosho* (February 1973): 26–31.

Matsubara Shin'ichi. "Joryū sakka ni okeru seiji ishiki" [The political consciousness of women writers]. *Kokubungaku: Kaishaku to kanshō* (March 1972): 58–63.

Mawatari Kenzaburō. "Joryū bungei kenkyū" [Studies in women's arts]. In *Kindai joryū bungaku ron* [On modern women's literature] (Nansōsha, 1973), 29–51.

Migishi Setsuko. "Onna no sekai" [The world of women]. *Bungei* (September 1951): 25–26.

Minemura Toshio. "Kigyō fujin zasshi keitai ron" [On the shape of the women's magazine business]. In *Sōgō jānarizumu kōza,* 9 (Naigaisha, 1931): 63–87.

Mishima Yukio. " 'Bangiku' kaisetsu" [Commentary on "Late chrysanthemum"]. In Hayashi Fumiko, *Bangiku* (Kawade shobō, 1951): 166–169 Reprinted in *Bungei* Special Issue, *Hayashi Fumiko dokuhon* [Hayashi Fumiko reader] 14/7 (June 1957): 46–50.

———. "Shimin bunko 'Bangiku': Kaisetsu" [Commentary on 'Late chrysanthemum': The people's literature]. In *Kindai joryū bungaku: Nihon bungaku kenkyū shiryō sōsho* (Yūseidō, 1983), 77–78.

Miyamoto Kenji. *Miyamoto Yuriko no sekai* [Miyamoto Yuriko's world]. Shin Nihon shuppansha, 1963.

Miyamoto Yuriko. *Bungaku ni miru fujin zō* [The image of women found in literature]. Shin Nihon shuppansha, 1973.

——— *Fujin to bungaku: Kindai Nihon no fujin sakka* [Women and literature: Modern Japanese women writers]. Jitsugyō no Nihonsha, 1947.

———. "Yabu no uguisu" [A bush warbler in a grove]. In *Gendai Nihon bungaku taikei,* vol. 5, *Higuchi Ichiyō, Meiji joryū bungaku, Izumi Kyoka shū* (Chikuma shobō, 1982): 455–461.

Miyoshi Yukio. "Kindai bungaku kenkyū no dōkō" [Trends in research on modern literature]. In *Nihon kindai bungaku kenkyū hikkei* (Gakutōsha, 1980), 9–14.

Mizuta Noriko. "Hōrō suru onna no ikyō e no yume to tenraku—Hayashi Fumiko *Ukigumo*" [Dreams and downfall of wandering women in a strange land—Hayashi Fumiko's *Drifting Clouds*]. In *Feminizumu hihyō e no shōtai: Kindai josei bungaku o yomu,* edited by Iwabuchi Hiroko, Kitada Sachie, Kōra Rumiko (Gakugei shorin, 1995), 303–331.

———. "Josei ron no yukue" [The direction of debates on women]. *Kokubungaku: Kaishaku to kyōzai no kenkyū,* Special Issue, *Josei—sono henkaku no ekurichūru* [*Écriture* of the changing female] 31/5 (May 1986): 64–71.

Moriyasu Masafumi. "Nihon bungaku ni okeru josei no ichi ni tsuite" [On the position of women in Japanese literature]. (Unpublished manuscript, n.d.): 1–27.

Morota Kazuharu. "Kindai joryū sakka no shōzō: Enchi Fumiko" [Portraits of modern women writers: Enchi Fumiko]. *Kokubungaku: Kaishaku to kanshō* (March 1972): 117–119.

Muramatsu Sadataka. "Hayashi Fumiko no dansei henreki" [Hayashi Fumiko's love life]. In *Sakka no kakei to kankyō* (Shibundō, 1964), 202–217.

———. *Kindai joryū sakka no shōzō* [A portrait of modern women writers]. Vol. 53 of *Tosho sensho.* Tokyo shoseki, 1980.

———. " 'Onna de aru koto' ron" [On 'the fact of being a woman']. In *Kawabata Yasunari kenkyū sōsho,* vol. 3, *Jitsuzon no kazō* edited by Kawabata bungaku kenkyū kai (Kyōiku shuppan sentaa, 1979): 168–182.

Muramatsu Sadataka and Watanabe Sumiko, eds. *Gendai josei bungaku jiten* [A dictionary of contemporary women's fiction]. Tokyodō shuppan, 1990.

Murō Saisei. "Bungei jihyō" [Commentary on current literature]. In *Insatsu teien* [A printing garden] (Takemura shobō, 1936), 237–249.

———. "Hayashi Fumiko no sakuhin" [The works of Hayashi Fumiko]. *Bungei zaisen* (May 1934): 82–89, 300–303.

———. *Ōgon no hari* [Golden needles]. Chūō kōronsha, 1961.

———. "Shimbun shōsetsu ni tsuite" [Concerning serial novels in the newspaper]. In *Insatsu teien* (Takemura shobō, 1936), 250–258.

Mushanokōji Saneatsu. "Hayashi Fumiko no shi" [The death of Hayashi Fumiko]. *Bungei* (September 1951): 18–19.

Nakamura Mitsuo. "Hayashi Fumiko." In *Nakamura Mitsuo sakka ron shū* [Collection of Nakamura Mitsuo's essays on literary figures] (Kōdansha, 1957), 150–160.

———. "Hayashi Fumiko ron" [On Hayashi Fumiko]. In *Gendai sakka ron sōsho: Shōwa no sakkatachi II,* edited by Nakajima Kenzō et al. (Eisōsha, 1955): 94–112. (Originally published in *Fujin kōron,* June 1953. Also reprinted as "Hayashi Fumiko bungaku nyūmon" [Introduction to the literature of Hayashi Fumiko], *Bungei* Special Issue, *Hayashi Fumiko doku hon* [Hayashi Fumiko reader], 14/7 (June 1957): 20–27.

———. "Hayashi Fumiko to sono bungaku" [Hayashi Fumiko and her literature]. *Shōsetsu kōen* (September 1951): 52–55.

Nakamura Murao. "Honkaku shōsetsu to shinkyō shōsetsu" [Serious fiction and mental attitude fiction]. In *Kindai bungaku hyōron taikei,* edited by Miyoshi Yukio and Sofue Shōji (Kōdansha, 1973), 11–16. (Originally published in *Shin shōsetsu* [January 1924])

Natsume Sōseki. "*Kōfu* no sakui to shizenha denkiha no kōshō" [Concerning a naturalist adventure and the intention behind *The Miner*]. In *Sōseki zenshū,* vol. 16, *Bekkan* (Iwanami shoten, 1967): 578–583.

Negoro Tsukasa. *Ōchō joryū bungaku no kotoba to buntai.* [The vocabulary and form of classical women's literature]. Yūseidō, 1988.

Nihon kindai bungakkan, ed. *Nihon kindai bungaku dai jiten* [Comprehensive dictionary of modern Japanese literature]. Kōdansha, 1977.

Niwa Fumio, Hayashi Fumiko, and Inoue Yuichirō. "Bundan ni deru kushin" [The difficulty of entering the literary world]. *Shinchō* 47/12 (1950): 114–128.

Nogami Yaeko and Amino Kiku. "Joryū bungaku to sakka seikatsu" [Women's literature and the writer's life]. In *(Taidan) Nihon no bungaku* [(Discussion) About Japanese literature] (Chūō kōronsha, 1971), 318–324.

Nomura Sawako. "Hayashi Fumiko den no shinjitsu no tame ni" [Setting Hayashi's biography straight]. *Shinchō* 57/10 (October 1960): 83–91.

Obara Gen. "Hayashi Fumiko ron: *Hōrōki* no jojōsei ni tsuite" [On Hayashi Fumiko: Concerning the lyrical quality of *Diary of a vagabond*]. In *Nihon bungaku,* Vol. 5 (Miraisha, 1956): 437–441.

Odagiri Hideo. *Gendai no sakka: Sono imi to ichi.* [Contemporary writers: Their meaning and position]. Tōjusha, 1972.

———. "Sakuhin kaisetsu" [Commentary on the works]. In *Nihon gendai bungaku zenshū,* Vol. 78, (Kōdansha,1967): 418–423.

Odagiri Hideo and Fukuoka Seikichi, eds. *Shōwa shoseki zasshi, shimbun hakkin nenpyō* [A list of censored Showa magazines and newspapers]. Vol. 1. Meiji bunken, 1965.

Ogata Akiko. "Kaisetsu" [Commentary]. In *Kindai joryū bungaku: Nihon bungaku kenkyū shiryō sōsho* (Yūseidō, 1983), 304–320.

———. "Kaisetsu" [Commentary]. In *Tanpen josei bungaku kindai* [Modern women's short stories], edited by Imai Yasuko, Yabu Teiko, and Watanabe Sumiko (Ōfūsha, 1987), 188–196.

———. Nyonin geijutsu *no hitobito* [The people of *Women's Arts*]. Domesu shuppan, 1981.

———. Nyonin geijutsu *sekai: Hasegawa Shigure to sono shūhei* [The world of *Women's Arts:* Hasegawa Shigure and her times]. Domesu shuppan, 1980.

Ōka Shōhei. "Kaisetsu" [Commentary]. In *Shōwa sensō bungaku zenshū* [Collected works of Showa war literature], 2 (Shūeisha, 1964): 490–496.

Okochi Akiya. "Kindai joryū sakka no shōzō: Setouchi Harumi" [Portraits of modern women writers: Setouchi Harumi]. *Kokubungaku: Kaishaku to kanshō* (March 1972): 122–125.

Ōkubo Norio. "Sengō bungakushi no naka no joryū bungaku: Hayashi Fumiko *Ukigumo* no ichi" [Women's literature in postwar literary history: The position of Hayashi Fumiko's *The floating clouds*]. *Kokubungaku: Kaishaku to kanshō* (March 1972): 47–52.

Okuno Takeo. *Joryū sakka ron: Shōsetsu wa honshitsuteki ni josei no mono ka* [On women writers: Does fiction essentially belong to women?]. Sanbunmeisha, 1974.

———, et al., eds. *Josei sakka jūsan nin ten* [An exhibition of thirteen women writers]. Nihon kindai bungakkan, 1988.

Onomichi dokusho kai, ed. *Onomichi to Hayashi Fumiko* [Onomichi and Hayashi Fumiko]. Onomichi: Onomichi Public Library, 1974.

———. *Onomichi to Hayashi Fumiko—arubamu* [Onomichi and Hayashi Fumiko—photo album]. Onomichi: Onomichi Public Library, 1984.

Ōya Sōichi. "Hayashi Fumiko ron" [On Hayashi Fumiko]. *Bungei annai* (March 1936): 30–32.

———. "Bundan girudo no kaitaiki" [Dismantling the literary guild]. *Shinchō* (December 1926): 78–83.

Saegusa Yasutaka. "Kindai joryū sakka no shōzō: Uno Chiyo" [Portraits of modern women writers: Uno Chiyo]. *Kokubungaku: Kaishaku to kanshō* (March 1972): 114–117.

Saeki Shōichi. *Kindai Nihon no jiden* [Modern Japanese biography]. Kōdansha, 1981.

Sai Manshu. "*Hōrōki* no koto nado" [On *Diary of a vagabond*]. *Bungei* (September 1951): 24–25.

Sakaguchi Ango. "Onna ninjitsu tsukai" [A ninja woman]. *Bungakkai* (August 1951): 88–90.

Sakurada Mitsuru, ed. *Hayashi Fumiko: Gendai Nihon bungaku arubamu* [Hayashi Fumiko: An album of modern Japanese literature]. Gakushū kenkyūsha, 1980.

Sata Ineko. *Sata Ineko shū.* [Works of Sata Ineko]. *Nihon bungaku zenshū* [Collected works of Japanese literature], vol. 39. Shinchōsha, 1961.

———. *Sata Ineko zenshū.* [Collected works of Sata Ineko]. Vols. 1 and 4. Kōdansha, 1978, 1979.

———. "Watakushi shōsetsu to kyakkan shōsetsu: Jibun no keiken kara" [Confessional fiction and objective fiction: From my own experiences]. In *Sata Ineko zenshū*, vol. 16 (Kōdansha, 1979): 122–126.

Sato Fumiko, ed. "Sokai no ki: Joryū sakka fujin undōka no baai" [Record of wartime evacuation: The case of the woman writer involved in feminist activities]. *Jūgōshi nōto* 8: 96–103.

Satō Haruo and Uno Kōji. *Kindai Nihon bungaku kenkyū: Shōwa bungaku sakka ron (ge)* [Modern Japanese literature research: On Shōwa period literature and writers]. Shōgakkan, 1943.

Seidensticker, E. G. "Hayashi Fumiko." Translated by Saeki Shōichi. *Jiyū* 5 (1963): 122–131.

Seki Reiko. "Dansei = dansei monogatari to shite no *Ningen shikkaku*" [Male = *No longer human* as masculine voice]. In *Dansei sakka o yomu: Feminizumu hihyō no seijuku e* [Women reading male Japanese writers], edited by Egusa Mitsuko, et al. (Shinyōsha 1994), 37–66.

———. *Higuchi Ichiyō o yomu* [Reading Higuchi Ichiyō]. Iwanami booklet no. 259. Iwanami shoten, 1992.

Sekii Mitsuo. "Kindai joryū sakka no shōzō: Kurahashi Yumiko" [Portraits of modern women writers: Kurahashi Yumiko]. *Kokubungaku: Kaishaku to kanshō* (March 1972): 125–127.

Senuma Shigeki. "Hayashi Fumiko." *Kindai Nihon bungaku no kōzō* (March 1963): 338–342.

———. "Taishō bungaku" [Taisho period literature]. In *Shinchō Nihon bungaku shō jiten* [Shinchō's concise dictionary of Japanese literature] (Shinchōsha, 1968): 689–694.

Setouchi Harumi, "Joryū sakka ni naru jōken" [Requirements for being a woman writer]. *Kokubungaku: Kaishaku to kanshō,* Special Issue, *Gendai joryū sakka no himitsu* [The secrets of modern women writers] 27/10 (September 1962): 96–99.

———. *Seitō* [Bluestockings]. 2 vols. Chūō kōronsha, 1984.

———. *Subarashiki onnatachi: Setouchi Harumi taidan shū* [Wonderful women: A collection of discussions with Setouchi Harumi]. Chūō kōronsha, 1983.

Shibaki Yoshiko. "*Chairo no me* kaisetsu" [Commentary on *Brown eyes*]. In Hayashi Fumiko, *Chairo no me* (Shinchōsha, 1954), 261–264.

———. "Kaisetsu" [Commentary]. In Hayashi Fumiko, *Meshi* (Kadokawa shoten, 1962), 217–221.

———. "Shinchō bunko *Chairo no me*"[Commentary on *Brown eyes*]. In *Kindai joryū bungaku: Nihon bungaku kenkyū shiryō sōsho* (Yūseidō, 1983): 104–107.

———. "*Ukigumo* no hito: shi—Hayashi Fumiko" [The person of *The floating clouds:* Teacher—Hayashi Fumiko]. *Shinchō* (October 1953): 66–71.

Shigeki Nobuo and Shōno Masanori, eds. *Orijinaru genban ni yoru Nihon no ryūkōka shi; Senzen hen* [The history of Japanese popular songs based on their original versions; prewar volume]. Bikutāongaku sankabushiki gaisha, 1977.

Shiina Rinzō. "Hayashi Fumiko no hito to sakuhin" [Hayashi Fumiko's life and works]. *Bungei* (September 1951): 22–23. Reprinted in *Kindai joryū bungaku: Nihon bungaku kenkyū shiryō sōsho* (Yūseidō, 1983), 84–85.

Shimada Akio. "Kindai joryū sakka no shōzō: Hirabayashi Taiko" [Portraits of modern women writers: Hirabayashi Taiko]. *Kokubungaku: Kaishaku to kanshō* (March 1972): 104–107.

Shimomura Chiaki. "Runpen—sono jittai, sono teigi, sono bungaku" [Lumpen—its essence, its definition, its literature]. *Shinchō* (May 1931): 1–7.

Shintō Junko. "Hirabayashi Taiko; Joryū de aru koto ni genkai wa nai" [Hirabayashi Taiko; There are no limits in being a woman]. *Kokubungaku: Kaishaku to kanshō* 27/10 (September 1962): 48–52.

Shioda Ryōhei. *Meiji joryū sakka* [Meiji women writers]. Seigodō, 1942.

———. *Meiji joryū sakka ron* [On Meiji women writers]. Nara shobō, 1965.

Sone Hiroyoshi. "Gendai bungaku ni okeru josei no hakken" [The discovery of women in modern literature]. *Kokubungaku: Kaishaku to kyōzai no kenkyū,* Special Issue, *Josei—sono henkaku no ekurichūru* [*Écriture* of the changing female] 31/5 (May 1986): 57–63.

Sukegawa Noriyoshi. "Kindai joryū sakka no shōzō: Ariyoshi Sawako" [Portraits of modern women writers: Ariyoshi Sawako]. *Kokubungaku: Kaishaku to kanshō* (March 1972): 120–122.

Suzuki Ichio. *Ōchō joryū nikki ronkō* [A study of classical diaries by women writers]. Ōbunsha, 1993.

Tachi Kaoru. "Kōtō kyōiku ni okeru joseigaku no: Dōnyū" [Introduction to women's studies in higher education]. In *Danjo kyōdō sankaku kei shakai no keisei to josei no kōtō iku* [Women's higher education and the model for joint participation of men and women in society] (Danjo kyōdō sankakukei shakai kenkyū kai, 1993), 161–168.

Takami Jun. "Shōwa no joryū sakka" [Women writers of the Showa period]. *Zadan, gendai bundanshi* [Round-table discussion: History of the modern literary guild] (Kasama shobō, 1976): 243–263.

Takemoto Chimakichi. *Ningen—Hayashi Fumiko* [Hayashi Fumiko, the person]. Chikuma shobō, 1985.

———. "Ningen—Hayashi Fumiko (1): Jippu Miyata Asatarō ni kanshite" [Hayashi Fumiko—the person (1): Concerning her real father, Miyata Asatarō]. *Hiuchi* 1 (November 1981): 199–222.

———. "Ningen—Hayashi Fumiko (2): Jippu Miyata Asatarō ni kanshite" [Hayashi Fumiko—the person (2): Concerning her real father, Miyata Asatarō]. *Hiuchi* 2 (May 1982): 192–213.

———. "Ningen—Hayashi Fumiko (3): Jippu Miyata Asatarō ni kanshite" [Hayashi Fumiko—the person (3): Concerning her real father, Miyata Asatarō]. *Hiuchi* 3 (November 1982): 3–27.

———. "Ningen—Hayashi Fumiko (4): Jippu Miyata Asatarō ni kanshite" [Hayashi Fumiko—the person (4): Concerning her real father, Miyata Asatarō]. *Hiuchi* 4 (June 1983): 172–204.

———. "Ningen—Hayashi Fumiko (1): Tsuminokoshi—Nomura ron" [Hayashi Fumiko—the person(1): On her break from Nomura]. *Hiuchi* 7 (April 1986): 94–113.

———. "Ningen—Hayashi Fumiko (2): Tsuminokoshi—Imai Tokusaburō sensei ni tsuite" [Hayashi Fumiko—the person (2): On her break with her teacher Imai Tokusaburō]. *Hiuchi* 7 (April 1986): 114–119.

Takenishi Hiroko. "Kaisetsu" [Commentary]. In *Kindai joryū bungaku: Nihon bungaku kenkyū shiryō sōsho,* vol. 20, *Hayashi Fumiko shū* (Yūseidō, 1983): 114–122.

Tamiya Torahiko. "Hayashi Fumiko no sakuhin" [The works of Hayashi Fumiko]. In *Hayashi Fumiko kessaku shū.* 1951. Reprinted in *Kindai joryū bungaku: Nihon bungaku kenkyū shiryō sōsho* (Yūseidō, 1983), 79–80.

———. "Kaisetsu" [Commentary]. In Hayashi Fumiko, *Meshi* (Shinchōsha, 1982): 220–226. (Originally published in 1954)

Terada Tōru. "Sannin no joryū sakka: Yuriko/Taiko/Fumiko" [Three women writers: Yuriko, Taiko, and Fumiko]. In *Gendai Nihon sakka kenkyū.* [Studies of modern Japanese writers] (Miraisha, 1954), 258–268.

Tokuda Shūsei. "Shinkyō shōsetsu to honkaku shōsetsu no mondai" [Issues concerning serious fiction and mental attitude fiction]. In *Kindai bungaku hyōron taikei,* edited by Miyoshi Yukio and Sofue Shōji (Kōdansha, 1973), 67–68.

Tokura Giichi. "Fujin katei tosho no shuppan kan" [Opinion on the publication of women's home books]. In *Sōgō janarizumu kōza,* vol. 9 (Naigaisha, 1931): 19–33.

Tomioka Taeko. *Fuji no koromo ni asa no fusuma* [Lavender garments and linen quilts]. Chūō kōronsha, 1984.

Toshizawa Yukio. "Joryū sakka ni okeru sei ishiki" [Sexual consciousness of women writers]. *Kokubungaku: Kaishaku to kanshō* (March 1972): 63–67.

Tsuboi Sakae. "Hayashi Fumiko san no omoide" [Memories of Hayashi Fumiko]. *Bungei* (August 1951): 22–23.

Tsuboi Sakae and Hirabayashi Taiko. "Hayashi Fumiko no omoide" [Reminiscences of Hayashi Fumiko]. *(Taidan) Nihon no bungaku* (Discussions) About Japanese literature] (Chūō kōronsha, 1971), 338–345.

Tsujihashi Saburō. "Kindai joryū sakka no shōzō: Yoshiya Nobuko" [Portraits of modern women writers: Yoshiya Nobuko]. *Kokubungaku: Kaishaku to kanshō* (March 1972): 111–114.

Tsukada Mitsue. "Joryū bungaku ko josetsu: Hayashi Fumiko o chūshin ni" [Prelude to women's literature: Centering around Hayashi]. *Joshidai kokubun* (January 1972): 31–42.

Tsurumi Shunsuke. "Tenkō no kyōdō kenkyū ni tsuite" [Cooperative research on political apostasy]. In *Tenkō ron josetsu* [Debates on explaining political apostasy], edited by Nakajima Makoto (Mineruba shobō, 1980).

Ueda Ayako, Ozaki Midori, and Yagi Akiko. "*Aouma o mitari* hyō" [Comments on "I saw a pale horse"]. In *Kindai joryū bungaku: Nihon bungaku kenkyū shiryō sōsho* (Yūseidō, 1983), 73–74.

Ueno Chizuko. "Atogaki" [Afterword]. In *Danryū bungaku ron* [On male literature], by Ueno Chizuko, Ogura Chikako, and Tomioka Taeko (Chikuma shobō, 1992), 400–405.

———. *Onna to iu kairaku* [The pleasures that are women]. Kesō shobō, 1986.

———. *Onna wa sekai o sukueru ka* [Can women save the world?]. Kesō shobō, 1986.

Ueno Chizuko, Ogura Chikako, Tomioka Taeko. *Danryū bungaku ron* [On male literature]. Chikuma shobō, 1992.

Uno Kōji. " 'Watakushi shōsetsu' shiken" [Confessional fiction: A personal view]. In *Kindai bungaku hyōron taikei,* edited by Miyoshi Yukio and Sofue Shōji (Kōdansha, 1973), 61–66. (Originally published in *Shinchō* [October 1925])

Usui Yoshimi. *Kindai bungaku ronsō (Jō)* [Modern literature debates, vol. 1]. Chikuma shobō, 1985.

Wada Yoshie. "Hayashi Fumiko." *Shūkan dokusho jin* (June 22, 1964), p. 3.

——— "Hayashi Fumiko, Hirabayashi Taiko nyūmon" [Introduction to Hayashi Fumiko and Hirabayashi Taiko]. In *Nihon gendai bungaku zenshū,* vol. 78 (Kōdansha, 1967): 424–430.

——— "Hayashi Fumiko, shusshō no nazo" [The mystery of Hayashi Fumiko's birth]. In *Kindai joryū bungaku: Nihon bungaku kenkyū shiryō sōsho* (Yūseidō, 1983), 131–135.

Wakuta Yū. "Ibuse Masuji to Hayashi Fumiko: 'Shūkin Ryokō' no haikei" [Ibuse Masuji and Hayashi Fumiko: The background of 'Shūkin Ryokō']. In Wakuta Yū, *Ibuse Masuji no sekai* (Shūeisha, 1983), 109–138.

Watanabe Sumiko. "Kindai joryū sakka no shōzō: Miyamoto Yuriko" [Portraits of modern women writers: Miyamoto Yuriko]. *Kokubungaku: Kaishaku to kanshō* (March 1972): 98–101.

Yamamoto Kenkichi. "Kaisetsu" [Commentary]. *Bungei* (October 1956): 375–379.

———. "Okamoto Kanoko no bungaku" [Okamoto Kanoko's literature]. In *Kindai bungaku hyōron taikei,* vol. 7, *Shōwa ki II,* edited by Takahashi Haruo and Hosaka Masao (Kadokawa shoten, 1972), 403–408. (Originally published in *Mita bungaku* [April 1940])

Yamasa Kin. "Hayashi Fumiko den" [A biography of Hayashi Fumiko]. *Santo Shimbun* nos. 1–22 (May 16–June 12, 1964).

Yasunari Jirō. "Shimbun to fujin" [Newspapers and women]. In *Sōgō jānarizumu kōza,* vol. 9 (Naigaisha, 1931): 1–15.

Yokozeki Aizō. "Hayashi Fumiko: Meshi ni nayanda odaijin" [Hayashi Fumiko: A princess in search of her next meal]. In *Omoide no sakkatachi* (Hōsei daigaku, 1956), 54–64.

Yonaha Keiko. *Gendai joryū sakka ron* [The debate on contemporary women writers]. Shinbisha, 1986.

Yoneda Sayoko. *Kindai Nihon joseishi* [A history of modern Japanese women]. Vols. 1 and 2. Shin Nihon shinsho, 1972.

Yosano Akiko. *Tokugawa jidai joryū bungaku: Reiko shōsetsu shū* [Women's literature of the Tokugawa period: A collection of fiction by Reiko]. Fuzanbō, 1916.

Yoshida Seiichi. "Kindai joryū no bungaku" [Literature of contemporary women writers]. *Kokubungaku: Kaishaku to kanshō* (March 1972): 10–17.

Yoshikawa Toyoko. " 'Feminizumu hihyō' wa seijutsu shita ka?" [Has "feminist criticism" come of age?]. *Nihon kindai bungaku* 52 (May 1995): 181–187.

Yoshiya Nobuko. "Juntokuin fuyo Kiyomi Oane: Hayashi Fumiko." In *Jidenteki joryū bundan shi* [Biographical history of the female literary world] (Chūō kōronsha, 1962), 50–71.

Yuri Sachiko. "Josei sakka no genzai" [Female writers today]. *Kokubungaku: Kaishaku to kanshō,* Special Issue, *Josei sakka no shinryū* [New currents in female writers] (May 1991): 71–81.

Sources in English

Ahmad Aijaz. "Orientalism and After: Ambivalence and Cosmopolitan Location in the Work of Edward Said." *Economic and Political Weekly* (July 25, 1992): PE/98–116.

Anderson, Joseph L., and Donald Richie. *The Japanese Film: Art and Industry.* Princeton: Princeton University Press, 1982.

Arima, Tatsuo. *The Failure of Freedom.* Cambridge: Harvard University Press, 1969.

Bernstein, Gail, ed. *Recreating Japanese Women, 1600–1945.* Berkeley: University of California Press, 1991.

Birnbaum, Phyllis, trans. *Rabbits, Crabs, Etc.: Stories by Japanese Women.* Honolulu: University of Hawai'i Press, 1982.

Bowring, Richard. "The Female Hand in Heian Japan: A First Reading." In *The Female Autograph: Theory and Practice of Autobiography from the Tenth to the Twentieth Century,* edited by Domna C. Stanton (Chicago: University of Chicago Press, 1987), 49–56.

———, trans. *Murasaki Shikibu, Her Diary and Poetic Memoirs.* Princeton: Princeton University Press, 1982.

Brownstein, Michael C. "*Jogaku Zasshi* and the Founding of *Bungakkai,*" *Monumenta Nipponica* 35 (1980): 3.

Bundy, Roselee. "Japan's First Woman Diarist and the Beginning of Prose Writing by Women in Japan." *Women's Studies* 19 (1991): 79–91.

Chabot, Jeanette A. Taudin "A View of Tokugawa Women and Literature." In *Women in Japanese Literature,* edited by The Netherlands Association for Japanese Studies, (Netherlands Association for Japanese Studies, 1981), 55–56.

Copeland, Rebecca. "Hiratsuka Raichō." In *Japanese Woman Writers,* edited by Chieko Mulhern (Westport, Conn.: Greenwood Press, 1994), 133–140.

———. *The Sound of the Wind: The Life and Works of Uno Chiyo.* Honolulu: University of Hawai'i Press, 1992.

Cranston, Edwin A., trans. *The Izumi Shikibu Diary: A Romance of the Heian Court.* Cambridge: Harvard University Press, 1969.

Danly, Robert Lyons. *In the Shade of Spring Leaves.* New Haven: Yale University Press, 1981.

Dunlop, Lane, trans. *A Late Chrysanthemum: Twenty-One Stories from the Japanese.* San Francisco: North Point Press, 1986.

Ericson, Joan E. "Hayashi Fumiko." In *Modern Japanese Novelists: Dictionary of Literary Biography,* edited by Van C. Gessel (Columbia, S.C.: Bruccoli Clark Layman, 1997).

———. "Hayashi Fumiko and the Transformation of Her Fiction." In *Currents in Japanese Culture: Translations and Transitions,* edited by Amy Heinrich (New York: Columbia University Press, 1997), 389–407.

———. "The Origins of the Concept of Japanese 'Women's Literature.'" In *The Woman's Hand: Gender and Theory in Japanese Women's Writing,* edited by Paul Schalow and Janet A. Walker (Stanford: Stanford University Press, 1996), 74–115.

Fowler, Edward. *The Rhetoric of Confession: Shishōsetsu in Early Twentieth-Century Japanese Fiction.* Berkeley: University of California Press, 1988.

Fujii, James. *Complicit Fictions.* Berkeley: University of California Press, 1993.

Garon, Sheldon. "Women's Groups and the Japanese State: Contending Approaches to Political Integration, 1890–1945." *Journal of Japanese Studies* 19/1 (1993): 5–41.

Gates, Henry Louis. " 'Authenticity' or the Lesson of Little Tree." *New York Times Book Review* (November 24, 1991), pp. 1, 26–30.

Gilbert, Sandra M., and Susan Gubar. *The Madwoman in the Attic: The Writer and the Nineteenth-Century Literary Imagination.* New Haven: Yale University Press, 1979.

———. *No Man's Land: The Place of the Woman Writer in the Twentieth Century,* vol. 1, *The War of the Words.* New Haven: Yale University Press, 1988.

Gluck, Carol. *Japan's Modern Myths.* Princeton: Princeton University Press, 1986.

The Gossamer Years: The Diary of a Noblewoman of Heian Japan. Translated by Edward G. Seidensticker. Rutland, Vt.: Charles E. Tuttle, 1964.

Gould, Stephen Jay. *The Mismeasurement of Man.* New York: W. W. Norton, 1981.

Hall, John Whitney, and Toyoda Takeshi, eds. *Japan in the Muromachi Age.* Berkeley: University of California Press, 1977.

Hane, Mikiso, ed. and trans. *Reflections on the Way to the Gallows: Voices of Japanese Rebel Women.* New York: Pantheon Books, 1988.

Havens, Thomas R. H. *Valley of Darkness: The Japanese People and World War Two.* New York: W. W. Norton, 1978.

Hayashi Fumiko. "The Accordion and the Fish Town," translated by Janice Brown *Winds* (Japan Airlines In-Flight Magazine) (December 1990): 38–49.

———. "Bones." Translated by Ted T. Takaya in *The Catch and Other War Stories,* edited by Shōichi Saeki (Tokyo: Kōdansha, 1981), 133–160.

———. "Borneo Diamond." Translated by Lane Dunlop in *Autumn Wind and Other Stories* (Rutland, Vt.: Charles E. Tuttle, 1994), 161–182.

———. "Downtown." In *Modern Japanese Stories,* edited and translated by Ivan Morris (Tokyo: Charles E. Tuttle, 1962), 349–364.

———. *The Floating Clouds.* Translated by Koitabashi Yoshiyuki and Martin C. Collcutt. Tokyo: Hara shobō, 1965.

———. "Journal of a Vagabond." Translated by S. G. Brickley in *The Writing of Idiomatic English* (Tokyo: Kenkyūsha, 1951), 19–23.

———. "Late Chrysanthemum," translated by John Bester. *Japan Quarterly.* 3/4 (October–December 1956): 468–486.

———. "A Late Chrysanthemum." Translated by Lane Dunlop in *A Late Chrysanthemum: Twenty-One Stories from the Japanese.* San Francisco: North Point Press, 1986.

———. "Narcissus." Translated by Joan E. Ericson. *Asian Cultural Studies* 21 (April 1995): 71–84.

———. "Narcissus." Translated by Kyoko Iriye Selden in *Stories by Contemporary Japanese Women Writers,* edited by Noriko Mizuta Lippit and Kyoko Iriye Selden (Armonk, N.Y.: M. E. Sharpe, 1982), 49–61.

———. "Splendid Carrion." Translated by Shioya Sakae. *The Western Humanities Review* (Summer 1952).

———. "Tokyo." Translated by Ivan Morris in *Modern Japanese Literature,* edited by Donald Keene (Rutland, Vt.: Charles E. Tuttle, 1956), 415–428.

———. "Vagabond's Song." Translated by Elizabeth Hanson in *To Live and to Write: Selections by Japanese Women Writers, 1913–1938,* edited by Yukiko Tanaka (Seattle: Seal Press, 1987), 105–125.

Hino Ashihei. *Wheat and Soldiers.* Translated by Baroness Shidzué Ishimoto. New York: Farrar and Rinehart, 1939.

Hirabayashi Taeko. "Self-Mockery." Translated by Yukiko Tanaka, trans. in *To Live and to Write: Selections by Japanese Women Writers, 1913–1938,* edited by Yukiko Tanaka (Seattle: Seal Press, 1987), 75–96.

Historical Statistics of Japan. Tokyo: Government of Japan, Japan Statistical Association, 1987.

Hoston, Germaine A. *Marxism and the Crisis of Development in Prewar Japan.* Princeton: Princeton University Press, 1986.

International House of Japan Library. *Modern Japanese Literature in Translation: A Bibliography.* Tokyo: Kōdansha, 1979.

Irokawa Daikichi. "Meiji Conditions of Nonculture." In *The Culture of the Meiji Period,* edited and translated by Marius B. Jansen (Princeton: Princeton University Press, 1985).

Iwamoto Yoshio. "Aspects of the Proletarian Literary Movement in Japan." In *Japan in Crisis,* edited by Bernard Silberman and Harry D. Harootunian (Princeton: Princeton University Press, 1974).

Japan Statistical Yearbook, 1993/94. Tokyo: Government of Japan, Statistical Bureau, Management and Coordination Agency, 1994.

Karatani Kojin. *Origins of Modern Japanese Literature.* Edited and translated by Brett de Bary (Durham: Duke University Press, 1993 [1980]).

Kato Shuichi. *A History of Japanese Literature.* 3 vols. Tokyo: Kōdansha, 1983.

Keene, Donald. *Anthology of Japanese Literature, from the Earliest Era to the Mid-Nineteenth Century.* Rutland, Vt.: Charles E. Tuttle, 1956.

———. *Dawn to the West: Japanese Literature in the Modern Era.* Vol. 1. New York: Holt, Rinehart and Winston, 1984.

———. "Japanese Literature and Politics in the 1930s." *Journal of Japanese Studies* 2/2 (Summer 1976).

———. *Japanese Literature: An Introduction for Western Readers.* New York: Grove Press, 1955.

———. "Japanese Writers and the Greater East Asian War." In Donald Keene *Landscapes and Portraits: Appreciations of Japanese Culture* (Tokyo: Kōdansha, 1971), 300–301.

———. *Modern Japanese Literature: From 1868 to Present Day.* Rutland, Vt.: Charles E. Tuttle, 1956.

———. *Travelers of a Hundred Ages.* New York: Henry Holt and Company, 1989.

———. *World within Walls: Japanese Literature of the Pre-Modern Era, 1600–1867.* Tokyo: Charles E. Tuttle, 1976.

Konishi Jin'ichi. *A History of Japanese Literature.* Vol. 1. Edited by Earl Miner and translated by Aileen Gatten and Nicholas Teele. Princeton: Princeton University Press, 1984.

———. *A History of Japanese Literature.* Vol. 2. Edited by Earl Miner and translated by Aileen Gatten. Princeton: Princeton University Press, 1986.

Levy, Ian Hideo. *The Ten Thousand Leaves: A Translation of the* Man'yōshū, *Japan's Premier Anthology of Classical Poetry.* Vol. 1. Princeton: Princeton University Press, 1981.

Lippit, Noriko Mizuta. "Japan's Literary Feminists: The *Seitō* Group." *Signs* 2/1 (Autumn 1976).

———. *Reality and Fiction in Modern Japanese Literature.* New York: M. E. Sharpe, 1980.

———. "*Seitō* and the Literary Roots of Japanese Feminism." *International Journal of Women's Studies* 2/2 (March 1979).

Lippit, Noriko Mizuta, and Kyoko Iriye Selden, eds. and trans. *Stories by Contemporary Japanese Women Writers.* New York: M. E. Sharpe, 1982.

Marx, Karl. *Capital.* Vol. 1. 1867. Reprinted in a translation by Ben Fowkes. New York: Vintage, 1976.

———. "The Class Struggles in France, 1848–1850." 1850. Reprinted in *Surveys in Exile,* edited by David Fernback. New York: Vintage Press, 1973.

Mass, Jeffrey P. *Lordship and Inheritance in Early Medieval Japan: A Study of the Kamakura Sōryō System.* Stanford: Stanford University Press, 1989.

Miki Soko. "Without the Spirit of Women's Liberation, What Is Women's Studies For?" *Onna Eros* [Women's Eros] (1977).

Miner, Earl. *Japanese Poetic Diaries.* Berkeley: University of California Press, 1969.

Mitchell, Richard H. *Thought Control in Prewar Japan.* Ithaca: Cornell University Press, 1976.

Miyake, Lynne K. "The *Tosa Diary:* In the Interstices of Gender and Criticism." In *The Woman's Hand: Gender and Theory in Japanese Women's Writing,* edited by Paul Schalow and Janet A. Walker (Stanford: Stanford University Press, 1996), 41–73.

———. "Women's Voice in Japanese Literature: Expanding the Feminine." *Women's Studies* 17 (1989): 87–100.

Miyoshi, Masao. *Off Center: Power and Culture Relations between Japan and the United States.* Cambridge: Harvard University Press, 1991.

Mizuta, Noriko. "In Search of a Lost Paradise: The Wandering Woman in Hayashi Fumiko's *Drifting Clouds.*" In *The Woman's Hand: Gender and Theory in Japanese Women's Writing,* edited by Paul Schalow and Janet A. Walker (Stanford: Stanford University Press, 1996), 329–351.

Morris, Ivan. *The World of the Shining Prince: Court Life in Ancient Japan.* New York: Penguin Books, 1964.

———. trans. *As I Crossed the Bridge of Dreams: Recollections of a Woman in Eleventh Century Japan.* New York: Dial Press, 1971.

———, ed. *Modern Japanese Stories: An Anthology.* Rutland, Vt., Charles E. Tuttle, 1962.

Mulhern, Chieko, ed. *Japanese Women Writers: A Bio-Critical Sourcebook* Westport, Conn.: Greenwood Press, 1994.

Murasaki Shikibu. *The Tale of Genji.* Translated by Edward G. Seidensticker. New York: Alfred A. Knopf, 1976.

———. *Murasaki Shikibu: Her Diary and Poetic Memoirs.* Translated by Richard Bowring. Princeton: Princeton University Press, 1982.

Nagy, Margit. "Middle-Class Working Women during the Interwar Years." In *Recreating Japanese Women, 1600–1945,* edited by Gail Bernstein (Berkeley: University of California Press 1991), 199–216.

Najita, Tetsuo, and J. Victor Koschmann, eds. *Conflict in Modern Japanese History: The Neglected Tradition.* Princeton: Princeton University Press, 1982.

Nakamura Takafusa. *Lectures on Modern Japanese Economic History, 1926–1994.* LTCB International Library Selection, no. 1. Tokyo: LTCB International Library Foundation, 1994.

Nijo, Lady. *The Confessions of Lady Nijo.* Translated by Karen Brazell. London: Zenith, 1973.

Nolte, Sharon, and Sally Ann Hastings. "The Meiji State Policy toward Women." In *Recreating Japanese Women, 1600–1945,* edited by Gail Bernstein (Berkeley: University of California Press, 1991), 151–174.

Okazaki Yoshie, ed. *Japanese Literature in the Meiji Era.* Translated by V. H. Viglielmo. Tokyo: Heibunsha, 1955.

Powell, Irena. *Writers and Society in Modern Japan.* Tokyo: Kōdansha, 1983.

Rimer, J. Thomas, ed. *Culture and Identity: Japanese Intellectuals during the Interwar Years.* Princeton: Princeton University Press, 1990.

Rodd, Laurel Rasplica. "Yosano Akiko and the Taishō Debate of the 'New Woman.'" In *Recreating Japanese Women, 1600–1945,* edited by Gail Bernstein (Berkeley: University of California Press, 1991), 175–198.

Roden, Donald. "Taishō Culture and the Problem of Gender Ambivalence." In *Culture and Identity: Japanese Intellectuals during the Interwar Years,* edited by J. Thomas Rimer (Princeton: Princeton University Press, 1990), 37–55.

Rubin, Jay. *Injurious to Public Morals: Writers and the Meiji State.* Seattle: University of Washington Press, 1984.

Ryan, Marleigh Grayer. *Japan's First Modern Novel:* Ukigumo *of Futabatei Shimei.* New York: Columbia University Press, 1965.

Schalow, Paul, and Janet A. Walker, eds. *The Woman's Hand: Gender and Theory in Japanese Women's Writing.* Stanford: Stanford University Press, 1996.

Sei Shonagon. *The Pillow Book of Sei Shonagon.* Translated by Ivan Morris. Suffolk: Penguin Books, 1967.

Sen, Amartya. "More than 100 Million Women Are Missing." *New York Review of Books* (December 20, 1990), pp. 61–66.

Sesar, Carl. *Takuboku: Poems to Eat.* Tokyo: Kōdansha, 1966.

Shiga Naoya. *A Dark Night's Passing.* Translated by Edwin McClellan. New York: Kōdansha, 1976.

Sievers, Sharon L. *Flowers in Salt: The Beginnings of Feminist Consciousness in Modern Japan.* Stanford: Stanford University Press, 1983.

Silverberg, Miriam. *Changing Song; The Marxist Manifestos of Nakano Shigeharu.* Princeton: Princeton University Press, 1990.

———. "The Modern Girl as Militant," In *Recreating Japanese Women, 1600–1945,* edited by Gail Bernstein (Berkeley: University of California Press, 1991), 239–266.

Tanaka, Yukiko, ed. *To Live and to Write: Selections by Japanese Women Writers, 1913–1938.* Seattle: Seal Press, 1987.

Tayama Katai. *The Quilt and Other Stories.* Translated and with an introduction by Kenneth G. Henshall. Tokyo: University of Tokyo Press, 1981.

Treat, John Whittier. *Writing Ground Zero.* Chicago: University of Chicago Press, 1995.

Ueda, Makoto. *Modern Japanese Writers and the Nature of Literature.* Stanford: Stanford University Press, 1976.

United Nations Development Programme. *Human Development Report.* New York: Oxford University Press, 1992.

Uno Chiyo. *Confessions of Love.* Translated by Phyllis Birnbaum. Honolulu: University of Hawai'i Press, 1989.

———. "This Powder Box." In *The Sound of the Wind: The Life and Works of Uno Chiyo,* translated by Rebecca Copeland (Honolulu: University of Hawai'i Press, 1992), 208–236.

Vernon, Victoria V. *Daughters of the Moon: Wish, Will, and Social Constraint in Fiction by Modern Japanese Women.* Berkeley: University of California, Japan Research Monograph, 1988.

Wittgenstein, Ludwig. *Tractatus Logico-Philosophicus.* Translated by D. F. Pears and B. F. McGinnis. London: Routledge and Kegan Paul, 1961.

Wolfe, Alan. *Suicidal Narrative in Modern Japan.* Princeton: Princeton University Press, 1990.

Index